To Diana and Kathleen Arnote
and, of course,
Angelique

Preface

The British Crown Colony of Hong Kong lies about two degrees below the Tropic of Cancer. About ninety percent of it is located on the mainland of Asia, with a common border with the People's Republic of China. The rest of it comprises 236 islands, some of them hardly more than huge boulders in the South China Sea. The island of Hong Kong is the home of the governor's residence, and is the beating heart of the burgeoning capitalistic free enterprise system, unlike any other in the world. Lantau, rugged and mountainous, as is Hong Kong, is the largest island. It is sparsely populated and incredibly beautiful.

On the other side of Victoria Harbor from Hong Kong Island lies Kowloon, said to be the most densely populated spot of land on earth. A railroad travels north from Kowloon through the more rural district of New Territories. The trains pass through a small town named Lo Wu and cross the Sham Chun River into the People's Republic of China. Passage across that border is closely regulated, with special visas needed for almost everyone.

For one hundred and fifty years, the Crown Colony of Hong Kong has grown, despite one obstacle after another, starting with the opium wars in the early days of its existence. Now it is a seething, prospering city-state, rampant with nearly unbridled free enterprise.

One does not have to travel very far beyond Lo Wu to see the stark contrast between capitalism and communism.

On July 1, 1997, under an agreement signed by the British and the Chinese in 1984 in Beijing, the Royal Crown Colony of Hong Kong will become Hong Kong, China.

As the date approaches, the problems involved in combining these two opposing economic and political systems are still unanswered, especially since the brutal suppression of the students at Tiananmen Square in 1989.

After several successive visits to Hong Kong and the People's Republic in the last ten years, I have become fascinated by the drama and the anxiety of the population of Hong Kong as the date approaches. The agreement signed in 1984 says precious little about how the diverse economies and citizenships are to be merged. True, there will be a British governor for another fifty years. But he will be without real power, some say merely a presider over a grievance committee by whatever name.

There is a concern, a fear, among the populace best illustrated by the peaceful protest of some two hundred thousand in the streets of Hong Kong after the suppression of the students. Many business interests have left Hong Kong. More have stayed. Others are still trying to figure out what to do.

As a writer of fiction, I found the setting of Hong Kong, about a year before the birth of Hong Kong, China, too compelling to ignore. So I have written a novel, created fictional characters and tossed them together in the puzzling, logic-defying, truly mysterious atmosphere of the Crown Colony of Hong Kong today.

Lacy Locke, financial analyst from New York; Brandon Poole, billionaire Hong Kong aristocrat; Claude Van Hooten, Dutch taipan; Moia Hsu, Beijing woman caught between two cultures worlds apart; Davy Wong, dissident student; Liu Wing, an officer in the People's Liberation Army; Mary Lulu, sexy American rock star, imported to Wan Chai: that's the main cast, plus the six million people who live in Hong Kong.

Almost every day the same thought crosses many of their minds. What will it really be like when, on July 1, 1997, the People's Liberation Army crosses the bridge at Lo Wu?

Chapter 1

DAVY WONG crouched low in the reeds. It was daybreak on the Sham Chun River, the natural boundary separating New Territories, the northernmost district of Hong Kong, from the People's Republic of China. During the night he had spent in the swamp, he had heard four distinct shots fired nearby, and once he had heard voices he estimated to be only a few hundred feet away. The past few hours he had heard nothing. He was shivering. His arm ached from a gash he had given himself while crawling under the razor wire fence near Man Kam To.

Davy strained to see the gash on his upper arm in the morning light and decided that it was superficial. It had bled freely the night before, but the blood was now congealed. He dared to peek out at the rise of land perhaps a quarter mile away, on the other side of the river in the People's Republic. At least three soldiers were scanning the broad marsh from a rocky crag bordering the river. He ducked down again, prepared to spend the day in the shallow muck if he had to. Freedom for him was still a mile away, near Sha Ling where the closed-area buffer zone between the People's Republic and New Territories came to an end.

Davy Wong lay on his back, staring up at the brightening sky, head propped on crushed reeds to keep his ears and mouth above water. Getting this far had been a miracle. He didn't want to blow it now.

Walking away from the detention camp near Hengyang had been easy, but he had been lucky. The truck that had taken him all the way to Guangzhou was loaded with cabbage and broccoli, so there was food. But luckiest of all, the driver had asked no questions. Several times he had cursed the regime and stared at him, probably trying to evoke a response. Once Davy dared to smile, his eyes meeting the driver's after another string of invectives about the regime in Beijing. From then on, the slender young man said nothing.

Now, lying in the swamp, Davy realized that the driver had probably seen the Wanted posters. After all, Davy Wong, a notable activist at Tiananmen Square back in 1989, had been the subject of a major search throughout South China since his escape. Sympathy for the students was well known to be rife throughout Guangdong Province.

His mute driver had dropped him off on the busy highway leading from Guangzhou to the east toward Shenzhen and Hong Kong. Now he was less than a mile from a safe haven. He again lifted his head ever so slightly. The soldiers were still surveying the vast swamp from their high perch. Davy glanced to the southeast. Clouds were pushing his way across the morning sky. Could he be so lucky to be blessed with rain or, better yet, fog?

He slapped at a pesky mosquito. He was shivering and hungry, but the day would bring warmth. He decided that he would endure anything until the soldiers broke their vigil. Freedom was only as far away as the first telephone he could reach beyond Sha Ling.

About an hour later he was jarred to attention by a volley of rifle shots in the distance. Though distinct, they sounded far away. Davy lifted his head to peek again through the reeds. The soldiers had vanished from the high ground, perhaps distracted by some movement farther to the west from where the gunfire came. Furthermore, the rocky crag on which they had stood was now barely visible in the thickening mist.

It began to rain. Davy rose and began to slog his way southward toward Sha Ling. Quicker than he expected he came upon another barbed wire fence. He walked slowly along the fence for a hundred yards or so and came to a place where it had already been breached by someone. He flattened himself to the ground and squeezed under the menacing barbs. Davy walked due south, trying to put as much distance between himself and the fence as possible.

If he had things figured correctly, he was now in Hong Kong. The second fence had marked the southern extremity of the closed area, the now porous buffer zone between the People's Republic and Hong Kong. The farther he walked in the rain, the easier he breathed. There was a spring in his step. He forgot his hunger and discomfort. He was free again!

. Still, he would have to be careful. Sometimes the People's Army was not deterred by boundaries. He came upon a farm road that led directly south and began following it. Then he froze. Back though the haze, he saw the outline of a truck rapidly approaching him. If they were looking for him, there was nothing he could do. He flagged his arm at the vehicle as it approached.

Thinking quickly, he yelled, "I am late for work. I need a ride to Taipo." He knew Taipo to be a couple of miles down the road. He had friends there.

The driver stared at him, eyeing the tattered shirt and the big blot of blood on the shoulder. The driver hesitated, probably realizing he had come from beyond the border as many did. Then, without expression, he jerked his thumb back toward the flatbed of the truck. Davy climbed aboard, joining four field workers. He nodded at them, but none responded, staring instead at the bloodstained shoulder.

The old truck jostled them southward until they joined a main road where the going was easier. The driver slowed down as he neared Taipo, peered through the glassless rear window, and jerked his thumb emphatically toward Taipo. Davy leapt from the truck and walked a quarter of a mile or so until he was in front of a small bake shop.

He grinned broadly as he went inside. The shop-keeper turned from his oven, beamed in quick recognition, put aside his baker's paddle and came forward to greet Davy Wong with enthusiasm.

"I think I see a miracle," the old man said as he scanned his strapping broad-shouldered visitor.

"I think that is a fact." Davy laughed, exhilarated by the lack of tension for the first time in days. "I need to call Hong Kong Central." The man led him into the living quarters behind the bakery and produced a telephone.

Davy Wong dialed the number of Brandon Poole Ltd. It was a private line that he hoped would find the industrialist at his desk.

"Poole here," a voice snapped.

"Brandon, you conniving capitalist! It is I, Davy Wong."

"Davy! I must be dreaming. Where are you?"

"I'm in Taipo. At Ling's bake shop. I've had a hairy hike down from Shenzhen. But I'm okay. They might be nosing around, so I am going to stay with Ling awhile."

"I'll have a driver there within an hour. Cecil Lo will pick you up. He'll take you directly to the Peak."

"Mr. Poole, is that wise for you?"

Brandon Poole laughed in his deep baritone. "We'll have a discussion about wisdom when I see you on the Peak. You'll be safe there. Cecil won't tell a soul you're in town."

"Thank you, Brandon. We have much to talk about." Davy hung up and turned to face the slender Ling.

"I may have another shirt around here that will fit. Let me look." Ling held a cup of tea in one hand and a plate of sweet pastries in the other. "Here, help yourself. When is the last time you ate?"

"I feasted on broccoli and cabbage just two days ago. Up north."

Ling frowned at his wounded shoulder as Wong doffed his shirt. "Barbed wire?"

"I don't see anything, do you?"

Ling shook his head. "No. As a matter of fact, I don't even know that you are here."

"Mmm . . . These are very good, Ling." Davy smiled as he began ravaging the tray of sweet goods.

Back on the rocky crag, General Liu Wing of the People's Liberation Army scanned the vast swamp, visibility now narrowed greatly by the steadily falling rain. Three soldiers stood nearby, rifles at the ready, peering off into the general direction of Hong Kong.

The soldiers were all uneasy and never once dared to suggest that pursuing the escapee had become a hopeless task. No doubt they wondered why the usually routine search for an escapee was commanded by a general. Their prey must have been someone very important.

The general spoke. "We will return to Guangzhou. If he made it across the swamp alive, he has succeeded only in getting himself bottled up in the steel trap of Hong Kong. He will be easier to find there than in China."

General Liu smiled confidently into the growing mist. The soldiers relaxed somewhat. They had fully expected a temper tantrum from the general at best. Each of them cautiously nodded his agreement with the general's assessment of the situation. Their quarry had obviously disappeared. Their general was quite wise.

Chapter 2

HALFWAY AROUND the world on Wall Street, New York City, at the same time General Liu Wing was giving up his pursuit, Lacy Locke sat exhausted in her office at New Worldwide Securities. The brilliant analyst, corporate guru for the Pacific Rim, was still at her desk at this late hour wading through the stack of books she had selected to prepare herself for a visit to Hong Kong. She had convinced her corporate superiors that the vagaries of the Hong Kong market, in the light of the takeover by the Chinese in 1997, demanded her personal scrutiny. Rumors persisted that the transition of the Crown Colony to Chinese sovereignty would be far from smooth and predictable.

Now the trip was only a few days off. A heavy appointment schedule with their clients in Hong Kong had been completed. She would visit all the companies that were candidates for their risky Pacific Rim mutual fund and try to assess their stability during the inevitable transition to Beijing control. All the details of her visit had been assembled in what promised to be a grueling schedule.

At the end of a long day, two pieces of paper remained on her desk. One concerned a visit to New

York by Brandon Poole, one of Hong Kong's most successful businessmen. Some assured her that he was a billionaire, a man whom all others watched. It had been arranged that he was to talk to a seminar of bankers and brokers about the future of Hong Kong. The meeting was to take place at the Waldorf just a couple of days before her scheduled trip. Lacy reluctantly cabled her acceptance to attend Poole's meeting before she left.

The other item on her desk was a folio of news items regarding one of their accounts, Phuket Color of Bangkok and Hong Kong. The fast-growing fashion clothier had embarked upon a highly visible campaign to open new markets, including the United States. A publicity release by Phuket Color stated that they had employed Chad Grissom, a well-known male fashion model, to exploit their line.

Lacy could not restrain an audible chuckle at one of the news items in the Phuket file. It seems that Chad Grissom had been squiring around Mary Lulu, the blatantly risqué new hard-rock blond bombshell. What made it newsworthy was the fact that Miss Lulu had appeared in public numerous times lately in the virtual buff, clad only in one of Chad Grissom's oversize powder blue Phuket Color sport coats.

Is that good or bad publicity? she mused to herself as she studied the outlandish news photo.

Lacy pushed the day's work aside. She stood and stretched. She actually looked forward to eating dinner at home with Adam tonight. He could be a credible chef when he put his mind to it.

Adam Locke was morning news anchor on a local TV channel. He was strikingly handsome, as a news anchor was supposed to be. That's what had drawn Lacy toward him in the beginning.

Lacy looked at herself in the mirror behind her office door before donning her coat. Her thirty-six years still looked like twenty-nine. She was tall and svelte, wore clothes like a fashion model. Shoulder-length jet hair, curled inward, sleek and bouncy. High cheekbones and wide-set hazel eyes made her look nothing like a popular conception of a financial analyst. Men got the wrong signals from her sometimes, but she couldn't help it. She was generally upbeat and liked to smile.

Now she adjusted her coat, still looking in the mirror. Yes, she and Adam had made a stunning couple in the beginning. Her face grew sober as she walked to her desk to retrieve her purse. "Damn!" she said aloud, and wished she wasn't going home to Adam. He's a philandering boob, a pompous airhead, she thought to herself for the zillionth time. Then she smiled. In ten days she would be alone in Hong Kong. "I just might stay awhile," she said aloud to no one. She rode the elevator to the street level, walked out of the building, strode boldly into the street and hailed a cab.

"That you, darling?" Adam called out from his study as Lacy entered the apartment.

"Yes, Adam. Who else could it be?" No smells came from the kitchen. That part of the apartment was dark. She sighed. That meant Adam had decided to go out for dinner. She walked into Adam's study, plopped down on a long leather sofa and put her feet up. "What's for dinner?"

Adam was studying some typewritten pages under the desk lamp. She knew him well enough to know that he had heard her question, but had chosen to ignore her until he finished whatever it was he was reading. Lacy kicked off her shoes.

"Nothing," he finally said. "We're going out. I've made reservations at Sean's."

"Let's see, it's Wednesday," Lacy mused. "That means lamb stew, some weird pasta creation, or some delightful haddock. Fuck Sean's, Adam." She decided to be bitchy.

"Lacy, I have something we must discuss." Adam straightened the papers he had been studying on his desk and fastened them neatly with a paper clip. "They are very serious about me running for governor."

Lacy turned to stare at him. The handsome masculinity that had first attracted her was still there. She studied the rugged features profiled by his desk lamp. "What for, Adam? Why would you really want to do that?"

"Because I think I can win."

Lacy stretched out on the long couch, clasped her hands behind her head and stared wide-eyed at the ceiling. The answer he gave her was fully predictable. She could picture the striking six-foot-two Adam, with his thick, wavy black hair and deep booming voice, standing behind a podium somewhere. The women in the crowd would be mesmerized by the charm that had swept her off her feet in the beginning. The meaningless words that rolled off his tongue would have his partisan audience cheering.

"I didn't ask you whether or not you can win, Adam. I asked you why you wanted to run. What is it that you believe in, Adam? What grand scheme do you have planned for us? How are you to make life better for your followers? What do you propose to do about the filth and all the marauding crazies that screw up the quality of life everywhere?" Lacy groaned audibly. "The truth of the matter, Adam, is that you have no plans at all. You just think being governor is a peachy idea."

"What in the hell do you mean by all that!" Adam stopped short, biting his tongue. "I'm sorry, Lacy. I'm doing this for you as much as me. I do realize what you mean, but when we get in the governor's mansion, solutions will come. I promise you."

"Like you promised we would eat in tonight?"

"I'm not really in the mood for that, Lacy. You know that what I really want to do is talk to you about running for office. I'd be a fool not to do it. I just wish you felt the same way. Think of yourself, Lacy. Think of the business opportunities it would open up." Adam sat on the arm of the couch, staring at her. Lacy's eyes were closed, her remarkably beautiful face expressionless.

"Adam, I have unavoidable, extensive travel plans all through the next year." Her eyes were still closed. "I would be of little use to you in a political campaign. Think about the press. What would you tell them about having a wife gallivanting all around the Pacific Rim while you are campaigning?"

"Lacy, you could defer those plans until after the election. I need you. With both of us pressing the flesh, we could shake hands with everyone in the state."

Lacy rolled over on her side. "All for what, Adam? What do you believe in? What solutions to you have? What about the drug problem? AIDS? Do you bother reading the papers anymore? Jesus, Adam! I saw a group of men hanging around on Seventh Avenue this morning, bare-chested, with their nipples pierced with heavy gold rings. They are part of your electorate too, Adam." Lacy had rambled on in a low monotone, her eyes still closed.

"Lacy, I'll attack all the problems one by one after we're in the governor's mansion. Right now, winning the election is our first problem."

Lacy snapped to a sitting position and then stood and stretched. "Your problem, Adam. Not mine. In fact, I say screw your election. Forget dinner for me. I'm going out to a movie. I'll have some popcorn."

"Lacy, I really don't have time for a movie tonight."

"No one asked you, Adam. Stay home and plan your campaign. You might say a prayer that none of your future constituents tries to rape me before I get home."

"Lacy, talk like that is stupid."

"Maybe you think so." She paused before leaving the apartment just long enough to open her handbag. She produced a small stainless steel .22 automatic, sleek and shiny. "I really don't worry much about your city, Adam."

Adam Locke stared at the gleaming automatic. "Are you insane? You don't even have a permit for that. You could be put in jail."

"Then hurry up and get elected, so I will have some political strings to pull. Good night, dear." Lacy Locke slipped the automatic back into her purse, left the apartment and closed the door behind her. No matter how polished and physically appealing Adam was, he had become a shallow, meaningless part of her life. Even his extramarital affairs no longer bothered her. She just didn't care.

Lacy walked several blocks before she reached the Plaza. She went inside, located a pay phone and dialed Eric Hanson's number. Eric was her administrative assistant. She had ignored him lately in the rush to prepare for the Hong Kong trip.

"Lacy! What a surprise. I was just going out alone for a snack."

"Join me, Eric. I'm at the Plaza."

Chapter 3

Adam Locke had started at WYNK-TV twelve years ago as a local newscaster based largely on his magnetic appearance and the baritone voice that went with it. From the very beginning, he had attracted attention. His ruggedly handsome demeanor along with the voice that rang with authority had gotten him promoted to morning news anchorman at WYNK-TV within two years.

Adam had the benefit of a liberal arts education that left him with a thin veneer of knowledge across a broad range of subjects. His luckiest day was the day he met Lacy at a holiday cocktail party in Manhattan. He had swept the brilliant woman off her feet before she had an inkling that Adam Locke was basically a handsome but also spoiled and lazy man. Even he realized that it was her drive and insistence that had pushed him to read about and study current events and politics until he could mesmerize and fool most of the people most of the time.

His ratings soared. The newsman had become the heartthrob of thousands of women who watched his suave presentation and wished that the men in their lives were more like Adam Locke.

Running for governor was a suggestion foisted on him by WYNK-TV's management when he began to get letters by the hundreds from listeners. They urged him to run after he had bemoaned the lack of qualified opposition candidates during a newscast. At first it was all a joke on the part of management. But when the letters and the urgings grew in number, Adam's market share grew. His management instructed him to ride the publicity wave as far as he could.

Tonight, Adam was puzzled. Lacy obviously had no real interest. She thought the idea of his running for governor was still just a joke. Also, she had never walked out on him like that before. Going to a movie alone? That wasn't like Lacy at all. He looked at his watch. There was plenty of time to go out and buy a box of fancy chocolates for her pillow.

The air was crisp and cool. It was a good night for a stroll. Bloomingdale's was still open. He wandered inside where he was immediately recognized by the flashy salesgirl behind a perfume counter.

"You're Adam Locke, aren't you? I wake up with you every morning." She smiled broadly. "Anything I can help you with? You know, you look exactly like you, if you know what I mean. Some celebrities who come in look totally different, and you aren't quite sure."

"Well, I'm glad I look like me," beamed Adam. "Where can I find fancy chocolates in your store? I know I've seen them here before."

She told him where to go. "Of course, you could give her perfume. It will last longer than chocolates."

"Thank you. Next time perhaps." He winked appreciatively at her and then wandered off to locate the candy.

Box in hand, he strode rapidly up Lexington Avenue. Darkness was closing in as he turned off Lexington toward their apartment.

Suddenly there was a rush of footsteps around him

and then a solid whack across his shoulders, narrowly missing the base of his skull. He later suspected it was a baseball bat that struck him. For one dizzying second he was aware of a street gang around him before he fell unconscious.

Lacy returned to their apartment shortly before one A.M. Adam was not there. This was very unusual. He had to rise early each day to prepare the morning news, so he hardly ever stayed out late at night. She began to prepare for bed. Several snifters of Grand Marnier at the Plaza had made her a little unsteady. Perhaps it was best that Adam was not there.

The phone rang. "Hello. Lacy? Sorry to wake you." It was Hampton Forbes, station manager of WYNK-TV.

"That's okay. I was awake anyway. Is Adam with you?"

"Lacy, first of all I'm told that Adam will be okay. But right now things are pretty rough. He was badly beaten by someone early this evening. They took all his identification, but someone at Lenox Hill Hospital recognized him and called the station. I've been trying to get you for some time."

"Oh my God! I was out for the evening . . . at a movie," she added nervously. "Are you at the hospital?"

"Yes. Perhaps you'd better come. I'll send my car for you."

"Give me ten minutes, Hampton. How bad is it?"

"He was out for a couple of hours, they say. He just came around. I think the sight of you would perk him up."

Lacy arrived at the hospital to find Adam lying in bed, his shoulders slightly elevated. His handsome face was heavily bandaged. "Oh Adam!" She hugged him for a while. He moaned an acknowledgment, but seemed to be unable to speak.

"He has a broken nose and has lost several teeth." Hampton Forbes spoke quietly from a chair in the corner of the room. "The bastards really did a job on him."

"Who? Hampton, who?"

Forbes shook his head. "The police don't know. Probably just hooligans. They took his wallet and his jewelry." He turned and picked up a package from the windowsill. "They didn't bother with this. The police found it next to him."

A plastic sack contained a box of chocolate truffles from Bloomingdale's along with a card. She read the inscription on the card. "Hi, hope you enjoyed the movie. Sorry I was a bad boy. I love you—Adam."

Chapter 4

LACY LOCKE stopped by Lenox Hill Hospital on her way to work the next morning. She was surprised to see Adam sitting up in bed sipping coffee and watching the morning news. "Adam! What a surprise!" Then looking more closely, she gasped, "Oh Adam, what did they do to you?"

The bandages on his face had been changed, leaving more of his features exposed. His nose was obviously broken. Both eyes were blackened and a deep cut ran diagonally across his left cheek.

"It's going to be okay, Lacy. Most of it is pretty superficial. They say I have a concussion, so I'll have to stay around here a couple more days. You should have been here earlier. They had a TV crew in here. You just missed me on the morning news."

Lacy glanced at the small TV screen. Babs Billings was doing the news. "Babs gets her big break, huh?"

"She's good job security for me, Lacy. She's butchering the whole thing."

"Adam darling," came the voice from the TV. "You get well real fast. I know everyone wants to hear your story as only you can tell it. We all love you, Adam."

"Bullshit." Adam Locke snapped the off switch. "She really wishes I would die."

"Shame on you, Adam. I can remember you telling me that Babs was very loyal to you."

"That's before they started putting her on camera now and then. Now she thinks she's the next Barbara Walters."

"Well, Adam, it really doesn't make any difference, does it? If you run for governor, Babs may get your job anyway." Lacy smiled as Adam stared at her with his blackened eyes.

"Hey, the boys think I should get back on the air as soon as possible, black eyes, broken nose and all. It would be the perfect opening for me to deliver a big blast about the gangs on the streets of the city. The way things are going, it will be the hottest issue in the campaign."

"And what are you going to do about the crime in the streets, Adam?" Deep inside, Lacy was rooting for a logical answer. Maybe, she thought, this experience had provoked some substantive thought about addressing the problem.

"You mark my words, Lacy. The time will come when we will put a stop to it all. What happened to me could happen to anyone, you know."

"How, Adam?"

"How what?"

"How are you going to put a stop to it?" Lacy decided to be bitchy again. "Oh, forget it, Adam. I'm late for work. See you tonight, on the way home from work." Lacy brushed his swollen lips with a kiss, and left the room.

She hailed a cab downtown. During the stop-and-go traffic on Lexington Avenue, thoughts of Adam vanished as she faced the excitement of another day preparing for the trip to Hong Kong.

When she entered the building housing New Worldwide Securities, everyone asked about Adam, stopping her repeatedly to bring them up-to-date as she made her way to her private office. Most of them were fans of Adàm and listened to him every morning. But of course they didn't have to live with him.

"Good morning, Lacy. How's our next governor doing?" Whitney Gordon, New Worldwide's senior VP, smiled broadly. He knew all too well what Lacy thought about the ballyhoo over Adam's candidacy.

"Oh Whit, for God's sake. I wish people would stop. The joke is over." Lacy leaned back in her big leather chair. "Adam's doing fine, I guess. He looks like a mess. But now he wants to start a crusade against crime."

"What's he want to do about it?"

"He doesn't know. But he does know that he's against getting bashed in the head."

Whitney nodded. "Well, that's a beginning. By the way, Lacy, I figured you'd be in late this morning, so I asked Eric to put together an update on all the Pacific Rim stuff that you will be looking into. The dollar lost ground again to the yen this morning."

"Don't worry about anything, Whitney. We are going to be in great shape." Lacy amazed herself sometimes. When she really believed something, she spoke with such authority that challengers sat silent, as if she were an oracle.

"Oh, I'm not going to worry at all. I'm going to Martinique for a few days."

"Will you be visiting the nudie beaches or will you be taking Mrs. Gordon?" Lacy liked to kid around with the senior VP. Too bad she didn't meet him before she met Adam, she often thought.

"Anita and I are going to climb old Mount Pelée. Maybe there's a guru up there who can tell us who will be our next governor."

"Whit, I'd much rather know how China is going to behave in the summer of '97, after they take over Hong Kong."

Whitney Gordon's face became serious. "Lacy, you're our expert on the People's Republic." He walked toward the door of Lacy's office. "Anita says to give Adam her love. We all hope he gets well fast, Lacy."

Lacy took time to sort through the updates on happenings in China and Hong Kong that Eric clipped from the wire services each day. The political situation seemed to be heating up. Three dissidents who had served sentences for two to three years as a result of their participation in the Tiananmen Square uprising in 1989 had again been taken into custody in Zhejiang Province and returned to prison for sedition. It was believed by Beijing authorities that another had escaped to Hong Kong.

Chapter 5

CLAUDE VAN HOOTEN stood at the window of his office in the Shanghai Bank Building, which towered above the Central District of Hong Kong. The prestigious location housed the offices of Phuket Color. The tall, reddish-blond Dutchman was proud of his company. He had deserted the Netherlands five years ago to take advantage of the Far Eastern labor market for development of his high-fashion enterprise and the Crown Colony had captured his spirit for adventure as well as his need for the unregulated, open business atmosphere.

He stroked his neatly clipped beard as he looked out upon Hong Kong from his lofty vantage point. He could easily spot the tram making its way up Victoria Peak. A preoccupation with the tram on a morning eighteen months ago had led him to Moia and the good fortune that had filled his life since then.

Van Hooten continued to stare at the tram as it reached the station at the top of Victoria Peak. It had been a similar sun-drenched morning, lacking the usual Hong Kong humidity, when he had walked boldly up to Moia Hsu and stood nearby to watch the beautiful woman. She was scanning the harbor with a small, ornate pair of roof prism binoculars and didn't notice him for some time.

When she finally turned and lowered the glasses to look at him, it was with the same warm smile that Van Hooten had now grown to know very well. Moia's classic features and waist-length, perfectly groomed jet black hair framed a face he knew he would never forget. She was much taller than most Chinese women, and the warm smile was full of confidence and boldness that were unusual.

"You picked a poor time of the day for that," she had volunteered, pointing at the small camera he carried. "The morning sunlight fills your lens pointing toward Hong Kong. Late afternoon and evening is a much better time."

"I'm afraid photography is not a field of expertise for me," he replied, much surprised that the striking woman would initiate a conversation.

Now, in deep thought, he turned his eyes from Victoria Peak and stared across the channel into Kowloon. He had seen Moia almost every single day since then except for the brief times she went unexpectedly to visit her family in Beijing.

To him, Moia was part of the enigma of Hong Kong during the mid-1990s. The summer of 1997—and the return of the Crown Colony to Chinese sovereignty—was less than one year away. Until very recently the date had always seemed too far in the future to worry about. But now, the time seemed to race by. The lowering of the British flag loomed somewhere in the recesses of the mind of most everyone who did business in the boiling capitalistic cauldron that was Hong Kong.

By now, most businessmen who had decided that the future held disaster had already exited Hong Kong with whatever assets they could take with them. Claude Van Hooten, however, was one of those who stayed. He had built his company, Phuket Color Ltd., up to the status of an emerging giant in the textile industry, specializing in fine Thai silk and selected synthetic fabrics. By the use of new production techniques and remote labor markets in Thailand and the People's Republic of China, Phuket Color would now be able to undersell a significant segment of the world market.

The fruits of all his planning were about to be realized, so he wasn't the least bit inclined to pack up and leave Hong Kong. Moia Hsu was a key factor in his decision. Her mysterious ability to deal successfully with the layers of bureaucracy in Beijing was a chief ingredient in their success this far. In his mind, the Chinese posed no major problem. Moia's assurances had more than allayed the fears expressed by his international counterparts. After the lowering of the flag, he gambled that Hong Kong would merely go on as it had gone before.

It was so obvious to Van Hooten. Beijing wanted a world-class marketplace for their emerging growth in production of products with worldwide appeal. He was convinced that Hong Kong's welcome mat would remain open to all serious investors and traders.

Van Hooten turned and sat down at his massive desk, where he was still afforded a view of Victoria Peak and far beyond, deep into the countryside of New Territories. On some rare clear days, he could see the tall buildings of Shenzhen looming in the mist inside the People's Republic.

Moia Hsu was stopping off in Shenzhen today on her return from several days in Beijing, and Van Hooten really didn't know why. The woman was a heavy contributor to the success of Phuket Color, but there was a part of her that always remained a mystery.

He had hired Moia about a year ago, mostly because of her multi-language ability. But she soon became a key to opening the doors they would need to establish manufacturing sources in the People's Republic. Somehow she got things done. But how she did it remained largely her own secret. At her strong insistence, he rarely crossed the border into China with her.

Van Hooten was suddenly distracted by a familiar knock on his office door. It was Moia's four quick light taps. He buzzed her in, then rose to greet her as she walked smiling to his desk.

"Moia, you surprise me! I thought this was your day for Shenzhen." He embraced her. It was always with a long, soft kiss that lasted for several seconds. The hint of jasmine that always accompanied her was in the air.

"I have good news, Claude." Her dark eyes fixed squarely on his own as she pulled her head away from him, still holding him with her arms around his waist. "Shenzhen wasn't necessary. But they want to see you in Beijing. It will be sort of a celebration to bring luck to our plans for Phuket Color."

"How soon is our visit? You have always chased me away from Beijing."

"Claude! You know better than that. Have I not done well?"

"I couldn't have done this without you, darling." He wrapped his arms around her shoulders and pulled her tightly against him. "But for you, I would have long ago joined the others that have abandoned Hong Kong."

"Claude, you will meet my family." Her expression became serious. "After all, my father is in the Trade Ministry. It is unavoidable."

"Tell me, Moia, does he know anything about us?" He spoke quietly, emphasizing the *us*.

"I have no way of knowing that. I've certainly never told him anything." Moia pulled away from him and walked toward the large window overlooking Victoria Peak. "My father is a highly intelligent man. There isn't much he does not know. You must remember, however, that this invitation comes from him. If he had any reason to dislike you it would never have been forthcoming."

"How long must we stay in Beijing?" Claude found

it difficult to share Moia's enthusiasm for the trip.

"Probably just overnight. Please don't worry, Claude. I will be at your side the whole time. Anyone who convinces the Trade Ministry that they can be of such great help to China is already a hero there."

Van Hooten forced a slight smile. Doing business with China was a complicated process. Moia understood that process. He had no reason to mistrust her judgment. "Very well, my love. I hope this visit can be arranged quickly. We have some financial and advertising people coming in from New York in about ten days."

"How exciting! I told you it would happen quickly, remember?"

"You certainly made the right move in hiring Chad Grissom," murmured Claude. "He's been wearing our wardrobe everywhere in New York. All the trade columns have picked it up since we signed the big contract. He manages his way into all the gossip columns. Just the other day he was spotted with Mary Lulu, the latest abhorrent sex rocker in the States. Of course they made a point of him being all decked out in Phuket Color stuff. One photograph in the tabloids showed Mary Lulu performing stark naked with the exception of Grissom's oversize Phuket sport coat."

Moia beamed. "You were complaining, I recall, that no one in New York or Paris had an inkling about Phuket Color. Now it is different. Questions are being asked about us, and we must have the right answers from now on."

Moia's sense of timing was flawless, thought Van Hooten. The publicity was superb. They had generated a lot of attention. Now they had to produce and follow up. "Grissom will be here for extensive photo sessions within two weeks. As luck would have it, a representative of our broker handling the new public issue of Phuket stock will be here at about the same time."

"Claude, we want them to have a perfect visit to

Hong Kong. We will handle them personally. If you don't mind, I will concentrate on the pretty boy, and you can dazzle the stuffy broker. Who are they sending?"

Van Hooten picked a letter off a pile on his desk. "Ms. Lacy Locke. It says here she is a vice president."

Moia shrugged. "I hope she knows what she is doing. We are relying heavily on the stock issue. The people in Beijing would be much more comfortable with a man."

Van Hooten nodded, then smiled. "The world keeps turning, my dear, sometimes despite Beijing. I am sure she must be very competent to gain such a position in that company."

"Careful what you say about Beijing. They already think you are a bloodthirsty capitalist." Moia walked to the door and locked it, then went to the window and tugged at a cord, closing the drapes. The dimly lit office was now illuminated only by the single lamp on Van Hooten's desk.

Claude Van Hooten chuckled quietly as he loosened his necktie. "Moia, absolutely no one can see through that window. We are over forty stories up, higher than all the buildings around us."

Moia twirled out of her long wraparound skirt and let the silk slide noiselessly to the carpet. Walking over to where he now sat on the edge of his desk, she put her forefinger to his lips. "Shhh, perhaps others are as curious as we are, Claude. There could be a tourist on Victoria Peak with a telephoto lens. The poor fellow would be driven mad by the sight of what is about to happen."

Moia slowly proceeded to unbutton his shirt, replacing each button with a soft kiss on his bare flesh. It was a ritual she insisted upon. Whoever left the other for any length of time was committed to be the amorous aggressor upon their return. It was the same for him when returning from the Netherlands or the United

States. "Six days is much too long," she whispered, kneeling to brush a kiss where his belt buckle had been.

Several minutes later, after removing his shoes, she rose to press herself against him for a moment before leading him to a massive leather sofa. At this point, Van Hooten, consumed with desire, took charge. He could carry their ritual only so far before becoming the aggressor.

Under him, she pushed mightily against him in mock protest. "That's not fair," she gasped. "I was the traveler. It is my time to have my way."

Van Hooten paused in his erotic fervor to stop her speech by pressing his mouth to hers. "Later, Moia, later," he mumbled. "Let's enjoy this insanity."

Chapter 6

As Lacy dressed for the day, she switched on the morning news. Adam had departed for the studio at four A.M., after nervously primping in front of the bathroom mirror for half an hour. He did look rugged indeed, certainly not the usual meticulously groomed newscaster his public had grown to expect. The breaking of his nose had caused both eyes to blacken and his left eye to swell partially closed. The deep scratch on his cheek proved difficult to camouflage with powder. He had awakened this morning questioning his decision to go on the air this way, but decided to go on with the plan after a phone call from Hampton Forbes urging him to do so.

"Oh my God!" Lacy exclaimed aloud, and then sat on the end of her bed when the camera first panned on Adam at the news desk. He had covered the least injured eye with a black patch, fully exposing the swollen left eye. The scar on his cheek was an ugly red. The powder he had been experimenting with at home had been washed away. The wound looked as if it had even been enhanced by makeup to appear more startling than it actually was. A polished wooden cane lay flat on the desk in front of him. She wondered who had supplied that touch. He had never had any problem walking normally since his release from the hospital.

"Good morning! I'm Adam Locke, and this is your morning news. For those of you who might be seeing me for the first time, this is not the way I normally look. All of this"—he paused to thump the cane against the desk—"is the result of a battle I had two nights ago waging war on the evil forces in our city. I was attacked and beaten repeatedly and systematically by a well-organized gang of toughs right in front of my own apartment. In looking at me, you are looking at an example of what is waiting for everyone daring to venture forth at night in this lawless city. More about that later on. Now the news . . ."

Lacy watched in disbelief as her husband proceeded to read the news. As bad as he had looked when he had left the apartment this morning, the makeup-enhanced image on the screen was infinitely worse. At first she felt sorry for him, then ashamed at his charade, and then she started laughing and giggling at the image of Adam Locke on the screen. To her he looked like a ham actor playing a bad role. At times he didn't even sound like Adam. The two teeth he had lost from his lower jaw gave him trouble enunciating certain words, though she hadn't noticed that when talking to him in person.

Lacy resumed her morning routine with Adam rambling on in the background. She decided that she just wouldn't look at the screen anymore. She thought of the coming day at the office. No doubt everyone would be aghast at Adam's appearance. She had certainly given them no cause to expect that. The black patch hiding his relatively uninjured eye made his whole visage one of rare hamburger.

"And now, folks, I have a personal commentary . . ." Lacy continued to apply her makeup while the voice of Adam Locke droned on in the background. "Some of our viewers may be aware of the movement afoot to urge me to run as a candidate for governor. Up to now I have considered this the supreme flattery of friends who like their news undiluted and straight from the shoulder. Now I find that the scoundrels who laid me low have made me seriously consider the possibility of running. It just wouldn't be like Adam Locke to turn and run in this battle with the hooligans in the street. And then there is my sweet wife, Lacy, who only this very morning urged me to do what was right for this great state of yours and mine and all of your children."

Lacy dropped her hands into her lap at the dressing table. She turned to look at the strange visage of her husband on the large screen. She rose, walked over to the headboard of their bed and pressed the off button for the giant screen.

"Adam, you silly bastard," she said loudly. "You've finally gone nuts. And I'm not going with you."

She stormed out of the apartment, still furious about Adam's fictitious claim of her endorsement. He knew better than to put words in her mouth. If there was any sacred ground left in their marriage, it was their respect for mutual individuality. They were each their own person, up until now.

Lacy strode into the lobby of New Worldwide Securities. Luckily, there were no close acquaintances in the elevator. When she reached her own office, however, Whitney Gordon came in almost immediately.

"I saw Adam on the news this morning. That poor man, I hardly recognized him. Lacy, you should have told me how bad it was. I would have been more in touch."

"Adam's just fine, Whit. I hardly recognized him myself. He looked pretty good when he left for the office."

"Oh?" Whitney stared at the obviously distraught woman. "Lacy, I take it you think Adam should try for governor. I was surprised to hear it this morning."

"Whitney, I was also surprised to hear it. Don't believe everything you hear on the news." She paused.

Whitney Gordon had always been a confidant. "I don't know what to do, Whit. Adam has begun to believe his own publicity crap. He doesn't have an inkling of what he would do as governor. In fact he would be chopped to pieces by his opponent."

"There must be trouble in paradise. I'm sorry, Lacy. Anything I can do?"

"Nope. I want to wrap myself up in the Phuket Color project as quickly as I can. The trip to Hong Kong looks better all the time."

"You're calling the shots there, Lacy. Get going anytime you want to. Several papers have been on the phone already this morning. Because of Adam's remarks this morning, they are looking to do a piece on you."

"They'll have to wait a long time. I have nothing to say. Adam said it all this morning."

Whitney Gordon shrugged and walked out of her office, leaving Lacy to immerse herself in all the information she could gather on Phuket Color. She was getting close to a final decision to include Phuket Color Ltd. in the short list of stocks to be offered by Worldwide Securities in a developing-market mutual fund.

Lacy studied the Cathay Pacific airline tickets to Hong Kong, which she had jammed into the developing-markets folder, noting the departure time just nine days hence.

Eric, her assistant, strolled into her office. "Lacy, do you have some time? I've been going over some stuff for you that needs your attention."

"You've got me, Eric. Let's go over it right now." Thank God for Eric, she thought to herself. He didn't permit anything to fall between the cracks.

"First of all, a Moia Hsu called. She is with Phuket Color in Hong Kong. She called twice and then insisted she talk to someone. She wants a photocopy of your passport. It has to do with procuring a visa for the People's Republic. I've checked and it seems to be a standard request."

"Really? I didn't know I was going into China. It must be something Phuket Color has planned. Go ahead and send it. If I don't want to go when I get to Hong Kong, I just won't go."

Eric made notes as she talked and then went on to discuss the items on his list which he checked off one by one. "This Moia Hsu also wanted to know if anyone would be accompanying you. I told her there wouldn't be. If there is any change in that, she asked to be advised. Oh yes, there is one other thing. She said that Chad Grissom, the model for Phuket menswear, would be on the same flight that you have scheduled on Cathay Pacific. Since it is such a long flight, she said you might want to kill a little time with him."

Lacy shrugged. "Anything else, Eric?"

"No, that's it. It all sounds so exciting. I wish I were going." Eric, a handsome young man in his twenties, said it as if he meant it.

Lacy smiled. No doubt that young Eric could be of great assistance. But she needed him in New York. "Someday, Eric, someday. You'll get your fill of travel if you stick with me."

Chapter 7

THE DRAGON Air flight from Hong Kong to Beijing was crowded. In fact, Moia had noticed that there were seldom empty seats anymore on flights from Hong Kong. Claude Van Hooten and Moia Hsu sat in the first-class cabin, spending most of the time in conversation. Moia was giving Van Hooten a crash course in Beijing politics as it affected relations with Hong Kong. She kept using the word *their*, emphasizing that what she had to say was not necessarily her opinion, but that of the Trade Ministry. She frequently used her father as a synonym for the Trade Ministry.

"My father has much respect for you, Claude. He thinks you showed great strength in your decision to keep Phuket Color in Hong Kong. Those who will abandon Hong Kong for Australia, the Andamans, or some other crazy place will be very sorry." Moia reached to grasp the back of Claude's hand, resting on the armrest between them. "I am told that we will be joined by many others like ourselves."

"Like ourselves, Moia?"

"Yes, entrepreneurs like you who have decided that Hong Kong has a bright future."

"Moia, the brightest part of my future in Hong Kong

is you. I wish sometimes I was just as certain about the commitment of the People's Republic as I am about yours."

"Claude. Shame on you. You promised me that once the decision was made, you would not look back. Ninety-seven will be a glorious year for Hong Kong and Phuket Color. Besides, as my father so often says, you cannot change the past. Madness comes to those who try." Moia lifted the back of his hand to her cheek and held it there affectionately.

Van Hooten turned to gaze at the profile of his beautiful companion. He hadn't expected this out of their relationship. He hadn't expected to fall in love with her. In fact, up to now, he had been uncertain about the reality of love. He had always been able to regard the women in his life as playmates, perhaps fancy bonbons, but nothing so emotional as to provoke the use of the word *love*. It is not too late, he thought, to change his commitment to Hong Kong. It would be difficult, but not impossible. He was reluctant to admit to himself that it was Moia Hsu who had tipped the scales toward Beijing as far as he was concerned. Van Hooten closed his eyes and dropped into a nap that didn't end until the plane bumped down heavily at Beijing Airport.

Once through customs, they were met by a nattily dressed uniformed chauffeur who led them to a black Lincoln Town Car parked outside the terminal. A rear window lowered to reveal the face of an older man with a small pointed white beard. "Father! What a pleasant surprise." She leaned into the open window to hug him. Van Hooten could see that the old man's eyes were focused on him during her greeting.

Moia turned to Van Hooten. "Claude, this is Dr. Ching Hsu. He is my father, and one of our hosts." The old man nodded, almost imperceptibly, and then turned his eyes back to his daughter.

Once inside the limo, Dr. Hsu and Moia had a brief,

animated conversation in Chinese, most of which escaped Van Hooten's understanding, though he could make out his name being spoken several times. For a short time Moia seemed upset about something her father said, but the displeasure was soon replaced with a smile.

"Father says we will be his dinner guests this evening with ten other businessmen. They represent other companies who are dedicated to the long-term development of Hong Kong."

Van Hooten mustered a friendly smile. "That's very nice of you, Dr. Hsu. I'm sure it will be interesting."

"Yes, it will be." This time Dr. Hsu spoke in perfect English. "Another guest will join our group for dinner." He looked intently at Van Hooten as he spoke. "General Liu Wing will be joining us. He is a close friend of my daughter. They see each other so rarely, I thought we should take advantage of their both being here in Beijing. General Liu has just returned from assignment in Tibet."

Van Hooten nodded and smiled. Moia turned to peer out the window at the broad boulevard that covered most of the distance between Beijing Airport and the complex of government buildings in the central part of the city. Moia explained that the highway had been completed with the hope of a host role in the 1996 Olympics. The Olympic bid went to Atlanta in the United States, but at least China now had one fine, if very short, highway.

Van Hooten sensed she was uncomfortable with her father's announcement, and wondered if General Liu was the subject of his remarks earlier when she had became upset.

The Town Car pulled into the circular driveway in front of the Great Wall Hotel. The gleaming hotel was situated in the midst of rather shabby surroundings, though Van Hooten did see heavy cranes rising from the ground nearby, indicating that replacement and renovation were planned for the immediate area.

Dr. Hsu stayed in the car as their baggage was being unloaded from the trunk. When they were ready to go inside, the rear window lowered again. "Moia, the driver will bring the car back here for your use during the day. He has instructions regarding dinner. There will be an afternoon trip to Badaling for all our guests. Perhaps you should join them."

"Thank you, father. I think Claude would enjoy that." Moia smiled as her father's face disappeared behind the descending window.

Upon checking in, Van Hooten was upset to find that he and Moia had been assigned separate quarters on different floors. He wondered if it were a case of father looking after daughter. He felt little warmth from the old man and hoped that Moia was correct in predicting that their stay in Beijing would be brief.

A tapping came at Moia's door less than a minute after she had closed it. She ran quickly to open the door, expecting it might be Van Hooten, but found herself staring into the smiling face of handsome General Liu Wing.

"Liu! What a surprise. Father said you would be joining us for dinner. Come in. Come in, I am unpacking."

Liu strode into the room, tossed his visored military hat onto the sofa, and swept Moia into his arms. "I miss you so much, Moia," he murmured as he kissed her forehead. Feeling a stiffness in her, he relaxed, held her loosely and studied her beautiful face. "Moia, you are the most attractive woman in China. I certainly saw nothing the likes of you in Tibet."

"Oh, Liu, please tell me what it is really like in Tibet." Moia saw an opening to change the subject.

"Tibet is not my cup of tea at all. But guess what, my dear, all of that is about to change. In fact, it can be like old times. Remember when we were both assigned to Shanghai?" The tall young general was smiling broadly, reminiscing.

"Whatever are you talking about? That was so many years ago. A lot of things have happened to us since then. Tell me about Tibet. I only hear rumors once in a while."

"To hell with Tibet! I am finished there. I have a new assignment. Hong Kong! I will be there in a few weeks."

Moia's face grew expressionless, pondering what that might mean. "Liu, that doesn't make sense. The People's Liberation Army in Hong Kong?"

"Of course not! Not the whole damn army, just me. I will be working as a special attaché for the Trade Ministry. That means we can resume our lives. Or at least we can see each other more often." Liu stared at Moia. She was strangely quiet.

"Liu, it's been a long time. I am happy for you, but our lives went on separate paths two years ago." She thought right then of telling him about Van Hooten. It would clear the air . . . maybe. She remembered her father's talk about Liu in the limo. Maybe Dr. Hsu had a hand in the general's reassignment.

"And in those two years, Moia, I have thought of you every day. Is there someone else, Moia?"

"Every day! I haven't heard from you for months and months. You could have been shot. There was killing in Tibet, I heard." Moia decided to delay any discussion about Van Hooten. She walked over to him and put her hands on his broad shoulders. "Welcome home, General Liu. And welcome to Hong Kong. We will have lots of time to talk about the future, won't we. As for right now, I have to meet Claude Van Hooten. They have scheduled a trip for our group to Badaling. Claude hasn't been there before. Why don't you come along?"

"Oh no. The last thing I need is another trip to the Great Wall. Enjoy yourself. The Dutchman should be very impressed. The dikes in the Netherlands are no comparison."

Moia could scarcely suppress a sigh of relief. Having Liu with them, and tramping the Great Wall together, would be a tense ordeal.

Liu recovered his hat from the sofa, walked back to Moia and brushed a kiss on her cheek. "Better take an umbrella. I think it is supposed to rain north of here. I look forward to dinner. Dr. Hsu says I'm to sit next to Van Hooten. What sort of capitalist is he?" Liu spit out the word *capitalist* as if it were a curse.

"Textiles, silk, and synthetics. Clothing for export. He loves to talk about his business. You will learn all about it tonight. He will find you fascinating. I'm sure he's never met a general in the People's Liberation Army."

"Those capitalist Hong Kong boys making their first trip to Beijing always ask the same questions. They all want to know right away what happened at Tiananmen Square, even though they've probably heard the story a hundred times. It's been over six years now. The day at Tiananmen is obscure as a flyspeck in the history of China."

"Are you sure about that, Liu? Is that Liu Wing's opinion or is it that of one of Deng's generals?"

"They are one and the same, Moia. Ah, my dear sweet bird, the vagaries of politics always mystified you. Maybe you have spent too much time in Hong Kong." Liu put on his hat as Moia opened the door. "Enjoy your visit to Badaling. I'm sure your account of the Great Wall will captivate the attention of our Dutch capitalist."

Moia closed the door, breathing a sigh of relief. The possessive tone of voice used by the young general annoyed her. Memories of their days in Shanghai swept through her mind. Their affair had burned alternately very hot and then very cold. At times their passion had been too compelling to deny.

Their physical attraction to each other had burned with the intensity of fire all during a long winter spent north of Shanghai at a time when Liu was in military study. Nevertheless, the body must recuperate once in a while from the exhaustion of passion. It was then that both of their minds worked overtime and independently. Ideologically, they were most often split in their beliefs as to what was the best course for China's future.

The telephone rang. It was Van Hooten. "Hello, dear. I have a lovely room. It's rather cold, however. It needs a little Moia for warmth."

"Claude, I must tell you that our time is planned ahead carefully for us. I have just read the schedule and it does not say anything about Moia warming your room. It says only that we must meet our group in the lobby in fifteen minutes for the trip to Badaling. Father is so certain that all newcomers to Beijing desire to see the Great Wall."

"I had something else in mind, Moia. But if we must, we must. Is your father going?"

"Dr. Hsu has other plans. I know that disappoints you." Moia laughed softly. "My father is not as tough as he might seem. He has only one child, you know, and a mere woman at that. Please forgive him for being himself. You will find him quite accessible on business matters."

"A mere woman?"

"China needs strong young sons. Remember that, Claude." Moia chuckled musically. "Also remember that I'm very happy about being a woman."

"Not as happy as I am," assured Van Hooten. "By the way, is there anything special about this trip to the wall that I should prepare for?"

"Bring along your camera and your trench coat. Badaling is in the mountains. It rains a lot up there this time of year. Don't worry about anything. It's only a little over an hour's drive. We'll be quite comfortable in the limo with another guest or two."

When Van Hooten hung up the phone, he walked to the window. The street in front of the hotel was a river of bicycles with only an occasional auto. All those people, he thought, with such a meager list of possessions. All of them were soon to be exposed to the wonders of the marketplace in Hong Kong. More than ever, he felt that his decision to keep Phuket Color in Hong Kong was the right one.

The drive to Badaling went quickly. Four Town Cars followed in close single file all the way to the mountain foothills at Badaling. The highway narrowed at that point where the Great Wall cut across the roadway. A tunnel through the wall took the cars to a parking lot on the other side. A row of tacky souvenir shops lined the roadway on both sides of the wall.

Van Hooten eyed the passengers as they alit from the other cars. From their speech and clothing, he drew the conclusion that most of them were American businessmen. That was somewhat of a surprise. Many of the Americans he knew had long ago given up on Hong Kong.

Moia led Van Hooten on ahead of the group, and the two of them were the first to climb the staircase to the top of the Great Wall. They walked a hundred yards or so eastward to the first guardhouse that straddled the wall. She turned the corner and tugged at Van Hooten's sleeve, pulling him into a sheltered alcove inside the guardhouse. Quickly glancing around to make certain they were alone, she hugged Van Hooten and then accepted his kiss, which burrowed deep into the hollow of her neck. Then she tugged Van Hooten into the open to await the others. Outside the guardhouse, the view of the massive wall winding with serpentine twists and turns along the ridge of the rugged mountains was spectacular.

Van Hooten looked at the wall, which stretched

many miles to the west of them, as far as they could see. "Moia, I must say, I have seen pictures and postcards of this very spot all my life, but it is still most impressive. The actual building of it defies logic."

Moia nodded in assent. "It goes on for over three thousand miles, you know. My father says China itself defies logic. It is not like other places. Even our Hong Kong is different."

They walked westward on the wall, continuing up a steep incline until they reached the next guardhouse. From there they could look back on Badaling and the extension of the wall disappearing into the east across the highway. The cloud cover broke for a few moments, inspiring Van Hooten to busy himself with his camera.

Far ahead of them a group of soldiers of the Liberation Army strolled along the wall in bright dress uniforms. In fact, Van Hooten noticed that there were several groups of soldiers visiting the wall that day. They made up a significant percentage of the visitors.

"Why all the soldiers?" he asked.

"It is a favorite place to visit for all Chinese. On weekends and holidays it gets very crowded up here. The Beijing garrison is large. Many soldiers from South China have never seen the wall."

Moia became silent and studied the group of military men that must have been a half mile beyond them. Among them was a very tall soldier in an officer's coat. The others clustered around him as he seemed to be pointing out objects in the distance. She opened her purse, hoping to find the tiny roof prism binoculars she usually carried. Then she remembered leaving them on the dressing table back at the hotel.

"I want to thank you, Moia, for insisting that I play tourist this afternoon. It is truly spectacular. We are also building an appetite for dinner this evening." Van Hooten kept clicking away with his camera as the clouds parted and opened spaces for shafts of sunlight to brighten the green mountains.

"Claude, I want to take a picture of you, right here in this beautiful spot," Moia declared enthusiastically.

He handed her the camera. She then clicked off a couple of shots of Van Hooten studiously contemplating the rugged terrain north of the wall. Next, she turned slowly until the camera's zoom lens was carefully adjusted to bring the group of soldiers a thousand yards above them into clear focus.

The tall soldier in the officer's coat was unmistakably General Liu Wing. The group of younger officers around him seemed to be listening intently to some point he was making. She clicked the shutter and then continued to pivot, taking several other shots.

She still held the camera tightly to her face. Inside she was seething and did not want to reveal her mood to Van Hooten. Liu had undoubtedly sped to the wall ahead of them. Perhaps he had even taken a helicopter. From his position on the wall, he could have watched them with field glasses or camera lens all the way from the stairwell in Badaling.

Able now to hide her disgust with Liu, she turned and handed the camera back to Van Hooten. "Claude dear, we have far outdistanced the others. I think we had better walk back and join them." They began their descent, quickly covering the distance back to the next guardhouse. Moia studied the spot where she and Van Hooten had embraced. She turned to where Liu and his soldiers were standing, now even farther away. No question about it, she told herself. If Liu had his binoculars or his camera out, he could have spotted their brief embrace. The odds were against it. But he could have.

"You are very quiet, Moia. Is it the company or is it something else?" Van Hooten was now walking beside Moia, who seemed lost in thought as they approached other members of their entourage at a lower level.

"I'm sorry, Claude. Silly man, you know it is not you. I guess I have a lot on my mind. The wall is sometimes depressing. Somehow it provokes too many thoughts about the old China. I prefer the new China."

"What do you mean?" Claude asked, not following her thoughts completely.

"Look closely at it." She swept her hand toward the distant mountains where the wall merged with the horizon. "All those hundreds of years. Zillions of man-hours of labor. Countless lives lost. And many scholars will say it was a failure. It kept no one in or out. China's enemies in the early days of the wall knew that it would be only as successful as the bravery of its defenders. Maybe it was Genghis Khan who said that. Ask General Liu about that at dinner tonight. I'm sure he fills his head full of such trivia."

"I would imagine that a man in the military here in China would have some very definite opinions about the wall," said Van Hooten. "I doubt if it has any military significance at all today. And it probably never did."

They were now rushing down the stairs, exiting the wall. Moia paused, touching his arm, then turned around when they were completely surrounded by the walls of the stairwell. When she was certain there was no one behind them or in front of them, she put her arm around his neck and pressed her lips to his. "I love you, Claude," she murmured. Then she released him quickly and sprinted down the stairs.

Soon they were walking back toward the parked limos. Urchins selling souvenirs, mostly painted rocks and plastic coins, tugged at Van Hooten's jacket. He smiled down at the grimy young entrepreneurs, wondering if their blatantly capitalistic endeavor would be the last they ever indulged in. For the sake of his own future, and that of Phuket Color, he hoped not.

The drive back to Beijing went swiftly. Van Hooten grasped Moia's hand firmly when their fingers touched beneath her raincoat, which lay on the seat between them. She squeezed his hand, then closed her eyes and appeared to sleep most of the way to Beijing.

Dr. Hsu's dinner guests that evening were taken to a banquet hall in a remodeled wing of the huge Beijing Hotel. The massive structure had served China through scores of years, housing at one time or another a good portion of the major political figures of the twentieth century. The hotel's proximity to Tiananmen Square and nearby government buildings made it a logical quarters for state visitors.

Besides Dr. Hsu and General Liu, Moia and Van Hooten were joined by several representatives of an American fast-food chain, a world-renowned manufacturer of farm machinery, and a major American automotive giant. As successful as Phuket Color Ltd. was at this time, the other companies dwarfed Van Hooten's comparatively tiny firm. In fact, he wondered why he and Moia were selected to dine with executives of all those billion-dollar corporations. It was well known that a number of truly small businessmen had been brought in from Hong Kong, but they were obviously being entertained elsewhere.

It had to be Moia's connection, he reasoned. Hsu's daughter, though a "mere woman," was apparently held in high regard by the Trade Ministry. Nevertheless, Van Hooten decided that he had every reason to feel flattered at the inclusion of Phuket Color among these giants.

Peking duck was served as a main course for their dinner, along with the usual endless selection of side dishes frequently served to visitors. It was as if the chef were saying, "Look! In China we can cook absolutely anything."

Despite all of this the dinner progressed swiftly, until the lights were dimmed and a projection screen drawn down on one wall.

The presentation by Dr. Hsu was very brief. Its gist was a pictorial review of the vast industrial growth purported to be happening in many remote provinces of the People's Republic. The program was supposed to inspire a feeling of kinship between those present at the dinner and those who were obviously already taking advantage of the vast billion-person labor market. "High-quality workmanship is the real advantage you gain over your competition when you invest in China. Because of our competitive labor market, it will be years before similar product can be duplicated outside the People's Republic." Dr. Hsu turned to look directly at Claude Van Hooten when he spoke.

Van Hooten found himself compelled to break eye contact with the old man. He found himself thinking about Hsu's "competitive labor market." The truth of the matter was that rural China was so vast, and the manufacturing projects were so widely scattered, that workers could be held to their employment by the meagerest of wages. There was in fact no competition as yet in this rudimentary struggle toward capitalism. The status quo would no doubt be maintained into the next century, given the authority of a vast military establishment numbering over twenty million under arms.

Hsu continued to stare directly at Van Hooten. "Gentlemen, my friend to my left, seated beside General Liu Wing, is Mr. Claude Van Hooten of the Netherlands." He paused. Van Hooten was taken aback. He couldn't even vaguely imagine why the trade minister had singled him out. "There is a word, *dapper*, used by our British friends." Hsu paused again. It was pretty well known that Hsu had no British friends.

"Mr. Van Hooten is a 'dapper' man. The fine silk he wears was grown and crafted in Guangdong Province by the finest tailors in the world, Chinese tailors." The old man remained serious. Several of the other guests smiled, probably amused at Hsu's using Van Hooten as a billboard to illustrate China's advance in the world textile and fashion market. Liu turned toward Van Hooten and smiled broadly, patronizing Hsu without saying anything.

Van Hooten felt impelled to say something. "Thank you, Dr. Hsu, for your flattering observation." Then addressing the others, Van Hooten went on. "Phuket Color has a retail shop in Hong Kong. I'm sure you will find our tailors, Chinese tailors, happy to serve you. In fact," he winked, "if you mention my name you will be treated with a handsome discount."

Everyone laughed. Dr. Hsu's deadpan delivery had set them up very well for a bit of levity, even though it wasn't very funny.

Several young women entered the banquet hall and distributed packets of reading material for each guest. Hsu rose from the table, thanked everyone for attending and expressed the thought that tomorrow's conference would be a very thorough discussion of the times lying just ahead for Hong Kong, complete with an open forum with questions and answers. All questions for the Trade Ministry should be submitted in writing, first thing in the morning. Dr. Hsu didn't seem a bit troubled by this strange interpretation of an "open forum."

It was about ten o'clock at night when Moia and Van Hooten were dropped off at the Great Wall Hotel. It was Moia's suggestion that they have a drink in the cocktail lounge just off the lobby before going upstairs. The lounge, subdued by warm, dark woods and dim lighting, seemed a perfect place to relax.

"So, my love, what did you think of Dr. Hsu?" Moia smiled as she asked the question.

"First of all, he is a gracious host, though his sense of humor is a bit hard to find. I felt a wee bit embarrassed by his personal commercial for Phuket Color."

"You shouldn't have been. That was father's way of saying to the others that China is opening its doors to companies both small and large. He is rather obscure at times."

"I suppose you are right, but he isn't a bit obscure about some things."

"And what might that be?"

"He looks after his daughter, like a great eagle sitting on a cliff overlooking his aerie."

Moia smiled gently and patted the back of Van Hooten's hand affectionately. "Is that bad?"

"I suppose not. No doubt he feels that it is his duty, and that it is natural and noble for him to protect the shining jewel of his family."

"Claude dear. This jewel would have much more luster if it were a son."

"You've alluded to that before. I'm sure you are wrong. He is obviously so proud of you."

"You will understand someday, Claude. The more time you spend in the People's Republic, the more you will know about fathers and sons." Moia smiled and grasped his hand. "Don't feel bad for me, Claude. Actually, I am quite happy. The magnificent Claude Van Hooten makes my life sing!"

Moia and Claude spotted General Liu Wing at the same instant. He strode up to the bar and stood for a moment, letting his eyes adjust to the dimness. Then, turning around, he saw the two of them instantly. "Well, what a surprise," he said. "Moia, you must be exhausted. It has been a long day on top of your flight from Hong Kong."

"Yes, Liu, it has. Claude and I were just relaxing, discussing father's meeting. The Americans were very attentive."

"Please join us, General. I've always found a glass of sherry promotes sleep. Although after tramping along your Great Wall, I'm sure I'll have no trouble." Van Hooten signaled for a waiter as Liu pulled up a chair.

Moia watched Liu closely at the instant Van Hooten

mentioned the wall. It was a perfect opportunity for him to declare that he had also visited the wall in the afternoon.

"I must confess I haven't been to Badaling in years. There are other vantage points along the wall that I prefer. What did you think of our treasure, Claude? Did it live up to expectations?"

"Yes, it did." Van Hooten paused and looked at Moia, who was staring intently at Liu, as if something was wrong. "Of course, Moia was an excellent guide, full of information. Before I asked a question, she had given the answer."

Moia rose abruptly from the table. "Gentlemen, my long day has caught up with me. I am going to leave you both here, while you have each other's company." As she picked up her purse, she glanced at Van Hooten's camera case, which he had carried with him all day. She couldn't wait to see the film developed so she could examine the phantom of General Liu facing them from the high guard post west of Badaling. "Sweet dreams, gentlemen."

Both men watched as she disappeared into an elevator in the hallway outside the cocktail lounge.

"Moia is a talented women," ventured Claude Van Hooten. "She has the business instincts of a successful leader."

"She is very attractive, also," General Liu observed. "I'm sure that hasn't escaped you. Right, Claude?"

Van Hooten felt ill at ease with the remark. He didn't know why. "I don't think we would get anyone to disagree with that."

They became quiet. Van Hooten finished off his sherry, and signed the check. "General, I must say good night. I'll want to be alert for the conference tomorrow. Will I see you there?"

"Oh, heavens no. I'm sure Dr. Hsu feels that a military presence is not desirable." Liu also rose from the table. "However, I will see you again one day. If I can help you with anything while you are in China, please let me know. Moia knows how to reach me."

He watched General Liu walk slowly out the front door of the Great Wall Hotel. He couldn't remember disliking anyone so much for no apparent reason.

Chapter 8

CECIL LO, past fifty years, slender and erudite, sat at a table next to a second-floor window overlooking Chinatown's Mott Street in New York City. Cecil had been asked to accompany Brandon Poole to New York for his seminar at the Waldorf. He accompanied Poole frequently on such trips as a security man. Brandon had asked him to meet him at Hing's, a small, quiet cafe that catered mostly to Chinese and a few others who delighted in food the way it would be prepared in Guangzhou, or Canton as it was called in the old days.

Brandon Poole was usually prompt. He expected to see him at the stroke of twelve. Lo sat reading the single-page report he had prepared for Poole, who had assigned him unexpectedly to shadow Lacy Locke when they arrived in New York. Poole had a mania for investigating people who might play a part in his business life. Actually this was sort of a Hong Kong syndrome these days. Everyone seemed to be watching everyone else.

The log prepared by Lo showed that Lacy had walked to Lenox Hill Hospital directly after leaving her apartment, no doubt to visit her husband, reported in the morning papers to have been mugged several days ago. After that she went to work at New Worldwide Securities in lower Manhattan. The wife of the high-profile newsman was evidently successful in her field. She was listed as a vice president for that company, which he found had impressive quarters on Wall Street.

Lacy worked long hours and usually went straight home to her apartment. One evening she had left her apartment to have cocktails with a young man at the Plaza. It seemed to be business related.

Cecil Lo finished reading his report again. Certainly not much there, he thought to himself. He wondered if Brandon Poole would think it worthwhile.

The thought had not left his mind when the tall, athletic-looking Poole entered the doorway, spotted Lo immediately and hurried to their table. Brandon Poole was the grandson of Sir Brandon Poole, who had gained a heroic reputation serving with Mountbatten in India when the British Empire still existed. Handsome young Poole, now in his late thirties, had become a permanent resident of Hong Kong. Years ago he had decided that he would make a lot of money there, and he had.

"Cecil! Good to see you again." Cecil Lo stood as Brandon Poole shook his hand, and silently nodded and smiled in response.

They both ordered lunch before Cecil Lo slid his brief report across the table, rather tentatively. Lo shrugged. "I hope you are pleased. Not much excitement here."

"That's good, Cecil. I'm not looking for excitement. I have enough of that in my life." Brandon read the report carefully.

"Good work, Cecil! Keep on her track for another day or so. This information is quite useful."

"Really?" Lo lifted his eyebrows. He hadn't expected such approval.

"Now, my friend, let's enjoy our lunch. It is always good to come back to Hing's. His family has the finest restaurant back in Guangzhou, you know."

After lunch, Brandon Poole waved goodbye to Cecil Lo as he hailed a taxicab on Mott Street. He glanced at his watch and then instructed the driver to take him to the Waldorf.

Poole decided that he was fully prepared to address the select group of investors having a primary interest in Southeast Asia, the People's Republic, and Hong Kong. The seminar had been arranged by a coalition of Hong Kong business interests that had made a decision to stay in Hong Kong beyond 1997. The seminar also had the unusual stamp of approval by the Trade Ministry in Beijing, who seldom expressed an opinion on such matters unless they directly involved the Chinese.

Poole was widely known in investment circles as a man who had accumulated a fortune in a few short years, not only with his investments but with his construction company. Its name was visible on rising cranes and construction sites throughout the Crown Colony and in the neighboring countries throughout Southeast Asia.

Brandon Poole surprised many by publicly vowing to keep his construction and exporting company in Hong Kong and "grow with the future," after the 1997 Beijing takeover. His was a prestigious name in this last vestige of empire, and his intention to stay put, announced early on, had surprised almost everyone. The exodus of others to Canada, Australia, and other places had no doubt been postponed by some, owing mainly to the decision of the man considered a premier expert in his field. Brandon Poole Ltd. had thrived spectacularly lately, even as the influence of the People's Republic was obviously growing every day.

Now, in his suite, Brandon relaxed for the short seminar which was to begin in about an hour. He reviewed the guest list, a total of sixteen people, most of them key people for brokerage houses specializing in Pacific Rim investments.

Near the middle of the alphabetical list of people attending was the name of Lacy Locke, VP, New Worldwide Securities. He decided that he would attempt to draw her aside and discuss the unusual and unexpected names of Hong Kong companies included in a proposed high-risk fund.

He was particularly curious about Phuket Color, the comparatively small company he knew from outside sources was building an immense factory in a remote area of Guangdong Province. It was partially owned and operated by Claude Van Hooten, the lone-wolf Dutchman who was rumored to have close connections in Beijing. Like himself, Van Hooten seemed to be dedicated to stay past 1997. He wanted to know why.

Brandon Poole entered the small conference room reserved for the meeting about fifteen minutes early. Three guests were already there, chatting by a window looking out on Park Avenue. One of them was a tall, breathtakingly beautiful woman with jet black hair and wide-set hazel eyes which instantly fixed confidently on his own.

"Hello. I'm Lacy Locke. I know you are Brandon Poole from your photographs in the South China *Morning Post.*"

"Aha! You've been reading the Hong Kong papers lately. Good for you!" Brandon Poole grasped her extended hand warmly. "It's encouraging to meet people who do their homework. Let's see now . . . you're with New Worldwide Securities."

"Mr. Poole, you've done your homework, too. But then I'll bet you always do. Is it true that you have personally constructed a third of Hong Kong?" Her eyes continued their aggressive contact with those of Brandon Poole.

"Absolutely not," he assured her with a deep laugh. "But rumors to that effect can do me no harm. Hong

Kong is so vast. There are many that have prospered as I have, and room for many more."

The two men who had been talking to Lacy were now joined by others who began to wander into the room. All stood absorbing the conversation between the two strikingly attractive people.

"Yes," intruded one man, "but will there be room after 1997?"

Brandon Poole glanced at his wristwatch. "Sir, it is three o'clock. I believe it is time for us to discuss the very question you ask. Let's get to work."

They all took chairs around the elongated oval conference table. Brandon Poole took a thick folio of notes, placed it in front of him and spent the next two hours extolling the future of Hong Kong. He referred to his notes only infrequently, and then only to quote appropriate numbers.

At the conclusion, he gave concise answers to several questions and then closed the meeting. "Gentlemen and lady, I must leave for another engagement. I hope you have learned a little. I also hope that I can see you in Hong Kong someday. If any of you ever make the trip, and you should, I will do whatever I can to help you get to know Hong Kong."

Lacy Locke lingered in the room until the others left. Smiling, Poole walked over to her. "Did you learn anything?"

"Of course I did. I learned that there are an infinite number of questions still to be asked. I'm leaving for Hong Kong in about a week. If you're there, would it be an imposition to ask them of you then?"

"I'd be very insulted if you didn't look me up immediately. Mind if I leave with you? I'm rather in a hurry." Riding down in the elevator, he found it impossible to keep his eyes off her. "Where are you staying in Hong Kong?"'

"At the Mandarin."

"Very good. It's only a short walk from my office.

Please call. I'll be expecting it. There is so much to talk about."

As they exchanged business cards in the lobby, Brandon Poole spotted Cecil Lo sitting in the lobby, eyes buried in a newspaper. When Lacy exited the lobby, Lo casually folded his paper and followed.

Brandon Poole returned to his suite, where he busied himself with his daily telephone calls to Hong Kong. He had decided to order dinner in his room in order to complete his business for the day. At nine P.M. he was to meet a friend, Sean Xiang.

Sean was a Hong Kong impresario visiting New York for the purpose of recruiting talent for several trendy nightclubs he owned back in Wan Chai and Kowloon. Sean had an eye for the outlandish that had made his clubs in Hong Kong the "in" places to go. His flashy clubs attracted the broad clientele of the city's ample affluent populace as well as the tourist trade. He had made a specialty of importing cutting-edge decadence from New York and Los Angeles to Hong Kong.

It was only a few minutes before nine when Brandon Poole concluded his work for the day and prepared to meet Sean in the lobby bar. Before leaving his room he carefully checked his airline tickets for his return to Hong Kong in the morning. He suspected it would be a late night, but he would have plenty of time to nap on the long flight. If you could pick one host in the whole world for a night on the town, it would be Sean Xiang. Brandon looked forward to the evening ahead. He almost never worked such frivolities into his busy schedule back in Hong Kong.

Sean was sitting in the lobby bar when Brandon walked in. The stocky, muscular man rose and pumped Brandon's hand vigorously. Despite his weight, he appeared to be very fit. All of his moves were decisive and energetic.

"You are looking very well, Sean. But you always

do. That's always puzzled me," said the grinning Brandon. "It can't be due to clean living."

"Shame on you, Brandon. You are jealous. You sit there in that big office in Hong Kong and count your money around the clock." He shook a finger back and forth in mock admonition. "However," he said assertively, "you will no doubt be rewarded in your Episcopal heaven."

"I'm afraid I can't count on that, Sean. It is much too late. My record is cluttered with deeds I wish I could forget." Brandon said it like he meant it.

"Cheer up, old man. Tonight we're checking out Satan's Niche. I am told that it is frequented only by the truly evil. In fact you can't get past the bouncer unless you qualify."

"Do we qualify?"

"No, Brandon, we don't. But in my business, I have close friends who do. We'll use them. That's your expertise, using people, right?" Sean nudged Brandon gently in the ribs with a pixie smile on his round face.

"Well then, I'd better fortify myself." Brandon ordered a drink for both himself and Sean. "Two Chivas doubles, neat."

"Ah, now there's a call for the devil. You even remembered what I drank on our last ill-spent night together."

A few minutes after ten, a taxi deposited them in front of an unmarked doorway in the West Village. A line of people trailed from the door a short distance to and around the corner. Many were business-people dressed in the usual dark suits. Most of the women wore tight, short, dark skirts or dresses that they had worn to the office, leaving their sneakers in a desk drawer in favor of spike heels. Some of the younger people were garishly costumed and with wild hairstyles. All seemed impatient to get into Satan's Niche.

Sean Xiang walked straight to the head of the line with Brandon Poole close behind. They were met by a broad-shouldered, bearded giant of a man, forming an impregnable wall across the door behind him. Sean slapped a folded twenty in the giant's hand. "Del Gaizo, I want you to meet Brandon Poole. He owns Hong Kong."

The giant smiled. "I thought *you* did, Sean. Go on in. If you can't find a table you like, let me know and I'll personally throw someone out."

Brandon Poole was amused by the patter between the two. He marveled at how Satan's Niche could be part of Sean's world when he lived ten thousand miles away. Sean Xiang was in high gear as usual.

They were seated at a table next to a large, square elevated stage in the middle of what was probably an old warehouse. The room, painted black, was lit by several naked lightbulbs dangling on wires from a high ceiling. The darkness of the decor absorbed almost all the light. Though the place was jammed, it was hard to make out anyone. It would take some time to adjust to the light.

Massive amplifiers stood like monoliths along the rear of the platform. Others were spaced strategically around the room. "I think we are in for some deafening cacophony, Sean." Brandon was eyeing the amplifiers warily.

"I'm sorry, Brandon. But you are correct. Such cannonading takes possession of all intelligent conversation and kills it. You must listen and watch the performers. However bad they are, they come across better than the music. The performer here tonight is the most bizarre imaginable. I am negotiating with her agent for an extended appearance in Hong Kong. I plan to put her in my new place in Wan Chai. Such decadence should be rewarded. Besides, Hong Kong hasn't seen anything quite like this one."

"What's her name?"

"Don't expect to recognize it, my friend. Her world is hardly in your universe. Her name is Mary Lulu."

"Really!" Brandon's face lit up with a faint smile. "Oh yes, she's supposed to be a hot item with some famous male model. Performs naked under his sport jacket."

Sean Xiang looked astonished. "Brandon, I can't believe you've joined the mad masses addicted to the tabloids."

"Believe me, Sean, she makes the financial pages too. Her model friend just signed a million-dollar contract with an obscure Hong Kong clothier with very little visible means of support. It has a few people wondering. There is to be a stock issue shortly for Phuket Color Ltd. It's headed up by a Dutchman, Claude Van Hooten. Ever hear of him?"

Sean shook his head. "No, I thought all the Dutch with money had already packed up and left Hong Kong."

Suddenly all the lights in the room went dark. A single powerful spotlight flashed toward the high ceiling and came to rest on a white rectangle, about eight feet by six feet. At first there was a faint humming noise, like a bumblebee. The buzzing grew very slowly in volume, taking about ten seconds to reach an earsplitting din. Then dead silence. Somewhere, barely audible, came the faint tinkling sounds of a piano. It was a Scott Joplin rag tune played slowly and deliberately, but increasing in volume just slightly every few seconds.

The white rectangle on the ceiling began to move. A transparent platform began to emerge from the rectangular opening, soon revealing that the suspended stage held a baby grand piano. Two long, shapely female legs planted in spike heels, leading upward inevitably to a perfectly sculpted derriere, clearly nude and visible, appeared below a short garment as the platform descended. It gave the illusion that the piano and the woman player standing in front of it were floating in the air.

The tempo picked up quickly as the small stage con-

tinued to descend. Soon it was clear that she wore a
loose, powder blue man's sport coat. A three-foot-long
blond ponytail trailed down her back and bounced cra-
zily as the beat picked up. Somewhere back of the
stage, drums, cymbals, and guitars began to pump deafening heavy metal through the amplifiers. Three muscular young male dancers clad only in powder blue
athletic supporters climbed onto the stage and began a
symbolic erotic worship directed at the descending
platform.

Sean Xiang glanced at Brandon Poole, formed an
okay sign with his thumb and forefinger, and mouthed
the words "Perfect for Hong Kong!"

Brandon shrugged and shook his head as the descent
of the platform stopped several feet above the main
stage. All at once, the woman turned around and faced
the audience. She stretched her hands high over her
head, permitting the sport jacket to open fully and expose a flawless naked figure. The music stopped, the
dancers froze on the stage and the crowd went wild.

The tall, Amazon-proportioned dancer then pursed
her lips, and touched them with her finger. "Shhh . . .
hush!" The crowd quieted, one by one. It took a while
as she pointed to a few of the more energetic cheerers,
and stared them into silence. Then for a second you
could hear a pin drop. "Hi there! I'm Mary Lulu. I love
to sing, dance, and fool around a lot."

The words ignited the crowd again, but once again
she hushed the audience with her exaggerated finger-
to-lips gesture. "First, I am going to sing."

She not only sang, but had a remarkable voice. Beautiful torch songs were in wild contrast to the garish appearance of her basically nude presentation. She
ranged from a low, throaty, sexy voice, to a soprano.

"No question about it, she has talent," murmured
Brandon. "Actually, Sean, she could make it as a
singer. Why all the rest?"

"Because there are lots of singers, but not many of

them have the ability to give the audience all the rest. I'm afraid artistry takes second place today in Hong Kong." Sean stared at her, then closed his eyes. The performer's stark nudity refused to separate totally from her voice. "You know, Brandon, not many could pull off an act like this without getting hooted unmercifully. That's talent, in this rotten world of ours."

"I suppose you're right, Sean. But don't the Mary Lulus of the world go off the deep end sooner or later?"

"Always! That's a tough part of my business, knowing when to dump them."

A sudden clash of cymbals and a loud reggae beat silenced their conversation. The descending stage now lowered her to the level of the male dancers. Mary Lulu then began to dance. She expertly undulated her way through an exotic routine that feigned the sated exhaustion of the male trio of worshipers, which stopped just short of explicit contact.

Then she turned her backside to the audience and began playing boogie-woogie piano. The combination of her fine piano playing and her elevated spread-eagled stance drove the crowd wild.

Brandon glanced around the room. "It's a good thing, maybe, that she is up on the high stage. This could get rough after people get a few drinks in them."

Sean grinned. "Then it becomes a job for Del Gaizo, the giant."

As the Plexiglas platform slowly began its ascent, Mary Lulu turned and faced the audience, once again spreading her arms wide, fully opening the powder blue sport coat. Then she deposited her derriere lightly on the keyboard of the baby grand behind her and began to jiggle her buns rapidly along the keys. The boogie-woogie began again, thus creating an illusion that it was the product of her rapidly jiggling derriere. The crowd cheered their approval as they followed Mary Lulu's progress all the way to the ceiling and into the dark rectangle.

In a few minutes, Sean and Brandon found themselves walking on Fourteenth Street. "Tell me, old boy," Brandon asked, "was that a roller piano, or does she really play boogie-woogie with her derriere?"

Sean Xiang grinned his big pixie smile as they crawled into a waiting cab. "I promise you, Brandon, that I will do research on that. I suspect it was a convenient tape, however."

Brandon Poole got out of the cab several blocks from the Waldorf, said good-bye to Sean Xiang, and decided to walk a few blocks for some much needed exercise. He walked left on Forty-eighth Street from Park Avenue, deciding to circle another block before entering the hotel.

By the time he reached the middle of the block, the street was void of any pedestrian traffic. Then someone stepped out of a doorway near the corner ahead and began walking toward him. Turning his head, he saw now that there was also someone approaching him from behind. Call it instinct, or maybe something buried in his mind from the old days in the Royal Marines, but he knew they were after him.

Brandon Poole slowed his step, deciding to deal with the person behind him first. He waited until he felt the touch on his clothing, then spun like a coiled spring and clotheslined a blow against the man's Adam's apple with his forearm, dropping him to the street. He turned swiftly to face the man ahead of him, who had stopped about twenty feet away, gaping at the groaning figure on the sidewalk. Then he wheeled around and fled. Brandon started after him reflexively. He took a few short paces and stopped.

He turned around, eyeing the motionless hulk on the sidewalk. He stepped around him and headed back toward Park Avenue. "Hell, I can't clean up their damned city," he muttered, thinking of the less hostile

New York he had visited in the past. As he turned the corner to head toward the Waldorf, he glanced back down Forty-eighth Street. The would-be assailant hadn't moved. He wondered if he had killed him. Unlikely, he thought to himself. But then he had done it before, back in the days of the Royal Marines.

Chapter 9

It HAD been a week now since the visit of Moia and Van Hooten to Beijing. One of the results of the conference was Ching Hsu's suggestion that Van Hooten see for himself the progress on the new Phuket Color factory being erected in Guangdong Province. Evidently the progress made thus far on the facility was impressive. Moia had reasoned that the main reason for her father's suggestion was that Van Hooten would be impressed and would probably communicate his optimism to business friends in Hong Kong.

Moia was napping now with her head on Van Hooten's shoulder as they clickety-clacked across the Pearl River on the bridge that led away from Guangzhou toward Foshan. The old train that crossed into the People's Republic at Lo Wu had made the trip west for many years, long before Canton had been renamed Guangzhou. Van Hooten had crossed the bridge once before. He had made the trip to Foshan to buy jade for a friend back in the Netherlands. As before, there were soldiers, apparently on sentry duty, at each end of the bridge.

Moia's eyes blinked open at the noise of the bridge crossing. "Oh, we are beyond Canton." Moia still hadn't broken the old habit of calling all the renamed cities by their old names. She closed her eyes again and snuggled close to Van Hooten.

"Why the soldiers?" he asked.

Moia blinked her eyes again. "I don't know. I guess they are protecting the bridge."

"Protecting it from what?"

"Claude! I don't know. They have so many soldiers. I guess someone thinks it's a good idea to keep them busy."

"Maybe it's your General Liu's idea."

"Hardly. I think he has other things to do. He was in Tibet, you know." Now she opened her eyes and stared at Van Hooten. "You don't like him, do you?"

"Does it matter?"

"No," she said quietly. "Now please let me sleep. We will travel by van from Foshan to the new factory. I have been over that road. There will be no sleeping there. It is hardly paved."

"It doesn't sound like much fun, a seventy-five-kilometer jaunt on an unpaved road. I wish we were going back to Hong Kong tonight."

"It will be very late. We will stay at the Dong Fang Hotel in Canton."

"By the way, does your father like it when you call the cities by their old names?"

"He used to frown. Now he doesn't bother. A lot of the people in Canton haven't changed either."

"What is the Dong Fang Hotel like?"

"It is old, but we will be comfortable."

"In separate rooms, I suppose."

Moia smiled impishly. "No. I made these reservations, not my dear father."

Van Hooten sighed. According to their schedule, it would be after dark before they finally got back to Guangzhou. "I hope it is all worth the trip. I do wish that we had waited until actual production had started. I'd feel a lot better if I could actually see product."

"Maybe you'll be surprised," Moia replied, unable to mask a smile.

"Don't tell me they are producing!"

"How would I know a thing like that?"

"You beautiful devil! I think you have a way of knowing everything."

The train lurched slightly as the brakes took hold. Moia now opened her eyes, pushed the lace curtains aside and looked out the window. "Claude, my dear, we are almost at the station in Foshan. Now you can quit worrying and asking questions. Have you ever been to Foshan?"

"Yes, I came here to buy some jade once. They have a factory here. I was able to get a large jade replica of a trotting horse for a friend in the Netherlands."

"A lady or a gentleman?"

"I believe I remember noticing that it was a gelding."

"Claude! I didn't mean the horse. I meant the friend." She dug her elbow playfully into his ribs.

Now it was Van Hooten's turn to smile.

They had scarcely stepped onto the platform in Foshan when a neatly uniformed young man introduced himself. "Mr. Van Hooten, I am Chou." He spoke that much in English, bowed slightly, then turned to Moia to continue in Chinese. "I will be your driver today, as soon as you are prepared to leave." A brief discussion followed between Moia and Chou, then he led them to a small Chevrolet van.

The American van was a surprise to Van Hooten, though lately, in the large cities, American cars were showing up more often. He regarded this as a positive sign. He felt that if ever China was to pull itself into the next century, it would need the assistance of the United States. "How long will the trip take?" Claude asked.

Chou looked at Moia, who repeated the question in Chinese.

"He says more than an hour," Moia interpreted.

"But the way he said it, I would guess more like two hours."

The first few miles went quickly over paved road passing through large produce communes. Because of the proximity of Guangzhou, it was fair to assume that their yield was probably destined for that huge South China metropolis. A little later the pavement deteriorated to gravel. Lack of maintenance produced an uncomfortable washboard effect. Then came a more narrow, rutted road through low farmland.

"Look!" Claude exclaimed, readying his camera. A farmer was working the land with water buffalo. "It's picturesque, but my picture would have looked the same a hundred years ago. It's hard to imagine a modern factory out here someplace."

"A factory, and lots of available labor, makes good roads a certainty very soon. You will see, Claude." Moia spoke with conviction. "If what is happening here happens in a thousand places all over China, China and its people will prosper. It is so exciting, my love."

Van Hooten was looking across the van through the driver's window as she spoke. There was a flicker of movement on the driver's face as he grew attentive. Van Hooten would have bet money that Chou had picked up Moia's careless use of the endearing term "my love." Later, when they left the van, Van Hooten decided that he would caution Moia to be more careful. Of course she would probably laugh at him and accuse him of paranoia.

Suddenly they cleared a wooded area that bordered on a rise in the landscape. Across a broad rolling hill they spotted a two-story building, covering perhaps twenty-five-thousand square feet in all. Lettered very neatly on a top corner was the name PHUKET COLOR. You could have expected to find just such a building in the outskirts of any modern major city in the world. Van Hooten thought of the sweatshop he now used in Bangkok, and felt a surge of energy. His excitement was more personal and limited, but nevertheless he now felt some of the exhilaration exhibited by Moia.

Chou turned off the rutted rural road and sped down the paved service road. The external portion of the structure was completed, ready for the occasional torrential rains that come to South China. It was painted beige with the lettering of Phuket Color in dark brown.

"Claude, it is beautiful. I am so excited for you. Isn't it wonderful!"

Claude nodded, obviously pleased and surprised. "The most wonderful thing about it, Moia, is that it exists. Now let's take a look inside."

Leaving the van, they walked briskly down an unpaved walkway to the door. A short, wiry man in khaki work clothes and steel-rimmed glasses emerged from the doorway to greet them. He stuck his hand out to grab Van Hooten's.

"Mr. Van Hooten, welcome! I am Sing Lee, manager of the construction team here." The man spoke impeccable English.

"Sing! I remember you well. We met at a planning meeting in Hong Kong, a year ago to this day. It looks like that was one meeting that was a success."

Sing Lee grinned. "Ah, you do remember. There were so many at the meeting. Construction had not started yet. This building was just a dream then." Sing turned and looked proudly at his work. "Come inside. We are actually a little ahead of schedule. I think you will be pleased with our progress."

Inside, they walked through a small office area that was barren of furnishings, except for a large desk covered with blueprints. "I have been working in here, and will vacate when the furniture arrives from Canton. It will be ready for your manager then upon request."

They walked through the door into the factory portion, which utilized most of the building. It was swept clean with open wiring dropping down at intervals from the ceiling. "Believe it or not we are all ready for the cutting and sewing machinery when it arrives."

Van Hooten was listening to every word, but his eyes were fixed on perhaps a dozen people, all busy at work in front of sewing machines and cutting tables set up neatly in a far corner of the open expanse. He walked toward the group ahead of the others. Lined up on a clothes bar behind the workers were perhaps a hundred men's suits made from fine silk. Sing Lee then actually ran ahead of them and lifted a plastic bag from the clothes bar. It was clearly marked *Claude Van Hooten* across an adhesive strip on the plastic.

"Sir, this is for you." Sing smiled broadly. "This is our first. I understand many thousands will follow it soon. Our production manager insisted on proving to you that, at least in some limited way, we are already operational."

Van Hooten took the garment bag from his hands. "Thank you, Sing. I will treasure it. Where is your production man? I would like to congratulate him."

"He had to make a trip to Foshan for supplies. I'll bet you passed him on the way. I will pass along your good words. He will be very proud."

Van Hooten passed the garment bag to their driver. "Please take this to the van for me." The man took the bag, and turned away without smiling. He walked a couple of steps, hesitated, then proceeded to the van. "Our man does understand English, doesn't he, Moia?"

Moia, watching the departure of the driver, looked thoughtful. She was no doubt thinking the same thoughts that were on Van Hooten's mind.

Van Hooten asked Moia to compliment the small group of workers in their native language before Sing Lee continued his tour of the new factory. They smiled appreciatively at her words, but kept right on sewing and cutting without cessation.

When they fell several paces behind Sing Lee, Moia whispered to Van Hooten. "Just think, Claude, these workers make even less than their counterparts in Bangkok."

"Not for long, Moia, not for long. Let's hope it lasts until we open all the markets."

Sing Lee proceeded to show them the fabric warehouse, a dust-free storage room, that took up perhaps a third of all the space in the building. To their surprise, it was about half full.

The rest of the tour took a little more time, because the computer installations that would connect them with Hong Kong and the world were not yet made. Sing Lee, who seemed to have a wealth of knowledge beyond that of the basic construction of the building, assured them that it would be in place within thirty days, along with the intricate worldwide inventory control system.

Within about three hours from the time they arrived at the factory, they climbed back into the van for the grueling journey to Guangzhou and the Dong Fang Hotel. Van Hooten smiled at the garment bag, which hung in the back of the van. "Do you suppose it will fit?" he whispered to Moia.

"I'll bet my salary on it," she replied, squeezing his hand behind the back of their driver.

Just before leaving the service road that led to the rugged road to Guangzhou, Van Hooten saw something he hadn't seen on the way in. Just ahead of them, parked against a stand of trees, was a tractor and a construction crane that had no doubt been used on the building. A sign in foot-tall letters along the crane proclaimed it was owned by BRANDON POOLE LTD., HONG KONG. He had seen the name next to countless construction sites around Hong Kong. Until now he didn't know that the People's Republic had used Brandon Poole to build Phuket's building, now to be leased to him for twenty-five years. The fact that the lease was a piece of paper that could be changed by the whim of someone in Beijing really hadn't bothered him until now. He squeezed Moia's hand gently. She was more and more becoming a part of the whole enterprise.

Chapter 10

Aꜰᴛᴇʀ ꜱᴇᴠᴇʀᴀʟ days, Adam Locke suddenly gave the morning news without the eye patch. He was his old handsome self, miraculously left unscathed by the vicious attack of the mugger.

His decision about campaigning for governor had been put temporarily on the back burner. It was still several weeks before election law required him to make it official. Supporters were actively getting petitions signed, trying to amass the thousands of names it would require to get him on the ballot. Only this morning he had discussed pros and cons with Lacy. Once he became an official candidate, he could no longer use his newscast as a pulpit for his ideas. If he did, equal time would have to be given to his opponent.

Lacy sat at her dressing table preparing for her day while listening to Adam read the morning news on the TV. The key word was *read*. That was Adam's real forte. The only problem he ever had with the news was when he eschewed the teleprompter. He had that lustrous baritone voice that could make a minor news story sound like a national cataclysm. Just this morning she had made this point with him. She had done it before, but this time he accused her of being seriously nonsupportive.

"You are suggesting that I am an unthinking and untalented robot," he had said.

"Adam, that is not fair. I couldn't do what you do in a million years. I admire your ability to make mundane, repetitive news listenable. It's just that when you start preaching about what a good politician should do, totally ad lib, you get in trouble. If you are going to do this thing, run for governor, you should take the time to do some extensive research and decide what it is you stand for. Maybe you need a sabbatical to map it all out."

"Lacy, my mind is on that all the time. You have no idea how much I've thought about it. It would be stupid to tip my hand to anyone as yet."

"I guess anyone includes me." She was sorry she said it. Another morning, another spat.

"Look, doll, if you don't know how I feel about things, nobody knows."

"Don't call me 'doll,' Adam. I'm your wife. I don't deserve some patronizing, sexist lunacy in the middle of a serious conversation. Look at yourself in the mirror, Adam. For God's sake, take off that eye patch! It's phony. It's dishonest, Adam." She had told herself many times before that serious arguments always ruined their days. Besides, maybe the handsome news robot wasn't capable of anything else. Nevertheless, she couldn't resist one more parting shot. "Take off the eye patch, doll! You're not reading the teleprompter very well. Believe me, people can tell."

He clammed up until he slammed the door and left the apartment. Now there he was on the morning news, all spiffed up. No scars, no eye patch. She couldn't resist a smile. "Thank you, Adam," she said, addressing the talking head on the screen.

Lacy flipped off the television set, leaving Adam pontificating in the middle of a sentence. She rose from the dressing table and walked into the bathroom, pausing to pick up the bathrobe Adam had left hanging on the back of a chair, as usual. She picked it up and started to hang it on the bathroom door, as usual. Her fingers touched something that was not terry cloth. Without thinking she pulled at the strange texture hanging from the pocket of the robe and gingerly held it aloft. The item was silky and lacy. It was a pair of women's panties, certainly not hers. She stuffed them back into the terry cloth pocket. She walked back to the dressing table and sat down, actually trembling with fury.

Adam had made a big deal the evening before about how Babs Billings, feeling so sorry for him, had come by in the afternoon with a container of soup and a deli sandwich. She returned to the bathroom, again took the lavender-colored panties from the robe, took them into Adam's den and draped them over the screen of his computer monitor. He spent a lot of time playing with his personal computer. This would give him something to think about.

Soon she hailed a cab downtown, still furious with Adam. She arrived in what seemed an instant, her mind totally preoccupied with her anger. She paid the cab driver, raced into the building and into an elevator.

At her desk now, she could do little more than stare blankly out the window. Adam had let her down one more time.

"Something wrong, Lacy?" Eric had entered her office without her even noticing him, and now stood at her side.

"Eric! I didn't even hear you! Nothing's wrong. I guess I was just thinking about the trip."

Eric deposited a folder on her desk that enclosed an itinerary and an ever expanding daily appointment schedule for her time in Hong Kong. Her selections of stocks for the new Southeast Asia Developing Market fund was still tentative. She noticed blocks of time were already set aside for Brandon Poole, Claude Van Hooten, and others, including major banks headquartered in Hong Kong.

Whitney Gordon tapped on her door. The CEO of New Worldwide Securities had a lot riding on the new venture.

"Come on in, Whit. I'm going over the latest data I have on the new fund. Talk about excitement! I hope I can take it. There is so damn much I don't know. I have only a few days left to educate myself, Whit, and then I'll be sinking or swimming in Hong Kong."

The soft-spoken CEO settled into a leather chair. "Lacy, thanks to you we'll have a flying start when we kick off this fund. Frankly, you've been so careful that I'm not so sure it is a high-risk fund. Similar mutual funds by other houses look like long shots at Belmont compared to this."

"Thanks, Whit, but there is a lot of risk here. I've been boning up on the whole Pacific Rim. The new fund is heavy with companies who deal with the People's Republic and Hong Kong. There is a wave of optimism about the future, a popular belief that 1997 will come and go, and Hong Kong won't skip a heartbeat. I'd like to know why. Frankly, I haven't seen anything that convinces me that substantive change has occurred since 1989 and Tiananmen Square. Do you know that a half million people demonstrated against that action in Hong Kong?"

"You've done your homework, Lacy. You're also right. It is a risk fund, but we'll be peddling it that way. I think you'll feel good about it by the time you get back. By the way, how's your Chinese?"

Lacy groaned. "Hardly the best, Whit, maybe the worst. I listen to tapes every day. Every time I spring it on my Chinese friends here in the city, they get a good laugh."

"Better laugh than cry. At least you'll get an A for effort. By the way, how did the seminar with Brandon

Poole go? He is bullish on the future of Hong Kong, I hear."

"He is. But he is different from a lot of the others. I guess he is incredibly rich. He's dealt with the Chinese for years. Old money and lots of new money. He's part of Hong Kong's aristocracy. His grandfather was knighted and served with Mountbatten of Burma. At this moment his construction expertise is badly needed in South China by Beijing. I have a gut feel he operates under different rules than many of the others. He's promised to spend some time with me over there."

Whitney Gordon sighed. "Be careful, Lacy. His history is that of a successful opportunist. In business, nobody bats a thousand. But Brandon Poole does." Whitney rose from his chair and got ready to leave.

"Thanks for the advice, Whit. I need as much as I can get."

"Lacy, my line is open to you around the clock. Remember that now, and when you get to Hong Kong." He strolled out the door.

Lacy could feel a level of excitement unknown to her before in matters of business. She could tell that behind his laid-back exterior, Whit was feeling it also. I'll bet Whit's another guy that bats a thousand, she thought.

Chapter 11

TERRY HARGRAVE, a Hong Kong superintendent of police, eyed the tall man closely. Hargrave was an old-timer. He had lived alternately through times openly corrupt and covertly corrupt. Right now it was the latter. A lot of people were asking questions. If there was skulduggery afoot, it was time to push it behind a curtain or under a rug.

Who the hell really knew what would happen to the Hong Kong police force in 1997? Despite verbal assurances, he couldn't imagine the communists not putting in their own superintendents of police. He had even heard that the People's Liberation Army would move right in and take over police duties. The fact that the governor called that a nasty, baseless rumor did little to dispel it.

That's why the tall man from Beijing bothered him. General Liu Wing of the People's Liberation Army. His credentials clearly stated that to be a fact. His civilian attire under these circumstances was completely in line with regulations. He was in Hong Kong in behalf of the People's Trade Ministry. That is what his credentials read. So, being convinced for the moment that the man was not in Hong Kong to take over his job, Hargrave smiled.

"Yes sir, this is an honor. What can I do for you?" He thus was following rule number one: Be nice to officials who might visit from the Beijing regime.

The tall man, still looking very much like a soldier, even in his civvies, also smiled. "Why is it an honor?"

Caught off guard, Hargrave fished for the right words. "Sir, you are a general. Forgive me, I have never before met a general of any army. What can I do to help you here in Hong Kong?"

General Liu reached into his jacket pocket and quickly produced a bulky object, which he slammed down on the desk. He lifted his hand to reveal a pair of heavy wire snippers. "You can stop your citizens from cutting holes in the fences near Lo Wu and Man Kam To."

The two towns were checkpoints along the border of the Hong Kong district of New Territories and the People's Republic. Hargrave thought for a moment. If there was any fence-cutting being done it would be unlikely that it would be someone in Hong Kong trying to get out. The problem was almost always the reverse.

"General Liu, I will most certainly take this up with the border sentries in that district. You can be sure of it."

Liu broke into a broad smile, then into heavy laughter. He actually walked around the desk and patted Hargrave on the back. "You are very quick witted, Hargrave, to give me an answer like that, when you and I know the streets are full of Guangzhou citizens who have cut their way into Hong Kong."

Liu's patronizing touch annoyed Hargrave. "Oh, I suppose that sometimes it happens either way, General, but I think you have stated it correctly."

"I admire smart people, Hargrave. So take possession of those wire snippers, and do what you can. But that really isn't the purpose of my visit today. I need a favor, just known to you and me. Is that possible?"

"I am a superintendent of police. My word is sacred, sir. I've spent a lifetime building a reputation."

"Well then, it is obvious we can trust each other." Liu pulled a small paper, attached to what could have been a passport photo, from his jacket and handed it to Hargrave. "This woman, Moia Hsu, is a citizen of the People's Republic. She is valuable to us—highly connected, you might say. I want you to watch her for a few days. Consider it a protection for her. However, in her case, she is not to be aware of any surveillance. Can you handle that?"

"Of course, General. It is a small thing. When will I see you again?"

"Oh, perhaps in a week or so. All I ask is that you keep a small journal of her movements." Liu reached into his jacket pocket and withdrew a wallet. He extracted two one-thousand-dollar Hong Kong notes and laid them on Hargrave's desk. "This should defray any expenses you might have. Hargrave, you certainly look Chinese, like one of my countrymen. Hargrave is a strange name."

"My father was British, sir."

"Well, Mr. Hargrave, I don't suppose you can do anything about that, can you." General Liu, turned on his heel and walked to the door.

He opened it and left without looking back, leaving Police Superintendent Hargrave feeling very uneasy. It was his first smell of things to come in 1997. He didn't like it at all.

Hargrave picked up the wire snippers and scrutinized the heavy metal. It was shiny. The two points actually glistened. The critical points of contact gave no evidence of ever having been used. He suspected that General Liu had bought them in a tool shop right there in Tsuen Wan. His real business today was Moia Hsu, who unfortunately for himself resided in his district.

The address was that of a villa located in the nearby countryside of New Territories.

He pondered for a few moments about whom he would assign to the task. Whom could he trust? Who on his staff would not boast to their girlfriends about being on assignment for a general from Beijing? Of course, he decided it must be handled by himself. After all these years on the force, he really couldn't trust anyone, especially in matters concerning Beijing. He memorized the address and decided that he would post himself near the villa early in the morning. Actually it would be a pleasant diversion from his normal schedule of supervising people who had grown accustomed to supervising themselves, while he enjoyed the horse races at Sha Tin.

The next morning he parked a small, dust-laden minivan at the edge of a small grove of trees a quarter mile from the villa supposedly housing Moia Hsu. The old van had been confiscated in a cocaine raid a couple of years ago. The department had received permission to retain use of it for occasions just like this. It looked like thousands of other small vans, popular for commercial use, making it ideal for his purpose. Hargrave, in field worker dress, kept his eyes on the villa, periodically using a pair of field glasses, scanning the living quarters and grounds for some sign of life. By noon, nothing had moved around the villa. His task had turned to complete boredom. The hardest part of the job, which would ordinarily be handled by a stringer for hire, was staying awake.

Hargrave looked at his Rolex, a gift from the operator of a Kowloon brothel some years ago. He had earned the handsome timepiece by having charges against the owner dismissed. Actually it had been merely a harassment raid to quell the noise after revelers got a bit out of hand one night. The owner probably would have got off anyway, but Hargrave felt it was his duty to accept the gift from the grateful entrepreneur.

Hargrave groaned. It was nearing one P. M. It was Saturday. He would see no races at Sha Tin today.

His vigil ran on into the darkness. He gave up, deciding to return the next morning. If General Liu were to ask him if had kept the vigil all night long, he would lie. He had made a study of every road, bush, and tree stump for miles around. There was no one near the remote villa observing him. He felt sure of that.

The next day, the villa appeared just as he left it. In the morning he drove the old minivan up the winding gravel road leading to the house. There were no vehicles parked anywhere around the living quarters. The house appeared to be shut tight. In fact, a massive lock and chain secured an iron gate. Noting carefully the position of the lock, he drove back to his cover behind the grove of trees.

By noon he had decided that it would be safe to turn his dismal job over to a stringer back in Tsuen Wan. It was time to collect a favor from a grateful pickpocket he had caught at Sha Tin.

Just before he was about to pull out of his covering grove, a black Mercedes sedan sped by, kicking up a long trail of dust on the gravel road. To his amazement, it turned into the long driveway which led to the villa. Training his field glasses on the car when it stopped in front of the gate, he spotted a woman get out of the car, then walk a few steps to the iron gate. She was tall, slender and, from a distance, beautiful. She wore one of those excessively short skirts which delighted Hargrave so much since they first came into fashion. If that were Moia Hsu, he could well understand the general's interest in her.

The woman opened the gate just enough to enter, leaving the Mercedes outside the wall. In a few minutes she returned from the house, carrying a small bag and several articles of clothing over her arm. She put the items in the backseat of the Mercedes, then went back and locked the gate. Soon she sped past him heading toward Tsuen Wan. His close-up view confirmed that it could be the woman in the photo General Liu had given him.

The woman drove aggressively. It was difficult for Hargrave to keep pace. Soon they were in heavy traffic in Kowloon. The pace slowed considerably. Finally she entered the tunnel to Hong Kong Island. Exiting the tunnel she again picked up speed and became more sure of herself.

Twenty minutes later he was still following her, not an easy task for anyone. But it was one of Hargrave's specialties. Thank God it was midday. The perpetual traffic jams due in an hour or so would have made the tailing impossible.

Now they were on Stanley Gap Road driving past the heights above Repulse Bay. Nearing Stanley, the Mercedes slowed to a crawl, then turned left into a driveway leading to one of the upscale villas in the heights above Stanley. Hargrave pulled his van over onto the shoulder and watched the Mercedes climb the winding drive up to the two stone pillars that marked the gates of an estate he knew very well. Only a few years ago he had been assigned to the Stanley district. The heights were a popular spot for the lavish estates of many of Hong Kong's wealthy. This one belonged to Claude Van Hooten. Supposedly, he had made his fortune in textiles and clothing.

The gates closed behind the black Mercedes. Now he had something to put in his journal. Moia Hsu from Beijing, after staying away from the villa near Tsuen Wan for an entire day and night, had returned to pick up some belongings and then had gone to the estate of Claude Van Hooten. He wondered what General Liu would think about that. It could mean something or nothing. At least he had something to put in his journal. Perhaps the general would be generous with him again. He looked at his watch, then stared up at the villa. He decided that he would find a spot near the driveway, but out of view from the heights, and stay there until after dark before heading back to his apartment in Tsuen Wan.

Chapter 12

BRANDON POOLE stared at the expanse of Kowloon out the window of the big 747, now on final approach to Kai Tak, Hong Kong's international airport. It was midmorning in Hong Kong, and visibility lacked the usual haze. Kowloon was teeming as usual, the roadways clogged with cars and people as far as one could see across the endless mixture of business, manufacturing, and residential quarters. Each time he arrived it seemed a little more crowded. The carefully planned expansion into the satellite cities, basically bedroom high-rises, some satellites housing a half-million people, seemed to do nothing to alleviate the glut of humanity in Kowloon. Of course, their continuing construction continued to fatten his own bank account.

The knuckle-whitening approach to Kai Tak, with its final descent between rows of apartment buildings just before touchdown, had become routine to him. Still, he would be glad when the new airport off Lantau at Chek Lap Kok would be completed. He was a veteran traveler, but the short runway at Kai Tak was a source of concern for too many pilots he had talked to in the course of his travels.

Brandon Poole badly needed rest after the flight

from New York to Los Angeles and the sixteen additional hours to Hong Kong. Still, he instructed his driver to take him to his office in Central District as he climbed into his Mercedes.

He had received a coded message while still in New York that Davy Wong wanted to see him on an urgent matter as quickly as possible. Anyone else he would have put off for another day, but not Davy Wong. He hoped that Wong hadn't gotten himself in trouble already, though he knew it would come eventually.

Davy had been a student in Beijing at the time of the bloodbath in Tiananmen Square, miraculously escaping soon after the tragedy, only to show up in Hong Kong a few days later. He had been one of those who had inspired the massive demonstrations in Hong Kong against the Beijing action. The size and fervor of the Hong Kong demonstration had shocked Brandon Poole and many others.

By now, the influence of the People's Republic had infiltrated so many facets of Hong Kong life that he would have guessed such a massive demonstration would have been impossible. But young activists like Davy Wong had the obvious support of hundreds of thousands who ran the risk of protest. After all, the People's Liberation Army was only a few miles away, at Lo Wu.

When Brandon Poole arrived at his office, Davy Wong was sitting in the reception room. "Davy, you rascal! Good to see you!" The two shook hands energetically. "Very good timing, Davy. Now let's see, how could you accomplish that?" Poole mused with mock wonder.

"I called Cathay Pacific, and then figured it all out," Wong said, smiling and tapping his temple with his forefinger. "I figured I'd better be here before Mr. Poole gets into his business papers. Then he would have no time for the likes of Davy Wong."

The compact, muscular Wong was bright eyed and

likable. He had conned Iris, Poole's secretary, into allowing him to wait without an appointment. "Mr. Poole, Mr. Wong says he has an appointment. I told him that I had no record of it, but he assured me it was true."

"It's okay, Iris. Davy speaks the truth. He may not tell you everything, but whatever he does say is true," Poole assured her.

"Thank you, Mr. Poole, for the compliment. Now I know I can tell you anything, and you will believe it," Wong said with a chuckle.

Poole motioned for Wong to follow him into his inner office. "Iris, don't put through any calls until Davy leaves. We don't want to be disturbed."

Once inside, the two took leather club chairs next to a massive carved rosewood coffee table. "So how is the rabble-rousing business these days?" Brandon Poole put the question to his now very sober-faced guest.

"I've been a good boy, perhaps too good. Oh, by the way, I have a job now. I work for this print shop in Wan Chai." He slid a card across the table to Poole. "I can be reached there."

"So, it sounds like you are getting ready to raise a ruckus. Over what?" Poole was an expert at getting down to business quickly.

"Mr. Poole, I can't get over how people are just sitting around idly, watching it all happen and doing nothing about it. The future is approaching like a runaway train, yet Hong Kong sits while no plans are made for transition. Everyone is waiting for Beijing, and they are waiting only for 1997."

"Oh, I suspect that Beijing has some sort of long-range plan. But who knows what? There is much fear in Hong Kong, Davy. Frankly, I held my breath when you fanned the massive demonstrations here in Hong Kong after the students died. I have to admit the protests were orderly. But Beijing and the rest of the world were preoccupied with what happened at Tiananmen

Square. I think one little screwup in your demonstration might have brought in the People's Army. You were lucky, Davy. The scope of the protest in Hong Kong was totally unexpected, and Beijing's attention was elsewhere."

"It was not luck!" insisted Wong. "It was calculated. Even the governor issued strong statements condemning the action of Beijing. But that is all. Still, after a big demonstration and a protest there are no talks at all going on to explain what is really going to happen in 1997. In July of that year we will gain China's sovereignty. We get Deng, we get a new flag, and we get the People's Army. Absolutely nothing else is clear. Doesn't this terrify you, Mr. Poole?" Wong gripped both arms of his chair and leaned forward as he asked his question.

"Davy, you know the facts as well as I. Details are as yet unclear. What concerns me most is that good entrepreneurs and good money are again leaving Hong Kong. People forget too quickly that there will still be a British-Chinese commission until the year 2047. As problems arise, they are supposed to work them out. If violence is avoided, I think a lot of the problems will be solved through the joint commission."

Davy Wong shook his head, frowning with teeth clenched. "There are many curse words to describe what I think of that theory, Mr. Poole. I won't use any of them." He paused reflectively. "Mr. Poole, would you like to become Chinese so that your nationality will be one and same with the red star that will fly over the Bank of China?"

"I will always remain British, Davy. I do know what you're driving at, of course."

"Perhaps you are a special case and have your reasons. But at this moment, most of the small-business owners out there, perhaps two hundred thousand of them"—Wong waved his arm at the expanse of Hong Kong out the window—"can neither be British, because of the edict of your government, nor can they be Chinese. Don't you think that's because Beijing has been training people, waiting in the wings, to go on stage in Hong Kong and take over? Of course it is!" Wong tapped his finger gently on the rosewood. "Some of them are already here."

"Anyone that we should be especially concerned with? I doubt it, Davy. We both know that many Chinese have been sent here to observe and learn. The expectations are that they will return to the provinces of China and help implement industry and manufacturing for the world market. I really believe that is China's hope."

Davy Wong continued to shake his head. "Mr. Poole, the positive thinker, you have always been that way. Even before your prime minister gave it all away, you thought it wouldn't happen. Remember?"

"I've always been at odds with the politicians in London. That's why I'm as far away from London as I can get. When politicians come to Hong Kong, I can't wait until they leave. Please don't ask me to account for Mrs. Thatcher's mistakes."

"Well, now someone else has come to town, Someone whom every Hong Kong subject should loathe even more than your queen and your prime minister."

"And who, pray tell, is that?"

"General Liu Wing of the Liberation Army. He is in Hong Kong. He has a specialty which he learned in Tibet. It is occupation, and the elimination of resistance." Wong arose and walked to the window to look across a harbor crowded with moored freighters amid the noonday humid haze now hanging over Kowloon.

"What is he supposed to be doing here?"

"Oh, he's here as a member of some sort of trumped-up trade mission. He's hidden himself away in a small hotel in Tsuen Wan. That in itself is scary. You know how those Beijing types love to revel in the capitalistic splendor of the Mandarin or the Regent."

"For God's sake, Davy. Maybe he is just on R-and-R leave or something. You're jumping to conclusions. I'll bet you'll find him in a day or two gambling at the tables in Macau, with some woman on his arm. That's becoming a favorite hideaway for the People's Army brass on leave."

"Not likely, but I'll know soon." Davy Wong grinned and popped his fist in his hand.

"Now what the hell are you up to, and why tell me?"

"Mr. Poole, you have always been a friend. I know of your great business commitment to China and to Hong Kong. I suggest you chew on this awhile before we talk again. Maybe by that time you will want to more actively support those who don't want to wait until Deng Xiaoping dies and a new question mark takes over."

Brandon Poole walked over to join Davy Wong at the window. "Thanks for keeping me posted, Davy. I'll poke around and try to find out what this general is really all about. So where are you headed? What are you up to?"

Davy now grinned broadly at his friend. "I'm going to spend a little time in Tsuen Wan. General Liu is going to have a perfectly miserable time in Hong Kong. Perhaps the bastard will want to go back to Tibet where things are now peaceful."

"Don't get yourself in any more trouble than you are in, Davy. One general in the People's Liberation Army is not worth the likes of one Davy Wong. They must have thousands of generals in that big army. How important can he be?"

"Ah yes, you are right, Mr. Poole. He is worthless. And he will be even more so when I finish with him."

"How many people are you this candid with, my friend?" Poole had unlimited admiration for the young activist, but wondered at times about his seeming lack of tact.

"You put it very well before, Mr. Poole. I tell the

truth as I know it to everyone. For security, some things must be left untold."

As he talked, Brandon Poole returned to his desk, fished out a slip of paper and copied something from it. "Davy, I want you to have this. It is a new code for the private tramway up to my place on the Peak. I mean it when I say you should use it if you ever need it while on the run." He handed the slip of paper to him.

Davy took the paper and studied it for a few seconds, and then handed it back to Poole. "I have it . . . up here." He tapped his forehead again with his finger. "I appreciate that, Mr. Poole. If someday my life becomes a typhoon, I will have a port for my personal storm." He then paused. "I worry about you also, Mr. Poole. How many people do you favor with carte blanche entrance to your place on the Peak?"

"Very few, Davy. The number of people in Hong Kong that I totally trust I could count on the fingers of a hand. Hong Kong today is not like it used to be. But you above anyone should remember that."

Poole walked the young activist to the bank of elevators outside his office where they shook hands and said good-bye. His reaction to Davy Wong's visit was that he felt he had overreacted. One Beijing general tucked away in Tsuen Wan didn't bother him that much. Poole stared out the window again at Kowloon across the harbor, crammed with millions of people. "God knows what all of them are up to," he mused aloud. His talk with Davy churned his thoughts. The massive demonstration after Tiananmen Square had jolted him as it did most others. Government was always left to the British and the hongs in Hong Kong. He hadn't realized that the people had that much political awareness, to cram the streets like that. Davy knew, though. His fingers were right on the pulse.

He felt good about giving Davy access to the Peak.

Access that could save his neck someday. The aeries of the superaffluent tucked away high on Victoria Peak would be the last place authorities would dare to look for a renegade activist.

Chapter 13

THE BIG 767 climbed into the air from Newark Airport and pointed toward California. Lacy kept busy on the flight from New York to Los Angeles by making necessary last-minute phone calls. She decided she liked flying better before telephones were standard on most planes. The reading material she had brought along was still in her briefcase. Most of it had to do with background history of Hong Kong.

There had been a last-minute tizzy with Adam, who seemed to realize only then that she would be away for at least two weeks and possibly more. He hadn't made up his mind about running in the primaries yet. That very morning he asked her to give him a point-blank answer, yes or no, as to what she thought. Of course, she said no.

"Do you think it is right to take off for the other side of the world for an extended trip before we've made this decision?" he had asked.

"It's your decision, Adam. You just asked what I think and I gave you an answer. You are still free to do what you want to do."

"Would you vote for me?"

"I suppose so," she had replied, rather tepidly.

"I suppose so! What kind of damn answer is that?"

"A truthful one. I'd have to factor in the burning issue of the lavender panties." Her biting remark left him red-faced and grumbling. He had denied any knowledge whatever of the lingerie.

Adam had left the house in a grim snit, which he carried right over into the morning newscast. So she did the right thing and called him from the plane, trying one more time to extract a confession from him. Babs Billings was about a size five, she opined. She hung up when he exploded with a series of invectives.

Lacy fetched the latest workup on Phuket Color from her briefcase. Eric had done a fabulous job of filling her in. The new workup included the latest available information on Phuket's competitors. She looked forward to meeting Claude Van Hooten. Some of his competitors looked formidable, if you considered only the numbers. Yet Van Hooten seemed recklessly confident about an uneventful transition to Chinese sovereignty. His future planning seemed to ignore the political questions that had caused others to be more cautious. One letter in the correspondence mentioned a possible trip for her to the People's Republic to visit Phuket's new factory. This explained Moia Hsu's mention of the possible need for a visa.

Managing the company's risky new mutual fund was the opportunity of her life, and she had long decided that she would give it her best shot. She would stay in Hong Kong as long as necessary, and go wherever necessary to gain the insight that would make the fund a success. If the fund was a loser, her own career would be a loser. The way she saw it, her future was wrapped up in understanding the uncertainties of Hong Kong's immediate future.

The trip was shaping up as a real adventure. Too bad Adam wouldn't take a sabbatical and come along. She had once asked, but he really didn't want to go. The morning news was his whole life. What would he do without it? Who would read the teleprompter? Weary of the study and the running hassle with Adam, she found herself dozing, awakened only when a flight attendant made the announcement to prepare for landing at Los Angeles International Airport.

The heavily loaded plane thumped down on the runway at LAX, jarring her from her thoughts. No sooner had she exited the aircraft than she heard herself being paged on the intercom. She picked up a nearby courtesy phone.

It was Chad Grissom, the model Phuket had hired as a spokesperson. He was waiting in the Admirals' Club. She entered the club and came face-to-face with him. She recognized him from the publicity photos in the Phuket dossier. He was young, handsome, with big blue eyes and two rows of gleaming teeth locked in a smile.

"Chad Grissom! What a pleasant surprise. How long have you been in California?"

"Just a few days. Here, let me help you with that." He reached out and grasped her loaded briefcase. "I thought I would take the initiative and meet your plane. Moia Hsu seemed to think it would be nice to know someone on the long flight. I think she's right." Grissom looked her up and down approvingly. "That's a lovely suit, Ms. Locke. You should be modeling for Phuket."

"Thanks, Chad. Please call me Lacy. Let's go to the international terminal. It's just a short walk. Perhaps we can switch to adjacent seats."

"Good idea. If I had been thinking I would have done that already." They walked together to the international terminal only a hundred yards or so from where they exited the American baggage area. After checking baggage through on Cathay Pacific, they still had a couple of hours to kill.

"Come on, Chad, I'll pop for lunch." Lacy pointed outside. "There is a pretty decent place in the Theme

Building. Nothing but fast food right here in the terminal. Are you ready for a walk? It's in that round building over there, kind of like a hovering flying saucer." She pointed to the structure, perhaps a quarter mile away.

"Lacy, you aren't leading me astray, are you?"

"Not in a million years, Chad. Phuket Color needs you badly." Lacy lead the way, striding rapidly toward the restaurant at the hub of LAX.

Cecil Lo stood near an entrance to the international terminal and watched the pair. He had seen them check luggage through on the same Cathay Pacific flight he was to be on. He looked up at the smoggy haze hanging over LAX on the warm day, frowned, and then walked swiftly to close some of the distance between them.

The young man hadn't been on the plane with Lacy. Who in the world could he be? They were walking rapidly now, away from the international terminal.

Cecil Lo watched the tall, svelte woman walking next to her new companion. Odd, he thought. Although he was never a good judge of men, he decided the young man was probably as attractive as she was. They seemed to know each other, but their body language indicated nothing personal. Lo wondered what her husband, the news anchor back in New York, would think about this young chap. Right now she was walking a little ahead and apart from him.

At least the flight to Hong Kong would be a little more interesting with a twosome to watch on the plane. He had spent a lot of years spying on people for Brandon Poole. Most of the time it was hopelessly dull. The stranger who had checked in on Cathay Pacific with her added a little spice to his chore, and perhaps good reading for Brandon Poole.

As they turned into the Theme Building, Lo lingered behind, giving them time to take the elevator inside.

Going inside, he took the special elevator servicing the restaurant level.

Once inside the restaurant, he positioned himself at the bar so he could watch the couple unobtrusively from a distance. They had been seated at a table along the window. Cecil Lo ordered a glass of fruit juice. Apparently they both ordered martinis.

There seemed to be a dearth of conversation between them. At one point Lacy withdrew a Michelin guidebook from her bag and began to leaf through it, pausing once in a while to point out something to the man. Cecil Lo decided that if they were lovers, the flame was burning very low.

In an hour, they were walking back toward the international terminal, a hundred yards ahead of Lo. He could only speculate as to why Brandon Poole was having the woman followed. Poole kept the women in his life to himself. Long one of the most eligible men in Hong Kong, he was spotted only occasionally with ladies in his box at the Sha Tin horse races, or dining privately at the yacht club. If a certain woman really mattered in his life, it was a well-kept secret, even from Cecil Lo.

Usually when Brandon Poole had people under surveillance it had something to do with money. He called his spying activities "investments in people." Once Poole told him that if it was really important, he wouldn't deal with anyone whom he didn't know more about than the person knew about him. That's what bugged Poole about his dealings with Beijing. Believable information was hard to come by. This fact had endeared Brandon Poole to Cecil Lo. He knew the bureaucracy in Beijing like the back of his hand. He knew the territory, as Poole would say.

Once aloft in the big Cathay Pacific 747, Lo adjusted his seat to a comfortable level, pulled down the window shade and assumed a position that permitted him to keep an eye on the pair, across the airplane and one row behind them. It wasn't the best vantage point, but it was the safest for the long flight. His seat had been carefully selected several days prior to the flight when Lacy Locke's name had first appeared on the passenger list.

Despite all the careful preparations he had made, the fourteen-hour flight yielded little of consequence. Soon after they reached cruising altitude, Lo was able to pry the young man's name from a flight attendant he knew. In fact the young man had already talked to her and told her he was a fashion model.

Lacy read a lot. Chad Grissom slept a lot. Several times he had slumped his head on her shoulder during his napping, and she had seemed to tolerate that. Of course, Lo couldn't watch them every moment, absorbing himself in his own reading, periodic food service, and an occasional nap.

Once he glanced across and saw them face each other in animated conversation. Then they both laughed, amused at something. That was the only such incident he saw and he couldn't draw any conclusions from it. On a passion level of one to ten, he would rate their relationship as a mere one.

Across the cabin, Lacy watched the little airplane emblem as it inched across the electronic map on the bulkhead of the first-class cabin. Their position was now off the north coast of Taiwan. The flight plan would take them southwest into Hong Kong. "Chad, look at the land out the window. It must be Taiwan." She pointed to the map on the partition.

Chad glanced out, shrugged and buried his attention in a copy of *GQ* a flight attendant had brought him. Geography was evidently not one of his interests. In fact, she had difficulty finding any interests at all other than his profession and his appearance. Both the female and male flight attendants had given him an abundance of attention the entire flight. It was mostly chitchat about movie stars or supermodels. Nothing like sharing a fourteen-hour flight to get to know someone, she thought. Of course, when he turned toward her with those blue eyes and handsome face, her growing boredom with his vanity would fade for a moment.

"So, Chad, what are you going to do first in Hong Kong? What are your plans?"

"You know, I don't have the slightest idea." He closed the *GQ* and stuffed it into the leather pocket in front of the seat, then fished around in a travel bag and produced a pocket calendar. "Nothing tomorrow. I guess I'll try to catch up on sleep. The next couple of days we will be filming some commercials for Phuket Color. In fact, I'll be doing a lot of that over the next couple of weeks."

"You must be happy about getting right to work, Chad. Where does all this take place?"

"Some place called Sai Kung." He paused to spell it out for her from the note in his calendar. "Supposedly, they make more movies in Sai Kung than anywhere else in Asia. It's on the shore in a place called New Territories."

"Hey, that's exciting. Maybe you'll get a screen test! Now there's something I never knew. You think of movies, you automatically think of Hollywood. I've never heard of Sai Kung." Lacy paused reflectively. "That scares me, Chad. If what you say is true, there must be a million things I don't know about the business world of Hong Kong."

"I never heard of it either, but they told me that because of the big movie industry in Sai Kung, all the technical talent and studios are available for the production of commercials. It's right on the coast. We're going to do some shooting aboard someone's fancy yacht."

"Sounds like I'm in the wrong business, Chad. Are

you dealing directly with Phuket Color on this?" Lacy's ears popped and she could hear the whining hum of wing flaps being deployed as they rapidly lost altitude.

"Yeah, Phuket Color has set up everything. My contact is Moia Hsu. Don't ask me to spell it."

"Moia," mused Lacy. "She's the one who's been in touch with our office for my appointments with Van Hooten. Sounds like someone who has many talents."

Again came the humming sound of the lowering flaps. The 747 banked steeply, lining up for the final approach into Kai Tak. Lacy caught her first view of Hong Kong over the wing tip. Rows of skyscrapers against a rugged mountainous terrain extended as far as she could see in either direction. The waters of Victoria Harbor sprawled in front of the panorama, filled with moored freighters and other watercraft of every description.

"Chad, I don't know what I expected to see, but it was nothing like this." Lacy marveled at the sight out the window. Then as quickly as the panorama had appeared, it vanished between the rows of tall apartment buildings in Kowloon, some of them so close you could see people moving around inside. The 747 touched ground and reverse thrusters roared as the big Cathay Pacific jet slowed rapidly and taxied to its home gate in Hong Kong.

Cecil Lo watched from a distance, after they had passed though customs. They climbed into a waiting Rolls-Royce supplied by the Mandarin Oriental Hotel. Interesting, he thought to himself. But a quick phone call revealed they would have separate quarters when they arrived. Not so interesting, he thought.

Lo then placed a call to Brandon Poole. He wasn't in, so he left a message that he was back in Hong Kong and at his service. The slightly built private investigator sighed wearily, took the steel-rimmed glasses from his eyes and rubbed them. It had been a tiring trip. He wondered if Brandon Poole would be pleased with what seemed like precious little to him.

He carried his luggage to a cab stand and asked to be taken to the Lion and the Rose, a small residential hotel in Kowloon that was home to Cecil Lo.

Chapter 14

It was a clear night. An onshore breeze had pushed the haze back across the land. On rare nights like this, from the heights above Stanley Gap Road it was possible to see the yellow glow in the sky from the lights of Macau across an island-strewn arm of the South China Sea. Claude Van Hooten had designed his house in the heights. It featured a broad sheltered veranda that curved along the sweep of rock that was the backbone of Hong Kong Island. The veranda faced due west, for the most part, offering a view of part of Hong Kong to the north, and the Colony's islands of Lamma and Lantau, which lay due west. The lights were dazzling on this particular night, all the way to the glow in the sky which was Macau.

"You know, Moia, at times like this I wonder why it is we continue to fight the battle. I have all this"—he swept his arm along the veranda, with its magnificient view—"and I have all this." He trailed his large hands delicately across Moia's nude breasts, barely touching her, causing goose bumps to rise around the perfectly sculpted mounds.

Moia shivered in the warm night and closed her eyes as she snuggled even closer to her attentive lover.

"Please don't stop doing that," she whispered. "I think that is better than anything."

"Anything?" asked Claude.

"Until you invent something better." She brushed her long hair back across her shoulder and smiled as he continued his delicate caresses. "And I know that you will." She shifted slightly to reach his lips with her own, causing the broad, flat hammock they were lying in to sway slightly on its tethers. Moia's dark eyes, now open wide, fixed unblinkingly on her lover.

"Why are you staring at me?" he asked.

"Because the night is still young, and we will be here, right here in the swing, for such a long time." She began to caress him as he did her. "And then, much later, because we are not in a hurry, we will go crazy, and then go crazy again. And when we stop, the lights of Lantau and Macau will be gone. And my dear Claude, it will be better than the last time, just because it always is."

"Are you absolutely sure of that?" Claude whispered as he began to burrow kisses in the hollow of her neck, and then move slowly down with his trail of kisses, adjusting his body expertly in the broad hammock.

Hours later they awoke to a faint morning light that shone on the beaches of Lantau in the distance. Macau was now totally invisible in the haze. Side by side in the hammock, they lay fully awake for a few moments before Moia swung her feet gingerly over the side until her toes touched the floor. She brushed her long, jet black hair with her fingers and looked over her shoulder at a smiling Van Hooten. She was always amazed that her tall rugged-looking lover could be so gentle. In business he gave no quarter, but in the bedroom or in this case a hammock, he was a giver of more than he received. "See, Claude, I told you so."

"Yes, I know. It was better than ever."

"I thought so too. Can it go on like that forever, Claude?"

"Nothing goes on forever, especially here in Hong Kong. But we'll try, Moia. We'll try." Moia stood, bent to kiss his lips gently, then walked off the veranda to the shower and dressing room inside.

Now, his mind at rest from their night together, he was beginning to contemplate the days ahead. The uncertainty of the future of Hong Kong as it affected the business community was always there. Their visit to Beijing had done little to assuage that uncertainty. More and more he was coming to realize that he was relying on Moia's confidence concerning the future. There was still time to escape Hong Kong with most of his assets. But Moia was so sure of everything.

How much impact her father had in Beijing was questionable to him. Dr. Hsu was a bureaucrat in a sea of bureaucrats in Beijing who seemed to be more important than many of the others. Did he really believe that, or did nights like last night with Moia cloud his business judgment?

Moia returned to the veranda in a few minutes, looking spectacularly refreshed in a sheer silk robe. She carried a tray holding a tea service and sat it on a table next to the hammock. Van Hooten was staring glumly at the hills northwest of his estate, where in the far distance he could catch a glimpse of Victoria Peak.

"Claude! You look so sad, almost angry." She walked over and put her arm around him.

He kissed her and forced a smile. "Forgive me. After a night of ecstasy, the realities of our existence in Hong Kong have crowded back into my mind. Thank God for us, for you and me. If we didn't have each other, this waiting around until 1997 would be unbearable."

Moia sat at the table and poured tea. "Do you want to talk about it, Claude? If you worry, I share that worry. I am also unhappy."

Moia had a way of getting right to the point. "Oh,

I'm sorry, Moia. Forget about it. I'll be good. I get a little moody now and then. The Dutch are like that."

Moia smiled. "No, no. I don't think being Dutch has anything to do with it. I've noticed something. You haven't been the same since we returned from the factory near Foshan. Frankly, I was amazed by the progress I saw. Now here you are moping at the start of a new day. I saw you last night, early in the evening, staring at the Peak with that same sadness."

"Do you know who lives on the Peak, Moia?"

"Lots of people. Lots of very rich people, but many neither as wealthy nor as successful as you, Claude. In fact, I'm sure you could live on the Peak if you wanted to."

Van Hooten laughed. "No, nothing like that. I wouldn't trade this for the whole damn mountain."

"Good, I would be very disappointed if you did. So why do I catch you looking so gloomily at the Peak?"

"Brandon Poole has a place there. Near the top, with a private tramway. I suppose that's the reason. I must do it unconsciously."

"Brandon Poole? Why should you care where he lives? Do you know him, Claude?"

"Ever so slightly. Remember the day when we were leaving the factory? There was a lot of Brandon Poole construction equipment stored near a grove of trees as we drove back to the main road."

"Oh yes, I remember. He is a very reputable and successful builder. Claude, I think you should feel good about him building the factory." Moia sat wide-eyed looking at her lover, trying to fathom his concern.

"Moia, my dear sweet lovely woman. This is business. If there is to be anything to worry about, it is my job alone to do the worrying. Now that I have said that, I will share some of my thoughts with you. I have much interest in Brandon Poole. He, above all others, is extremely bullish on the future of Hong Kong come July 1, 1997. In fact, he has gone out of his way to travel around New York, London, and other places selling potential investors on the wisdom of investing in Hong Kong companies.

"When I saw the construction equipment at the factory I began to put some thoughts together. I have dealt before with China in matters concerning construction. I always knew Brandon Poole was involved, but thought that lots of others participated also. In fact, I was led to believe that by Beijing."

"So? Isn't he the best?" Moia asked.

"Perhaps. But he has also gone far out of his way to publicize that he's staying in Hong Kong. When a man says that, I automatically look for good reasons, so I can add them to my own.

"Follow this, Moia. Poole builds our factory, using labor all furnished by the People's Republic. The cost of labor is probably a tiny fraction of what it would be here in Hong Kong. He brings in his foremen and engineers. Then the Chinese make a deal to buy the finished building at a specific price, probably fifty percent under what it could be without enforced government labor.

"So the Chinese buy the building from Poole and then they lease it to me, long term, for a cost much less than I would pay in Hong Kong or Bangkok. So Poole runs away with his bag of money, puts it in the Bank of China here in Hong Kong, and I'm held to a long-term lease with the People's Republic, held by the Bank of China."

Moia had followed him carefully. "Claude, I think you worry needlessly. So Poole builds you a fine building. He is probably doing it for others all over China. He takes his profit immediately, which is smart. You then have access to the same low-cost labor market that built the building. Everyone profits, and China has product to export. In many years the labor-market prices will become closer to those in Hong Kong. By then Phuket Color will be a giant." Moia smiled confidently.

"I hope God is listening to you right now, Moia. Quite frankly I would rather owe my factory leases to Brandon Poole than to the People's Republic. What happens if Deng dies, and someone changes all the rules? Brandon Poole has all his money, probably in a Dutch bank eventually. I then owe my very soul to the People's Republic."

Moia's great dark eyes grew serious as she thought about his words for a few moments. "Claude, in that case, if Deng Xiaoping dies, it will be even better. It is widely accepted that Deng does not have all his faculties now. Don't quote me on that. My father would get very angry." Moia kissed Claude on the lips, and laughed softly. "Sometimes lovers share things they should not. I love you, Claude."

"Enough to marry me?" It popped right out. Van Hooten didn't even think about it before he said it.

"Yes, Claude. But we must wait. Do you understand?"

"Of course." His spirits soared. Moia was a wonder. Not only had she given him some optimism about the future, but she been so damned logical and honest about it. "I'll wait, but the absolute deadline is July 1, 1997."

"Claude! Nonsense! We will have a child before then."

He swept his arms around her and maneuvered her once again toward the hammock, where they sank down in each other's arms until soft music from the wake-up system filtered through the villa.

A short time later, Van Hooten drove his Mercedes down the winding roadway to Stanley Gap Road, and turned right for their drive to Central District. There was very light traffic at this early hour. Behind him a small minivan kept its distance on the winding road.

"Moia dear, I am going directly to the Mandarin. Lacy Locke will be having breakfast with me. As you well know, she is handling a stock issue for us with New

Worldwide Securities. I hope she is impressed, not only with Phuket, but with the stability of Hong Kong." Claude glanced at Moia, very quiet since leaving the villa. "Any last-minute thoughts about what this Lacy Locke should be told?"

"Claude! I was thinking about our night together, and you interrupted my thoughts. That was cruel. It was such a perfect night." Then out of the blue came a totally unrelated question. "Do you have other women in Hong Kong?"

He looked at her again. She was absolutely serious. "Moia, you know much better than that."

"Well, most men of means in Hong Kong do have several women. You never talk about the races. Whom do you dine with at Sha Tin? Who sits in your box and looks beautiful?" She looked at him now with a faint smile.

"You know I hate the races, Moia. I haven't used my box for over a year. I give access to clients and visitors. Frankly my gambling urges are more than sated by my investments in future styles and Phuket copies. I'm much better at it than I was with horses. Now will you consider answering my question about any last-minute things to discuss with Lacy Locke?"

Moia thought for several seconds. "No. You will charm her and you will say all the right things. Phuket Color has been a big success already. The factories in Jakarta and Bangkok are at capacity, waiting for Foshan to take the overload. Perhaps she should visit Foshan."

"We'll see. I don't know how a factory that has just opened and is operating at one percent of capacity would impress her. She'd be more impressed with the big operation in Bangkok."

"Maybe," Moia answered slowly. "But Bangkok is now. Foshan is the future. I think your Lacy Locke is interested in the future. Is she attractive, Claude?"

"I have no idea. You know I've never met her. She's married to a TV newscaster, I hear."

"Being married don't matter, Claude. She is an American. I hope she is an old biddy." She grinned impishly at him.

"So how is your day shaping up, Moia?" Van Hooten pulled the Mercedes into his garage in Central. "I'm not going up to the office. I'll hoof it over to the Mandarin."

"Chad Grissom will be up to the office shortly. We'll drive to Sai Kung with our production people. Over the next few days they will be filming commercials near Sai Kung. I guess I'd better keep a close watch on that."

"Oho! You've been chipping away at me, and here you'll be showing the good life to Chad Grissom." Claude, laughing now, leaned over and gave her a quick hug.

"Relax, Claude. I think he is actually very ugly," she teased. "He just happens to have the gift of being photogenic. I suspect he is probably gay."

"You don't lie very well, Moia dear. See you tonight." He watched her walk from the car to the elevator corridor. This daughter of Beijing was like no other woman ever, in his whole life.

As he glanced in the rearview mirror preparing to back into his parking space, he saw the small minivan that had followed at a distance all the way from Stanley Gap Road. It was at the curb across the street. Van Hooten switched off the engine and casually got out of the Mercedes. He began walking, then running, to the door of the garage level. But he was not quick enough. The van bolted ahead down Queens Road, and by the time he got to the door it was too late to identify the plate number.

Van Hooten walked slowly back to the garage to finish parking his car, once again feeling uneasy. The delightful time spent with Moia had cajoled him out of his moodiness. Now it had returned.

He glanced at his watch, then began to walk the several blocks to the Mandarin Oriental. He remembered what a dealer in Macau once said when a customer, looking very nervous, finally bolted from the table after repeated glances over his shoulder. "You can always tell those big guys from Hong Kong with the heavy pockets. Everybody's got a tail on everyone else in that league."

Of course the question was, who was the man in the minvan following, him or Moia?

Claude Van Hooten arrived at the Mandarin Oriental at 8:30 A.M., the precise time for his breakfast meeting with Lacy Locke. The hostess led him to a corner table in the dining room, where Lacy Locke sat engrossed in a copy of the South China *Morning Post*.

"Ms. Locke, your guest is here." The hostess pulled a chair away from the table to accommodate Van Hooten.

Lacy stood immediately and extended her hand to the tall Dutchman. "Well then, you must be Claude Van Hooten, the beating heart of Phuket Color."

Van Hooten laughed easily. "Well, I've never been called a beating heart before. Perhaps I am in a way, but we have many talented people at Phuket Color." He studied the woman in front of him. Startling was a word that came to his mind. Black shoulder-length hair and large hazel eyes, alert, penetrating, and beautiful. Certainly not the stereotype of a world-class financial expert.

"Let's hope that you can make this heart beat faster, Ms. Locke. A successful stock issue would certainly help us immensely. A new factory will be constructed near Shanghai quite soon, and the plant at Foshan is now operational. Of course, you'll be given the details of all that. Is this your first visit to Hong Kong?"

"Yes it is. I am overwhelmed! It all looks so exciting

and prosperous. I'm sure I'll pester you with a million questions. Just let me know if I get on your nerves. By the way, please call me Lacy. Please, let's order breakfast. I'm famished and still don't know what day it is. Losing a day to the international date line is a new experience for me."

Van Hooten eyed the dazzling woman as she took her chair again at the table. The dress she wore was tasteful but did nothing to disguise a supple and fit woman. Phuket Color certainly had a number of items that would be sensational if worn by this Lacy Locke.

"Well then, Lacy, welcome to Hong Kong. I know a little about your New York. Been there a few times on trips back to my Netherlands. On the surface the cities have many similarities. But they are quite different when you dig in a bit. As questions come up, please be quite candid. If I can't answer them, I'll find someone who can."

"Thank you, Claude. I will do that." They paused for a few moments to order breakfast. Van Hooten looked amazingly young to her for having his reputation of success. The tall Dutchman, probably over six-four, had a lean stature and a chiseled face, made younger by a cleanly trimmed beard and short reddish-blond hair. His piercing blue eyes moved a lot, seemingly taking in everything.

"So, Claude, you say our two cities are different. What single thing is the most different?"

"Oho! You put me on the spot before I have been fed. Well, let me see," mused Van Hooten. "That's an easy question, really. As I have read and observed, New York is a true melting pot. I saw such large numbers of many nationalities there. Hong Kong is ninety-eight percent Chinese. When dealing with people here, one does well to remember that. Their customs, religions, and plain superstitions must be acknowledged and hold influence over anything else."

"Ninety-eight percent! That is shocking to me."

"Lacy, we do have common ground. That common ground is capitalism. Unrestricted capitalism, the compelling drive to make money, is unleashed with a fervor stronger than most religions. In recent years the Chinese here in Hong Kong are among the most wealthy and influential. To be an entrepreneur of any size has its status." Van Hooten paused. He wanted to be accurate. The rapt attention of the beautiful woman almost demanded that.

Lacy shook her head and shrugged. "It does make you wonder, doesn't it. It certainly isn't compatible with the politics of the People's Republic. It's easy to see why so many have already packed up and left Hong Kong . . . but you, Mr. Van Hooten, have made up your mind to stay. That takes guts, sir."

Van Hooten grinned broadly at her choice of words. "Well, I think that is putting it much too strongly. I've been in Hong Kong for many years. So have others who are staying put. It's hard for you to understand me today, but I think you will before you leave Hong Kong. Others like me have an investment in the People's Republic. A superficial answer to your question would be to state that they just plain need our help. Pardon me, Lacy. I must sound like I'm preaching."

"Claude, please go on. Remember, I am asking people to invest money in a number of companies in Hong Kong. I want to believe what you believe."

"I'm afraid that's impossible at a meeting like this. I would have to be a clairvoyant to be absolutely certain of anything. It will take you some time to get a real feeling as to what is going on here in Hong Kong. Over the next few days I think a lot of what you see will strengthen your belief in Hong Kong's future, I promise."

Lacy smiled warmly. "Thanks, Claude, I'll try to be a good student."

"And I'll do my best at teaching." No doubt about that, Van Hooten thought to himself. Breakfast with

Lacy Locke was certainly different from the usual such event with Hong Kong's pesky financial sharks. "There is one thing to always keep in mind, Lacy. Across that border, less than thirty kilometers from where we sit, are one and a quarter billion people under the Beijing regime. Most of them have absolutely nothing, materially, when compared to that man right there." He motioned toward a passing waiter. "They are becoming aware of what they are missing. If they fail to put a few capitalistic principles into use, the carnage at Tiananmen Square will look like a Sunday school spat, compared to what will happen."

"Claude, I don't know whether you've made me feel better or worse."

"While you are here, be sure you cross the border at Lo Wu. There is a fairly reliable train to Guangzhou. Perhaps you know it as Canton. They are permitting me to build a factory near there, just as they are letting thousands of others do all over China. The regime must let it happen. They've gone too far to back down." Van Hooten realized that he was now, indeed, preaching. "Enough of this, my dear. See for yourself. I will personally see that you get to my new factory in Foshan. It is but a day's trip." Van Hooten now attacked his breakfast.

"I wouldn't miss it for anything. Thanks, Claude. I have so much to learn, and whether you know it or not, you've given me a flying start. By the way, I met a young man on the Cathay Pacific flight who said he was doing some work for you, a Chad Grissom."

"Oh yes. We've signed Chad to be our spokesperson in the United States. In fact he's in Sai Kung with my assistant today. They are working on a catalog and shooting some film we might use later on. What did you think of him?"

"He's a gorgeous boy, Claude. I suspect he's a real professional at what he does. Who picked him out for you?"

"Moia, my assistant. Actually she is much more than that. I count on her a great deal. I want you to rely on her also. You will no doubt meet her while you are here in Hong Kong. In fact when we go over all the financial details later in the week, I'll make certain she is there."

After breafast they chatted for a moment in the lobby of the Mandarin.

"Claude, thanks again for everything. Good company and a fine breakfast have totally cured my jet lag."

"If I were you, I would take it easy the first couple of days. That's the best cure."

"I do have one question. Are you familiar with a man named Brandon Poole? I'm seeing him later today."

"Really! Yes, he did some construction for me. I don't know much about him personally. Big, big firm. He's sort of a legend around Hong Kong. Everyone tries to figure out what he's up to next. He seems to be leading the fight to convince others to stay."

"Like yourself?"

"Not really, he's a real activist on the matter."

The two shook hands and parted.

Cecil Lo, slumped in a big leather chair in the lobby of the Mandarin, polished his steel-rimmed lenses with a special cloth he carried. He put them back on and watched Lacy Locke return to the elevator bank of the hotel. Women who walked and looked like that had titillated him all his life. This one reminded him of an old favorite he saw over and over again in an old American movie, Jennifer Jones. Now, in his old age, he was forced to follow a woman like that day and night.

He wasn't the only one, though. Claude Van Hooten shared his malady. Lo saw him glance at her several times before he walked out the door.

Cecil Lo often speculated as to why Brandon Poole

was having her followed so closely. When he asked him once, Brandon had said that he couldn't tell him, because then he would only look for certain things. He had said it was important that he knew everything.

Chapter 15

D<small>R</small>. H<small>SU</small> sat at the head of the small conference table in Beijing. As several members of his committee filed into the room, he stared out the window of the government building which held his office. Only a block away, Tiananmen Square was bathed in bright sunlight. The line of red banners shone brilliantly, flapping in a stiff breeze.

The usual groups of tourists milled around in the immense square, most with lens covers dangling on cameras pointed at Mao's tomb and the soldier's memorial. The steady stream of tourists moved across the square toward the Forbidden City, in these days no longer forbidden. Hsu wondered why it had taken so long. The precious contents of the city were gone, looted by the plundering Chiang Kai-shek and taken to Formosa long ago. A few soldiers strolled here and there, some of them also carrying the inevitable camera.

The small group had now taken their seats at the table. Ching Hsu stood, still staring out toward the square. "Tell me, my friends, do you see what I see out there?"

One by one they shook their heads. It was a tradition

of the old man that he would ask a question and then answer it when he started each meeting. After all, he was the chairman of a committee on the economic transition of Hong Kong.

Ching Hsu walked away from his chair and swept his arm at the scene on Tiananmen Square. "I see hundreds, maybe even thousands of cameras out there, some of them costing a year's wages in Beijing. And how many have a sign that says it was made in the People's Republic? Oh, perhaps there are a few. But if there are, would any of you wish to own one of those cameras?"

The group was silent, intimidated by his question. "The effort to mass produce high-quality photographic equipment in China is so disappointing. As you know, this effort is only one of ten projects this committee is working on presently. However, as you will guess from the empty chair, the chairman for that committee has been dismissed. When we meet next time, you will greet our new expeditor for the committee. In less than a year, Hong Kong will be expected to exhibit and export the best product that the People's Republic can produce. Everyone in this room must meet his goals, so reasonably set by this committee."

Ching Hsu took his chair, picked up a telephone and asked for a young assistant to bring the garment manufacturing project folders into the room and distribute them. The material for the photography project was placed neatly in front of the empty chair.

On top of each folder was a two-page report, featuring pictures of a new clothing factory near Foshan. Li Pao, the chairman of that committee, read the report in a low monotone. Proud workers were shown presenting a fine silk suit to their company president from Hong Kong. In the background, a dozen tailors were working diligently at sewing machines and cutting tables.

"Of course, some of the committees are ahead of

schedule," Ching Hsu interrupted in a louder tone of voice than Pao's. "The products of the factory you see in the photograph will soon be flooding the markets in Hong Kong, and within months all over the world." Ching paused, watching each project member examine the report, each nodding in approval of the apparent success. He was well aware that at least two members of his committee knew that his daughter, Moia Hsu, was involved somehow in the Foshan factory. He was careful to note that those two members lavishly praised the project to the others around them.

"This," continued Ching, "is the kind of progress I want to see from each of you when we meet in thirty days."

The meeting continued for most of the morning, torturously, for most of the members had not got beyond the planning stage. Layers of red tape bound the Beijing regime to traditions that rendered many of them powerless when dealing with provincial authorities.

The project head for Foshan had an advantage that slashed though the obstacles. They had Moia Hsu. Li Pao, who sat in the chair of the clothing production expeditor, was a merely a figurehead. But those who knew dared not bring that up.

Ching Hsu's style would demand another empty chair at the next meeting. Few felt confident that the empty chair would not be theirs.

Ching finally arose from the table and excused himself from the group. Glancing at his Rolex, a gift from Claude Van Hooten, he returned to his private office. Within minutes a phone rang. It was a private line known only to a few superiors and a handful of others of his own selection.

"Good morning, Dr. Hsu." It was the crisp voice of General Liu Wing.

"Ah, it is not such a good morning here in Beijing. I had to dismiss the administrator of the photographic development project. It was sad to see even one person confused and inept after all our training. However, the others will learn from his pitiful failure."

"Dr. Hsu, because of your wisdom, the project will go forward with great speed."

"General Liu, they need only follow the example of the developments in Foshan. I have had photographic documentation of that success given to each member of the committee. One by one, they praised the effort."

"As they well should, Dr. Hsu. Your leadership has set such a fine example."

"Perhaps it is the military discipline I gained in the past from being in your business, General Liu. I will not tolerate a committee member that does not have it. Please see that Moia is praised for her assistance to Li Pao. Such a message would be welcome from you, General."

"Of course, Dr. Hsu." He willingly accepted Hsu's remark as a virtual order to see Moia personally. "I have a very small problem. I have not been able to locate Moia at her villa in Tsuen Wan. Her service for China goes on day and night, just like her father's." Thinking quickly, he decided, for the moment, to spare the old man the information he had from Superintendent Hargrave. He would wait for the right moment to inform him of her all-night "service to China" on Stanley Gap Road.

"Thank you, General Liu. I am pleased to hear of her diligence. Make an effort to see her. She needs diversion from such furious activity. By the way, how is your own work going along in Hong Kong?"

Liu hesitated. He felt the old man was fishing. He doubted very much if he knew of his true assignment in Hong Kong. "Very well, Dr. Hsu. Hong Kong is moving steadily toward their needed sovereignty of the People's Republic."

The old man no doubt knew a deliberately evasive reply when he heard it. So after a bit of further small talk, they ended their conversation.

* * *

No sooner had Liu hung up his telephone in his small apartment in Tsuen Wan, than it rang. It was Super-intendent Hargrave checking in right on time.

"General, Hargrave here." His voice was somewhat of a whisper.

"Hargrave, please do not address me as General. You will not use my name. I'll only remind you once. With all the electronics around Hong Kong, you surely realize that any conversation can be a public one. Sometimes I wonder how you became a superintendent of police. The future of Hong Kong will greatly benefit by Beijing authority."

Hargrave held the small portable phone tightly against his ear, trying desperately to eliminate the noise of the harbor in the background. "Yes sir. You are right, of course," agreed Hargrave nervously. The trip on the Star Ferry from Central District to Kowloon would take less than ten minutes and already they were halfway. "I have news to report. About twenty minutes ago, Moia left her office in Central, I would say at ten A.M. A young man was with her, oddly dressed in a powder blue sport coat and running shoes. I think the ladies would say he is a handsome young man."

"Hargrave, will you speak up. I can scarcely hear your whispering. What about this young man?"

"They walked to the Star Ferry terminal and boarded this ferry we are on right now. In fact she is pointing out the sights to this young fellow. Now he has a camera trained on Victoria Peak."

"Strange, indeed." Now Liu was whispering. "Stick with them when they get to Kowloon. Call me back when you get a chance. Don't lose them!"

"I'll do my best, sir."

"I hope that is good enough, Hargrave. . . . Oh, one other thing, did she return to Stanley Gap Road again last evening?"

"Yes sir, she did. Late-night work, I surmise. She was carrying a heavy briefcase."

"Hargrave, just give me the report. I'll do the surmising. Did Van Hooten drive her to the office?"

"Yes," answered Hargrave quickly. The bad memory returned, reminding him of Van Hooten almost identifying him at the garage. Yet he was certain that he had gotten away in time, unless the Dutchman had the eyes of an eagle. He had parked at a station house in Central, and walked back to stake out the building.

"Then she left over an hour later with the young man, and without Van Hooten? Do I have it straight, Hargrave?"

"You've got it right, sir. I suppose the young chap entered the building while I was parking my van." Hargrave wondered to himself why it was all right for Liu to use his name, while he couldn't use Liu's. Some people in Hong Kong made a pastime of eavesdropping at random on the hundreds of thousands of portable phones.

"Hang with them, Hargrave, and keep me posted."

Liu hung up, and Hargrave folded the phone into his jacket pocket just as the big Star Ferry bumped along the pilings lining its berth in Kowloon. He followed Moia and the young man through the crowded ferry terminal and watched them walk to an area utilized by limos and liveried vehicles.

He would have to act fast. Running through the heavy traffic, he flung open the door of a commercial limo and climbed in. He flashed his superintendent of police credentials and stuffed some money into the protesting driver's hands, motioning emphatically toward the limo now leaving the area. The driver reluctantly pulled out to follow the vehicle, which seemed to be in no great hurry.

A few minutes later, they had circled several blocks and were heading north on Nathan Road. The pedestrian traffic surged across each intersection, Nathan

Road at this point being a mile-long shopping mall jammed with tourists and locals. After a few blocks the limo stopped across from a large Friendship Store, one of several department stores in Hong Kong controlled by the Beijing government and featuring products of the China beyond Lo Wu.

Moia and her companion got out, had a few words with the driver, then walked across the street to the store. Hargrave's driver edged near the curb a few yards behind and gave a palms-up. What do we do now?

"Wait, they will be back. Their chauffeur is waiting."

The driver shrugged and pointed toward the no-parking instructions.

"Relax, my boy. You are with the police." His driver slumped in his seat and turned on a radio. He ran the tuner up and down the dial, until he located a station playing loud nerve-jangling American rock.

Hargrave cringed. Hong Kong was falling apart. He didn't understand it anymore. In fact he didn't even understand the job he had been drawn into. Why was he following these people? General Liu made him very nervous. He was due for a holiday. He decided to put in for it immediately. He would enjoy a few days at the casinos in Macau. Racing days came and went at Sha Tin and Happy Valley, and he had no time for either.

After perhaps fifteen minutes, Moia and the young man appeared again, exiting the Friendship Store and walking toward their limo. The young man carried a gift-wrapped package. The two made a handsome couple, Hargrave decided. Numerous pedestrians glanced discreetly at the pair. Now Moia was smiling and talking to him with great animation. He wondered how the general and Van Hooten would react to this scene.

With his passengers back in the limo, the driver proceeded a little farther on Nathan Road, then veered right on Argyle Street. For a moment Hargrave panicked. They were headed for Kai Tak Airport. One or both of them must be leaving Hong Kong. But the driver passed the normal exit to Kai Tak and now proceeded full speed until he turned on Clear Bay Road and drove far into the countryside of New Territories.

Soon they had the waters of Sai Kung Bay on their right. In another fifteen minutes, they reached the community of Sai Kung, the energy-charged film capital of the Far East. The limo finally made a sharp right into the gates of a sprawling marina. Moia lowered the rear window, flashed some identification and was waved onto a small parking area just past the gate.

Hargrave's driver again gave his What now? gesture. "Pull up to the guard and let me handle it," Hargrave instructed. He then showed the guard his superintendent of police credentials. "That is a beautiful sailing vessel over there. I happen to be a fancier of such things. Do you mind if I take a closer look?"

The guard waved him through immediately and they pulled into a parking place very near the limo. Hargrave donned dark sunglasses and a crumpled cotton hat that served as a rain hat at times and left the cab. "Stay here," Hargrave advised his driver. "You're hired for the day." He slipped him a couple of more bills.

Hargrave let the couple get a good head start and then ambled casually, a hundred meters behind. In his crumpled head cover, the pudgy Hargrave looked like anyone but a superintendent of police. To his surprise, Moia and her companion walked directly up to the gangway of the huge sailing vessel and climbed aboard. They were met by a man in yachtsman's garb, and then suddenly surrounded by half a dozen bikini-clad young women, who seemed very happy indeed at the presence of the young man.

Scrutinizing the vessel, Hargrave saw that the helm and cockpit were located amidships, and a large elevated aft deck was set up with extensive filmmaking equipment. Cameramen were busy setting up, and a director was advising a lighting crew in the location of large reflecting devices to highlight details on the aft deck. Obviously, they were making a film, and from all the attention he was getting, Moia's companion had a major role in it.

Hargrave watched for a while and then decided to find a vantage point much farther away where he would less likely be noticed.

A little later, the young man, who had disappeared for a short time, reappeared dressed in a sharp business suit and a flaming red tie. Someone produced a bottle of champagne and passed glasses all around to the bikini-clad group, now cavorting on the deck around the trousers of the actor now proposing a toast. Moia, standing to one side, had also been given a champagne glass. She occasionally burst into fits of laughter as the moviemaking progressed. Obviously she was amused with the action on the aft deck.

Hargrave frowned, wondering what General Liu would make of all this, and how he would react.

Chapter 16

Cᴇᴄɪʟ Lᴏ got on very well with Brandon Poole. Certainly in the far-flung holdings of this business titan throughout Hong Kong and Southeast Asia, Brandon Poole dealt with the elite among his peers, in business and in government. Cecil Lo, private investigator, was certainly one of the lowest in the social pecking order of Hong Kong whom Brandon saw regularly.

Cecil had heard Brandon say more than once, "Treat every man with respect who treats you with respect, no matter his station in life." With Poole, these were just not idle words. He meant them.

Cecil thought of those words now as he sat in his humble flat in Kowloon, waiting for Brandon Poole to knock on his door. He shook his head in disbelief. Imagine, him hosting the great Brandon Poole. Of course, he could never tell any of his friends that Poole came to chat at the Lion and the Rose. None would believe him.

When they had first met, Cecil was serving under Brandon as an officer in the Royal Marines. One day, young Brandon Poole had noticed his combat ribbons and asked that he discuss each one. From then on, in the military and then out, he had served Brandon Poole to the extent of his ability. It was usually exciting and sometimes actually fun. This latest assignment, poking into the life of Lacy Locke, was about the dullest he could remember. Yet he was sure Brandon had his reasons, and he gave it all he had. Still, he felt he had dug up precious little for all the expense involved. And he now wished he had much more information to supply as he anticipated Poole's knock on his door at the spartan Lion and the Rose.

There it was. A solitary knock, followed by three rapid light taps, a B in Morse code. B as in Brandon. It always brought a faint smile to Cecil's face. He opened the door quickly.

"Cecil, you old scoundrel, you waited for me. Sorry I'm running late." There was a hearty handshake. It was their first face-to-face meeting since lunch at Hing's in New York.

"I felt it prudent to wait," replied Cecil with a hint of a smile. He eyed Brandon appreciatively. His tall, fit frame was covered in workman's clothes, his heavy hair hidden under a billed cap that had NY on the front.

Brandon smiled as he caught Lo looking at the cap. "It's a New York Yankees baseball hat." He tossed it on a small table. "You're welcome to it, Cecil."

"Wouldn't think of it, sir. I'm afraid it would blow your disguise. Now let me guess. I'll bet you came by subway."

"Right, Cecil! All the way from the station at Tsim Sha Tsui. Cecil, you are a marvel. I'm not going to ask how you know. I will just marvel at the fact that you do know."

The old investigator chuckled and shook his head. "The great Brandon Poole, with a fleet of Rolls-Royces at his command, no one would believe it. By the way, that, sir, is not much of a disguise. The work clothes should have been dirtied and laundered a few times. Anyone would know that they came right out of a box, and then they really start looking you over."

"Thank you for the advice, Cecil." Poole sat down in a chair across the table from Cecil Lo. "Now, what can you tell me about our Ms. Lacy Locke?"

"She is absolutely beautiful, sir. But you know that because she attended your seminar in New York. I've prepared this written report. Perhaps you'd better read it before we talk." He slid the report across the table and watched Brandon scan the two pages.

"So she made the trip with Chad Grissom. Interesting. Do you think she is really smitten with this chap?"

"I really doubt it, sir."

"Oh, come now, Cecil. You report that they were inseparable, at the airport in Los Angeles, the restaurant and on the plane. You report that occasionally he slept with his head on her shoulder."

"Think about it, Brandon. If she really had a thing for him, it would have been her head on his shoulder. Oh, I could be wrong, but her attitude was more of tolerance than affection . . . all a case of body language. You'd have to see it to agree. There is something strange about that young man. When I put my finger on it, you will know."

Poole nodded. "What about the breakfast with Claude Van Hooten? I don't suppose you could get close enough to actually hear them."

"You know that voice of Van Hooten's. I was able to hear quite a bit. He seemed to be giving her a rundown on Hong Kong. From all I could tell, he was pumping her up about the wisdom of staying put in 1997. Van Hooten is a salesman, sir. That's the way I read him."

"And he has something tough to sell, Cecil. He is trying to raise a lot of money from a stock issue. He believes that Lacy Locke can help him. And she can." Poole paused, thinking back to their brief meeting in New York. "But I want to know why Van Hooten thinks he is perfectly safe in tomorrow's Hong Kong.

If others had his enthusiasm, more would be staying."

Cecil Lo listened thoughtfully. "Sir, I am naive about his business, the rag trade as they call it, but why don't you just ask him?"

"Van Hooten is a maverick. He has always been one. He's in a tough business that I don't pretend to understand. Imagine trying to keep track of styles and fads that change from day to day. He might share generalities with you, but you'd never get inside his mind."

"Sir, I still think he would be flattered by a call from Brandon Poole. Let's face it, he wouldn't dare refuse a meeting with the likes of Brandon Poole."

"We'll see, Cecil. . . . We'll see. If he has a good reason that I don't know about for staying in Hong Kong after 1997, I want to know exactly what it is. And if it is a good reason, or perhaps reasons, I want to buy Phuket Color, lock, stock and sewing machines. I'd then pay him more money than he ever dreamed of to run it for me!"

"Damn! Now that is exciting, sir. Brandon Poole is on the hunt again." Cecil Lo slapped his palm on the table.

Poole pushed away from the table and stood up, extending his hand to Cecil Lo. "Cecil, keep up the good work. Follow Lacy Locke around for a couple of more days. Give me a report on Friday. And then we'll make life more exciting for you. I'll make arrangements to get you on a plane to Bangkok on Saturday."

"Bangkok, sir! I often remember the old days, sir, when we were working undercover for the Crown. The quarters we selected were in the midst of a virtual brothel. For a while there, sir, I thought I had lost you. Tell me, Brandon, do you ever take time for such R-and-R anymore?"

Brandon responded with a reminiscent grin. "Shame on you. I had long forgotten that bit of nonsense until you brought it up. I can see you are bored, Cecil. You need a little of that Thai spice."

"I'll be ready, sir." He walked a few steps to the door and opened it for Poole.

"Cecil, you probably know this, but I'm meeting with Lacy Locke this afternoon. You can pick up your tail on her when she leaves my office."

Cecil grinned. "I had already planned to do that, sir." Cecil walked him to the door of the Lion and the Rose. He backed into a doorway soon after Brandon Poole left and started walking toward Nathan Road. He trailed him closely until he entered the subway stop that would take him to a train back down through Kowloon, under the harbor, and to an exit near his building in Central District.

He walked back to his flat to prepare for his afternoon assignment. Brandon Poole had picked up his spirits. Maybe Hong Kong would survive after 1997. Brandon was on the move, preparing to buy another company.

Another thought flickered across his mind. He sensed that Poole's interest in Lacy Locke might be a tad personal. After all, her business mission seemed to be perfectly understandable. Why this preoccupation with how she spent every minute of her time?

Chapter 17

GENERAL LIU WING drove his rented Volvo up to the gate of the villa near Tsuen Wan. Mist hung heavy in the air of New Territories on this morning. He got out of the car and walked over to inspect the padlock that held the heavy chain blocking entry through the massive iron gate. He flipped the lock to make sure it was closed and then turned around to scrutinize the countryside around Moia's villa.

The grove of trees in the distance where Hargrave usually parked his minivan, barely visible in the mist, was apparently empty. That probably meant that Moia wasn't at the villa. Hopefully Hargrave was on the job and knew where she was.

The powerfully built Liu grasped the crossbar of the gate and easily vaulted over into the compound. He circled the entire villa, stopping frequently to inspect windows and doors. Everything was tightly closed and locked. Peering inside the large glass doors that opened into the kitchen, he found everything neatly in order. Liu guessed to himself that the villa had been unoccupied for several days. Hargrave was probably right about her and about the Dutchman's estate on Stanley

Gap Road, he thought. The capitalist pig was teaching her the habits of ruttish swine.

Liu removed a notebook from his jacket and addressed a short note to Moia. "My dear, I missed you. Too bad, it was a perfect day to hide ourselves away in the countryside. Remember the dark, rainy days in Shanghai? Affectionately, L.W."

Liu slid the note under the front door of the villa. He checked the time of day, then walked back and vaulted over the iron gate. He had just enough time to meet Li Pao's arrival at Kai Tak from Beijing. The nominal administrator of the Foshan project would join him for the trip to Thailand. It was no secret in Beijing that Moia ran the project, and Li Pao could be spared for a few days. Li was a true servant of the People's Republic, handpicked by Dr. Hsu to assist in the Hong Kong transition.

Now caught up in the heavy traffic along Argyle Road, Liu found himself brooding over Moia's apparent infatuation with the Dutchman. He wondered when it all started. When did she become engulfed in the web of western decadence? Her commitment to him during their Shanghai days had been complete. He and their friends fully expected that Moia and he would spend their lives together. How could she do this to her father and crush the spirit of a general of the Liberation Army? At first he tried to push his jealousy out of mind by reasoning that Hargrave, himself a toady to capitalistic decadence, was letting his depraved thoughts run wild.

Now he had the report of their driver to the factory in Foshan, reporting an obvious intimacy between the couple as he chauffeured them to the remote location. He smacked his hand against the steering wheel of the Volvo until it stung from the abuse. Now he had the mission to Bangkok to worry about. Moia would have to wait. Still, then and there he vowed to himself that the Dutchman would not have her! As it was now, he would have to invoke upon himself the greatest discipline to accept her back into his life, soiled virtue and all. And this had to be done before the rumor mill in Hong Kong made her despicable affair public knowledge.

He finally reached Kai Tak and pulled into the parking area used by a few Beijing dignitaries. Now, pushing Moia from his mind, he proceeded to the customs and arrival area servicing Dragon Air. Despite the fact that the heavy traffic made him late, Li Pao was just at that moment clearing his luggage through the customs table.

"Sorry, General, we had some nasty weather. The pilot had to fly around it. I didn't expect to be this late." The slightly statured Li Pao seemed a little flustered by the imposing presence of the general.

Liu turned on his warmest, most patronizing smile. "The weather can be a formidable adversary, Li. Even Deng Xiaoping would have difficulty changing the weather. Actually we have just enough time to bring each other up-to-date before our flight leaves for Bangkok."

The two crossed a narrow walkway which led to a hotel across from the terminal, and seated themselves in an isolated section of the lounge.

"And how is Moia? Dr. Hsu asked that I pass along his greeting to her."

"Rest assured that I will do that, Li." The general saw no purpose in sharing any thoughts he might have concerning Moia with Li Pao. Pao supposedly had connections far beyond his assignment to Dr. Hsu in Beijing.

"I understand that you are quite familiar with the Phuket Color garment factory in Bangkok." General Liu put his question in the form of a statement, every moment watching the eyes of Li Pao, a splinter of a man, compared to most.

"When Claude Van Hooten contracted for that facility, I went down there to lay it out. It was a thorough renovation. Most of the old machinery had to be replaced. For years they had been manufacturing work clothes and uniforms for the Thai army. They had no ability to mass produce the high-fashion requirements of Phuket Color. In six months, I had it renovated and working at capacity."

"High fashion? Who wears this clothing, Li? Is it something I should have in my closet?"

Li Pao shrugged his bony shoulders. "Not really, General. They hardly befit such a distinguished servant of the people." Li paused for a few moments, uncomfortable under the penetrating eyes of Liu Wing. "Parisians wear them. Londoners and Americans, especially. The best of shops in New York, Rio, Berlin, and along the French Riviera all feature the latest fashion from Phuket Color."

"Li, you have just listed all the places where capitalists school their youth in decadence, rather than history."

"General, I neglected to mention another place. Right here in Hong Kong, Phuket does its biggest business."

Liu Wing scowled. "Only for a little while longer, my friend. I feel sorry for you, Li. The other committees are involved in farm machinery, earth-moving equipment, computers, photographic excellence, and you are in charge of costuming the rich for their fun and games. Do you ever think about that?"

"Of course I do. I think of the money that it will bring into China, all to be spent wisely under the supervision of Beijing. It is a small thing, perhaps, when compared with the things you mention. But it is money easily made for little cost. China has to walk, before it can outrun the others. I have heard Dr. Hsu say that."

"Dr. Hsu is a wise man," Liu agreed. "It is obvious that he has taught us well." The general looked at his watch. It was time to check in on their flight to Bangkok.

He watched Li Pao ahead of him as they threaded their way through the late afternoon departure crowd at Kai Tak. The little man was like a thousand other bureaucrats in Beijing. If things were to be left to them, it would take China another hundred years to realize its potential and gain retribution from its old enemies. Maybe Li Pao would change his mind after their nasty little assignment in Bangkok was completed.

The flight to Bangkok from Hong Kong went without much conversation. The crowded Thai Air 727 did not lend itself to discussion of the mission ahead of them. Pao read from a newspaper brought from Beijing. Liu dozed, occasionally waking up to ogle the flight attendants. They all seemed uniformly attractive to him. It was as if Thai Air had a factory somewhere and turned them out of a mold. Once he had visited Ching Mai in northern Thailand and marveled at the women there. He dozed off again, dreaming of that factory somewhere near Ching Mai.

After a long ride from the airport through the narrow streets of Bangkok, the general and Li Pao checked into the White Lotus, located along the Chao Phraya River, a capricious main artery of Bangkok that often floods beyond its banks.

That evening, as the dusk closed in, they walked together a dozen blocks from the hotel. Li pointed out an old building to the general. The long, narrow structure was in poor repair. Cracked windows and paint peeling from damp, rotted wood gave the building a hopeless character that hardly matched the public image of its ultratrendy tenant. A small sign painted on the glass pane of one window carried the logo of Phuket Color.

General Liu studied the surrounding buildings all in similar stages of decay. "So this is the money machine of our capitalist, Claude Van Hooten?"

"Yes, General, along with two others, one in Jakarta and a small facility in Hong Kong."

"China can be quite proud of that magnificent new air-conditioned structure near Foshan," boasted Liu. "I'd say that this miserable structure fairly begs to be burned down, before it falls down. Wouldn't you say so?"

Li Pao could only nod his head. He was thinking about the people crowded in their workspaces in front of their machines on any workday.

That night they went to a dinner theater near the Oriental Hotel, just up the river from the Sheraton. Liu scowled as he scanned the crowd, heavily laced with Australians, Americans, and Europeans, no doubt most of them tourists. There were very few Asians.

After dinner the house lights dimmed for a program of Thai dancers. The performers were beautiful, absolutely exotic. General Liu smiled in appreciation as they went through a gentle but rather sensuous routine with undulating hips sheathed in silken gossamer. Then Liu was specifically drawn to watching the feet of the dancers. They were uniformly large.

"They are men!" he exclaimed.

Li Pao nodded his agreement. "I thought you knew. They are widely acclaimed for their artistry, you know."

General Liu turned and scanned the faces of the crowd. "It figures, my friend. Men performing as women, to satisfy the peculiar appetites of their capitalist visitors."

"General, I have heard of similar exhibitions in China," Li said, not quite willing to admit that he had actually sought them out and witnessed them on occasion.

"Li, I am pleased that we have witnessed this. It makes it all the easier to accomplish our mission tomorrow."

Li Pao remained silent. It was impossible for him to assess the general's logic at this point.

Chapter 18

THE ENERGETIC young male assistant, impeccably dressed in a dark silk business suit, opened the door to Brandon Poole's opulent, spacious aerie. His office, wrapping around the corner of a high floor of the highest building in Hong Kong, sprawled in front of Lacy Locke.

A huge polished rosewood desk sat on an ornate Mongolian carpet that covered all but a bordering foot of polished teak floor. Leather couches were angled so the view out the windows offered Victoria Peak and the harbor. Heavy drapes were pulled wide to expose the view, best at this time of day. Brandon Poole circled his desk to welcome Lacy.

"Ms. Locke, welcome to Hong Kong. It is my pleasure to meet again the star of my seminar in New York." The tall, fit Brandon Poole smiled affably as he reached out to grasp Lacy's extended hand. The handsome man's confidence and assertiveness registered even more strongly on his own turf, against the sweeping panorama outside the windows.

"Brandon, I took you at your word, so here I am. The view from your office has already made my visit worthwhile. May I take a look?"

Lacy walked over to the floor-to-ceiling windows and gazed out toward Victoria Peak, which looked almost close enough to touch. Turning slowly, she followed the coast of New Territories until it became Kowloon. Scores of ships were moored in Victoria Harbor. "It's truly breathtaking. It all seems so . . . artificial . . . yet alive."

"Ah, spoken with the brilliant logic of a woman, which most often offers a refreshing perspective." Poole was now standing at her side. "Over there"—he swept his arm across Victoria Harbor—"I identified over seventy freighters this morning. Seven of them are owned by Brandon Poole Ltd.," he said quietly. "Last evening there would have been nine. One is off for Singapore, and another to Brisbane."

"I had no idea you were so heavily involved in shipping. I thought you were the construction maven of Hong Kong. How exciting!" She became very conscious of the perfectly groomed Poole, who towered at her side.

"When one hangs around Hong Kong for any length of time, money accumulates. You wonder what to do with it. You find yourself dabbling in many things. There is nothing illusive about opportunity here." Poole spoke the words matter-of-factly, without braggadocio.

"Dabbling! Nine freighters! I'd hardly call that dabbling, Mr. Poole. That sounds more like dedicated commitment." Poole was now holding her wrist as he elevated his hand and pointed toward a location high up on Victoria Peak.

"Now look right there." Brandon extended a finger to point. "You can see my house."

Even from this distance, she could see that the house was spectacularly situated on a rocky crag that jutted from the dense foliage around it. "How do you ever get up there? It looks virtually inaccessible."

"I suppose a service road would be possible over

a period of time, utilizing my best engineers, but I have opted for a small private tramway. Fortunately, weather here in Hong Kong permits year-round use of such things."

Poole led Lacy Locke from the window to a small couch positioned directly facing his desk, then circled his desk and sat down. "Hong Kong is a money machine, and you are here to take advantage of it. Right, Lacy?"

"I suppose so, but in a roundabout way. My specialty is in risk-taking mutual funds. Nevertheless I feel obligated to do all I can to see that my investors make money. I must tell you, Brandon, that your Hong Kong is the most challenging market of all. In their mutual funds, Worldwide Securities includes companies located in countries all around the Pacific Rim. Analyzing most of them is fairly simple. But Hong Kong! The future is not readable to most people." She paused to look out the window toward Kowloon. "But the place seems to be bustling, moving onward at a furious pace. It's as if so many people know something I don't know. It seems that 1997 has been pushed into the subconscious of everyone. It is really business as usual, Mr. Poole?"

Poole chuckled easily. "My, my . . . that was quite a little speech. I'm still trying absorb it all." Brandon Poole slid a desk drawer open and produced several sheets of paper, clipped neatly together. He slid them across the desk to Lacy. "That is a copy of Her Majesty's government's treaty with the People's Republic of China. Read it sometime, and then you tell me what it says."

"Brandon, you don't think I would be here right now if I hadn't already read it, do you? I think it is terrifying."

"Welcome, Lacy! Welcome to our royal club. I think the membership includes almost everyone in Hong Kong." Brandon Poole's eyes met Lacy's openly agressive stare. Women like this with such beauty mixed with business acumen were certainly a rarity in Hong Kong. Her features were flawless. He found himself diverted momentarily by the attractiveness of the woman. The obvious intellect of Lacy Locke only enhanced her beauty, which needed no enhancing at all.

Brandon Poole stood up and walked a few steps to point a finger at a large map of the world that nearly covered one wall. Appropriately for him, Hong Kong was positioned in the center of the massive map. Large adhesive dots in several colors were scattered over the chart, identifying the many far-flung interests of Brandon Poole Ltd. "Here you have Canada," he said as he pointed to it. "And way over here, India," he said, taking a few steps. Pointing again he continued. "And South Africa. I could go on and on if I wanted to. All of these places, once part of the British Empire, were schooled in suffrage and government before they ceased to be colonies. Their future never lay hidden in the shroud that hangs over Hong Kong."

"Brandon, you must have some hunch. Look how you have invested in Hong Kong."

"Lacy, notice all those colored dots circling our world. Only a few of them are right around Hong Kong. Such is the intentional decentralization of Brandon Poole Ltd. In the past, Hong Kong has been administrated by the governor in partnership with the most powerful business interests here. Business has always ruled the day, unencumbered by any restraining influence that might arise from a one-man, one-vote democracy. Capitalism has run wild, unfettered by any governmental restraint. The people simply have never been troubled with the idea of governing themselves. In contrast, the People's Republic, our sovereignty in 1997, has endless lists of rules governing the behavior of its subjects."

"What about the legislative committee?" Lacy was

beginning to wonder why anyone in his right mind would stay after 1997.

"Once again you are talking about an institution that is ninety percent appointed by business interests, with no defined power in our glorious future." Poole tapped on his desk lightly with the flat of his hand. His blue eyes dug into Lacy's and refused to let go. "I suppose that now you'll tell me that our governor will persist until the year 2047, and you are right. Also, there will be a six-man grievance committee to study all problems. That's all true, Lacy. But neither will have any defined authority. The ability to make any significant decision stays in Beijing."

"Then why are you staying? I distinctly got that impression at your seminar in New York." Lacy was determined to push for some sensible reason.

Brandon Poole sighed heavily, and then pointed out the window to a point where New Territories fused in the humid haze with the People's Republic. "First, and always the most important reason for anyone, they need me. Brandon Poole Ltd. has a staff of construction engineers that are unmatched by most others. I can build things fast, and they won't fall down. Such talent has number-one priority in the People's Republic."

"And what else?"

"They respect me. I always deliver."

Poole's logic and self-confidence thus far made sense. She broke eye contact with him, arose from her chair and walked over to the world chart, studying the small dots clustered around Hong Kong. There were several inside China, one near Shenzhen, another near Foshan. Each dot was labeled clearly with tiny hand lettering. *Phuket Color* appeared on the Foshan location. North, just south of Shanghai, another dot was also lettered *Phuket Color*.

Poole idly studied the woman facing away from him, looking at the chart. She moved, as his impresario friend Sean Xiang loved to say, like a jaguar. Her suit was tastefully tailored, yet did nothing to subdue the flawless figure of the woman it covered. She would certainly look well at his table at the Yacht Club, or in his box at Sha Tin.

"Brandon, you have Phuket Color's new factory marked near Foshan. I thought you didn't know much about Claude Van Hooten. Isn't that what you told me in New York?"

"We've never exchanged more than pleasantries. The factory was just completed under a contract with the People's Republic. They in turn will lease it to him over a long term. I have never been there, though I approved the plans submitted by my engineers. I have no desire to get into the real estate business in China. It doesn't seem to bother Van Hooten."

"Do you respect him?"

Brandon Poole had walked from his desk to stand beside her. She turned, this time initiating the duel with his deep-set blue eyes. "Yes. He has been very successful. Fashion is a highly competitive field, something I don't pretend to understand. I do, however, know success when I see it." He paused and moved a couple of steps away. "Like you in that suit. It's perfect. But I certainly couldn't create it. Give me a building, a road, or a dam any day."

"Thank you, Brandon." Lacy found herself a little uncomfortable with the obvious compliment and decided to keep the conversation on Van Hooten. "Do you think Van Hooten's business is safe for post-1997?"

"I would say that his future, like mine, is determined by how much Beijing needs him. He evidently feels very confident, but I really can't put my finger on any reason why he should be." Brandon paused, thinking about the energetic Dutchman. "But I am sure there is one dominating reason. Some day, when the fat is in the fire, we will know what keeps him here. There are hundreds of others, you know, and they all have separate reasons for feeling they have Beijing's blessing."

"Well, I will be meeting him again this week. We are about to handle a Phuket stock issue in our mutual fund, you know. I will try to determine why he is so confident about the future. Of course, he asked the same question about you at breakfast this morning."

"Really?" Brandon Poole chuckled quietly. "Hong Kong today is a place alive with rumors, almost none of them remotely true. Everyone has their own reasons for making up their mind whether to go or stay. And they don't share them with anyone. Everyone zealously guards what they consider to be their competitive edge. Secrecy and then surprise, those are the ingredients of success here." Poole became silent for a few moments, and watched Lacy as she contemplated what he had said.

"And now, Ms. Locke, now that I have shared my secrets with you, I would like to show you more of Hong Kong. If you are willing, I would consider it a priority and a privilege to help you get the feel of it, to catch the fever, so to speak. If money is your game, you should learn as much as you can about the playing field. The excitement is almost unbearable here in Hong Kong."

Listening to the words fall from the lips of a ranking member of the Hong Kong aristocracy had captivated her. To plumb the vagaries of Hong Kong, one could have no better teacher than Brandon Poole. "Okay, Brandon," Lacy challenged, "teach me about Hong Kong."

Poole nodded his head in approval of her quick response. He looked at his wrist to check the time. "It is almost three-thirty. How does your schedule look for this evening?"

Lacy checked her calendar for the day. This evening she was to have a late dinner with Chad Grissom. Pretty Boy was going to give her a report on the events of the day. He would be returning from the movie colony at Sai Kung and would no doubt have much to say about the filming of commercials for Phuket Color. Also he would be able to give her a rundown on the Phuket personnel working with him. It was important, but hardly so compared to an evening with Brandon Poole. "Brandon, I have nothing on the docket that can't be changed."

Poole smiled broadly. "I like that, Lacy. Quick decisions, well made. Why don't I call for you at the Mandarin at six. We'll start off at my place by having dinner on the Peak. Then we'll work our way down through Hong Kong. The later it gets, the lower we'll go."

"I'd love dinner at the Peak, Brandon. But you'll have to convince me about all the rest." Now it was Lacy's turn to smile.

"Lacy, I suppose I have been a little presumptuous. But after all we are both busy people. If you want my character reference, I suggest you call the governor. He doesn't have much else to do these days."

They both laughed as Brandon picked up the telephone. "Chelsea, I'm bringing a guest for early dinner, about six-thirty. Surprise us with something special. We'll dine on the deck." There were a few questions from the other end which Brandon answered with a succession of "Fine" or "Good girl" responses. When he hung up, his secretary buzzed him. Another appointment had arrived and was waiting in the anteroom.

Lacy made ready to leave. "You didn't give Chelsea a lot of time for something special, Brandon. I hope this isn't too much trouble."

"Nonsense, Chelsea has worked for our family since long before I was born. She still does her best work when confronted with a crisis. You'll love her."

As Lacy was shown out of his office, she couldn't help but feel elated. Brandon Poole's hospitality had overwhelmed her. She idly wondered if she would have received the same attention had she been a man. Probably not, she decided, remembering his unyieldingly aggressive eye contact. Brandon Poole was quite sure of himself. He, no doubt, was used to getting about everything he really wanted.

Chapter 19

IT WAS late afternoon of the day following the arrival of Li Pao and General Liu Wing in Bangkok. Li Pao was strolling through the grounds of the royal palace amidst hundreds of tourists, most of them continually clicking away with cameras and video recorders. To help him blend with the crowd, he also carried a small Nikon, with its lens cap dangling. He was slightly early for his scheduled meeting with Wally Pei. Pei was an operative who had served Beijing well. It was through his efforts that some of the more inflammatory dissidents of the Tiananmen Square riots had been identified. Now it was again his turn to serve the people.

General Liu had retired for the evening with an exotic mandolin player, who had held him entranced during cocktails at dinner that evening. It seemed that her artistic talents ran far beyond the melodious plucking of her strings. Liu dealt openly with a pimp who had approached him, obviously noticing his blatant ogling. The general's swiftness at arranging for the transaction had amazed Pao. Generals were driven by the drive to procreate much more than others, he decided. He tucked the incident away in his mind, making a note later of the exotic's identity. He wondered if Moia Hsu or her father knew of the proclivities of her general.

Actually it was comfortable to be away from the general for his meeting with Wally Pei. The ornate grounds of the royal palace were a pleasant diversion. The endless intricate architecture in reds and golds surrounded with giant demonic statuary certainly outdid his native Beijing's sobering Forbidden City.

Li Pao arrived at the temple of the Emerald Buddha, situated in the midst of the royal palace grounds, at their appointed time, slipped his shoes off and placed them in the long racks outside the temple. He walked in, knelt before the giant Buddha, hand carved from a single chunk of jade. It was one of the most visited and sacred relics of Thailand.

Almost immediately, Wally Pei materialized at his side. Looking discreetly around him, Li Pao set his camera between them on the floor. When a minute elapsed, Pei arose and left the temple carrying the camera with him, lens cap still dangling.

Picture-taking was forbidden in the temple. Pei had suggested the location to eliminate any possibility that they might be photographed together by others. Pao had thought it a needlessly far-fetched idea. But Wally Pei had been selected to run this part of the operation.

Outside, a few minutes later, Li Pao resumed strolling around the palace grounds, pausing to play tourist here and there. Wally Pei had vanished as quickly as he had materialized in the temple. Now the timer had been set on their plans. There was no turning back. Wally Pei had vanished with the camera shell that was filled with the tiny but sophisticated incendiary devices.

Late that night, after midnight, the streets of Bangkok screamed with sirens as firefighting equipment rumbled through the area south of the tall hotel where the general and Li Pao were staying. After the din had died down, Li's phone rang a half-dozen times and then stopped.

He slipped on a robe and walked down the hall,

where he knocked on the general's door as he had been instructed to do. In a few moments, General Liu opened the door far enough to allow Li to see inside. His exotic companion was sitting on the edge of the bed, looking sullen and bruised, a far cry from the delicate young woman he had seen playing so beautifully earlier in the evening.

"Everything is fine," whispered Li. "It is over."

"Good! If you don't mind, Natasha and I will celebrate. See you in the morning." Liu closed the door.

Li Pao returned to his room. It occurred to him that he disliked the general immensely. Li found it impossible to sleep. He thought of the cramped quarters of the Phuket Color factory and hoped his information had been correct. Occasionally, they would run a late shift to pare down the backlog of orders. Tonight that would have been a disaster.

Chapter 20

HARGRAVE HAD long abandoned his vigil along the water's edge at Sai Kung, near the mooring of the luxury sailing yacht. The air-conditioned limo made a much more comfortable observation post. Periodically, he would train his small roof prism binoculars on the frivolity evidently being filmed on the yacht's aft deck. They seemed to be filming the same thing over and over again, with the young man and some of the women changing clothes quite often.

Moia Hsu sat in the shade of a sun dodger sipping at an icy drink and watching the proceedings. Occasionally, the young man who seemed to be the director of the activity would go over and appear to explain something to her. Once the young actor walked over and kissed her full on the lips. Moia stood and squirmed away from him, laughing and shaking her head. Everyone seemed to get quite a kick out of that.

However, there seemed to be nothing special about the kiss, inasmuch as the young man seemed to be showering kisses on all of the ladies as the cameras recorded everything. Hargrave felt a surge of arousal that hadn't bothered him in years as he eyed the jiggling and seeming merriment of the bikini-clad group.

What a life this young fellow had, he thought. The movie colony and beaches at Sai Kung had never been part of his life in Hong Kong. But now it was too late for all that.

His thoughts were interrupted by another limo which pulled up several parking spaces away from his own. A bronzed young woman emerged and immediately commanded all of Hargrave's attention. Tall, perhaps five ten or so, he would guess. At first Hargrave thought she wore nothing but a sheer nylon coverup, but as she turned briefly he could see a strategic patch of white, held by a white bikini thong, showing sharp contrast to the sun-bronzed, flawless figure. A long blond ponytail bounced saucily from hip to hip as she strutted toward the gangway.

The young man rushed to meet her halfway, and then greeted her with a hug and a long kiss. Hargrave noticed that the camera crew turned their attention to the scene immediately. He trained his binoculars on Moia. She continued to sit quietly on her chair, observing the arrival of the young woman without expression.

"Some party there, sir." His limo driver, who had been dozing, had been reinvigorated by the arrival of the incredibly statuesque blonde.

"That blonde certainly makes a man thankful for good eyesight," Hargrave murmured. He continued to watch for a few moments as the filmmaking continued. The newly arrived blonde had been introduced to Moia, and now sat next to her watching the others. Hargrave couldn't help but wonder what was going on, and how he would explain all this to General Liu. Liu had said that Moia was "well connected" in Beijing. What in hell was she doing here amidst such goings-on?

Aboard the sailing yacht *Sai Kung Eagle,* Moia was suddenly grateful for her dark sunglasses. They gave her an opportunity to scrutinize Mary Lulu, the bombshell from New York. There was so much of her, all of it physically flawless. The photos forwarded to her from American tabloids were hardly adequate when compared to the real thing.

The woman turned and stared unabashedly at Moia, eyes moving from head to foot. "Moia, you are beautiful. You are exquisite. If I could look like someone else, I would want to look like you."

"Thank you. . . . That was so nice to say." Moia was speechless for a moment. "But I don't think for a minute I would ever look so dazzling in one of our Phuket sport coats as you do."

"I don't believe it. Remember, when I wear a Phuket Color sport coat, it is all I wear. Something about the powder blue job makes men go nuts." She again studied Moia, this time reaching over gently to lift her dark glasses. "Aha, to complement those eyes you would have to wear another color. Then I'm sure it would have the same effect."

Moia laughed quietly. "I could never make myself do that. I mean wear nothing but a Phuket sport coat, other than perhaps with a husband or lover."

"Moia! that's brilliant. We've talked only a couple of minutes and you have discovered the whole secret to my act. I do in public what most women reserve for their lovers."

"Oh, you sing and dance quite well. I've heard!"

"So do a lot of other people," Mary Lulu said barely audibly, and then abruptly changed the subject. "Chad says you are a big wheel with Phuket Color. You guys are making some real noise out there. You picked a great spokesperson when you selected Chad. Isn't he a doll? Look at him. I'd just love to get him down and wear him out."

"What!" In China or Hong Kong, Moia had never heard words like this, especially from a stranger. "He is nice-looking, but I hardly feel like that about him."

Then she found herself unable to restrain a smile.

Mary Lulu sensed her embarrassment. "I'm sorry. I was just making a little joke. It's all part of the act. My friends get a kick out of me being 'on' all the time. Actually Chad and I are good for each other. When we're seen out in public together, people go wild. The cameras start clicking and the presses start rolling."

"And Phuket Color sells more suits and sport coats," added Moia. "So all three of us prosper."

"Moia, I like you." She put an arm around Moia's shoulders and squeezed her for just a second.

Moia couldn't help but smile at the performer, and decided that she liked her also. She was blatant and bizarre, but Moia got the feeling that she was just being herself. "Chad didn't tell me that you were joining him in Hong Kong."

"Joining him!" Mary Lulu turned toward her, looking puzzled. "Coincidence, doll, coincidence. I'm here on my own gig, at the Typhoon Club. I told Chad that back in New York, so when I got in last night, he invited me out to watch the shooting of commercials. I told him no, but I came anyway." Then she leaned over and whispered in Moia's ear. "Between you and me, I don't even think Chad digs us babes."

Chapter 21

LACY TOOK more than the usual amount of time selecting what to wear for the evening with Brandon Poole. Once she even toyed with the idea of calling the whole thing off. It was rather brash of him to offer such an invitation, she thought. Yet he had conducted himself in a thoroughly businesslike manner. To refuse would foolishly toss away the opportunity to have the gates of Hong Kong thrown open to her from a perspective few would ever have.

Brandon Poole, in a way, exemplified the ultimate success possible in Hong Kong. His aristocratic heritage was that of one of the movers and shakers who had created the fortune-building city-state from the dregs of the opium wars. Besides, Lacy liked him. His decisive toughness had evidently gained the respect of Beijing. Yet, if she read him correctly, he had diversified enough to wait out another year or so before setting his go-or-stay position in stone.

Finally, she decided on a light wraparound navy dress. Knee length and flattering, it seemed just the thing for a humid Hong Kong night. She had tested it on Adam and he had liked it. A minor pang of guilt surfaced. She hadn't thought of Adam all day. Maybe her long hours in the office had contributed to the cooling of her ardor. Too many late nights and too many "headaches" might have helped drive him to an affair with Babs Billings. No, she thought, it was his pompous attitude and blatant dishonesty that really irked her.

She looked at her watch, and wrestled with the time difference. In New York it was morning of the same day, and Adam would be leaving for his stint on the news. She made a mental note to try again in the morning, when it would be evening in New York.

Exactly at six the phone rang in her room in the Mandarin. It was Brandon Poole. He was in the lobby. She made one more check with the mirror before she left the room, and decided that she had not yet adjusted to the time change. She headed for the elevator, thinking, What the hell, it's just another business dinner, an everyday occurrence in New York. Yet she felt nervous.

Lacy spotted Brandon near the entrance to the lounge in the lobby. He was talking to two well-dressed gentlemen in what appeared to be a serious conversation. She hesitated for a moment and then walked over to them.

He immediately grasped her hand. "Gentlemen, this is Lacy Locke, New York investment specialist. Now tell me, gentlemen, wouldn't she create quite a stir around the Hang Seng stock market?"

The two men nodded approvingly, obviously diverted by the attractiveness of Brandon's "investment specialist."

"Ms. Locke, it is a pleasure. Welcome to Hong Kong," said one of them. "You are in very good company here." He nodded toward Brandon Poole.

"This is a rare treat for us," said the other. "Brandon spends so much time getting rich, that we seldom see him anymore."

"Please call me, we will get together," Brandon assured them, "but right now Ms. Locke and I have to run." He motioned toward the door.

Outside, a chauffeur held open the door of a Mercedes and the two climbed in. Quickly they were winding through narrow streets, working their way north toward the Peak.

"I suppose I cut those chaps off a little abruptly, but we have little time to waste, and they can talk on forever without saying much of anything."

"Brandon, they did speak well of you. You must appreciate that."

"So they did. Incidentally, the two of them are about to fly the coop, leave Hong Kong. They aren't sure of themselves and keep pestering me to give them good reasons to stay." Brandon paused to point out the window. "That's Ladder Street. Endless antiques, curios, and just plain junk. Rather unique, though." Stair steps replaced a street and extended upward for several blocks. "Perhaps a place to spend a couple of hours before you go back to New York someday."

"Someday? Brandon, you make it sound like I'll be here for a while."

"Stranger things have happened in Hong Kong. Actually, Lacy, it's your kind of place. For anyone obsessed with making money, there is no place like it. I meant what I said about the Hang Seng market. Hong Kong could get mighty lonely if Van Hooten and I were the only ones left."

Lacy was relieved to see that Poole was now smiling at his observation, obviously meant as a jest. "Brandon, look out there." The Mercedes had now climbed to a height where the dazzling lights of the waterfront of the Island and Kowloon were strewn endlessly below them. "I am sure that you will have plenty of company. What is it? Six million people out there?"

"Yes, six million people. Almost all without a vote, most without any real citizenship, and most with not an inkling of their future beyond a year or so. Our money machine exists only at the whim of a few old men about a thousand miles from here."

"Yes, Brandon, but this afternoon you convinced me that Beijing needs you, and that they are aware of that. You even said there were many others like you. If you believe that, why worry?"

The Mercedes, now threading up a series of short hairpin turns, stopped abruptly. They were in the middle of what appeared to be a small cul-de-sac surrounded by a heavy growth of underbrush. Visible through some of the bushes on one side was an eagle's view of Hong Kong. Lights shimmered across an expanse extending from the far reaches of New Territories to the north, across all the islands of Hong Kong strewn in the South China Sea to the south.

"It's gorgeous," murmured Lacy, following Brandon Poole across a small parking area.

In the semidarkness, lit at this point by only the moon and the stars, she could make out two narrowly spaced rail tracks that ran from the cul-de-sac to a point that looked to be about two hundred feet up a very steep cliff. Poole activated a remote device he had pulled from his pocket and a small, open tramcar that could seat perhaps four people emerged from the darkness on the mountainside.

"Our chariot awaits, my lady." Brandon helped her into the small contraption and pressed some buttons, and they began a slow but steady ascent up the private tramway. "Lacy, in a few moments you will understand one of the important reasons that keep me in Hong Kong. The first plans for this villa were laid out almost a hundred years ago by Sir Brandon, my great-grandfather. I find it difficult to adequately express my feelings for this estate. I can only say that I feel like I belong here, and am part of it. Does that make any sense to you, Lacy?"

"Oh Brandon, of course it does. It's your home, your roots. You will make everything else happen as it should, and you will stay here as long as you want. And Hong Kong will be all the stronger for it."

"That's an optimistic assessment, Lacy. You are very good at that. You can verbalize the obvious to someone who has trouble finding it."

Brandon hugged her protectively as the tramway lurched to a stop next to a deck that sprawled around the villa, which stairstepped upward several levels into the mountainside. She had the feeling that she was moving into another world, one of light, air—and privilege.

Brandon guided her to a sliding door where a slightly built woman appeared. Gray hair was piled neatly in a bun. She moved with a quick step and a beaming smile on a pleasant, aging face.

"Chelsea, we're right on time. I want you to meet Lacy Locke. She is visiting the Colony from New York."

"Well, bless you, child. It takes something very special to get Brandon home early enough to take his meal here. How he can spend so much time in that old office, I will never know." The effervescent little woman smiled warmly and then turned to reenter the villa. "Brandon, when you are ready to be served, just let me know. It is very nice out on the north deck." Chelsea smiled and reentered the house.

"Brandon, she is absolutely precious. You are so fortunate."

"Lacy, if you don't mind, she's a wee bit like having your mother around all the time. My father knew her in Wales and brought her to Hong Kong. She never went back. She can get pretty bossy at times, but she really runs this household as if it were her own. But Chelsea has a heart of gold and heaven help anyone who tries to voice a bad word about Brandon Poole. Of course, she only knows me from my life here on the Peak. She knows little about the troubles of the Crown

Colony and the business world. If she knew more, she'd expect me to fix them."

Brandon Poole took Lacy by the hand and led her around the deck to the northeast side of the villa. The view of Hong Kong and New Territories from there was perfect on this clear night. He pointed northward. "There, see that glow in the sky? That's Shenzhen. That's the People's Republic. They've been only thirty kilometers away for the the last hundred and fifty years. That's one reason I don't like to come up to the Peak on a clear night. I see that damnable glow in the sky."

In a few moments Chelsea began serving dinner on the north deck. It was delightful. A gentle breeze wafted in from across Victoria Harbor. For the longest time, Brandon paid little attention to the chilled soup and lobster salad prepared by Chelsea. He couldn't resist pointing out all the points of interest visible from the lofty villa, describing each one with an oral historical footnote. It was obvious that he took great pride in Hong Kong and relished the task of describing the unique colony to Lacy.

"Now, Lacy, perhaps you can appreciate my personal stake in Hong Kong. Between you and me, when I talk of leaving Hong Kong, I am probably talking about something I could never bring myself to do. So many of the others do not have the generational heritage that I do. It is easier for others who have come and prospered, say in the last twenty-five years."

"So, Brandon, would it be so hard to tell others that your reasons for staying are probably different from theirs? As you told me before, the key to it is for them to make themselves indispensable to Beijing."

"Lacy, you are a good pupil. If only they would listen as closely as you do. Sadly enough, even if they do listen, they still expect me to make their decision for them." Brandon paused, now picking away at the delicious lobster salad.

"Now you take your client, Van Hooten," he said. "I respect him because he has made a total commitment to stay after 1997. He's made it on his own, and kept his reasons to himself. Lots of guts, as I hear you Americans say. And, my dear Lacy, from my perspective his decision was a bad one. But obviously, not from his."

Lacy couldn't resist smiling. "Perhaps you two should get together. He wonders why you are staying and now you are wondering why *he* is staying."

"Really, did he ask that?"

"No . . . not in so many words. He called you an activist in getting others to stay. But I gathered he is not at all sure why you *are* an activist."

"Is it so difficult to understand, Lacy? Hell, I don't want to find myself here all alone. If people can be truly helpful to Beijing and I can make them believe that, perhaps they should stay. I think also that it pays to be diversified. That's part of my speech. You heard it in New York."

Conversation then turned to less demanding things, like the magnificent gardens around the villa. Now and then a large tramcar would appear, making its way up to the very top of Victoria Peak in the distance. From Brandon's villa, several hundred yards away, it was a startling sight, suddenly emerging from the foliage on the mountainside, like a giant caterpillar inching its way toward the top.

"It's the oldest such railway in the world," Brandon said. "There's a restaurant and observation deck up there, with the usual trinkets for tourists. You can probably skip it, now that you've seen Hong Kong from here."

Lacy became quiet, sipping at the orange brandy Chelsea served after they had dined. Now and then Brandon would spot something else of interest and describe it to her in his deep, unique English voice. She was overwhelmed with Brandon's hospitality and the romantic setting of the cliffside villa. Wisely, she pushed the snifter of brandy to one side as he continued his informative travelogue.

"Down there is Statue Square," he said, pointing to a cluster of tall buildings. "The Cenotaph is in a small park hidden by those structures. It is a monument to the dead of Hong Kong's wars. Even today, one can occasionally see flowers placed there to honor the students who were killed on Tiananmen Square in 1989. The reaction of Hong Kong was one of horror. That event, more than anything else, caused the go-or-stay issue to top everyone's priority list."

Brandon turned to look at Lacy, sober faced in rapt attention to his ramblings. "I'm sorry, Lacy. I have become much too serious for this beautiful evening. Let's leave the Peak before we lose the entire night."

"Brandon, I am absolutely fascinated. I could listen to you all night."

"That would be cruel, my dear. Let's be off."

They said good-bye to Chelsea and walked quickly to the private tramway. Brandon's chauffeur emerged from nowhere and climbed into the tramcar to ride down to the parking area with them. Brandon gave him instructions in Chinese on the way.

They drove down the series of hairpin curves and proceeded through the now mostly empty streets of the business district. Finally they reached a small pier in Wan Chai at the water's edge. Brandon once again gave their driver instructions in Chinese, then helped Lacy out of the Mercedes onto the darkened pier lit only by the running lights of a small lighter, moored to the pier with lines tended by two crewmen. White letters on a dark hull of the small bargelike vessel read BRANDON POOLE LTD. One of the crewmen assisted Lacy as she stepped onto the lighter, bobbing slightly in the light chop. Lettered neatly on the dark jumpsuits of the crewmen was, again, BRANDON POOLE LTD.

"Not very elegant, Lacy, but it will surely get us there," assured Brandon.

"Get us where, Brandon?" Lacy asked as they were seated on a single bench to the stern of the small vessel. A dozen small boxes of cargo were piled neatly on the deck in front of them. She could feel her pulse racing with excitement. This might be a perfectly ordinary outing for Brandon Poole, but it certainly carried the flair of adventure for her.

"I'm sorry, Lacy, I should have explained. At this hour one of my lighters is the best transport out to the vessels in the harbor. The *Kowloon Eagle* entered the harbor only yesterday. The freighter is one of the finest of its kind. Right now it is moored at a great vantage point for us to see the harbor."

"This is quite a treat, Brandon. I'm afraid I am pretty ignorant when it comes to boats," she said, trying to relax as her flimsy dress billowed often in the harbor breeze. The lighter was skipping over the gentle chop, already rapidly approaching the silhouette of a large freighter moored directly ahead. She looked at Brandon Poole, all six foot four of him now standing at her side, giving orders to the crewman at the helm. He was dressed in a dinner jacket and shoes buffed to a gloss that occasionally glinted a reflection of harbor lights. If her apparel was unlikely, so was his.

Soon they were putting slowly around the fantail of the huge freighter. High over her head were the words BRANDON KOWLOON EAGLE, and in smaller letters below, *Hong Kong*.

As they pulled alongside, a gangway was lowered to deck level of the lighter. "Give me your shoes," instructed Brandon. "The gangway is rather steep for heels."

Lacy emitted a laugh that she couldn't contain as she handed the imposing Brandon Poole her shoes. "I'm sorry. I didn't mean to laugh, Brandon. But all this is pretty awesome."

"And so are you, young lady," was his unexpected reply. "Now walk ahead of me up the gangway. Hold on to the line. I am right behind you."

Once aboard, they were greeted by the captain. "Captain, I want you to meet Lacy Locke. She is from New York, here to absorb the wonders of Hong Kong."

The captain's easy smile put her at ease. Behind him crewmen seemed to be moving about energetically. "Forgive me, Mr. Poole. Your visit was unexpected." He looked at his wristwatch. "In another thirty seconds, the vessel will be ready for your inspection."

"At ease, Captain. I want to show Ms. Locke the bridge and one of the staterooms. Then we'll stroll around the deck for a few minutes, and then we'll be off. Sorry for any inconvenience."

"At your service, sir." The captain saluted the couple and waved them toward the bridge ladder.

The view from the bridge was truly spectacular. The *Kowloon Eagle* was moored about midharbor between Hong Kong Island and Kowloon. Beyond a promenade along the waterfront in Kowloon, Lacy got a glimpse of the historic Peninsula Hotel, long a favorite residence for visitors who included countless heads of state and world dignitaries. One by one, Brandon pointed out other landmarks as they circled the bridge. He spoke with pride about several state-of-the-art instruments at the helm which made the *Kowloon Eagle* one of the finest freighters in the world.

Returning to the main deck, they walked to the bow. Brandon stood beside her, put his arm around her wrist protectively in the light breeze and pointed to several dots of light high up on Victoria Peak. "There, right there is my villa where we dined." Poole paused as a small junk passed by under full sail in the light wind.

"It's breathtaking, Brandon. Pictures I've seen on postcards and travel folders have all come to life. Now where do you suppose that junk is going?" Lacy was a bit taken aback by Poole's familiarity but suddenly it felt right. She decided she'd let him keep his arm where it was—for the moment.

Brandon eyed the tiny vessel now gliding past the bow pointed toward the South China Sea. "He carries some small cargo. See the boxes strapped to the fore-deck? He is probably on a run to one of the outer islands, Cheung Chau or Lantau. He is hardly rigged for a long voyage on the open sea. Actually Lacy, he is an entrepreneur, just like hundreds of thousands of others in Hong Kong."

Lacy stared at the tiny craft as it moved away from the massive, gleaming freighter. "Do you think he aspires to be like you, Brandon? What does he think when he passes a great ship like this one?"

"He keeps a very neat vessel and probably is a good provider to his family. But as far as becoming another Brandon Poole, he has a long, long road ahead of him. I doubt if he ever thinks in those terms."

A fresh breeze, gently cooling, wafted across the harbor through the evening air. Lacy held her arms across her bosom, clasping elbows. Her thoughts raced back to an outing several years back she had made with Adam. His TV station had tossed a company party on the Fourth of July on a party boat which had circled Manhattan on a clear night. Adam had just been made news anchor, and he was at his handsome, pompous best. He had drunk too much and was eagerly accepting kisses of congratulations from all the young women from the TV station.

She remembered how at first she'd felt a little jealous and then embarrassed when Adam and the TV station's weathergirl put on a smooching exhibition that was talked about by everyone for the rest of the night. On the way home she had told him that it was disgusting and that either the heavy drinking had to stop or she would leave. The next day she forgave him against all better judgment. But soon after that she realized that his behavior that night was the real Adam, and there would be no changing him.

"Lacy, you are awfully quiet. Am I boring you with my travelogue. I'm sorry."

"Oh, no, Brandon. Really, I enjoy every word. I . . . was just comparing this to a trip I once made at night on a boat that circled Manhattan. I would say that your Hong Kong is every bit as dazzling."

Another junk, this one under power, passed near their bow, engines clanging suspiciously and emitting a low roll of exhaust across the water. Brandon raised one arm to point to the red flag atop the masthead. "The flag of our future sovereignty, Lacy. He's on his way up to the mouth of the Pearl River, probably to Shenzhen or Guangzhou. Now, which of those last two vessels would you rather be on?"

She turned toward him, smiling. "I'd rather be on the *Kowloon Eagle*, Brandon. I think it is much more seaworthy than either. I love your Hong Kong, Brandon."

He could feel her tense up slightly, but she did not pull away from his loose grasp. "Then why don't you stay for a while, Lacy. Tell the big boss back in New York that you're taking a sabbatical. I would love to show you how business is really done in Hong Kong."

She pulled away from him slowly. "Brandon, all this"—she swept her hands around the harbor—"is another world to me. I've never felt so much like a child, since, well, I was one. Please, let's get back on land. I think I've done enough seafaring for tonight. I'll always treasure this evening on the bridge of the *Kowloon Eagle*."

Poole dropped his arm to his side and grinned down at her. "Just don't forget what I said, Lacy." He walked to a point where he could signal a deck officer and ask him to ready the lighter for transport. "And now, my dear, it is time to resume our little tour of Hong Kong. There is one more stop we should make before you get safely back to the Mandarin. I think you'll find it amusing, for a lot of reasons."

"Thank you, Brandon." She slipped off her heels and walked toward the gangway to the lighter, thinking that Brandon Poole was, indeed, a gentleman. But that, of course, made him more fascinating and diverting.

The small lighter skipped along rapidly over the now flat water. As they approached their pier, the glistening skyline of Central District to the north was mirrored almost perfectly in the water.

On shore, she saw their limo waiting. It was the only vehicle in the small parking area. The strange little man who was their chauffeur stood next to the limo. He had his chauffeur's cap pulled down across his forehead. That was the way he had worn it when he had joined them at the villa and shared the tramway to the parking area.

"Where to now, Brandon?" Lacy asked as they climbed into the limo.

"Relax, my dear. It's not far. In fact it is right here in Wan Chai. You have a tight schedule, I know. So this may be your rare opportunity to see a little of our nightlife. Frankly, I never find time to go, nor would I especially recommend it. However, it should be part of any education for understanding the complete Hong Kong.

"Cecil, take us to the Typhoon Club."

The driver nodded and turned onto the now very quiet streets of Wan Chai. However, they had driven only a few blocks when a glow of lights lit up the street ahead of them. Scores of garish neon signs, most of them in Chinese characters, pulsed and blinked above the sidewalk. Down a narrow side street, a small blue neon sign in English lettering identified the Typhoon Club. It stood alone on the darkened street with a long line of patrons waiting to get in.

The limo moved directly to the doorway. The chauffeur got out and spoke a few words to the giant of a man monitoring the entrance. In a moment, he nodded to Poole, and he and Lacy got out of the limo and walked to the doorway. The ever smiling impresario Sean Xiang appeared almost immediately.

"Brandon, this is an honor. Welcome to the Typhoon Club." Sean clasped his hand warmly, and then escorted them to a semicircular red leather booth facing an elevated stage just a few feet away. Sean, bent low, spoke to Poole in a whisper and nodded toward Lacy. "Very, very nice, you old fox. I thought you never found time for such things."

"Sean, this is Lacy. Sean here is the P. T. Barnum of Hong Kong." Lacy beamed at the personable impresario. "Lacy is a financial wizard from New York, Sean. She is here to help us make a pile of money before the time runs out."

"Now that is good news, Miss Lacy. Perhaps you can share a tip or two that I can take to Hang Seng." Sean smiled broadly.

"I am afraid, Sean, that there is only one financial wizard at this table." Lacy glanced toward Brandon Poole.

Sean bent next to her ear and whispered, "I think you're right, Miss Lacy. He may be the only wizard left in Hong Kong." He then straightened up and addressed both of them. "You caught us in intermission. Very soon you will see our new feature act, fresh from Miss Lacy's native New York. Brandon, is this young lady old enough to witness such frivolity?" He looked at Poole with mock concern, and winked at Lacy.

Brandon laughed easily. "If Lacy doesn't like the performance, I'll merely blame it all on your bad taste, Sean. She's making a study of Hong Kong, which would never be complete without a visit to the Typhoon Club."

The house lights were dimmed to pitch black. A voice, clear and true, emanated from somewhere high above them, a torchy version of a popular song from the old musical *Cats*. A single spotlight formed a dot near the ceiling. The spotlight's orb grew larger and larger until it focused on the gorgeous blond singer, perched on the lid of a grand piano, seemingly suspended in space. Her legs were elevated and crossed, Petty Girl style. A powder blue men's sport coat was draped over one shoulder.

"Ladies and gentlemen, Miss Mary Lulu!" The crowd roared its approval as the piano descended to the stage.

Lacy shook her head in disbelief and gently elbowed Brandon Poole as he watched her face. "Brandon! You devil. You knew all about Mary Lulu and her Phuket sport coat. Why didn't you tell me? I didn't even know she was in Hong Kong." Then Lacy remembered what she had read about her act in New York. She wondered if Brandon Poole knew what was ahead.

Now the piano was on the stage, less than twenty feet from their ringside booth. Mary Lulu stood, wearing only a bronze suntan, spike heels, and the sport coat still draped on one shoulder, long blond hair trailing to her waist. The crowd cheered wildly in approval.

"Gee, folks, I'm sorry," intoned Mary Lulu in a throaty voice. "I didn't quite finish dressing." She then twirled the sport coat off her shoulder, put it on and slowly buttoned the two buttons as the crowd shrieked with approval.

Lacy covered her eyes with her fingers and then peeked out between then.

"Lacy, I'm sorry. It's a little raw. Perhaps we'd better leave."

"Oh no you don't, Brandon, how then would I ever know what goes on in Hong Kong at night?" She turned to look at Poole. The imperturbable Englishman was actually reddening.

Brandon sat with her through the entire routine,

which was almost a duplicate of the one he'd attended with Sean Xiang in New York. The ear-splitting rock group supporting the scandalous Mary Lulu aroused the deafening approval of the crowd. When the finale came, and she started playing the piano with her derriere, Lacy and the usually sedate Brandon Poole were laughing with the crowd.

Then Mary Lulu walked over to a corner of the stage as a spotlight swung on a darkened booth. A young man was standing, applauding vigorously. It was Chad Grissom. Mary Lulu tossed him the powder blue sport coat, blew him a kiss and ran off the stage.

"Brandon, that was Chad Grissom, Phuket's model and spokesperson."

Poole was grinning. "I'm, glad you enjoyed that, my dear. Now, can we leave?"

"Of course. We could have left anytime, Brandon. Thanks for indulging me." Without thinking, she kissed his cheek. Somehow it just seemed like the thing to do.

The limo was waiting outside. The chauffeur, whom Poole called Cecil, took Poole aside, and the two of them had what appeared to Lacy a quite serious conversation. When he got in the limo with Lacy, he seemed to be deep in thought.

"Something is upsetting you, Brandon. I can tell."

"Business in Hong Kong is full of surprises, Lacy." He became quiet, again in deep thought. "Lacy, I want you to know that my villa on the Peak is always open to you. Perhaps you would like to spend the night there. Chelsea makes a lovely breakfast."

From any other man, she would consider that a flat-out proposition. But with Brandon Poole, she wasn't sure. Something had changed his demeanor since his conversation with the chauffeur before he got in the limo.

"Thank you, Brandon, but the Mandarin serves a fine breakfast. The night has been exhausting. I feel like I know so much about Hong Kong."

"Cecil, take us to the Mandarin." He lapsed again into deep thought for a moment and then looked at Lacy. "Perhaps you'll join me for dinner at the yacht club later in the week."

"Of course I will. In fact I'll count on it."

The short drive to the Mandarin was void of conversation. When they pulled up in front, Brandon said, "Cecil, give us a few moments, please." Cecil left the limo and went over to strike up a conversation with the doorman.

"Lacy, I know that you are vitally interested in Phuket Color. I don't want to see you make a serious mistake. While we were in the Typhoon Club, Cecil received a report which came from reliable sources. I can't tell you how I know, but I know. There was a major fire in downtown Bangkok tonight on the premises of the Phuket Color factory. There was heavy damage. The fire came between shifts, so I am told there were few casualties."

Lacy stared at the sober-faced Poole. "I'm meeting with some of their people tomorrow. Thanks for telling me. I'll let you know if I learn anything further."

Brandon Poole clasped her hand tightly in his for a moment. "Lacy, I must ask you to keep the source of this information in confidence. Good night, Lacy. Sorry a perfect evening had to end this way."

She got out of the car, smiled, waved good-bye and walked into the Mandarin.

Cecil Lo climbed back into the limo. "When did that call come in from Reggie in Bangkok?" asked Poole.

"Less than an hour ago, sir. He insisted on talking to you before he says any more."

Poole frowned. "I don't know that I trust Reggie all that much. He's been pimping young artists into the big hotels again, I hear. I'll try to reach him from the Peak. By the way, Cecil, you can drop our tail on Lacy

Locke. I want you to get down to Bangkok as quickly as possible and find out what the hell happened to the factory. And give me a report on Reggie. Maybe we don't need him anymore with Phuket burned out."

Chapter 22

THE MOB was not unruly. They just mixed with the customers and quietly did their job." Tommy Ching, the store manager, was talking to the superintendent of police. "There were at least ten of them moving through the aisles between clothing display tables. By the time we discovered what they were doing, they had left the store. One of our clerks chased them to the Tsim Sha Tsui subway station on Nathan Road, but then lost them in the crowd."

"Was anyone injured?" queried Hargrave.

"No, no one was injured."

"How about the damage? Has that been fully assessed?"

"Damage was limited to about fifteen tables of merchandise. However, it consisted of cashmere sweaters, skirts, blouses, and ladies' fashion goods of the highest quality. Perhaps two hundred thousand in Hong Kong dollars."

"Let's take a look." Superintendent Hargrave scratched his chin and spoke to his assistant. "I was told that this happened at a store in Central District a few days ago. However, the damage there was limited to one table of high-priced sweaters."

The store manager led them on an inspection of the high-fashion store, one of a score of such upscale shops along Nathan Road in Kowloon. The area that had been ravaged was roped off from the other merchandise. Several investigators were examining the contents of the display tables.

Hargrave stood at the shoulder of one policeman as he lifted several cashmere sweaters from the table. Gaping holes appeared in some of them. Others had tiny holes, as if they had been eaten by moths.

"Acid," proclaimed the policeman. "I suspect some variety of sulfuric acid. It is extremely dangerous and volatile. Apparently they had some sort of small glass vial that let a few drops at a time seep out. It would have been important that they not get any on themselves. It would cause an immediate flesh burn."

"How much of the goods on the table is actually unsalable?" Hargrave asked, thinking ahead to the necessary vandalism report.

The investigator shook his head. "Almost everything was damaged in at least some small way. It's amazing how the acid mixture ate its way through stacks of things."

"Tell me," Hargrave asked the distraught manager, "have you had a squabble with anyone lately? Perhaps a disgruntled worker, or even a customer?"

"I have asked the same question to my department managers. None reported any such difficulty. It was an organized mob, not the work of a single irate person."

Hargrave kept busy at his notebook as the manager talked. He looked at his Rolex. It would soon be time to meet the general. Liu had been gone for several days. This was the day he was to show up in Tsuen Wan. He turned to leave instructions with his chief investigator. "Question all the salesclerks who might be able to identify members of the gang who did this. Someone must have a description. I want one of these gang members brought in before nightfall."

"Yes sir," the investigator replied smartly. "There were so many of them. It shouldn't be difficult to find one of them. And he will talk," he assured Hargrave with confidence.

Hargrave left the scene. He had to hurry if he was to keep his appointment with General Liu. He headed the minivan north on Nathan Road, passing the giant Beijing-owned Friendship Store. Never any trouble there, he thought to himself. There had been a rash of smaller incidents like this lately. But he had seen no purpose in listing them to the store manager. Strange, he thought, the Beijing-operated businesses never had these problems. Or perhaps not so strange.

He veered slightly out of his way to take one last look at Moia's villa. He had posted a lookout there just in case she showed up, which she never did. The villa on Stanley Gap Road must be quite cozy, he thought. The Dutchman knew a good thing when he saw one.

Hargrave saw his man, parked in the grove of trees just as he had been instructed. Slumped over the wheel, window lowered all the way, he looked suspiciously like he was asleep.

"Hey, you!" he called again and again. The man didn't move. Hargrave got out of the car and walked over to the old Mazda. "Jesus! No wonder," he murmured. A gaping wound was open alongside his temple. Hargrave felt for a pulse. His stringer was cold dead.

Hargrave opened the door of the Mazda and examined the wound closely. He surmised that the man had been sleeping when someone had hit him with a hard blunt object. There was no evidence of a struggle. He guessed from the gouge in the flesh that a section of iron pipe or the barrel of a handgun could have been the weapon used.

Hargrave returned to his minivan to call the station house for assistance. He would report it just as it had happened. He had passed by and seen the driver slumped over the wheel. There was no reason for anyone to know that he was using the Sha Tin pickpocket as an operative.

When his men arrived, he briefed them on his discovery, placed the case in their hands and told them to keep him informed. Privately, he figured that he would hear no more about it. Few would be concerned about the loss of another petty thief.

By the time he reached his substation near Tsuen Wan, he was forty-five minutes late for his meeting with General Liu. Hargrave was shocked to see the general sitting in his office, at his desk, reading through one of the reports that lay on it. Not even his own commissioner would dare do that.

"General, you have made yourself comfortable. The routine matters of this small substation must be quite boring to you." It took a massive effort for Hargrave to be even somewhat pleasant.

"Quite to the contrary. I find all police work fascinating, Hargrave. If small crimes and small criminals are taken care of properly, they never become big problems." Liu tossed the papers he was perusing back on the desk. "You are quite late, Hargrave. But perhaps Hong Kong is better off because of it."

Hargrave didn't miss the sarcasm in Liu's voice. "There was a little trouble in the countryside this morning, General. A man was done in as he sat in his vehicle. As a matter of fact, his misfortune occurred very near Moia Hsu's villa. I called in investigators to handle the matter. It took time. I got here as quickly as I could."

Liu stared icily at Hargrave. "This kind of thing is beginning to happen all too frequently in Hong Kong, Hargrave. Have you boys let things get out of hand? In Beijing the culprit would be jailed within hours."

"Have no concern, General. My men are digging into several leads right now."

"Really?" The general asked the question as if he wanted to know more.

Hargrave decided to change the subject. "I am sorry I'm late. But I want to assure you that I have been pursuing the Moia Hsu matter around the clock."

Liu stared at him with his usual intensity. "And what do you have to report?"

"I suspect that Van Hooten has set up some sort of a workstation in his villa on Stanley Gap Road. Moia spends many hours there, many days from early evening until morning."

"A workstation, now that is interesting. You think like a Britisher, Hargrave. You've spent your life in Hong Kong and you think like a Britisher. One of the most beautiful women in all of Hong Kong spends her nights with a flaming capitalist for days on end, and you conclude they have set up a workstation." Liu paused, stood up and frowned down at Hargrave. "Tell me, Hargrave, have you ever been with a woman?"

Hargrave reddened. "Certainly. But of course I am no longer a young stallion like one of those thoroughbreds at Sha Tin."

"Did you ever set up a workstation with a young lady in your small apartment while in the service of Her Majesty?" Liu leered lasciviously at Hargrave.

"I'm afraid I am much too busy for that, General. Such frivolity is better accomplished while on holiday in Macau." Hargrave grinned nervously, feeling uncomfortable with Liu's persistence.

"Too busy! Hargrave, you've just put your finger on it. A capitalist, say like Claude Van Hooten, is not too busy at all. In fact the capitalist carefully builds time into his schedule for decadence. The money they have bled from the people is spent in the corruption of our Beijiing women, in this case Moia Hsu." Liu slammed his hand on Hargrave's desk, making him jump.

"Sir, I can only speculate on that."

"Speculate?" Liu sighed heavily. "Hargrave, a competent detective must fill in with his brain what his eyes do not see."

"It is difficult sometimes, General."

"But not for a man of your brilliance, Hargrave," Liu said with a patronizing smile. "Now tell me what else do you have to report?"

"I followed Moia to Sai Kung." Hargrave was relieved to get away from the subject of Van Hooten. "She went there early yesterday morning by limo, accompanied by a young American named Chad Grissom." Hargrave fervently hoped that the security guard at the marina had given him the correct information. "He must be a movie star, sir. They were later joined by a tall, extremely attractive woman. Moia sat in a chair on the aft deck of a sailing yacht moored in the marina and watched as a film crew took movies of the others."

General Liu stared wide-eyed at the superintendent of police. He decided the story was too bizarre for him to concoct. "Others? Who were the others?"

"Beautiful young women, sir. Perhaps a half dozen or so. They wore very little clothing and posed quite provocatively, I might say, with the young American."

"And Moia watched?"

"Oh yes, sir. She never removed her clothing as the others did."

"Of course she didn't!" Liu shouted. "Moia is not like the others!" Again he slammed his hand on Hargrave's desk. He watched Hargrave twitch nervously at his display of temper. "Sorry, Hargrave, but such behavior is appalling to me. What happened next?"

"Well, sir, they sipped champagne on the aft deck for a while and then resumed filming."

"Sipped champagne?" murmured Liu, trying to modulate his temper.

"Yes, General. At about five P.M. they ceased filming. Moia, the man called Grissom, and the tall blond actress got into Moia's limousine and returned to Central District. Grissom and the actress were deposited at the Mandarin Hotel. Moia continued on to the villa in Stanley."

"To spend the night at her workstation with Van Hooten, no doubt." Liu forced a smile. "Hargrave, I must be leaving now. Unless something special comes up, we'll meet here next week at the same time. This is for your continuing investigation." He pulled an envelope from his pocket, stuffed thick with Hong Kong banknotes, and pushed it across the desk to Hargrave.

"I will stay right on the case, sir." Actually Hargrave was beginning to feel dismayed about the continuing investigation for the general. He had little time for anything else.

Liu got up and walked to the door, and then turned around. "One more thing, Hargrave. I wouldn't waste a lot of time on the investigation of that chap you found at the roadside in Tsuen Wan. Consider your priorities, Hargrave."

"I will, sir." Hargrave heaved a sign of relief when the general left his office. He stared at the tall soldier until he left the building and turned a corner. Accepting his generous bribes had been a mistake. To accept the bribes of legitimate businessmen, or even felons wanting a favor, was one thing. But to be bought by the Beijing officer was a mistake he could not live with. His ulcered stomach growled furiously.

Chapter 23

It was five A.M. Claude Van Hooten, unshaven and clad only in a bathrobe, stood on his deck in Stanley, staring southward at the far horizon where the leaden waters of the South China Sea met the fainter light of another dawn. It was as if he were trying to see all the way to Bangkok for something that would explain the devastating news he had just received from his manager there.

"Damn it!" he cursed, throwing his hands at the distant sky. "Eleven dead. There may be more. It will be weeks before even a small portion of the factory can be made operational. At a time like this, why?"

Moia sat nude, cross-legged, statuelike, in the broad hammock. She hadn't spoken for several minutes. Immediately upon receipt of the news, she had tried to reach Li Pao in Beijing. As yet, she had not been able to contact him at home or at his office. His wife would only volunteer that he was away on business. Moia suspected that it was likely that she did not actually know where he was.

Li Pao had been a capable administrator for her, but it had always bothered her that he had been foisted on her and her father by a higher authority in Beijing.

Now, when it was urgent, where was he? "Claude, my dear, anger does not help. You cannot change what has already happened."

"I am afraid that even the wisdom of Confucius does not help, Moia. What can we do? Or can we do anything?" Van Hooten rubbed at the bristles on his chin. "It was all coming together, Moia."

"I must go to Foshan, Claude. We cannot wait another sixty days for them to achieve maximum production. You were too gentle with them on our visit. It must happen within a few days. I will explain the urgency to my father. Dr. Hsu will demand it, and it will be done." Moia lifted her head high and smiled confidently at the pacing Van Hooten.

Van Hooten shook his head slowly. "The plan is to have the local population trained into their positions. You cannot make excellent tailors and seamstresses out of office workers and field workers overnight. It will take time to train and phase them in." Van Hooten shrugged. His usual confidence was waning rapidly.

"I have two plans, Claude. May I explain them to you?"

His face broke into a faint smile as he looked at the nude Moia sitting with legs crossed, balanced in the center of the hammock. They had been locked in one of their erotic embraces, lost in savoring the slow sensual ecstasy they had perfected together, when Van Hooten's private telephone line continued ringing until it broke their blissful compulsion. Now her mind was switched in another direction, with the same intensity.

"My dear Moia, you have two solutions? We really only need one. By all means share your thoughts with me."

"I have heard it said in Beijing that we have warehoused enough uniforms for our military to clothe our army for twenty years. We will merely borrow some of these workers for use in Foshan."

"Moia, think about what you have just said. You are

expecting the military bureaucracy of the largest standing army in the world to stop making uniforms, and then switch to high-fashion garments to be worn by Americans and Brits at play."

"Not all of the workers, Claude! Just a few of them. For the good of China."

Van Hooten furrowed his brow. Moia had always been good at selling her Beijing superiors her ideas that were obviously "for the good of China." But to his knowledge, she had never taken on the military. It was hardly the thing to do if one's survival depended on it. "Moia, with all due respect, I would like to hear idea number two."

Moia sprang from the hammock, and ran a few steps to face Van Hooten, who was now staring toward Victoria Peak in the distance. She looked up into his face with her great brown eyes alive with enthusiasm. "I was thinking of the Thai workers. Most of them will not be working until repairs are made in Bangkok. We would demand that the authorities in Beijing allow them work permits for Foshan."

"Moia, that would be harder to sell than plan number one. China has no shortage of workers. To get them to approve a mass emigration of three hundred Thais is almost unthinkable, even for the good of China. Besides, my sweet Moia, I can tell you that not one in ten of those Thais would come. They don't give a damn about the good of China."

"Perhaps, Claude, I should go to Bangkok and talk to them."

Van Hooten beamed down at Moia's nude form now pressing against him. There was no question that this remarkable woman had great persuasive powers, but they would probably be lost on the several hundred Thai women he had seen at the factory in Bangkok. Van Hooten opened his bathrobe and enclosed Moia inside. She gently undulated against him.

"Claude," she said softly, "do you remember exactly

what we were doing when the telephone rang?"

"Exactly? Let me think for a moment." Van Hooten was startled at his own arousal, following the bad news from Bangkok.

"It's not important, Claude. I think it would be best if we started all over again." She brushed her lips lightly against his chest.

Van Hooten swept his arms under her, carried her to the hammock and joined her as it swung slowly on its tethers. "Those were excellent ideas, Moia. We'll get back to them, I promise you."

Chapter 24

Davy Wong had run far. It was difficult to modulate his breathing so that it was not audible. He opened his mouth wide trying to exhale without a sound. Investigators were moving through the night market in Kowloon, systematically searching each retail stall. They had started at both ends of the nighttime shopping complex, working their way toward the middle, where Wong hid in Eddie Sing's trash box under empty cartons and wrappings that had once held watered silk blouses and scarves shipped from Guangzhou.

Wong could now hear them questioning his friend, only inches away on the other side of the thin wood of the refuse bin.

"This man, have you see him?" The policeman held a photo of a sober-faced Davy Wong in front of him.

Eddie Sing inspected the photo as other police poked behind the curtains of his stall. One of them was now resting his arm on the refuse box which held his friend. Though the photo was that of Davy Wong, it was void of the effervescent personality that one naturally associated with Wong. It was probably taken from a passport photo or a mug shot taken in the Beijing jail.

"No," Eddie replied, pretending to peruse the photograph with great care. "I have not seen this man."

"Do you know him?" The policeman persisted.

Eddie shook his head slowly. "No, I have never seen him." The policeman now peeked behind the trash bin. "What did he do?" Eddie asked, trying to engage the policeman in conversation before he could open the bin.

"He killed a worker near Tsuen Wan this morning. He is very dangerous. You are to report him to us the instant you see him. We saw him enter the night market only a few minutes ago."

"Oh, I will, I will," repeated Eddie, feigning anxiety that a killer could be loose in the night market. The group of policemen then abruptly moved on to the next stall. Eddie leaned on the trash bin, then casually opened the lid and tossed some packing paper on top of the heap that concealed Wong.

"They are still nearby," he whispered to Wong. "You must wait until it is safe. I will let you know."

Wong sat quietly in the corner of his hiding place contemplating his predicament. He had no idea why the police were after him now. He was totally ignorant of any killing in Tsuen Wan which was evidently being attributed to him. He marveled at the coolness of Eddie Sing. For him to provide cover for an accused murderer, no matter how trumped up the charges might be, was courageous indeed.

Wong realized that his decision to enter the narrow streets of the night market had been a mistake. The usual throng of tourists that flooded the nighttime shopping mecca was not there owing to the evening shower. He had been spotted easily, and all of a sudden policemen appeared from everywhere. He would certainly remember the loyalty of Eddie Sing.

"Now, Davy, now!" Eddie rapped on the box and Davy emerged from the litter. "You should be able to make it to Nathan Road now, Davy. The way is clear."

Davy vaulted out of his haven, grinning at Eddie

Sing. He paused in the shadows of the stall to salute his friend with a big thumbs-up from both fists, then turned and walked rapidly toward Nathan Road.

On Nathan, he walked briskly toward the Star Ferry terminal, thankful that this main artery was crowded with enough people to give him cover.

Boarding the Star Ferry for Central District, he mingled with the throng of passengers and seated himself among them. The water was flat in the harbor this evening, the only movement being the swells caused by the wake of a Kowloon-bound ferry and a few other vessels moving in the harbor. Davy eyed Victoria Peak silhouetted against a now moonlit sky and hoped that Brandon Poole would not be upset with what he was about to do.

They were within a couple of minutes of docking in Kowloon before he noticed the two policemen. They had descended two ladders leading to the lower deck and were systematically working their way row by row through the lower deck. He slouched down in his seat and feigned sleep for a few moments, pulling the small billed cap down over his brow. One of the policemen continued past his row. The other had began a chat with a young lady, part of a group of what appeared to be American tourists.

Davy Wong continued in his feigned sleep as the huge Star Ferry began bumping along the wooden pilings abutting the station in Central District. As he expected, the passengers all surged toward the exiting gangway at once. He arose slowly and tried to move toward the middle of the pack as it crowded into the ferry station. He continued to mingle with the crowd as it moved rapidly through the station and then outside.

Now he was running toward the taxi station outside when he heard the police.

"Stop! Stop!" they yelled from a hundred feet behind. Ahead of him other policemen were waiting near the taxi stand. Just when the traffic looked the most dense, he plunged ahead into Connaught Road, dancing agilely between the passing cars. The police, thankfully, were not quite as willing to follow his daredevil path. By the time they made it across, Davy Wong had vanished in the alleys and back streets of the hillside leading toward the Peak.

He moved upward through the underbrush and emerged in the parking area of Brandon Poole's villa. He opened a small box on a post and pressed the numeric code that Poole had given him. Above him, he could hear the small tram descending.

Before he got inside the tramcar, he paused to study the underbrush around him. When he decided that he had totally eluded his pursuers, he sat down inside and breathed a heavy sigh of relief. Once again he had been lucky.

Brandon Poole was waiting for him as the tramcar inched its way into its bay near the top of the Peak. "Davy, it's you. I figured it had to be. No one else who has the code would call at such an uncivil hour."

"Sorry, Brandon. The bastards were after me. I left them dodging traffic down on Connaught Road." Davy Wong grinned at his friend.

"Why, Davy, why this time?"

"I overheard them talking down in the night market in Kowloon. Someone was killed near Tsuen Wan. They are telling people that I did it."

Poole frowned. No one could run forever, especially an activist like Davy Wong. Hong Kong wasn't that big. Sooner or later he would get caught. "Why do you suppose they are doing that, Davy?"

"I think they want me bad now. Remember, I told you about General Liu Wing living in Tsuen Wan. I've been poking around. Followed him to Kai Tak a couple of days ago. He boarded Thai Air for Bangkok with Li Pao, a Trade Ministry representative I once knew, from Beijing. Maybe they saw me. Of course, I am still wanted for questioning about Tiananmen Square."

"That was a terrible chance you took. They could have picked you up at Kai Tak. Beijing has people going through there day and night. Why, Davy?"

"I had to find out more about General Liu. It doesn't make sense that a man of his rank should be holed up in Tsuen Wan." Davy Wong followed Poole into the villa.

"Does it make sense to you now, Davy?"

"What if I told you that General Liu is up to some sort of a terrorist campaign designed to undermine the strength of certain Hong Kong companies that would be highly profitable if wholly owned by Beijing?"

"I would think, Davy, that you are wrong. I would suspect that Beijing would much rather have these companies stick around with all their assets intact, come 1997. Why suspect the general?"

"I called one of my good friends in Bangkok. On the evening before the fire at Phuket Color in Bangkok, the general and this Li Pao took a long walk. They stood in front of the factory site for over fifteen minutes before returning to their hotel. That night, while the two of them were attending a Thai dance exibition, the factory burned. The very next morning they left, returning to Hong Kong."

Brandon Poole stared at Wong and then shrugged. "I suppose you find it hard to believe that the general and his companion would fly all the way to Bangkok, see a dancing exhibition, and then return the next day to Hong Kong. Somehow you connect them with the fire."

"Yes, Brandon, I can feel it. I know that it is so."

"And this is what you risked your life to tell me this evening? I admit that the trip is odd. But I am not sure about the conclusions that you have reached. It will take much more than you have discovered to encourage the Thai government to charge a Beijing general with anything at all."

"Just remember what I told you, Brandon. General Liu Wing is much more important than you think. You will see."

Chapter 25

"Lacy, I've decided not to run for governor." Those words were the first spoken by Adam Locke when he picked up her call in New York.

"Hello, Adam," she replied coldly, ignoring the predictable lack of warmth in his greeting.

"Did you hear what I said, Lacy? I've made the big decision. I'm not running for governor."

"Good for you, Adam! I think you've made the right decision."

"No, it's the wrong decision. But it is one I have to make. I'm a little short in donations to my campaign fund. I'd have to raise over three million. The guys with the fat wallets in this town don't know what's best for them." Adam groaned, obviously distressed.

Or maybe they do know what's best, Lacy told herself. "Relax, dear, you've had a lot of fun with the idea. It helped build your ratings. Now you can blast everyone. What's in the campaign fund now?"

"About eighteen grand. It'll all have to go back." There was a brief silence as Lacy still waited for her warm greeting. "Lacy, I hope you're watching what you eat over there. I don't want you catching anything."

"How thoughtful of you, Adam. Actually the food is

quite wonderful here. You would have a ball."

"That's not what I've heard. There is all kinds of stuff floating around over there," Adam insisted.

"Floating around? Adam, walk over and take a peek at the East River at low tide. How are you making out all by yourself?"

"Just fine, Lacy. Babs Billings has been a jewel. You've got her figured wrong, Lacy. She had me over for dinner the other night. I'm returning the favor tonight. A little shoptalk to kill the time, if you know what I mean."

Lacy pictured the busty blonde who had filled in for Adam on the morning news when he was in the hospital. "Adam, you once said that she wanted your job so bad she could taste it."

"Lacy, she's a twit and a lightweight. I'm not going to worry about that."

"A twit, a lightweight, and a jewel. Those are all your words, Adam. Think about it. I don't want you to catch anything while I'm gone, Adam."

Adam roared with laughter. "No danger of that, honey. She does serve good pasta, though."

"Thanks, Adam."

"Thanks for what?"

"The 'honey.' Do you realize that's the first endearing word you've had for me? I get the feeling that I'm not missed, Adam."

"You know better than that. When are you coming back?"

"I have no idea. It will be a longer stay than I first envisioned. Besides, I'm enjoying myself." She decided not to tell him about the gracious attention paid her by Brandon Poole. She'd save that for another time. "Adam, I have a great news story for you. It's your kind of a thing. A great exclusive for the morning news. I want you to do it for me."

"Lacy, we have network people over there. Nothing much comes in from Hong Kong that we can use."

"Then they've got their head in the sand, or they're chumming it up too much in the pubs. I'll write it up and send it by special pouch. Promise me you'll use it, okay, Adam? I guarantee it will be picked up by all the wire services. It's big, Adam."

"I'll use it, Lacy. Just be sure you get the facts. I warn you, financial stuff usually goes over like a lead balloon. But for you, I'll do it."

"This isn't exactly financial stuff, but everything that happens in Hong Kong has something to do with money. You'll see when you read my . . . our story."

"Just don't make it too obvious, Lacy."

"How am I supposed to respond to that, Adam?"

"Lacy, I'll be glad to do the story. Just don't make it an obvious puff piece for Worldwide Securities. The boys upstairs can spot a shill a mile away."

"Shill! Adam, you're a bastard. Do you really think I would embarrass you?"

"I'm sorry, baby. I've got to be careful. You know what I mean. Write it any old way you want to, and I'll put it on the air. Jeez! There's no reason to get upset."

"Adam, I might as well tell you that I feel very upset about this conversation. Maybe we can do better the next time. Bye-bye." Lacy hung up the phone, angry with herself for letting the conversation deteriorate.

She walked over to the window of her room and pulled the drapes wide open. Victoria Harbor was bustling with activity this morning. The gleaming *Brandon Kowloon Eagle* was by far the largest of many vessels in the harbor. Now it was surrounded by a half-dozen large lighters, waiting their turn to lade cargo.

As she stared at the freighter's faraway bridge, where she had stood the night before, her mind raced over the events of the evening. The dinner on the Peak, the trip out to the freighter, and the surprise visit to the Typhoon Club and Mary Lulu, all spiced with the attentiveness of Brandon Poole, had overwhelmed her. Brandon had reached her in a way that few men had.

Slowly and very surely, he was growing to be a giant in her eyes.

The one unpleasantness had been at the end of the evening when news of the fire in Bangkok had been mysteriously communicated to Brandon. She wondered whether Van Hooten would tell her about that, later this day.

Lacy studied the Baedeker's map of Hong Kong. The Mandarin Hotel was just three blocks from the large bank building which held Van Hooten's office. Outside, the morning sun was shrouded by fog. She decided to take an umbrella in case of a shower, and walk to her appointment.

Room service brought her breakfast precisely at eight o'clock along with the copy of the South China *Morning Post* she had requested. She had ordered tea service, an assortment of bakery goods, and fresh juice, deciding that she didn't have time to be more adventurous.

The *Morning Post* carried a brief story of a fire in the garment manufacturing area of Bangkok. It said that there were fatalities, but the number was unknown at the time the story was written. Phuket Color was not mentioned by name, nor was the extent of the damage. Brandon Poole had given her more information than the short report contained. Van Hooten must know of the tragedy, she reasoned, but she wouldn't mention it until he brought it up. It made their meeting potentially quite meaningful. The fire, if it was extensive, might have a direct bearing on the inclusion of Phuket Color in New Worldwide Securities' mutual fund.

She sipped at her tea and again stared out the window at the *Kowloon Eagle* riding at anchor. Brandon Poole was constantly on her mind. She could remember every time he had casually touched her. Always gentle, always in the spirit of thoughtful assistance. Yet there was this quiet whimsical look about him whenever he fixed his eyes on her during conversation. He was easy to be with. She found herself looking forward to their next meeting, really for no definite business purpose. She decided that she liked him. Maybe she even admired him.

Another article in the newspaper caught her eye. Near Shenzhen, there had been a battle between some migrant workers and local villagers. Regular construction workers near Shenzhen had rioted in a protest against the hiring of migrant workers for about a dollar a day, about half what the regular villagers received. Police had opened fire on the migrants and killed several of them. Some were reported to have died because the local health authorities refused to treat them.

It seems that local construction companies hired the migrants often as a cost-cutting device. Her thoughts again turned to Brandon Poole and she wondered whether Poole ever made use of the migrants instead of local available labor. She made a note to ask him about this. Also, she felt uneasy that there were civil riots so close to the border of Hong Kong. The story added to the uncertainty she felt about the future of Hong Kong. Yes, she would have to ask Poole about that.

Now walking outside the Mandarin Hotel she turned right, toward Statue Square. Studying the massive buildings beyond the square, she pinpointed the one that housed Van Hooten's office and began strolling toward it in the warm, moist air.

A crowd of perhaps one hundred fifty to two hundred people, many of them carrying placards, was marching in orderly file in front of a domed building just off Statue Square. She changed direction, enabling her to walk near the apparent demonstration. Most of the placards were in Chinese and made no sense to her.

She picked out one sign written partly in English, making out the words COLONIAL PASSPORT. The man carrying this sign stood apart from the group and was talking rapidly in Chinese as he paced along beside them. Then she noticed several policemen carrying batons, standing quietly and watching the group from several hundred feet away.

As a group, the demonstrators were quite orderly, just pacing in a long oval path and occasionally moving their placards up and down. It was certainly nothing like the various activist groups she was used to seeing in New York, given to shouting and intimidating passersby.

Lacy walked slowly, studying the group, trying to fathom the meaning of the demonstration. With interest, she noted that the passing pedestrians, most of them no doubt office workers on their way to work, paid the demonstrators no attention at all. She passed the group, crossed Statue Square and entered the lobby of the skyscraper near the northwest corner of the square. Lacy produced a card and announced herself to a security guard, who immediately called Van Hooten's office to receive clearance for her visit.

The small elevator zipped quickly up forty floors. When the door opened she was met by a small, slender woman neatly dressed in a short black skirt and a white blouse buttoned to the collar, similar to the garb she had seen on many women down on the street.

"You must be Lacy Locke," she said with a smile, "looking for Claude Van Hooten."

"Yes. Good morning."

"Please come with me." She led Lacy down a narrow hallway to a door marked only with the number 4000 and opened it on a spacious reception area. A large window on one side looked out on Victoria Peak in the distance. The young receptionist moved behind her desk and announced her arrival to Van Hooten. A large Phuket Color logo, cast in chrome, hung behind the reception desk.

"Lacy, welcome!" Claude Van Hooten emerged from his office and extended his hand to Lacy. He was beaming. If he had a disastrous fire on his mind he certainly didn't show it.

"Good morning, Claude, what a lovely office. Now I'm certain there really is a Phuket Color."

"Oh very much so, Ms. Locke. Come into my office. I want you to meet my assistant. We've been getting some material prepared for you."

Inside the office, he led her to a small conference table next to a broad window that also looked out on the panorama of Victoria Peak. A strikingly attractive Chinese woman looked up from her work.

"Lacy, I want you to meet Moia Hsu. Moia is the marketing and operations executive of Phuket Color and one of the main reasons for our phenomenal growth."

Moia stared at Van Hooten, smiling faintly, appearing embarrassed at his praise. "Mr. Van Hooten is given to exaggeration sometimes," she said, rising to extend her hand to Lacy.

"Moia, I want to thank you so much for helping Eric in New York to plan my visit. Everything has gone just smashingly so far." Exotic, thought Lacy, as they shook hands. Moia Hsu was the very personification of the word. Marketing and operations was a strange combination. She decided that Moia must have plenty of talent backing up the beautiful exterior.

"It was my pleasure," assured Moia. "He seemed like a fine young man over the telephone." The three seated themselves at the conference table. Moia had arranged a half-dozen file folders in front of her. The neat files were the only things lying on the highly polished rosewood table.

Van Hooten accepted the file which Moia slid toward him. He positioned it in front of him unopened and nodded toward Moia, who moved her head affirmatively.

"Lacy, this is hardly the way I anticipated beginning this presentation," he began, "but we've had a bit of difficulty, which should be explained as a preface to this meeting."

Lacy glanced at Moia, whose wide eyes were riveted on Claude Van Hooten as he spoke. Already she could sense a bond between the two. The meeting had been carefully planned.

"Last night there was a fire in Bangkok. One of the buildings affected was a factory leased to Phuket Color. There was enough damage to cause an immediate work stoppage. I understand that there was some loss of life. Frankly, I do not know at this time when production will resume in Bangkok. I expect to have a complete report later this morning. I tell you this up front, because we want you to fully understand the implications of the fire, and realize that it will cause no more than a few days in loss of production. It is important that you know these facts as they originate from us, and not wild speculation from some other source."

"Oh Claude, I feel so bad about the fire. Perhaps we ought to postpone this meeting. Your minds must be occupied with this." Lacy sat erect, preparing to get up from the table.

"No, no, no," protested Van Hooten. "We are quite able to move forward, even in the midst of this tragedy in Bangkok. Moia and I have spent long hours this morning devising alternative production plans for the next few weeks. It comes at a time in our existence when we can absorb the blow, perhaps without missing the shipment of a single order."

"Really? That would be miraculous, wouldn't it? Everything I've learned about Phuket Color names Bangkok as its primary source of production."

"That was true yesterday, but not today. Don't forget, we have a small factory right here in Hong Kong that can double its production in a matter of days. And don't forget this is Hong Kong. There are more tailors and seamstresses per square mile than any other place in the world. Much work can be easily farmed out."

Van Hooten paused and turned to Moia, who was listening attentively. "Moia, please tell Lacy why there really is little concern over the stoppage in Bangkok."

Moia opened one of the folders she had lined up in front of her. "The facility in Bangkok was quite old. Some of the machinery was archaic, dating back to the 1940s and before. Within sixty days, we had already planned to move our primary production to Foshan in the People's Republic. Now we will do that in under thirty days. The factory in Foshan is already producing far ahead of schedule. As I suggested to Eric, you must go there and see for yourself. It is but a day trip."

Lacy listened, rapt at the gentle and concise summation from Moia Hsu. "It is amazing that you can cope with a tragedy like this so easily."

"It could only be done in Hong Kong," Van Hooten interjected. "Now Moia, tell Lacy about Shanghai. As you have guessed, no doubt, Moia here furnishes Phuket Color with great expertise in dealing with the People's Republic."

Just for an instant, Lacy saw what looked like a spark of agitation flicker in Moia's brown eyes, but it quickly faded into a faint smile. "We are building another factory near Shanghai. Construction has started already, and now will be expedited."

"You're telling me that the fire in Bangkok really has no impact on the future of Phuket Color." Lacy made the statement directly to Van Hooten.

"Lacy, in a strange way it even strengthens the future of Phuket Color. Like it or not, Phuket Color is now totally committed to Hong Kong and the People's Republic beyond 1997. Bangkok was sort of a safety valve that made an exit from Hong Kong a possibility, however slight." Van Hooten's voice trailed off as he appeared to be in deep thought, just realizing perhaps the implications of what he'd said. Moia too seemed in deep thought, eyes again riveted on Van Hooten.

"So it sounds like you have the situation well in

hand," Lacy agreed. "Now I can't wait to see all the goodies. I mean things like gross sales, profits, nets, costs, inventory, all those things that give an investor either a headache or a smile."

Moia laughed softly. "Goodies. I've never heard them called goodies before, but they are all here in these folders, ready to be studied at your leisure. Perhaps you would like to go over them with me right now."

"Yes, I would. I must admit that the garment business mystifies me. I flew over here in the same plane with a chap who is to be your spokesperson, Chad Grissom. Very attractive, but I'm curious about a million-dollar investment in such a man."

"A million dollars?" Moia again laughed softly. "Don't believe everything you read in the press, Ms. Locke. He does fill out our clothing beautifully, does he not?"

"That he does well!"

"He is in Sai Kung today. They are filming some promotional footage. No doubt we will have a tape for you before you leave Hong Kong. Shall we get started."

Moia moved next to Lacy so that she could read along and answer questions as they leafed through the financial reports. It became obvious to Lacy that the woman's mind took no backseat to her beauty.

Claude Van Hooten rose from the table. "Lacy, I am going to tend to other things for a while and leave you in Moia's capable hands. I'll be joining you both for lunch at the club." Van Hooten strolled out of the office, still seemingly absorbed in deep thought.

The next couple of hours were spent in heavy study of Phuket's financial history over the past three years. The company had had a meteoric rise in the Asian market, and all the testing that had been completed for Western Europe and the United States had resulted in success. By the end of the session with Moia, Lacy was ready to believe that Phuket Color was indeed on the move.

At twelve sharp, Lacy, Moia, and Van Hooten met at the elevator and headed for luncheon at Van Hooten's club, the Old Lion. As they walked across Statue Square, occasionally a head turned to glance quickly at the two striking women. Lacy asked Van Hooten about the demonstrators, fewer in number now, but still parading near the domed building to their left.

"They are protesting in front of the legislature. It really isn't a legislature, but it's all we've got now. The governor, who no longer really governs, sits and listens to various problems that need addressing. There is no general suffrage in Hong Kong, so only a few of the members are elected. Nothing comes of it, but as I say, that's all we've got until the Chinese show up in full force in 'ninety-seven." Van Hooten shrugged.

"And the protesters?" persisted Lacy.

"Lacy, there are a couple of million people in Hong Kong who live here by virtue of a British colonial passport. It used to be that the passport was a ticket to England, or one of the other reaches of the empire. Now it is virtually worthless as far as getting the right of abode anywhere. All these people would like some sort of assurance about their welcome here and elsewhere after 1997. Do I confuse you?"

"Not at all, Claude. It only makes me rather glad to be an American."

Lacy noticed that Moia Hsu was very attentive but totally noncommittal about his assessment of the protesters. She had usually deferred to Van Hooten's role of leading the conversation, but hadn't hesitated to chime in to further articulate some of the points he made.

Lacy quickly noticed that the throngs of people around them in Central District were almost totally Asian. People who were obviously European or American were a rarity. "I find Hong Kong incredibly exciting, Moia. Were you born and raised here?"

"No, not in Hong Kong." Pausing for a second, she added, "I spent most of my youth in Beijing and was educated in Shanghai and Canton." She changed the subject quickly. "There is the Cenotaph," she said, pointing to the memorial with a scattering of flowers at the base. "It honors Hong Kong's dead in the two world wars."

"Nowadays, most of the flowers placed there are in honor of the students who died at Tiananmen Square," added Van Hooten.

It was the only remark Van Hooten offered during the balance of the walk to the Old Lion Club. He seemed deep in his own thoughts. Lacy marveled at their ability to put together such a positive presentation in the face of the tragedy in Bangkok.

"Moia." Lacy decided to question her about the disturbing article she had read that morning. "In the *Morning Post* today, I read about a riot of villagers against migrant construction workers near Shenzhen. Does this kind of thing ever interfere with your own expansion plans?"

As they walked, Moia was silent for several seconds. Lacy thought she was not going to answer her. Then with a smile that Lacy thought was somewhat ingenuous, she spoke.

"I too read the story. Sometimes these reports are not totally accurate. There is a totally free labor market in the People's Republic of China. If people are willing to work for a certain price, so be it." Having said that, Moia picked up their pace toward the club, offering no further insight into the riot.

Lacy felt that she had been shortchanged by her terse response. She wanted to say, What do you mean, so be it? For a dollar a day! But she remained quiet and decided she would pose the same question to Brandon later.

Chapter 26

GENERAL LIU WING called Hargrave at five A.M. in order to be sure he would catch him before he left for his vigil on Stanley Gap Road.

"Hargrave here," he answered gruffly as he glanced at his clock, irritated at being awakened a full hour ahead of time.

"I'm going to give you a break today, Hargrave. Perhaps you'll relish the free time. You can go out and catch some criminals. I have heard there is a whole new breed of pickpockets at Sha Tin."

The crisp, sarcastic voice of General Liu jolted him awake. "I'm at your service, sir. But I welcome the time to get some of my routine affairs in shape." Hargrave glanced at the racing program he had purchased the night before, hardly expecting to actually use it.

"You can resume your surveillance of our beautiful friend tomorrow morning. Do you have anything to report to me, Hargrave?"

Hargrave scrambled unsuccessfully for his notes. "Nothing much, sir. She had lunch with Van Hooten and a woman I had never seen before at the Old Lion Club. The woman was very attractive. She carried a briefcase. I suspect it was all business."

"And afterward, Hargrave, what happened then?"

"They all went their separate ways. The woman left them, walking across the square, and Moia and Van Hooten returned to their office."

"And no doubt left for their workstation in Stanley later on."

"Yes, sir. It was quite late. I haven't had much sleep, sir."

"Well then, enjoy your day off, Hargrave. I'll be seeing you at the usual time later in the week."

Liu hung up the phone, churning inside. They might as well be living together, he thought. Hell, they *are* living together. "It's time to put a stop to that!" he raged aloud, popping a fist solidly into his other hand.

He rose to dress for the day in the clothes he had purchased for the occasion, loose-fitting khaki work pants and a matching shirt. He rolled the long sleeves up into a tight roll over his biceps, then jammed down a fisherman's hat until it rested near the bridge of his nose.

He stared in the mirror, rubbing his fingers on a three-day stubble of beard. He looked nothing at all now like a general in the People's Army.

Within minutes he had walked to the rail station in Tsuen Wan and boarded a subway to Central. Liu made his way to the ferry terminal that served the islands south and west of Hong Kong.

There he purchased a ticket for Cheung Chau, one of the smaller islands that had became a favorite for him and Moia years ago. They had visited Cheung Chau upon his graduation from military school, traveling from Shanghai at the suggestion of Dr. Hsu. They had found the beaches and the remoteness of the small island a welcome change from the hustle and bustle of Hong Kong and Shanghai.

Davy Wong waited patiently until General Liu Wing boarded the small ferry so that he could seat himself as far away from him as possible. He was much puzzled by Liu's choice of destination. Remote Cheung Chau was basically a fisherman's island. Tung Wan beach, bordering the east coast of Cheung Chau, served as a weekend haven for family picnics. The line of restaurants along the beach was crowded with weekend visitors, but usually very quiet during the week. No vehicular traffic was allowed. Though the island was small, travel by foot to Tin Hau Temple near the southwestern tip could take an hour.

A fresh breeze buffeted the small ferry as it drew away from the lee side of Hong Kong Island. Tiny whitecaps in the open stretch of the South China Sea made the going a little unstable and most of the passengers stayed in their seats. General Liu made his way to the small concession stand and bought a container of hot tea, then made his way back to his bench near the bow.

The stocky Wong sat on a bench with several other passengers in the aft section sipping at a container of coffee he had bought in Central. He was dressed in nondescript work clothes, soiled and not as new and natty as the general's. A light floppy-brimmed sunhat covered his mop of thick black hair.

He looked down at himself, satisfied that he looked more like a working fisherman than Liu. He had never directly confronted Liu face-to-face and Wong decided that it would be very difficult for Liu to recognize him from the Wanted posters that had been circulated a few months after Tiananmen Square back in 1989.

He stared at the back of Liu's head a dozen rows ahead of him. The unkempt stubble of a beard that he had noticed on Liu puzzled Wong as much as his odd destination. It was almost as if the Beijing general was going incognito. Now who could he be deceiving? Wong continued his safe appraisal of Liu, who was now staring at a copy of the *Morning Post*. Wong knew that the story of the fire in Bangkok was in that paper. He would have given anything to watch Liu's eyes as he read the story. But that was not possible.

The small ferry bumped along the pilings as it made its dockage in Cheung Chau. Liu crowded in with the others as the gangplank was lowered. Davy Wong was in no hurry. He could afford to give Liu a head start. It was not likely he would lose him on this small island. In fact, it was just as important to make himself as invisible and unobtrusive as possible as it was to keep Liu in sight.

To his surprise, the general seemed in no hurry to get anywhere. He ambled idly by the weathered storefronts along the harbor. He stopped at a teashop, bought a sweet roll and tea, and then settled down in a rickety chair at one of the small tables out front. Davy slouched on by and walked quite a distance before casually turning down a side street. Now he found himself staring at shop windows and killing time. Most of the shops were still closed. It wasn't that easy to idle and keep taking a peek at the general now and then, who seemed to be waiting for someone.

Finally, in the distance Davy saw another ferry coming in from Hong Kong. He cursed to himself. The general could have saved them both an hour's sleep. Why hadn't he taken that ferry?

This ferry was more crowded than the one Davy had taken. These were people who had spent the night in Hong Kong, most of them tourists here to see the rafting of junks they had seen only on postcards before. Many of them would make the long hike to Tin Hau Temple at the tip of the small island. There were a few fishermen loaded down with gear and new supplies they had brought from Hong Kong.

And there was a woman, a beautiful woman, dressed in light-colored slacks and a summery cotton blouse. Long jet black hair tumbled down her back, slightly windblown from the morning's fresh breeze. She was obviously a Chinese woman of means. Wong could tell that in an instant.

All the passengers were now ashore. The woman turned to the left, toward him, and then walked a couple of hundred paces directly to the small table where General Liu was sipping tea.

He rose, grasped her wrist and brushed a kiss on the back of her hand. It was done in haste, with no visible response from the woman, who now sat down across from him at the small table. She seemed sober faced, and appeared unresponsive to his broad smile.

Wong strolled along the waterfront to a point where he could clearly see the features of the woman in profile. Then it hit him. It was Moia Hsu, Van Hooten's sidekick at Phuket Color. He had seen photos of this beautiful woman in the *Morning Post* several times. Business articles telling about the success of the company were usually accompanied by photos of Moia Hsu at Van Hooten's side.

Wong's mind began to race with speculation. What business at this remote place could she possibly have with General Liu Wing? The general was now speaking, doing most of the talking. She remained stone faced, attentive but unresponsive. In fact, she glanced now and then at the ferry making ready for the return to Hong Kong Island.

The couple watched the ferry leave the pier, then rose and started walking to the south along the harbor. Soon they turned inland and took a pathway that closely followed the shoreline. Wong decided to follow them, but had to keep them at quite a distance. There was absolutely no way to get an inkling of their conversation.

Moia did nothing to encourage Liu's occasional stab at resuming some of the familiarity they'd had in Shanghai. It was important to her that they remain in public, where any show of affection by Liu would be held in poor taste.

"Moia, I remember the holidays when we came here from Shanghai. In fact we walked this very path all the way to Tin Hau Temple, where we watched the sun come up. There was haze on the sea, and it rose like a big orange ball. Remember, we counted the seconds it took for the sun to pop free of the water. How many seconds was that, Moia?"

"Of course I remember. It is a lovely memory. But we behaved like children, didn't we?" She smiled faintly, the first smile since leaving the Hong Kong ferry. "Of course, we were children. I knew nothing of the world. I knew nothing of politics. Peking was the most fabulous place in the world. Now, Liu, that is the way I feel about Hong Kong."

"And it will soon be Hong Kong, China. Isn't that wonderful, Moia? It's as if an erring daughter is coming home after a hundred and fifty years of frivolity."

The allusion to her own expatriate status was unmistakable. Moia froze in her tracks, letting the general stroll a few paces ahead. "I can't believe that you really said that. Is that what you want me to talk about? Is that why you asked me to meet with you? Do you want all the details of my personal life?" Moia exploded all the questions, then strode past him in anger.

Liu quickened his step to follow her. All at once she spun on her heel ahead of him.

"Tell me, Liu, what am I coming home to? Is it a fantasy we had on the beach when we were young and stupid? Is it Deng Xiaoping and his heartless politics of vagary? Why should I be happy about my world being turned upside down?"

Liu glanced around him. There were a few other strollers on the pathway, but none so near as to overhear her tirade. "This Dutchman, he is a pygmy in Hong Kong. I am telling you, Moia, he has built a house of cards. He cannot survive."

"Oh yes he can! Your China needs the jobs and the money. It needs a thousand companies like his to move into the next century. I intend to stay here in Hong Kong and help make that happen. Now tell me, General, who is a hero to China? Is it some general who marches off to Tibet and slaps a few backward people down their mountains, or is it someone who helps build the economy of China?"

Liu's unshaven face was reddening as he clenched his fists. Several hikers on their way to Tin Hau Temple passed by the now strangely quiet couple. He took a couple of steps toward her and spoke through clenched teeth. "It's all capitalist poison, my sweet. My God, Moia, have you forgotten everything you learned from your teachers?"

"Liu, when I saw you a few days ago in Beijing when Claude and I came to Dr. Hsu's meeting, I thought at first that we might be friends. After the trip to Badaling I changed my mind. Do you know why?"

Liu narrowed his eyes, thinking back to that day. "I have no idea what your thoughts are, Moia."

"I saw you with a group of soldiers about a half mile ahead, standing at a guard station on the Great Wall. Why did you deny going to the wall, Liu? Were you following me?"

"That is preposterous! My sweet Moia is inventing lies. Not surprising. Lies are a product of capitalist guile. I'm disappointed, Moia." Liu shook his head as if in disbelief. "But I still love you, Moia. Our times together in the future will wipe out all these bad thoughts."

"Liu, we have no future together. You might as well know. Claude Van Hooten and I are planning a life together. Someday I want to have his children. I can't make it any clearer than that."

General Liu Wing looked dumbfounded. His eyes narrowed and glistened with hostility. "Forgive me,

Moia. How can you do this to Dr. Hsu? How can you abandon China?"

"Forgive me, General Liu, didn't you just point out that Hong Kong will return to China, the 'erring daughter' you spoke of. Father knows I will be ready to serve China in her newest city as I know best how to do. You are free to march away to some glorious battle and win it. Unless things change there will be all sorts of places for you to gain ribbons. Perhaps Russia, Japan, or Taiwan—or perhaps one more time in Tiananmen Square."

He scowled as she touched what was always a sensitive issue with her. "You will change your mind, my sweet. By the way, do you know that Van Hooten is already on the rocks? Two nights ago his clothing factory in Bangkok burned to the ground." Now he was smug, almost gloating, waiting to see her squirm.

"How do you know that, Liu?"

"My sweet, it is all over this morning's *Morning Post.* I read it on the ferry from Hong Kong."

Moia remembered reading the same article several times. No mention was made of Van Hooten or Phuket Color, only that several buildings had burned in Bangkok that night. "General, I read that article myself only this morning. It mentioned nothing of Phuket Color, only that there was a fire. How did you know it was Phuket?" She stared at Liu in silence, reluctant to believe what was apparently the truth. "I'm going to walk back and take the next ferry to Hong Kong. Good luck in your battles, General." Tears that she did not want Liu to see gushed from her eyes as she strode past him.

Liu reached out and pulled her to his chest, then forced a kiss against her rigid, unyielding lips. "Be careful in your journey, my sweet."

She jerked away from the general and ran back along the path toward the ferry landing in Cheung Chau. He stood and watched her until she was out of sight.

Davy Wong pretended to study an outcropping of

rock next to the path as the distraught woman rushed by him. For a moment he almost followed her, but once she boarded the ferry, he turned back down the path and followed it all the way to the end.

General Liu Wing was sitting on a garden bench near the much-visited temple of Tin Hau, the patron saint of fishermen. He sat alone like a statue for the longest time, staring off at an open stretch of the South China Sea.

It was much later before Wong followed him slowly back to the ferry landing, where they both boarded the next ferry for Hong Kong.

Chapter 27

STEAMY BANGKOK was not one of Cecil Lo's favorite places, especially in the summer. The haze that hung over the waterlogged city was oppressive. As a youth he would have thought nothing of that. Any discomfort would have been tossed aside in favor of a quick plunge into a search for round-the-clock excitement in the back streets of the exotic city.

Now the slender investigator was far past his physical prime. Working for Brandon Poole was more a challenge to the mind rather than a reliance on his quickness and physical prowess, which had carried him well into the early years he had worked for Poole. Sometimes he wondered if Poole had forgotten that he was no longer the foot soldier he had known in the Royal Marines.

Of course, working for Poole had great advantages. His current assignment had taken him from New York to Bangkok. Poole insisted that he always travel in the mode of a gentleman. Not bad that he could take advantage of the amenities offered by the Sheraton Towers, to gain respite from his business in humidity-laden Bangkok.

He placed a call to his old friend, Captain Pierre

Boucher, an investigator for the Bangkok police. Boucher and he had shared information and helped each other in the past. He wasn't in at the moment, so Lo left a message.

He lay back on the bed, clasped his hands behind his head and contemplated plans for the evening. Before nightfall he would hope to contact Reggie. But first he would venture out to the scene of the fire, so that he could give Van Hooten an eyewitness report.

It was worse than he anticipated. The corner window on the third floor which carried the Phuket Color logo was about the only portion of the building that had survived. Debris still filled the sidewalk, and barriers had been put up by the police to prevent scavenging in the dangerous ruins. Lo estimated that the loss was very close to one hundred percent. The ruins would have to be leveled.

Lo reluctantly returned to his hotel. Pierre Boucher was awaiting him in the lobby bar. Pierre's dark brown eyes, almost black, seemed to dance with enthusiasm as he extended his hand. The usually dapper Boucher's white shirt was wet with perspiration.

"Greetings, my friend. It is not often one gets the pleasure of a summons from the great Cecil Lo." Boucher smiled broadly. "In reality, Cecil, I would have entered this air-conditioned paradise on the request of Satan himself today."

"I hardly expected to see you so quickly. Nothing quite that urgent, but it is good to see you looking so well. Sorry to keep you waiting, but my curiosity forced me to visit the scene of the Phuket fire."

"Aha! When I received your message I would have bet that you were here because of the fire. Those busy taipans you work for want the inside story, I'll bet." Boucher grimaced and shrugged. "It is a sad puzzle, my friend. I am intrigued by your coming all the way from Hong Kong to look at a burned-out building."

"Well, you know a little about Brandon Poole. He

wants his information from as close to the horse's mouth as he can get it."

"Cecil, here in Bangkok I have been called a horse's ass many times, but never a horse's mouth. If I could talk to horses I would move to Hong Kong and spend all my time at Sha Tin."

"You really ought to do that sometime, Pierre. Brandon has boxes, very elegant, at Sha Tin and Happy Valley. I'm sure he would welcome you." He saw Boucher's face turn glum as he mopped his fingers through his heavy black hair.

"I promise I will do that some day. But now we are having our problems in Bangkok. Everything bad seems to happen in my district. I'm thinking about asking for a transfer." He paused and leaned forward in his chair so that he could speak to Lo without others hearing. "The Phuket fire, very bad. It was arson."

"Really? How can you tell? These old buildings, it doesn't take much to get them started."

"There were four separate fires, widely spaced, that started burning within seconds of each other. Some very hot device was used. Probably magnesium with timers." He looked around him, now whispering to Lo. "We are trying to keep this quiet here in Bangkok until we have caught the bastards who did it. It is a terrifying situation. The condition of many of the old buildings is very similar to those that burned. There were three companies destroyed, but all of the devices were placed inside Phuket Color. The others burned because of their proximity."

"Are you close to an arrest?"

Boucher shrugged and shook his head. "No. I am hoping you may have some tiny bit of information. More than curiosity brought you all the way from Hong Kong. Am I right, my friend?"

Now it was Lo's turn to lean forward and whisper. "On the day before the fire, a General Liu Wing, of the People's Republic, came to Bangkok and stayed in a small hotel just down the block. He traveled with a bureaucrat named Li Pao. They left the morning after the fire. Brandon thinks if their steps can be traced while they were here, they might lead us to the arsonist."

"I presume you received all of your information about the fire from the press up in Hong Kong. Beyond that, I can show you the statement of the shop manager. What else do you plan to do?"

"Just between you and me, as the taipans say when they are lying to each other, except we have better social graces, Brandon has a stringer on his payroll here in Bangkok. He supplies information from time to time that is sometimes useful, but most times not. I know him only by the name Reggie."

"Reggie!" Pierre bolted upright and stared at Lo with a look of disbelief. "I'm surprised at Brandon Poole. If he is the Reggie I know, he is a chap who finds devious ways of getting on many a fool's payroll. He is little more than a common pimp."

"That's our man," smiled Lo. "Limo driver, jewel merchant, and common pimp. I am sure Brandon is well aware of his ilk. But sometimes such a person becomes useful, if you are careful to be the user and not the usee."

Both men saw Reggie at the same time. A dark, squat little man looking more European than Asian entered the hotel. He took only a step or two toward the front desk before he spotted Pierre sitting with Cecil Lo. He walked in their direction with a smile on his round face that aped the smile buttons that Cecil had seen lately in a fast-food restaurant in Hong Kong.

"Aha!" His fat cheeks jiggled as he spoke. "Mr. Cecil Lo, I am at your service. I received your call only minutes ago." Then he turned his eyes dubiously toward the policeman. "And good cheer to you, sir."

"Reggie," began the deadpan policeman, "we can either adjourn somewhere to a private room, or you can come down to the station house. Mr. Lo has some very serious questions."

"If you don't mind, sir, I would rather avoid the station house. It brings back some unpleasant memories." Reggie's jowls jiggled again as he chuckled.

"Well then, let's go up to my room," offered Lo.

The three went up in a crowded elevator without speaking and entered Lo's room. Cecil drew the drapes wide and stared for a moment at the broad river floating with mud and debris from a recent storm. He then opened the service bar, uncapped a large bottle of Perrier and filled a bucket with ice. "Help yourself, gentlemen. You may see something else there that you prefer." He then sat in a straight-back chair and turned to address Reggie, who had slumped into a leather club chair.

"The morning before the big fire, two men arrived from Hong Kong and stayed at the White Lotus, just down the block from where we are. They were Chinese. One, a very tall, muscular man, perhaps six feet two or three. He carries himself like an army officer. The other, quite the opposite, a little runt of a man, perhaps nearer my size."

Reggie beamed. "You must mean General Liu Wing and Li Pao."

"That's right. How come you know that?" Lo was surprised with his instant candor.

"Davy Wong had me meet their plane and follow then around. He called me from Kai Tak."

"And you told Davy about their long walk to the Phuket Color factory on that day."

"Yes, and that is all."

"Excuse me, Cecil, just who is this Davy Wong?" asked Boucher.

"He's from Hong Kong. Reliable, I know him."

"Reggie," Lo began again. "They were in Bangkok for about thirty-six hours. You've told us of only the first six. What about all the rest?"

"That is all. That is what I told Davy Wong. I also informed him when they flew back the next day. There is no more." He shrugged, avoiding Lo's persistent stare.

"If you don't mind, Cecil. I've had some experience with this." Pierre Boucher stood, stretched, walked over and stood directly in front of Reggie.

Whap! The sharp blow from the back of Pierre's hand found its target, the fat cheek of Reggie. "Thirty hours! I want to know about the thirty hours you haven't told us about. If you don't tell me, I will take you to the station house right now and charge you with starting the big fire in Bangkok."

Reggie cringed as Pierre cocked his hand for another blow.

"Okay, okay. I can tell you only a little more. The little man, he booked a tour of the royal palace, right here in the hotel at the concierge desk. I did not follow him. I stayed to watch the tall man. He stayed in his room. That is all."

Whap! Pierre Boucher let go with another blow. "Who was the woman, Reggie!"

"Oh yes, yes. There was a woman. I get him a woman. She plays mandolin at the club down the street. I saw Liu Wing looking at her, and I made the offer. She is a very nice girl and he seemed like a nice man."

"I want to talk to her. Take us to her."

"Oh, I don't know whether . . ."

"Now! Do you hear? Now!"

"I will try, sir, I will try." He guardedly put his hand to his face, fearing another blow from Pierre Boucher's strong right hand.

They exited the hotel and walked about four blocks in the stifling heat. Reggie led the two men down a narrow alley to a rusted old fire escape. They climbed two floors, and then stepped through an open window, parting a dingy pair of lace curtains. A young girl partially covered by a sheet lay sleeping on a small bed.

"Natasha!" Reggie's loud summons caused the girl to awaken and bolt to a sitting position, struggling to cover her bare torso with the sheet. She looked at the three men, wild eyed and fearful.

"Reggie, no, no, no more! I've had no sleep," she begged.

Cecil Lo looked at the small woman in the dim light. Actually, aside from her being understandably disheveled, she was quite attractive. Lo glared at Reggie. It was the height of incivility, he thought, to barge in on the young woman this way, no matter what she did for a living. "Young lady, I want to apologize for frightening you." He glared again at Reggie. "Captain Boucher and I would like to ask you a couple of questions."

She cringed on the bed, staring at Boucher, who seemed to frighten her most of all.

"Perhaps you would rather dress and come down to the station house and talk there," Boucher suggested quietly.

"No, no, please, I will tell anything, if I know it. Please ask me here." Natasha clearly wanted no part of the station house.

Cecil Lo watched as she rubbed her eyes. She was much more alert now, wide awake, but still appeared frightened. Lo looked at Boucher and then Reggie.

"Reggie, I want you to go down the fire escape and wait there," instructed Boucher. "Don't try to run away. We both know what will happen to you if you try."

"Yes sir. I will be right there if I can be of further service."

Cecil Lo waited until Reggie left the room. "Natasha, on the night of the big fire, where were you?"

"I played music at the Lotus Club. I play there every evening."

"And after you played? I think you had better tell

us, Natasha. Eleven people were killed in that fire." Lo instinctively felt compassion for the girl.

"I know nothing about that. I had a date."

"With whom?"

Natasha looked at the curtains swaying at the open window, making sure Reggie could not hear her. "Reggie told me about a general from Beijing, and that he would pay well to see Bangkok. He was not a nice man. See this." She pulled the sheet away to reveal a large bruise on her breast. Then she lifted her dark hair to show another bruise on her neck. "The man did not want to see Bangkok, he just wanted me like all the others."

"Natasha, where did you go?"

"To the White Lotus. The general was staying there."

"When did you leave him?" Lo asked, feeling sorry for the bruised young woman.

"Not until the next morning." She rubbed at the bruise on her neck. "He was bad, and he paid me only fifty baht. He promised me a thousand baht. I told Reggie about that."

Pierre Boucher hadn't taken his eyes off the young woman. "Is there anything else that happened during the night? Did you ever see anyone else, perhaps?"

"No . . . Oh, wait a minute, there was something. Early in the morning his friend knocked on the door of the room. The general opened the door wide and I saw him. He told him that it was all over, or something like that. The general told him that he would stay with me and celebrate."

"What was all over?"

"I don't know. The man did not say. I was very tired. The general would not let me sleep because he could not. All the noise from the fire equipment seemed to excite him. He kept running to the window, trying to see."

"Anything else?" asked Lo gently.

"Nothing." She shook her bowed head, a pathetic picture in the dimly lit room.

"Thank you, Natasha. If you remember anything else, you must see me. Understand?" Boucher said. "Is Reggie bothering you?"

"No." She hesitated. "None of this is Reggie's fault."

Lo peeled off a couple of hundred baht from a roll in his pocket and handed it to Natasha. "Better have someone take a look at that neck."

"It will be all right." She smiled faintly and rubbed again at the mark on her neck as the the two men exited to the fire escape.

Reggie was squatting sullenly on the first step. "Go," commanded Boucher. He didn't need a second invitation. He walked quickly away and disappeared around the corner.

"Pierre, we seem to have learned precious little," Lo said as they walked slowly back to his hotel. "We know two things that are not totally explainable. Why did Li Pao go to the general's room at five in the morning to tell him it was 'all over'? Did he mean the fire?"

Pierre shook his head. "Since they went there to inspect the location in the afternoon, perhaps he meant the fire. But it is not certain."

"Look at it this way," Lo said. "If it was not the fire, what else would have brought Pao to the general's room at that hour? What would be that important?"

Pierre shrugged. "It defies an answer without interrogating Li Pao. There certainly isn't enough to go on to allow an inquiry with Beijing authorities. They are seldom cooperative. You said there were two things that were not explainable. What is the other?"

"Why in heaven's name would Li Pao go as a tourist to the royal palace?"

"That is easy. It is truly a place with unparalleled beauty. If you haven't been, you should go, and you will see why."

"With all due respect, would you go if you had mayhem on your mind for that very evening?"

"Absolutely not. But then I do not have a mind that could contemplate the burning of such an occupied building."

They had reached the front door of the Sheraton. The two investigators shook hands. "I hope to see you in Hong Kong one day, Pierre. I'm perfectly serious about sharing Brandon's hospitality at Sha Tin or Happy Valley. Meanwhile let's keep each other posted. It was a hideous piece of arson that must be solved."

"I will not rest until it is, my friend."

"Tell me, do you plan to talk any more to Reggie about this matter? The man is obviously a petty scoundrel. Brandon is a little nervous about using him in the future."

Pierre smiled. "He has good connections with the subculture. Also he slaps around easily and sings like a bird. I'll use him until he destroys himself. People like that are quite useful, Cecil."

Chapter 28

Brandon Poole listened to Davy Wong's peculiar story. In tailing General Liu all the way to Cheung Chau, he had stumbled on a liaison between the general and Moia Hsu.

"You are absolutely certain that it was Moia Hsu?" Poole paced his office, staring out the window at the far reaches of New Territories, in deep thought.

"Yes sir. It would be almost impossible to mistake her, sir. She is singularly beautiful. Her photograph was in the papers only recently. It was taken at Sai Kung where they were filming commercials for Phuket Color."

"I saw that," replied Brandon, still turning over the entire story in his mind. "And you are sure that their mood toward each other seemed hostile, for the most part?"

"Brandon, it is difficult to explain. They acted as if they knew each other quite well, but she resisted his efforts to become close. She walked alone all the way from the temple of Tin Hau to the ferry. When I returned to Tin Hau, he was sitting on a bench, staring at the sea."

"Not exactly a lovefest, I gather. Strange that she

should sneak away for such a meeting. Apparently they did not want to be seen." Poole rubbed his chin and sat at his desk. "Moia Hsu is fairly recently from Beijing. Perhaps the general knew her there. She has connections in Beijing that have been useful to me from time to time. Her father is a midlevel bureaucrat with the Trade Ministry. Perhaps that lubricates Van Hooten's building of factories in Foshan and Shanghai."

Davy Wong nodded. "That would make sense. But why the meddling of the general? Is he overseeing things? Is Van Hooten in his pocket?"

"Those are good questions, Davy. I suspect, however, that it is something much simpler. Perhaps the general has been rejected by Moia. Perhaps she was an old flame in Beijing." Poole hesitated for a moment. "According to you, that is the way they acted. However, I have decided one thing for sure. It is time to get together for a discussion with Van Hooten. I'm thinking about buying his company, Davy. But first I want to know what makes him tick."

"Very good thinking, Brandon. But how about the fire in Bangkok? Is Phuket worth buying anymore?"

"I suspect it is, Davy. My construction site engineer in Shanghai reported only this morning that he was offered large incentives to bring the factory in far ahead of time."

Davy Wong rose from the couch in Poole's office. "If you don't mind, sir, I'm going to get back to the general. Police in Hong Kong were recently given a new list of my friends who escaped Tiananmen Square. My guess is that the general is here to prod them into action and I am convinced that the murder charge that they have pinned on me is his doing."

"Be careful, Davy. They've been sleeping up in Beijing for a long time. Don't give them Davy Wong as a victim."

Poole showed the grinning Davy Wong to the door. He looked at his calendar and asked his assistant to get

Claude Van Hooten on the phone. Tomorrow was race day at Happy Valley. He would like to trap Van Hooten in his private box for a few hours. Van Hooten could bring Moia along, of course. Poole smiled at his little scheme. He would bring Lacy Locke along as well. All that chemistry in that small private room should evoke far more interest than the horses below.

Claude Van Hooten returned his call in a matter of a few minutes. He had never received a phone call from Poole before and was flattered and puzzled that he was so honored now. The deep, crisp voice fairly boomed into his earpiece. "Claude, how does it feel to be the one of the world's most successful designers? All I read is Phuket Color, whenever I open a paper or a magazine."

"Believe me, Brandon, I leave the designing to my experts. And I am proud of them. We keep forging ahead despite the difficulties. You must have read about our fire in Bangkok."

"Yes, I did. It must have been quite a blow."

"I'd be lying if I said it wasn't, but we'll get by it. Fortunately, I have some usable alternatives and very fine people."

"I called for two reasons, Claude. First I have instructed my operation in Shanghai to move heaven and earth to meet the incentive deadlines for your new facility there."

"I just now received those assurances from Shanghai myself. I want to thank you, Brandon. You would have heard from me if it were otherwise. Incidentally I recently visited Foshan. Things looked really fine. I had no idea Beijing was using your company exclusively until I saw all your equipment out front. In fact, I must tell you that I see Brandon Poole Ltd. all over the place whenever I cross the border."

"Things are going well, which brings me to the real reason I called you. I think it is high time that the two of us got together and talked. Nothing but good can come of exchanging a few ideas. Success talking to success can't lead to anything but more success."

His suggestion took Van Hooten off guard. He hesitated. Comparing Brandon Poole Ltd. to Phuket Color was a little like comparing a soccer ball to a pea. "That's very flattering, Brandon. I'm looking at my calendar here. Let's set a date."

"I have a novel suggestion. I have this box at Happy Valley that I haven't used in months. You and I have both met with Lacy Locke. Lacy, you know, is trying to absorb all the vagaries of Hong Kong capitalism in a short visit from New York. I suggest we all meet tomorrow at Happy Valley. Why not extend the invitation to Moia Hsu, also? She has worked so well with our construction team in Foshan."

"Tomorrow? Let me look over things for a moment." Moia by this time was standing at his elbow. Van Hooten hastily scribbled *Poole—Lacy—Moia—me, Happy Valley tomorrow.* She responded by tracing a large X through tomorrow afternoon on their calendar.

"We . . . we'll have to shuffle some things around a little bit, Brandon. But yes, I look forward to it. We'll be there."

"Good, my assistant will call you with the details later. The ladies should enjoy themselves, and you and I will get an education amid lovely surroundings."

Van Hooten hung up the telephone and stared at Moia, now sitting across from him. "I wonder what that is all about. It's very nice of him, but Brandon Poole never does anything without very good reasons. Any ideas?"

Moia shook her head negatively. "If we go to Happy Valley, we will be with Brandon Poole for several hours. I don't know anyone in Hong Kong that would refuse such an invitation. Consider yourself fortunate, my dear Claude. I think it will certainly build confidence with Lacy Locke. That is our chief concern. In fact, you cannot refuse. What would Lacy Locke think if you did?"

"You are right, Moia, as always. I don't know why, but I feel like celebrating."

Moia rose, walked over and locked the office door. She drew the drapes facing Victoria Peak. Moving slowly, she unfastened a satin belt, then she twirled once and permitted her wraparound silk dress to slide to the floor. She came over and sat on Van Hooten's desk in front of him and brushed her hands through his hair. Then the celebration began.

Chapter 29

Brandon Poole's phone call reached Lacy Locke as she was having breakfast at the Mandarin. An extension was brought to her table at her request. Did anyone ever refuse a call from Brandon Poole? she wondered.

"Lacy, I'm so glad that I caught you before you started on one of your busy days. Our friends Claude Van Hooten and Moia Hsu have agreed to join me tomorrow afternoon at Happy Valley. All of us think that you should be there. I have private quarters there with a splendid view of the racing. It would be a perfect spot for you and me to learn much about your new clients. Incidentally they seem quite bullish on the future of Phuket Color, despite the fire in Bangkok."

"Brandon, my schedule. . . . Wait, let me look." She located her calendar in her briefcase and flipped it open. Two Hong Kong banks were on the agenda for tomorrow afternoon. She would have to change it. The opportunity was just too fascinating. "Brandon, it sounds fabulous, and probably much more enlightening than the bankers I have on my schedule. I look forward to it."

"Wonderful! I'll pick you up at noon at the Mandarin. I can't tell you how much I enjoyed our last evening together. I promise you we won't end up with the likes of Mary Lulu this time."

"Brandon, I hope not!" She couldn't suppress a burst of laughter. "By the way, is it apropos to talk business at these things? I think horses are beautiful, but that is about all I know about them."

"My dear, there is more business accomplished in the boxes at Happy Valley and Sha Tin than in all of the offices of Hong Kong. You'll see what I mean."

"Thank you, Brandon. I can't wait. I'll change my schedule. I'm getting a little weary of talking to your bankers here in Hong Kong anyway."

"Any of them worth talking to will be in Happy Valley tomorrow." Brandon chuckled in his deep baritone.

"Really."

"Yes, it may sound like a condemnation, but horse racing is almost a national sport here in Hong Kong. It's quite a spectacle. You'll love it even if you don't look at a horse."

"Oh, I intend to bet, Brandon. I expect you to have a hot tip," she warned.

"The hottest tip I could give you, my dear, is Brandon Poole. I recommend betting on him anytime."

"Brandon, that's outrageous."

"But it's true. See you tomorrow, Lacy."

What an egoist, she thought, as she put down the phone. Brandon Poole was certainly one of a kind. She marveled at his ability to bring the four of them together on such short notice.

She checked the time. She was already due for her first appointment. This bank was one of the more important institutions she had scheduled. She was grateful that it was not one of those planned for tomorrow that would have to be changed.

She found the bank building an architectural wonder. A spacious public lobby lay beneath the whole of it, an air-conditioned respite for the thousands that used it for a thoroughfare. Towering escalators ascended to the working floors of the bank amid the shining spectacle of granite, metal, and tinted glass.

Imposing, intimidating, thought Lacy. The historic old bank had long been one of the dominant institutions in all of Asia. She wouldn't like to work in such a building. But then it must be little different from working in the World Trade Center or the Citicorp Building back in New York.

She was directed to a bank of elevators that eventually led her to the office of Christopher Holoway, a vice president assigned to New Worldwide Securities' account. From the arrangement of the endless number of offices, she suspected that he was one of many vice presidents. It was hardly like talking to the seat of power in the old bank.

"Welcome to Hong Kong, Ms. Locke. I have prepared an account update for you, as requested by your letter. You speak of substantial new business. We see no problems with that. Your account is in impeccable order." He reached across the desk to hand her a folio. "Enjoying Hong Kong, are you? Is it your first trip?"

"I'm enjoying it very much. It is such an exciting place to be these days."

"Enjoying our fine shopping, I'll bet." The man manufactured a weak smile. From the tone of his voice, he evidently saw no need for further serious conversation.

She stared at the lean man in the dark suit until he broke eye contact. "I've had no time for your shopping as yet, Mr. Holoway. By excitement, I mean the transition into 1997. How do you see that all playing out?"

The man folded his hands, then met her gaze for only a few seconds. He obviously didn't expect serious conversation with a mere woman. "Splendidly, Ms. Locke. We foresee no major problems."

"Wonderful, I'm so happy to hear that. A few years ago when Jardine Matheson moved their headquarters from Hong Kong, a lot of others followed. Is the exodus over, Mr. Holoway?"

"Ms. Locke, this institution works in complete harmony with the People's Republic. Hong Kong will remain as it has always been, a corridor for investment in all of Asia. As far as we are concerned, there is no exodus."

"Very good. We expect to market the securities for several clients involved in manufacturing in the People's Republic through the Hang Seng market. Our business with you is now quite small. It should increase perhaps tenfold."

"Really?" Holoway folded his hands as he studied the numbers on his copy of the information he had given Lacy. There was no doubt that she now had his attention. "Ms. Locke, if you don't mind, I would like you to meet the head of my department. Tenfold—that is exciting."

He left his desk and returned several minutes later with his boss, obviously Chinese. He was tall and exuded confidence with an affable smile, possessing the personality and communicative attributes that Holoway was lacking. "Mr. Holoway tells me you are the renowned Lacy Locke." He continued to smile and winked at his remark as he shook her hand. "I am Winston Chen, at your service."

Lacy beamed. "Renowned! Really, Mr. Chen, how could you possibly think that?"

"Oho! Some very important people speak well of you, Ms. Locke. People like Claude Van Hooten. And there's that old devil on the Peak, Mr. Brandon Poole."

"That's nice. Your Hong Kong is so full of mystery. It helps to have men like that helping me to understand it." It amazed her that both Van Hooten and Poole would bother to pave the way for her visit.

"Add me to that list, Ms. Locke. Is there anything at all I can do for you? Holoway here was telling me that you were concerned about the departure of Jardine. That happened back in 1986, you know. However, Jardine still maintains a significant presence in Hong Kong. Now some of the people who left have returned. Hong Kong is a big pot of money, Ms. Locke. It's all here for the sharp wits, and hard work."

Winston Chen led Lacy to his office where they spent the next hour in conversation. Holoway vanished. Chen glanced down at his watch. "Oh my, I am talking too much. You must get on with your day, Ms. Locke. Remember, the People's Republic is very much a part of many of the banks in Hong Kong. It is not apparent to all, but it is better that way."

He rose and led her to the door of his office, which had a magnificent view of Kowloon across the harbor. "One last thing, Lacy. May I call you Lacy?"

"Of course."

"One last thing." He looked around him as they stood in the hallway and then spoke, almost in a whisper. "Forget about that big fire in Bangkok, Lacy. It's not important."

"Thank you, Winston. I feel so much better now that I have heard that from you."

Her path back to the Mandarin took her once again through Statue Square. There was another small cluster of protesters, perhaps a dozen. The crude signs they carried said something about Tiananmen Square and dissidents being held in Beijing. Brave lads, she thought to herself. It was strangely comforting that the small demonstration was permitted.

Chapter 30

Hargrave reread the letter from the commissioner of police. It had been hand delivered, not even entrusted to the usual postal service. "The petty crime in your district has trebled in a matter of weeks. Then there is the matter of the homicide near Tsuen Wan. We have not seen a single follow-up report covering your investigation. Repeated attempts to reach you at the station house on certain afternoons have met with complete frustration. Mutual friends have pointed out that these afternoons coincide with race days at Sha Tin. We must have a satisfactory response to this inquiry within forty-eight hours, or the entire matter will be turned over to the Investigative Commission."

Hargrave cursed, then belched. His stomach was aroar with discomfort. He reached into his desk drawer for a handful of those miracle antacid pills his counterpart in Kowloon had recommended. Sha Tin! He hadn't been to Sha Tin or Happy Valley in weeks. It was deceitful for the commissioner to put such speculation into writing for the record. The man who called himself General Liu Wing was ruining a lifetime of service to the Royal Hong Kong Police.

He folded the letter carefully, jammed it into his left

rear trouser pocket and carefully buttoned it shut. The shadowing of Moia Hsu had to stop, he reasoned. The general's demands were just too time consuming, and couldn't be assigned to subordinates who would want a piece of the action.

He sat at his desk and rubbed his forehead, trying to recall the documents the general had used for credentials the first time he had approached him. What if the documents were forged? What if he were not a general at all? His real attraction to the man had been the frequent flow of envelopes stuffed with money. The sums of money had grown larger each time. Liu had to have resources far beyond his stipend as a general in the People's Army.

The next time he met the general face-to-face, he decided he would simply say no. Yet how could he? Not many superintendents survived the notorious scrutiny of the Investigative Commission. If he lost his position, he would probably lose his pension. He needed the general's money. In fact he needed more of it. Pressures of the job had made him ill. He could belch his ulcerous gas at will now. Perhaps he would do that in the general's face.

He looked at his Rolex. It was almost three o'clock. It was time to start the evening shadowing of Moia Hsu. He made up his mind that this would be the last time. Hargraves locked his office in the station house, went outside and climbed into the dusty old van, pointing it toward the harbor tunnel from Kowloon to Hong Kong Island.

Negotiating the traffic gave him some time to think. He had heard whispers that numerous members of the Royal Hong Kong Police had been corrupted by the infiltration of Chinese from the People's Republic. They were preparing for 1997 in any way that they could. The commissioner himself had cautioned all about the possibility in a recent luncheon celebrating the retirement of a superintendent.

He wondered how many others had thrown caution to the wind and taken envelopes of money from strangers from Beijing. After all, "Royal Hong Kong Police" was likely to be a misnomer after 1997. There would be nothing royal about it. Right now he envied that superintendent who had retired.

All at once he started to perspire heavily in the chill of the air-conditioned old van. It came with the thought that perhaps the general had no official reason at all for the surveillance of Moia Hsu. Perhaps it was an affair of the heart, a raging jealousy over Van Hooten's control of the beautiful woman. He recalled how testy the general had become when he had tried to sugarcoat the report to him about all the time spent at the mythical "workstation" in Stanley. If it was a personal matter, reasoned Hargrave, he had burned all his bridges. Beijing was getting no feedback on Hargrave's cooperation, and now he had the commissioner on his neck.

Flashing his credentials, Hargrave commandeered a parking spot several hundred meters from the parking garage where Moia Hsu usually parked. He walked the distance to the garage and checked to make certain that the vehicle used by her and Van Hooten was in its place. It was.

He retraced his steps, then sat quietly in the van, turning the air-conditioning up to maximum on this sweltering day. He had become absorbed in the list of Happy Valley entries for the next afternoon, looking up just in time to see the shiny Mercedes pulling out from the garage ahead of him. He lifted the roof prism glasses to his eyes and verified the number easily. It was Moia Hsu, alone in the Mercedes.

Hargrave eased the van into traffic and followed her at a comfortable distance. He noticed that she was driving slower than usual despite the light traffic. From her movements thus far it appeared that she was taking her usual route toward Van Hooten's villa on Stanley Gap Road.

Then all at once she veered unexpectedly. She entered the tunnel that would take her through the mountain to Aberdeen on the southwest side of Hong Kong Island. After slowing to pay her toll, she hesitated for a moment, letting some of the more impatient drivers pass. By the time Hargrave paid his toll, she was only a couple of hundred meters ahead of him.

Moia Hsu glanced in her rearview mirrow, slowing until the old Mazda van occupant paid the toll. Then she stepped on the gas pedal and wove through traffic, putting several cars between them and trying not to make it too obvious that she had him spotted.

She picked up the car phone and pressed the button for Van Hooten in his private office. "Claude dear, now we know. He is not following you, he is following me. It's the same old Mazda we've seen several times. I say let's go ahead with our plan."

"Moia, I can't tell you how nervous I am about this. I have the police on the other line. They are waiting at the power station already. For heaven's sake, be careful. If there is any difficulty, step on the gas and lose him."

"Don't worry, my love. This is exciting. I can't wait to see who he is. Perhaps we'll have a new reason for celebrating this evening."

Van Hooten chuckled loudly. "You are a gutsy woman, my dear. Be careful."

"Gutsy? That is not a very nice word. You can do better than that."

Moia sped a little faster and the Mazda, now a quarter of a mile behind her, began to pass cars to keep pace. Having cleared the tunnel, she drove the Mercedes along Wong Chuk Hang Road, the main connector to the community of Aberdeen.

Then she slowed down considerably to make certain that the Mazda followed her next move. She turned right and picked up the cloverleaf to Aberdeen Island.

The Mazda followed obediently as she crossed the bridge road to the island, and then slowed down as she passed along the harbor road, busy with traffic from the boat people rafted along the lee side of the Aberdeen harbor. The Mazda was now close behind.

Within several minutes she sped into the dead-end road that led to the gates of the power station at the end of the island.

The Mazda stopped about a hundred feet behind her, trapped by the dead end. Within seconds a police van pulled out of the gate of the power plant, speeding toward the Mazda. The police spun around and blocked the exit behind the dusty old van. Moia smiled at the scene in the mirror. Her pursuer was trapped.

Moia backed the Mercedes part of the distance to the Mazda, got out and walked toward the four policemen, now stationed around the van. One of them was examining the credentials of the driver.

The policeman turned and walked toward Moia with the documents in hand. "Miss, there is some mistake. The driver is Mr. Terry Hargrave, a superintendent of Hong Kong police. In fact, I did not need these." He waved the documents at her. "I know him personally."

Moia saw one of the other policemen begin the walk back to his own van. Hargrave was staring at her with a hint of a smile on his face. She strode past the policeman and confronted Hargrave behind the wheel. "You have been stalking me for days! I demand to know why!" Moia was furious. None of the policemen seemed willing to support her.

Hargrave glanced at the policeman as he returned his documents, then turned to address Moia. "There's some misunderstanding, lady. I'm out here on some police business at the power plant." He turned again to the policemen. "Sorry for all the trouble, boys."

"You, sir, are a liar. You followed me all the way from Central District, through the tunnel and down to the end of this dead-end road. Not only that, you have been following me for days. I have another witness to that." She turned to the policeman. "I am pressing charges against this man. I don't care who he is. He has no right to stalk me and harass me, day in and day out."

"Miss Hsu." The policeman was nervously contemplating the thought of pressing charges against a superior. "Suppose I take your complaint and release Superintendent Hargrave on his own recognizance. Then we can investigate this matter and reach the proper conclusions."

Moia shook her finger in the face of the young policeman. "I remind you that I called for the police from my garage in Central. That man was parked up the street waiting for me. I am the reason that you are here, and I do not intend to drop charges. I demand a full investigation."

The policeman shrugged and began making some notes. Then he turned toward Hargrave. "Superintendent, you may proceed on your way. You will be given a copy of this woman's complaint when it is available. Good day, sir."

Hargrave stared icily at the policeman and Moia. Then he started the Mazda and proceeded to enter the driveway to the power plant.

Moia started the drive back to Central District, wondering whether or not the complaint against Hargrave would ever be filed by the young officer. She called Van Hooten from her car phone immediately to report the unusual outcome of their plan.

"Hargrave!" exclaimed Van Hooten in disbelief. "I know him well. He used to be assigned to the Stanley district. It's unbelievable. Don't worry, dear. We'll push the charges all the way. I won't permit the matter to drop. After all, we have to know why the hell he was following you. Someone either asked him to do it, perhaps paid for it, or maybe he is just enamored of you. Either way we've got to know."

Moia sighed. "Thanks, love. I guess for the time being, the man wouldn't be stupid enough to continue his nonsense. See you soon." Moia hung up and drove leisurely back toward Central through the Aberdeen Tunnel. Hargrave was guilty of her complaint for sure, she thought. And he certainly didn't seem like a compulsive stalker. She had had experience with men like that and he didn't fill the bill.

That meant he was following her for some other reason. She remembered what Van Hooten often said about the corruption of the police in these times. According to him, they were demoralized by uneasiness over 1997. Bribery was a common thing. If money was the key to Hargrave's loyalty, perhaps a little private questioning by one of Van Hooten's friends was in order.

Moia's thoughts turned to General Liu Wing as she approached Central District. She hadn't heard from him since leaving him sitting alone with his thoughts on the bench at the southern tip of Cheung Chau. Perhaps he would be deterred for a while. But come to think of it, there was a man who had the capability of becoming a real stalker. She thought of the day at Badaling when she had visited the Great Wall with Van Hooten. The general never gave up. The military had taught him that. She couldn't rid herself of the feeling that Hargrave's dogged surveillance might involve General Liu and wondered, if he *was* involved, how sane he might be to pursue her like that.

Chapter 31

IT WAS Saturday afternoon, race day at Happy Valley and blazing hot. Even so, that did not cause Cecil Lo to doff his jacket as he waited at the base of Brandon Poole's private tramway on the Peak.

Poole stepped from the tramway, jacket held neatly in one hand. He grinned impishly at Lo. "I take it you have made a list of all the winners for this afternoon. Ms. Locke would appreciate that. She would think of you as a genius, and therefore think much more of me for having the wisdom to employ you."

Expecting his question, Lo returned his smile and extended his hand, offering a slip of paper listing winners for every race that afternoon. "These come from my special source in Kowloon. Obviously I cannot reveal his name. The word would get around and his horses would pay little or nothing. I did stop at the temple in Central to make an offering on behalf of the list."

"Good work, Cecil." Poole folded the paper carefully and tucked it into his shirt pocket. "Tell me, Cecil, how many times have we gone to the races over the years?"

"Oh . . . perhaps five or six times," Cecil replied after some thought.

"And how many winners have you picked for us in all those times?"

"I can remember only one, sir, back in 1984. I remember it well. It was about the time Margaret Thatcher was in Beijing. I remember so many people were talking about it."

"And on that dismal day in history, we won at Happy Valley. Ah, Cecil . . . we were still losers on that day. In fact every blessed person in Hong Kong lost more than they bargained for on that day."

"Yes sir, I know," Cecil murmured quietly, thinking of the treaty that would bring down the curtain on Hong Kong.

Lacy Locke looked like a princess. That was the first thought that went through Brandon Poole's mind as she stepped from the elevator in the Mandarin. She wore an airy dress, loose and slit high. "My dear, you look like a princess of the Crown should look."

"Thank you, Brandon. I haven't spent an afternoon at the races in years. I have no idea what the uniform of the day should be."

"I think you've just created it. I will be the envy of Happy Valley."

Outside they climbed into the Mercedes. Cecil Lo smiled, touched his cap and tended the door.

"I think you will find this fascinating, Lacy. I wouldn't drag you there unless I thought it was important for you to witness." Poole turned himself slightly, so that he could look directly at her when he spoke.

"Horse racing here in Hong Kong plays a big part in people's lives. You could almost say that it is our national sport. Oh, there is some cricket and some soccer, but horse racing here draws crowds that would fill your Yankee Stadium on most days. It becomes a mathematical game that occupies people's minds when they stop making money for a few hours."

"Brandon, that's negative! Do you mean we are not going to make money wagering?"

Brandon beamed. "I've already taken care of that, my dear." He dipped into his shirt pocket and produced Lo's picks for the day. "I suppose it is a little unfair of me, but these are the day's winners. There is only the mere formality of running the horses around the race course." Poole looked ahead. Cecil Lo was shaking his head, almost imperceptibly.

Lacy looked over the list of horses. "I guess I should have gone to the lockbox and taken out all my money."

Lo glanced in the rearview mirror. "Perhaps it's good that you didn't, ma'am. Our hospitals and libraries would go wanting."

"Oh yes, Lacy, in the unlikely event that you lose, the money goes to a long list of noble causes here in Hong Kong. The Royal Jockey Club would like you to think that losing is really winning."

"Not in my book, Brandon. Winning is everything. I think Vince Lombardi said that."

"Vince who?"

"Aha, there is something the great Brandon Poole does not know, that I know. I will tell you before I leave Hong Kong."

"I'll have to ask Van Hooten today. A lot of people think he knows everything. After he tells me who Vince is, maybe he'll tell me flat out why he's staying in Hong Kong."

Lacy watched Poole's demeanor grow serious. He had a way of doing that often, she thought. His droll sense of humor could switch into dead serious thought at any moment. "Tell me, Brandon, is it protocol to talk business while we are watching my horses win?"

"Of course. Why do you think Van Hooten would wipe out a complex schedule and come running to Happy Valley? His box has been empty for years, they say." He furrowed his brow for a moment in deep thought. "Lacy, I'll bet you're a pro at mixing business with ostensible pleasure. You'll read the situation right away. It's like a long dinner at '21' or the Water Club in New York. In the boxes at Happy Valley and Sha Tin, business actually heats up. It's as fascinating as . . . well . . . perhaps Lacy Locke."

There was an awkward pause. Poole himself was certainly no slouch at mixing business with pleasure. "What do you think about Moia Hsu?" she asked, changing the subject.

"I think she is absolutely brilliant. Notwithstanding that her father is a minor prophet back in Beijing, she could make it on her own anywhere. Van Hooten may or may not be very fortunate."

"May or may not, that's pretty cryptic, Brandon."

"Yes it is. They live together, you know."

"No, I didn't know."

"Well, anyone that matters in Hong Kong knows, so I'm not gossiping. But knowing the traditional feelings of so many in her father's generation in Beijing, I wonder if Van Hooten has the situation in hand. God knows! I understand it. She's brilliant, she has connections, and she's beautiful, almost as attractive as Lacy Locke."

"Brandon, that is very nice of you to say. But I have seen this woman, and believe me, she is in a league all to herself."

"And that's nice of you to say." Brandon paused, again in deep thought. Cecil Lo was now threading the Mercedes through the heavy traffic of Happy Valley. Brandon reached across the seat and grasped her hand in his own. "Lacy, I have some information about Moia Hsu that I would rather keep to myself, until I get her reaction. The afternoon may not be all peaches and cream. If the party suddenly goes sour, please forgive me. But perhaps it won't."

"You know how to put a person on edge, Brandon. Now be positive. I found Moia Hsu very pleasant. I think perhaps you worry too much."

Brandon smiled. "Believe me, Lacy, I find even the worry and the concern fascinating. Hong Kong today is like an enraged giant. Everybody snooping, clawing, punching, working like mad to squeeze every dollar out of Hong Kong before the end either comes or doesn't come." He squeezed her hand firmly once again and then pulled away. Lo had pulled into a valet parking slot. They had arrived at Happy Valley.

An elevator carried them to a row of private boxes facing the race course from the top level of the massive grandstand.

Brandon Poole led Lacy along a narrow passageway and found that the door to his private box was slightly ajar. He opened the door to find that Van Hooten and Moia Hsu had already been shown to the box. "Welcome, Claude! It's been much too long. I'm so glad you are here early."

The two men grasped hands enthusiastically. Van Hooten then introduced Moia to Brandon Poole. Brandon beamed appreciatively. All that he had heard about her bewitching beauty was true. "My dear lady, it's about time that you have finally graced one of the boxes of the Royal Jockey Club. Claude here has kept you hidden from us. News of your success at Phuket Color is almost legendary, even by Hong Kong standards."

Moia smiled as she listened to Poole. "No, no, you have it wrong, Mr. Poole. Claude Van Hooten makes all the decisions. I merely administrate. Phuket Color is Claude's success."

"Said with diplomacy and grace, my dear. I am aware that you have both met Lacy Locke. Lacy here not only has to measure our success, but she has to figure out what makes Hong Kong tick. Her customers must be induced to bet on the future of Hong Kong, and then buy endless quantities of Phuket Color and Brandon Poole Ltd. stock."

"Here, here! I'd like to make a toast to that. When

Lacy finds out what makes Hong Kong tick these days, I pray that she will tell us." Van Hooten winked at Lacy and tilted an imaginary glass to his lips.

Poole pressed a button to summon a waiter who appeared almost instantaneously. "Bring us a selection of all those goodies you are famous for, and make sure that the wet bar is ready for action."

"Yes sir." The black-tied waiter swung into action with no further instruction.

Lacy was drinking in the scene. She knew little about race tracks. She could remember going to Santa Anita once, and to Belmont back in New York. Recently she had attended a party at the Meadowlands in New Jersey. But Happy Valley bore little resemblance to any of them.

Brandon's box was more like a tiny air-conditioned apartment. Farthest away from the window was a full-service bar. There was a handsome leather couch, several club chairs, and some stools along a ledge across the window facing the track. Video monitors above the bar kept the latest odds posted along with the probabilities for all sorts of exotic betting. Outside, a giant television screen and tote board were set in a lush green-grassed and flowered infield. Happy Valley could accommodate crowds of tens of thousands and was already buzzing with activity.

"Brandon, how does one actually go about betting on a horse? *Investors' Daily* is much easier reading than this program." She saw Moia smiling at her. "Moia, I feel incredibly stupid. Is there a secret to all this?"

"The secret is to keep your money in your purse. Then at the end of the day it will all be there." Moia studied the racing program carefully. "But I'm not going to do that either. In fact, Lacy, in honor of your visit I am going to bet on a horse bred in New York. She's running in the first race. See, right here, Long Island Girl."

"No kidding!" Lacy circled the horse's name on the program. "I was born on Long Island!"

"Wonderful!" Moia beamed. "The gods would not permit the horse to lose. Such a coincidence must be heeded."

Van Hooten groaned. "Moia, I think that kind of handicapping might well bankrupt Phuket Color."

"Claude, I think perhaps we should support the ladies. Such a coincidence must have divine origin. Cecil will be here about ten minutes before the first race. He will make all of our wagers." Brandon Poole winked at Van Hooten, who nodded his assent.

"We certainly don't want to make the gods angry, my dear." Van Hooten fished a couple of banknotes from his wallet and handed them to Moia. "The horse is forty to one. But after all, this is a charitable institution."

Brandon Poole chuckled in his deep baritone as Cecil Lo entered the box. "Folks, I must tell you that Cecil here has availed himself of the knowledge of the best handicapper in all of Hong Kong, and supplied me with this list of winners. Perhaps you'd better take a look at it before plunging ahead. Cecil, how come you missed Long Island Girl in the first race?"

"She's forty to one, sir. A miserable lot. I wouldn't risk it, sir." Cecil studied the program carefully and kept shaking his head. "No sir, I wouldn't do it."

"Cecil, where did you find this all-knowing handicapper of yours?" asked Van Hooten.

Poole waved his hand toward Cecil. "If you don't mind, Cecil, let me tell them the story."

"Yes sir," assented Cecil, looking very much relieved.

"It seems that there was this old handicapper in Hong Kong who lost favor with his clients after a disastrous season. He was so much in disrepute that he moved to one of the outer islands. We found him a few years ago and also found that he hadn't lost his talent at all." He winked an aside at Van Hooten.

"And where did this oracle go? Which one of the islands?" Lacy asked the question in all innocence.

Poole paused and met the eyes of Moia Hsu, who was listening in rapt attention to her host. "Cheung Chau. He finds Cheung Chau a good hideaway."

Moia blinked. If Poole hadn't been staring at her he would have missed it. The hint of a smile on her face vanished for only an instant and then returned.

"Really?" asked Van Hooten. "I'd swear you're serious. I thought you were putting us on. I didn't think anybody lived on Cheung Chau unless he was a fisherman, or perhaps a monk. Of course there are all those boat people who wouldn't know one end of a horse from the other. Now tell us the truth, Cecil, is Brandon serious about that?"

"Mr. Poole is very serious, sir." Cecil smiled and started picking up betting slips from everyone.

Good man, thought Brandon Poole to himself. Cecil got away with affirming only that he was serious, not truthful. "Cecil, if you don't mind, I'm going to ignore your pick and bet on Long Island Girl also. Forty to one would buy you a new suit at Phuket Color."

Cecil Lo shrugged and took their money, mumbling something undiscernible under his breath. No doubt he was wondering how these titans of Hong Kong business could be so stupid when it came to horses.

Their waiter returned with a large tray of selected miniature seafood delicacies, and popped the cork on a bottle of Dom Pérignon. Van Hooten toasted to the speed of Long Island Girl. The lack of late betting had made her odds almost sixty to one now.

Cecil Lo looked at the tote board and grimaced, regretting the small wager he had placed on the impossible horse in deference to their guest from New York. He watched the others sipping champagne and quipping at each other with lighthearted small talk. Lo had always considered cocktail conversation one of the lunacies of mankind. Yet Brandon Poole had once told him that he learned more from being attentive to such goings-on than he usually learned from an elaborately planned business agenda.

"Oh, she's beautiful!" exclaimed Lacy. She stood at the window and pointed toward Long Island Girl, now entering the track. The bay filly was very frisky. It seemed that the jockey had all he could do to keep her in hand.

"Yes she is," agreed Brandon. "But then I suspect beautiful fillies are somewhat like beautiful women. It takes more than mere beauty to make a stir in the world. Now let's consider Moia and Lacy. Can you imagine their success happening without inventive minds and hard work?"

"Brandon! You are comparing us with horses! Shame on you. Moia, in the United States that remark would be considered sexist and demeaning." Lacy turned around and found that Moia had ventured to the corner of the window and at this moment was paying little attention to the group.

Moia was staring out toward the hills of Hong Kong, looming in haze across the race course. She looked serious and detached. Turning her attention to the others, Lacy saw Brandon Poole also contemplating Moia. Something was going on. Whatever it was didn't seem to bother Van Hooten. He was lolling in a club chair, sipping champagne. He seemed totally dedicated to spending a frivolous afternoon.

The first race began as a field of ten horses raced past the grandstand on their way to cover a mile and a quarter. The horse on Cecil Lo's list easily finished first. Long Island Girl charged down the stretch determinedly, but still finished four lengths behind the leader.

"Oh damn!" Lacy squealed. "She tried so hard."

Cecil Lo kept his smile to himself. His small wager

had been for place, second position, and had paid handsomely.

"Very good, Cecil," Brandon whispered. He had bet a thousand dollars on the winner picked by Lo. His bet on Long Island Girl was only fifty dollars. Then in a louder voice he said, "Cecil, we stand in awe of your little old handicapper from Cheung Chau. If everyone had taken your advice and had not been distracted by the beautiful filly, we would all have won money."

"I have a confession to make." Van Hooten grinned at Cecil, who had placed his bet. "I had the winner. Amazing that some obscure oracle from Cheung Chau could be the hero of the day."

"I must confess that I also won," Cecil Lo offered unexpectedly. "I did bet on Long Island Girl, but to place. I have you to thank, Ms. Lacy."

"Bravo, Cecil!" Brandon Poole saluted the slender investigator. "However, it is proven that your Cheung Chau handicapper bears consideration for the rest of the program."

"Brandon has that right," exclaimed Van Hooten with enthusiasm. "Thank you, Cecil. Tell us now, are you pulling our leg? Did your tip really come from Cheung Chau?"

Cecil glanced quickly at Brandon Poole, not quite certain what his boss was up to. Brandon instantly came to his rescue. "Claude, it seems that many strange things are happening on that little fisherman's island lately. I heard only yesterday that a general in the People's Liberation Army was spending time there. Albeit he was not in uniform and apparently on holiday. But why sleepy little Cheung Chau? Rather unusual, don't you think?" Brandon saw that Moia was standing again at the window, staring without visible expression again at the rugged hills in the distance.

Van Hooten shrugged. "I suppose we might as well get used to that sort of thing. As we get closer to 1997, more and more of the mainlanders will discover the charming little recesses of Hong Kong."

Brandon Poole looked steadily at Van Hooten, his mind going over the strange report given him by Davy Wong. If Van Hooten knew anything about that, he was certainly doing a good job of concealing it. He decided to take one more shot before dropping the subject.

"Moia, you qualify as an expert on the People's Republic. Why do you think such a notable would seek out Cheung Chau?" Brandon spoke softly, but with a persistent tone that almost demanded an answer.

Moia, apparently in sober consideration of the racing program, lifted her dark eyes to meet Brandon Poole's. "I would guess that it means next to nothing. I think that his being there has a simple, logical explanation. As far as Hong Kong goes, I see nothing threatening about that. I think Claude is right. We'll see more of it during the transition." Moia lowered her head, as if to scan the racing program for the second race, and then immediately changed the subject. "Cecil, I defer to your genius. I'm sticking to your choice in the second race."

"Cecil, you have gained a fan. I will abide by the young lady's choice," Poole said easily, deciding to bring down the tension a bit with his beautiful guest before he dropped another bomb her way. If Van Hooten had any inkling of the building tension between them, he certainly hid it well. This probably meant that the Dutchman knew nothing about her stroll with the general on Cheung Chau.

Lacy sipped at her glass of champagne as she listened to the conversation. Perhaps it was the letdown after all the excitement of the first race, but she had detected the tension between Brandon Poole and Moia. Somewhere buried in Brandon's gentle and easy manner was the persistence of a prosecuting attorney she had once heard in a Bronx court. "Cecil, two hundred on your choice. I'm not sure I like his name, Rapscallion, but I once heard that horses have no inkling of their name anyway."

Rapscallion won, and Cecil Lo became a hero and adviser of all for the rest of the afternoon, even though he eventually had more losers than winners.

Brandon Poole turned on the charm. Lacy noticed that the strange tension that had built between Moia and Poole had eased. Everyone seemed into the racing program, mixing the conversation about horses and horses' names with sipping the constant flow of fine champagne. Then Poole dropped another salvo.

"Claude, I think you and Moia have done a magnificent job with Phuket Color." Poole got their attention with this observation, coming amid the lighthearted banter of late afternoon. "In fact, I'll state on the record that I consider Phuket Color a most tempting candidate for further diversification of Brandon Poole Ltd."

Everyone, including Lacy, looked at Poole, stunned with the surprising assertion.

Van Hooten set his champagne glass on the table and pulled himself erect in his chair. He laughed almost boisterously. "Oh come on, Brandon, be serious. You know I just lost my most productive factory in a fire. We'll pull through in top shape. But I must emphatically state that Phuket Color is not on the block for any sort of fire-sale price. In fact I have never once entertained the idea of a sale at *any* price."

Moia Hsu, appearing much elated, walked over and sat on the arm of Van Hooten's club chair, obviously in agreement with his quick and strong response.

"Now, Claude, I understand your position perfectly. But these are unusual times. There is a haze out there." Brandon waved his hand toward the north. "I am aware of your commitment to stay put in 1997. But if you ever change that, and many others have, I just want you to know that I'm here, and I'm willing. You name your price. I will consider it carefully, probably pay it and hire you and your staff to run it on a long-term and lucrative basis."

"Thanks, Brandon." Van Hooten looked at Moia, now close by his side, her arm around his shoulders. "I'll always remember this moment, because I know you are an honorable man. Perhaps I'll kick myself many times in the future for not prolonging this conversation. But I have a commitment to Moia here, to Hong Kong and to China that I intend to keep. Thanks again, Brandon."

Moia brushed her hand through Van Hooten's hair and then kissed him squarely on the lips. It was an amazing public display for an uptown Beijing woman.

For a moment, Lacy Locke thought she was going to shed a few tears. The poignant moment topped anything that she had seen on the silver screen. "Cecil," she called, breaking the tension, "I'm going along with your pick in the next race. Do you mind if I go with you? I would like to see how it's done over here."

Cecil glanced at Poole and saw no objection. "It would be my pleasure, Ms. Locke. Perhaps it will bring us luck." He collected betting slips from the others and left with the gorgeous Lacy on his arm.

"Your boss is a dynamic man, Cecil. Is he hard to work for?" Lacy posed the question as they threaded through the crowd at the betting windows.

"Mr. Poole is very demanding. . . . He is also generous." Cecil Lo paused thoughtfully. "He also most often gets what he wants."

"How about Phuket Color?"

"Probably so, Ms. Locke, probably so."

They returned to Poole's private box to find everyone all smiles. Brandon Poole was talking about his favorite toy, the big freighter *Brandon Kowloon Eagle*. "Lacy, I was suggesting to Claude that they would enjoy a tour of my new freighter as a pleasant diversion some evening. What do you think?"

"Oh, it's beautiful. I know absolutely nothing about such things, but anyone can tell that it is a magnificent ship. I've been on cruise ships that were not so impressive as this." Of course, she'd never had Brandon Poole with his arms around her, protecting her from the breeze on those cruise ships, either, she thought. "If I were you, I would go. They should do it at night, Brandon. The lights of Hong Kong are simply dazzling from the bridge."

"There, my friends, the voice of experience. I will call you and arrange it soon. Let's see if we can get the skipper to do something a little special for us."

The next race then commanded their attention. Cecil's pick nailed the win by a nose at the wire. He paid a low price, but put everyone in a fine mood for the trip home.

Leaving early to beat the large crowd to the roadway, the four of them shared an elevator to the ground level. Brandon Poole was standing in the rear of the elevator just a little bit to the right of Moia Hsu in front of him. Lacy stood along the side wall of the elevator so that she could see both their faces clearly.

"Oh, by the way, I almost forgot," Poole said in an offhand manner. "I know it's a strange coincidence, but the Chinese general visiting Cheung Chau was also in Bangkok on the night of the fire. Now that is odd, isn't it?"

In the midst of a pleasant smile, Moia Hsu's expression hardened, her eyes narrowing with anger. The elevator door opened and she marched out with Van Hooten close behind. Van Hooten waved back and then the two of them disappeared into the crowd.

Lacy saw it all clearly. "Brandon, shame on you. You seem to take delight in tormenting Moia. You have a knack for pushing all her wrong buttons. She left us furious, you know."

Brandon Poole smiled down at her. "I know, my dear, and I'm sorry. But I guess that all comes under the category of business here in Hong Kong."

"Brandon, it wasn't nice at all. Everyone had a fabulous time, and then right at the last, whatever you said had the effect of jabbing her with a sharp stick."

"Lacy, perhaps she needed it. She can be as devious as she wants with me. But she should level with Van Hooten about her friend, the general from Beijing."

"What? Are you sure?"

"Absolutely." Ahead of them Cecil was holding open the door of the Mercedes. "Come, let's get out of here. Chelsea is concocting something special."

"Brandon! I really should get back to the Mandarin."

"Nonsense! All God's beautiful people need one of Chelsea's wonderful dinners."

Cecil Lo closed the door, climbed in front and the Mercedes sped toward Brandon's tramway lot on the Peak.

Lacy sat quietly, wondering what she could do, short of throwing a fit, that would change the course of the evening. Her mother had always insisted that there was a way to say no to any man. Of course, her mother probably didn't have to contend with a Brandon Poole. Then she remembered Chelsea, and how matronly and sweet she was. All of a sudden she was looking forward to dinner on the Peak.

Chapter 32

DAVY WONG stood for a moment on the dock looking over the huge number of sampans in the harbor at
Aberdeen. Where was Chang? The old man was not in
his usual spot on the far edge nearest the channel. His
battered sampan blended so well in the impoverished
fleet that finding it quickly would be virtually impossible.

There it was! The old man's short low whistle, repeated several times in the growing dusk of the evening. A hundred yards to his right, Chang's sampan was
putting slowly his way toward the provisions dock. The
engine purred softly. Though the old man's vessel was
not much to look at, he prided himself on its seawor-
thiness.

"Chang, you had me worried. You should not play
hide-and-seek with your friends," Davy said as the old
man expertly nestled the *Lila Mae* alongside the dock.

"I saw you coming long ago." Chang's face was crin-
kled and creased far beyond his age from his constant
exposure to the weather. The old man had lived out-
doors all of his life, most of the time on the sea. "Come,
I have made fresh coffee."

"Chang, your coffee tastes like no other in the world.

Are you absolutely sure it is coffee?" Davy sniffed suspiciously at the steaming mug.

"The finest. A Beijing freighter brought it all the way from Brazil, just for Chang. It is the same coffee that is served to guests of Deng Xiaoping in Beijing." The old man winked, and if one looked carefully one could see a sly smile on his wrinkled face. He sipped heartily at the near-boiling liquid.

"Ah, old man. No wonder China has so many problems getting along with the rest of the world. They should force-feed this stuff to the People's Liberation Army instead of their guests."

The old man grinned approvingly at Davy. "We must be careful tonight," the old man warned, suddenly becoming very serious. "Patrol boats are everywhere. They are stopping many for safety checks. We must take the long way to Kowloon, around Stanley. The harbor is not a good place for Davy to be tonight."

"I don't care how long it takes, old man. I must get there. The Star Ferry is a trap for me now. Police are everywhere, hunting for me, poor, unimportant Davy Wong. I must run like a flea on a lion's mane." Davy paused, watching the old man expertly guide the sampan through the narrow spaces between row on row of boats, most of them long past any hope of marine usefulness.

It was a slum, a storehouse of humanity drawn to the magnet of Hong Kong by some vague hope for the future, far exceeding their existence on all those leaky sampans. Lately their number had swelled from the influx of boat people from Vietnam and the Chinese mainland. Survival was now their game, and the implications of 1997 probably never crossed their minds. The boat people of Hong Kong had survived regimes well back into history.

"Look out!" Davy shouted, as the old man challenged the wake of a fancy-fitted junk bearing down the main channel. It was the time of evening when such ornate craft brought load after load of tourists from Central and Kowloon to Big Jumbo and all the other floating restaurants in Aberdeen. Their skippers seemed to have little regard for the havoc created by the heavy wakes, and the near disaster they inflicted upon the tiny vessels in their path. "Fool!" Davy yelled, and shook his fist at the helm of the passing motorized junk.

"Davy, it is of no concern!" The old man shook his head vigorously and pointed to the bench along the taffrail. "They have a powerful radio," he added. "They best mind their business and we mind ours."

"I'm sorry, old man. You are right. I will wait for the day that he finds a hole in his fancy boat." He grinned at the old man, then hunched down in low profile as the sampan clipped by a harbor marker and veered southward into the safety and darkness of the South China Sea.

Forty minutes later the old man bumped gently into a commercial dock just north of the Star Ferry terminal in Kowloon. "Careful, Davy. You know where I'll be."

Davy saluted him with gusto, stepped onto the dock and quickly vanished from the old man's sight. He made his way to Haiphong Street and a few minutes later mixed with the crowd entering the subway station at Tsim Sha Tsui. Within minutes he was slumped in a doorway from which he could see the police station house in Tsuen Wan, and all who entered it. He reasoned to himself that he would be safest here, waiting for Hargrave to leave. The army of police that were seaching for him would never look just across the street.

It was now past nine o'clock. Davy was a little surprised with Hargrave's diligence. Most officers of his rank delegated late night duty to others, especially in these times when many felt that their careers were facing extinction. Their morale was such that many were just marking time, expecting the People's Liberation Army to take their jobs.

Davy was distracted by the heavy step of a pedestrian, boot heels clicking on the pavement. Who was this? "Unbelievable," he murmured aloud.

Striding up the street with the same imperious walk he had seen on Cheung Chau was none other than General Liu Wing. He leapt energetically up the two steps in front of the station house and walked inside. His tall, lean figure and military bearing were unmistakable.

Inside the station house, Liu nodded at the officer at the desk. He asked for Superintendent Hargrave in a voice loud enough to be heard by Hargrave, sitting at the desk in his office, door ajar.

Hargrave stared at the tall officer outside and then motioned him to enter. Liu closed the door behind him. "Good to see you, General. There is something we must discuss." Hargrave put on his official face, determined not to be intimidated by the general.

Liu smiled patronizingly at Hargrave, as if amused at his attempt to take charge of their conversation. "Well now, that is interesting, Hargrave. I was just thinking the same thing. I was thinking that you haven't given me much useful information lately about citizen Moia Hsu. I suspect that she has eluded you, or perhaps you have run out of lies to tell about her." Liu popped his right fist into his other hand, glared at Hargrave and sat down across the desk from him.

"I have no idea what you are talking about, General. A man would be very foolish to be anything but honest with such an important representative of the People's Republic. That is why I must tell you about my misfortune." Hargrave hesitated. After thinking the matter through he had decided to tell Liu as much as he dared about the incident at the power plant.

"This morning I picked up my surveillance of Moia Hsu as you had directed. In fact I followed her to the gates of the power plant in Aberdeen. Regrettably, she detected me and called the police from her car phone. It was a slightly humorous situation, General. There I was with my own comrades behind me.''

Liu scowled at Hargrave, no doubt thinking that the story was too amazing to be untrue. ''And what else, Hargrave.''

''Nothing much, sir. I told my police to return to their station, and told Moia Hsu that I had police business at the power plant.''

''And Ms. Hsu believed you?'' The general had a strange half smile on his face.

''She had no choice, sir. But nevertheless it makes it impossible for me to trail her in the future.''

''Of course, Hargrave.'' The general smiled. The Moia I know, he thought, would not give up her charges so easily. ''Best we lie low for a while. That will give you time to catch up on your regular duties.'' Liu removed a packet of money from his jacket pocket and slid it across the desk.

Hargrave looked dumbfounded. The bribe was much thicker than usual. ''Perhaps you didn't understand, General, I have blown my cover with Moia Hsu.''

''I understand that perfectly well, Hargrave. We're all human. I am very excited about you getting back to your regular duties, like finding Davy Wong for us.'' Liu paused dramatically to let the words sink in. He leaned over the desk and slammed a fist down upon it, causing Hargrave to jump. ''Find out where he is, Hargrave. My friends in Beijing want to have a long chat with him. He's a bastard. A lot of the blood of 1989 is on his hands, you know.''

Hargrave's face twisted unavoidably as he belched loudly. ''Sorry, General. I haven't been myself lately.'' He fumbled in his desk drawer for the vial of antacid pills. ''Davy Wong, you say . . . I haven't heard that name in some time. I don't know if he is even in Hong Kong.''

"Liar! Everyone knows he is in Hong Kong!" Liu shoved the packet of money against Hargrave's chest. "A lot of fools here call him a hero. They are wrong, Hargrave. I'm not asking you to bring him in. Just find him and tell me where he is. That's all. The people of China would be pleased with that information."

General Liu rose from the desk, turned on his heel and left Hargrave's office. Hargrave's stomach rumbled noisily as he belched again. He made a quick decision to leave the office. Working up a reply to the commissioner's letter had taken all day. Now he had accepted a bribe to produce Davy Wong, the Beijing dissident who was virtually a local hero. It looked like time was running out on him faster than for Hong Kong itself.

Hargrave put on his uniform jacket and stuffed the packet of money inside. He primped in front of a mirror for a moment, carefully combing his graying hair and mustache. Outwardly he looked like the royal servant he had sworn to be in his youth. But inside he was rotten, he thought. If there was a heaven, he no longer had a chance to get there. He put on his cap and walked outside. He walked across the dark street and turned to his left . . . and came face-to-face with Davy Wong.

Hargrave swept his eyes in both directions, now growing accustomed to the darkness. It hadn't been long. The general might still be in view. But he wasn't. "Davy Wong, that's you. I'd know you anywhere."

"The face has been on enough posters, Superintendent. I guess everyone in Hong Kong has seen it at one time or another. Can we talk, sir?"

"Sure, Davy. Care to go back in my office?"

"I'd rather not, sir. No need to bother with that. I've been a little curious. I've heard the communists want me on their side of the border. I just wonder if they have pestered the police about it, sir." Davy now walked alongside the superintendent on a darkened side street.

"Davy, it is the job of the Royal Hong Kong Police to protect the people of Hong Kong, not to turn them over to the communists. That's their problem if they want to question you. However, I'd advise you to stay on this side of Lo Wu."

"Thanks, Superintendent. One other thing. I hear they have some important people wandering around Hong Kong. There seems to be a Chinese general in town. I wonder what he's here for."

"I have no idea, Davy. I'll check around and let you know. Where can I reach you these days, Davy?"

"Superintendent, I think you're lying about the general. After all, he walked out of your office only a few minutes ago." Wong stepped in front of Hargrave, his usual jovial face an icy stare. "I think you are a disgrace to the Royal Hong Kong Police, Hargrave. What business did he want with you?"

Hargrave belched loudly. The unpredictable, muscular Wong, standing in front of him with fists clenched, scared the wits out of him. "He wanted you, Davy. I told him I didn't know whether you were in Hong Kong or not."

"How much money did he give you, Hargrave?" Davy moved close enough to smell his rotten breath.

"What are you suggesting?" Hargrave whispered. "How dare you . . ."

Davy thumped him solidly on his chest, right on the bulging inner pocket of his jacket. "I know how they think, Hargrave. And I know all about you. My advice to you is to spend the rest of your days here in Hong Kong beating up on the pickpockets at Sha Tin."

"The rest of my days! Now, young man, what are you trying to say?"

"You're the detective. Figure it out." Davy Wong tapped him once again on the chest, then walked rapidly to the nearest alleyway and vanished.

Hargrave belched nervously again. Davy Wong used to be a friend. Now, if he were told to select one friend in all of Hong Kong, he could not do it. He stood quietly for a moment, stomach rumbling noisily. He cursed himself for not having the guts to nab Davy Wong right there and hold him for the Chinese, but then he really hadn't the guts for anything these days.

He walked slowly back toward the station house and reentered his small office. He reached under the desk and produced a suitcase he had packed very carefully over the past few weeks. He had accurately reasoned that he might want to leave Hong Kong in a hurry sometime soon. Outside again, he placed the heavy bag in the dusty old Mazda, got inside, revved the engine and pointed himself toward the Macau ferry terminal in Central District. Maybe it was time to leave Hong Kong.

Chapter 33

MARY LULU had the crowd in the dimly lit Typhoon Club cheering boisterously. Every movement of her body brought a clap of their hands in unison. The coy face, then a sly wink and a furious snap of her pelvis, again and again until the old building shook with the raucous response of the crowd. She moved sensuously along the stage until she reached a female dancer pretending to be bound as a slave girl, sitting on the stage, hands clasped behind her back, body swaying slightly to the rhythm of the statuesque dancer above her.

Mary Lulu began to lower herself slowly toward the dancer below her as the mob cheered her on. Abruptly, she stopped and stood erect, shaming the crowd with the motions of her fingers. "I know what you want!" Mary Lulu intoned loudly as the audience was provoked into silence. "You want me to sing a naughty little song." And she began.

In the farthest corner of the cabaret, General Liu sat entranced by the actions of the steamy entertainer who had been with Moia at Sai Kung. Hargrave's description of the dancer didn't do justice at all to the torrid presentation he was now witnessing.

"She is an American?" He asked the question of his waitress.

"Yes sir. I think she is. She is so beautiful, is she not, sir?"

General Liu Wing scrawled a few words in English on a card that he produced from his jacket. Perhaps the time spent laboring in English instruction in Shanghai would now be put to good use, he thought. "Here, my darling." The handsome general handed the card to his server. "Will you see that Miss Lulu gets this." He handed the young woman the card with a hundred-dollar Hong Kong bill for her trouble.

"I will try my best, sir."

"Your best? I expect you to do it, young lady."

"Yes sir." She glanced up at Mary Lulu, who had now finished taking her bows and was heading toward the stage exit.

"Hurry, girl! Now!" ordered Liu.

The waitress ran quickly after the disappearing Mary Lulu. Liu smiled appreciatively at the waitress. Not bad either, he told himself. Perhaps he could arrange a threesome. From the descriptions Hargrave had given him about activities on the boat, the obviously decadent American would be game for anything. American women were like that. He was sure of it. After all, the newspapers of the world clearly documented their shameful debauchery.

The general watched another performance without any acknowledgment to his message, noting that Mary Lulu was giving a lot of attention to a young man sitting in one of the curved leather booths at the edge of the stage. At the baudy climax of the performance, arrayed only in Venuslike nudity, bronze suntan glistening to accent her perfection, she strode to the young man's table.

The young man smiled, showing gleaming teeth as he applauded. Then he doffed his powder blue sport coat and wrapped it around her shoulders. Mary Lulu opened wide the front of the jacket and pushed against the willing youth, wrapping him in the garment with her as the crowd cheered wildly.

The house lights darkened to pitch black. When they came on a few seconds later, Mary Lulu and the young man had disappeared.

The general pondered what to do. He was not used to being ignored. The young man was handsome, he supposed, by some trivial standard, but was certainly no competition for a man of his stature. Liu snapped his finger at the waitress who had supposedly delivered his inquiry.

"You forgot, didn't you?"

"Oh no, sir! She read your message, and later I saw her read it again. She smiled, sir."

"Smiled?"

"Yes, as if she liked it. And then she put it inside a tiny beaded bag in her dressing room."

The general stared at the ample bosom of his messenger, then produced another card from his jacket. He scribbled several words on it and passed it along to the waitress. "Here, no woman could refuse such an invitation from a general in the People's Army, could they?"

The young woman read the message and blushed. "Sir, you are so funny. I think she will like this."

"Funny?"

She nodded her head, smiled at him, blushed again and ran off toward the dressing room. Within minutes she returned and extended an invitation on behalf of Mary Lulu to visit her dressing room. "Come, sir. We must hurry, it is only ten minutes until she goes on stage again."

Liu stood and straightened up his civilian clothes as best he could. The suit was quite flattering, but showed its struggle against the humid Hong Kong night. It was that side trip to Kowloon to visit Hargrave that had taken the edge off his usual crisp appearance. His waitress stopped at a doorway down a long hall and knocked several times. The door opened, and Mary Lulu stood in a loosely draped silk robe, eyeing the general up and down as he entered.

"General? How do I know that? Where is your uniform?" She circled the general, who now stood in the middle of her dressing room. "Not bad, not bad at all. But I like my generals in uniform. Tell me, General, do you always write such shocking little notes to perfect strangers?"

"You are hardly a stranger, my dear. I have invaded you with my eyes. I feel already that we know each other." He studied the woman intently. She was almost as tall as he was. "Forgive me, you do have reason to suspect. I can imagine that you have all sorts of men approaching you, claiming to be someone of importance. I can hardly blame them."

Liu let her examine his passport and the People's Liberation Army credentials he fished out of his jacket. She smiled at the general, now gaping at her nakedness, as she allowed the silken robe to fall partially open. "Macau, General, I have only limited time in Hong Kong and I have never seen Macau. Perhaps you will take me there. I have always wanted to learn baccarat. Perhaps you can teach me and then we can talk about your naughty little notes. Do you always advertise so outrageously?"

"Of course not. But then I've never been provoked by such a performance as yours before." Liu paused for a moment trying to say something that would make the most of his remaining minutes with her. "I would love to show you Macau sometime."

"Sometime? Tomorrow is my only leisure day. Will you take me tomorrow? You must understand that I work late hours here, but by noon I will have had my beauty sleep."

"You scarcely need that. When and where can I call for you?" He stared at the beauty. She had tossed her robe aside and was costuming herself for her next number with a few strategically placed adhesive fig leaves.

"General! A gentleman would turn his back. I must prepare for my next entrance."

"I'm sorry . . . I'm not used to this . . . environment." He almost said "American decadence."

"Well then, pick me up at noon. I'm at the Mandarin. How shall we get to Macau?"

"By hydrofoil. I'll make the arrangements. You do me such great honor. I can hardly wait."

She smiled provocatively at the tall officer. "Ah, but we must wait. By the way, do you mind if I bring Chad Grissom along? The poor boy has never seen Macau."

"Chad Grisssom?"

"My friend in the blue sport coat."

"Your friend? Absolutely not!" Liu reddened, but he was not about to conduct a tourist's tour of Macau for her youthful colleague.

"Relax, General. No need to get upset about it. He can take his holiday here in Hong Kong quite easily. He wouldn't bother us, though. Chad marches to a different drummer, as they say. He hasn't much use for little girls like me."

"God help him, then. I much prefer that you and I go alone together."

"Obviously. Your scandalous little note made that clear." Mary Lulu walked to the dressing room door, prepared now to go on stage. "So it's you and me, at noon tomorrow at the Mandarin." The general was still ogling her near nudity. "You will recognize me, I'm sure, even though I will have my clothes on. See you then, General."

Cecil Lo, standing at the crowded bar in the Typhoon Club, had watched the little drama before him. The notes to the waitress and now the trip to the dressing room by General Liu made his new assignment interesting. The general certainly had a penchant for beautiful women. The trailing of Lacy Locke halfway around the world had proved to be a dreary task most of the time. Apparently that was over, with Lacy nestled alone with Brandon at the Peak. Now he had been assigned Wong's task of pursuing the general, with the hope of finding out what he was up to in Hong Kong.

Lo sipped at his glass of mineral water. He thought about Davy Wong for a moment. He was on the run. The communists were getting quite serious about the roundup of dissidents, and evidently Davy was high on their priority list. He glanced at his watch. Liu had been in the dressing room over five minutes now. The waitress who had served him was now passing his way.

"Excuse me, miss." Lo extended his hand, with a thousand-dollar Hong Kong note woven as a ribbon between his fingers. He had found this to be an international gesture that was sure to solidify quick friendships.

"Yes sir. This is not my station, but can I be of help?" Her eyes fixed quickly on the banknote.

Lo leaned over and spoke directly into her ear. "The tall gentleman, at the booth over there, he went backstage. Can you tell me something about him?"

The waitress tittered for a moment and then put her hand in front of her mouth. "He says he is a general in the army of China. He is very generous." She shrugged her shoulders, then smiled broadly.

"Why did he go backstage?" Lo now held the banknote by a corner and held it toward her. Glancing around, she took it and stuffed it quickly into her cleavage.

"He sent the singer a note. He asked her for a date." Again she smiled broadly. "It happens sometimes in here."

"What did he write?"

"It was very private, sir." She smiled and looked directly into Lo's eyes as he peeled another banknote from a roll in his hand. "He said that she reminded him of a delicious soufflé, and he would like to have her for breakfast." The waitress giggled softly as she stashed the other banknote on top of the first one.

Capitalism was certainly alive and well here in Hong Kong, Lo thought. "And did the lady accept?"

She shook her head. "I don't know, but I betcha she did."

"Try and find out."

"For you, anything, sir." The waitress walked off toward the service bar just as the general emerged from the dressing room corridor and took his seat once again.

Lo sat glumly, staring at the general, who was apparently going to watch another performance. He was hoping that he would leave. The waitress almost immediately served him a drink, and then engaged him in conversation. She was beaming as she passed next to Lo.

"They are going to Macau tomorrow. In fact, he asked me to meet them by the hydrofoil terminal at noon and join them. Can you believe that?" She shook her head in disbelief.

"Are you going?" persisted Lo.

"Never! My husband would not permit that." She giggled softly. "In fact, he would probably kill me."

"Good for you. You are a wise young woman."

"Not so wise, perhaps. But I have a wonderful husband." She smiled and strolled off to tend to her other customers. Lo wondered whether she was telling the truth. Generally, scruples had taken a nosedive in Hong Kong lately. It was as if everyone was trying to sample everything before the world ended, or at least before 1997.

Chapter 34

ANOTHER DECK of Brandon Poole's sprawling aerie, one that overlooked the skyline southward from the Peak, was set with candlelight and crystal. The dazzling lights of Hong Kong Island seemed to stretch forever in the clear night. Chelsea had served a magnificent dinner, a beef Wellington with an herb crust of her own creation. Lacy decided that it could have been served successfully at any fine restaurant in the world.

They dined leisurely as Brandon told her what he knew of General Liu and his long walk with Moia on Cheung Chau. He didn't tell her how he knew, just what he knew. "I got the distinct feeling, just as you pointed out, Lacy, that Moia was uncomfortable with my remarks. Van Hooten seemed to show no concern at all about the casual mention of Cheung Chau."

Lacy reflected over their afternoon at the races. "I would say you're right, Brandon. But what does it mean? Van Hooten and Moia are not married. Perhaps she took a day trip to the island just to relax, ran into this general, and shared conversation as they walked. From what you say, it was hardly a romantic tryst."

"No, it wasn't," Brandon agreed. "But it looks like more than coincidence that this same soldier was in

Bangkok the night of the burning of Van Hooten's factory."

Lacy shook her head slowly. "I guess it is one of Hong Kong's mysteries that I'll never know the outcome of." She watched a large jet airliner, its landing lights pinpointed in the distance as it lost altitude on the approach to Kai Tak. The arriving plane reminded her that she had been in Hong Kong several days now and that her business decisions regarding Phuket Color and other prospective clients were still not made. The complex issues surrounding the future of Hong Kong made business assessment extremely difficult. She decided to ask Poole point-blank about her concern.

"Brandon, do you see a big growth for Phuket Color? Will it survive the changeover in 1997?"

"My dear, you heard me offer to buy his company today on the condition that he and Moia stay and run it. That should answer your question."

"And the fire doesn't deter you?" Lacy persisted.

"Not at all. A temporary setback, that's all it was. Van Hooten seems to lead a charmed life with the Chinese. I suspect that Moia has much to do with that."

Chelsea served a selection of fruits with a sorbet. She brought a bottle of Grand Marnier to their table. "Will there be anything else, Mr. Poole?"

"Chelsea, consider your day at an end. Lacy and I can do quite well from here on."

"Ms. Locke, I hope you are enjoying your stay in Hong Kong. No one knows more about it than Brandon Poole." Chelsea beamed a matronly smile at both of them, then left the deck.

"She's a jewel, Brandon. You are so lucky to have her. Such unqualified loyalty must be a great comfort to you. She absolutely adores you. I would like to steal her and take her back to New York."

"Don't be fooled, Lacy. She can be a real pain in the neck sometimes. If I didn't let her run this household like it was her own, she would probably leave."

Brandon leaned back in his chair and brushed his hands through his thick black hair, replacing an unruly lock that was prone to pitch forward over his brow.

"Forgive me, Brandon, but I'm curious. Was there ever a Mrs. Poole?"

"I'm afraid not. Between the military, the time I've spent at sea, and the business, it just never happened." He paused reflectively. "I came close once, way back, right after I left the Royal Marines. But Hong Kong was not her cup of tea. I'm afraid I lost her to London."

"Then it wasn't meant to happen. It looks to me like living here is much like riding on a roller coaster. You either love it or want to leave it."

"Could you live here, Lacy?" Brandon leaned forward and grasped her hand in both of his own. His deep blue eyes bored intently into her own.

She felt slightly uneasy. His direct manner reminded her of his persistence with Moia at Happy Valley. "I . . . I suppose I could. It's exciting, Brandon. The business world, the freedom to wheel and deal is . . . electrifying. And I have met so many brilliant business people. Hong Kong is like a big poker game where almost everyone can win."

"Aha! You *do* have the fever. And that brings me to the real question."

Brandon paused, staring out over Victoria Harbor, his eyes coming to rest on his giant freighter. He was now grasping her hand even more snugly in his own. "I think it would be wonderful if you would have my son."

"Brandon!" She pulled her hand gently from his. Whatever she had expected him to say was certainly nothing like what he actually said. "How could you ever think . . ."

"Stop! Let me talk for a while. I've watched you all the way from New York. Remember our exchange at the seminar? I've never been so overwhelmed with a woman. You could easily take a year's sabbatical from your firm. I would set you up to handle my important financial affairs. You would pursue your interests, make lots of money and we could have our son. I suspect I've never been in love, Lacy, until now."

Lacy felt her pulse pounding. She was fighting off hysteria, alternate urges to laugh or to cry. She looked inside the villa past the doorway where Chelsea had vanished. She stood up and walked toward the rail around the deck, then turned to face Brandon, still sitting, his eyes never leaving her. "Brandon . . . it's preposterous. I am flattered by how you feel, but it is an impossibility. I think you'd better take me back to the Mandarin."

"Nothing, my dear, is impossible in Hong Kong." Now he was smiling at her, sprawling leisurely in his chair. "Relax, you have many days to think about this. The more you think about it, the more you will realize that I'm right."

All of a sudden she felt greatly relieved. She reassured herself that Brandon Poole was a gentleman. She felt certain he had no intention of going about the process of fathering a son this very evening. She felt comfortable directing a smile toward him. "Brandon, thank you for a supreme compliment. But don't count on me agreeing with you. For starters, there's the matter of Adam." She started laughing uncontrollably after she said it. To her amazement Brandon was laughing with her.

"Ah yes, my dear, I suppose we'll get down to talking about Adam sooner or later. But don't worry about that right now. In fact now that I have dropped the bomb on you, so to speak, let's leave the Peak. I'll get you to the Mandarin soon enough, but first I have a little side trip planned, something that may make you better understand Hong Kong."

"It's getting late, Brandon," she said, more relaxed now that they were leaving the Peak.

He looked at his watch. "It's not too late, in fact it

is just about the right time if we hurry." He walked to where she stood at the railing, bent slightly and kissed her cheek. "I want to compliment you for hearing me out. I guess my proposition was a little unexpected. At least you didn't vault over this railing and try to scramble down the Peak."

"You do know how to surprise a lady, Brandon. Please, can we go now?"

Brandon walked ahead of her down the dimly lit path to the private tramway. Lacy smilingly recalled that her advisers in the office had told her that Brandon Poole was worth perhaps two billion dollars. It would be a great story to tell one day. But then, who would believe her?

Cecil Lo was not at his usual place in the Mercedes, so Brandon climbed behind the wheel. On the way to the garage, he contacted Lo by car phone to tell him where he was leaving the Mercedes. There was a long conversation in which Lacy heard him mention Macau several times. Beyond that she couldn't make sense of it.

"Cecil's going to Macau tomorrow," he said without going into detail. "I'm afraid our Cecil likes to gamble a bit."

"I've always heard about Macau. In the States, there were some great old motion pictures about Macau, filled with intrigue. They were made before my time, but I've watched them on TV."

"I've seen one or two of them. Actually Macau is very much like that. Not a lot there, if you're not a gambler. Macau is next on China's list of acquisitions. Actually the People's Republic is very much a presence in Macau right now." Brandon fished around in the console compartment and came up with a New York Yankees baseball cap, which he jammed on his head. He removed his jacket and tossed it in the back seat. "Not much of a disguise, but it should do for a few minutes."

Lacy stared at Poole and smiled. "You're right, it's not much of a disguise, Brandon. However, I like it. You look like a tall first baseman."

"That's nice, Lacy. I think that is the first compliment you have paid me."

Brandon parked in his garage in Central, and they walked a block or so to the subway. The sleek train, moving almost silently on its tracks, came by within a few moments. The train to Tsim Sha Tsui would take them under the harbor to Kowloon.

Lacy marveled at the sterile efficiency of the subway. As sleek and clean as it was, she couldn't help smiling when she looked at Brandon Poole sitting next to her. She wondered if the billionaire would ride the subways in New York. "Do you ride the trains often, Brandon?"

"Almost never. But we can get where we are going in minutes. Besides, I thought you might get a kick out of it. Too bad about your subways in New York. I can't say I would ride them again."

Now Lucy found herself staring at her unlikely companion. If you studied him very closely, there was almost always a hint of a smile on his handsome face. She couldn't help but chuckle aloud as she recalled his shocking proposition. She leaned close and whispered her thoughts. "Brandon, say the impossible happened, and it won't, what if we had a daughter instead of a son?"

"Then some day she would be as lovely as you are. I would feel like a king."

Lacy smiled and shook her head. Brandon Poole's words were rarely predictable. Within ten minutes the train pulled in to the station in Tsim Sha Tsui, in the heart of Kowloon. Exiting to the street level on Nathan Road, they walked a few blocks north, passing scores of shops featuring cameras, designer clothing, jewelry, and art curios, all upscale and brilliantly lit.

"Lacy, there are probably a thousand entrepreneurs

right here on Nathan Road. All of them make money off millions of tourists each year. New space on Nathan Road is at a high premium. You'd find nothing remotely like this in Beijing." Now Brandon Poole was striding rapidly, his long strides keeping him constantly a half step ahead of Lacy.

Her day had started with a visit to the bank early this morning. Then there were the races at Happy Valley, the dinner on the Peak that produced Brandon's incredible suggestion. Now they were almost running down Nathan Road at ten-thirty at night. Did the man ever stop? she wondered. She grasped his arm as they stopped for traffic at Jordon Road. "Brandon, please, can we slow down a little? I should have worn my sneakers for the whole day."

Brandon stopped and faced her. "I'm sorry, Lacy. Forgive me. I just wasn't thinking." He looked down at her feet. "Only a couple of short blocks to Temple Street and the night market."

"The night market?"

"Yes, it's another perspective of entrepreneurship in Hong Kong. It opens in the evening and closes around midnight. Citizens of Hong Kong and a few tourists shop hundreds of stalls for necessities for their families, many times negotiating for their own price. Each stall represents a private business, one of a quarter of a million in Hong Kong. Our little jaunt will give you a quick look at the gamut of retail commerce in the Colony." Having said that, Poole began walking again at a more leisurely pace until they reached Temple Street, teeming with activity at this late hour.

They pushed their way northward through the crowd of people, most of them haggling over the price of merchandise in the small stalls. "Look!" Lacy pointed to a rack of women's blouses. "Phuket Color, I'm sure of it."

"Probably overruns, or odd lots," Brandon observed. "I suspect that if you look hard enough, you'll find some of the most prestigious designer names in the night market."

Lacy quickly struck a deal for one of the blouses for seven dollars. "I'll tell Van Hooten where I got it, when I see him again," she said, smiling over her bargain.

Brandon Poole chuckled aloud. "Lacy, you gave in too quickly. I'll bet you could have got it at half the price."

Brandon Poole's face became serious as they approached the next block of Temple Street. A crowd was milling in the street. There was loud yelling in the distance, now getting closer. Then there was visible pushing and shoving as a contingent of Hong Kong police pounced on a strapping man, desperately trying to escape their grasp. Now they had him pinned to the street directly in front of where Brandon and Lacy stood.

They stared down at the still-struggling man. Brandon Poole gasped. "My God!" he muttered under his breath, "it's Davy Wong." Now Davy was staring right at him and Brandon could see the recognition in his eyes. Poole gave him a quick thumbs-up, grasped Lacy's hand and walked quickly toward Nathan Road.

"Brandon, do you know him?" Lacy spoke between breaths as she ran along beside him.

"Yes! He is a good friend. I have to get to the commissioner right away. Those damn communists want him back in Beijing. I'm sorry, Lacy, to spoil our evening. But this demands fast action."

"Of course, Brandon, whatever you say."

Reaching Nathan Road, Brandon stepped into an alcove in a storefront to one of the now-closed retail stores and took a small cellular phone from his rear pocket. He dialed a number quickly and waited, staring at Lacy with the half smile she had come to expect as natural.

"Brandon Poole here, sorry to bother you at this hour, but it's urgent. The police have just picked up

Davy Wong in Kowloon. There was a real tussle in the night market." A pause followed as Brandon listened for what must have been a full minute. "I want him freed. I don't care what it takes. Davy Wong wouldn't harm a flea, much less kill someone. I'll take the responsibility. Sending him across the border would be the same as a prison sentence or perhaps even an execution." Then came another short pause as Brandon listened. "I'll be on the Peak in a half-hour. Bring me up-to-date then. I expect good news."

The two were back in the Mercedes in Central within a quarter hour. He paused in front of the Mandarin, allowing the attendant to open the door. Leaning over, he framed Lacy's face with his large hands and kissed her aggressively on the lips.

To her surprise, she let him linger for a few moments before she pulled away. "Good night, Brandon. I hope things work out with your friend."

"They will, my dear. I would not permit anything less." He waved as the attendant closed the door after she got out. She could hear the engine revving to high speed as he pointed it toward the Peak. Then, inexplicably, she thought of Adam and wondered what she really felt toward either man. Lacy felt confused—and knew she'd have to make a decision soon.

Chapter 35

CLAUDE VAN HOOTEN rolled and tossed. He found it impossible to sleep. The day at the races had been both relaxing and stimulating. Brandon Poole's verbal offer to buy Phuket Color had come right out of the blue. In his view, it was a supreme compliment coming from one of Hong Kong's most respected businessmen. There was no doubt that Poole had the cash to conclude such a deal if he wanted to respond.

It was a shot in the arm when he most needed it. As much as he tried to downplay the Bangkok fire, it was more than a minor disaster, coming when it did. He had played it pretty cool, not really responding to Poole with any more than a thanks-but-no-thanks kind of a reply. But there was no question in his mind that the offer was real, and one that he had to consider in view of the vague and turbulent times ahead for the Crown Colony of Hong Kong. Hell, Hong Kong was a sea of intrigue and indecision. A lot of companies would welcome such a gesture from the likes of Brandon Poole.

One thing bothered him. Moia had not been herself since they had left Happy Valley. At sometime during the height of their enjoyment of the races, she had withdrawn into a shell. At first, he wondered if it was something he had said, but he could think of nothing. He thought back over the afternoon.

There had been the idle talk about Cecil Lo's mysterious tour on the island of Cheung Chau. He had regarded it as droll humor from Cecil Lo, long a shadowy servant of Brandon Poole. In the past he had heard stories of Lo being a private investigator of note. But he had assumed that the aging Lo had long left that life behind him, if indeed it had ever existed. He recalled that Poole and Moia had exchanged idle talk about People's Republic notables spending holidays in the obscure corners of Hong Kong.

Van Hooten rolled over in bed, pounded his pillow into a fluffy ball, and lay back again, staring out the glass doors. Moia was sitting on the veranda alone, back toward him, staring off into the South China Sea. Evenings and nights at Stanley had always been a source of rest and renewing of strength for their long business days. Tonight, however, Moia was distant. Something was on her mind that she was not sharing with him.

Van Hooten rose, donned a robe and walked out on the veranda. He sat at the table next to Moia. She smiled weakly, and in silence she poured a cup of tea from the brew she had made. "I can't sleep, dear," she said. "I know why, but I don't think you do."

She turned to face him, eyes wide, very serious. Then she shrugged and sighed. "Perhaps it is my fault."

"Oh? I thought it might be Poole's offer for Phuket. Forget it. We will regard it as a compliment and nothing more. It was very nice of him."

"No, it isn't that. It was quite a compliment, one that you should remember as time goes by. He is a powerful man." Moia touched his hand on the table. "I have done a bad thing." She stopped abruptly and dabbed at unexpected tears with a napkin.

"Tell me about it, Moia, if you want to. Nothing could be that bad."

"In the box at Happy Valley, did you hear Van Hooten say that a mainland general was seen on Cheung Chau?"

"Yes, now that you remind me, I do. Lots of Chinese officials are exploring Hong Kong these days. We can't expect much else, I'm afraid."

"Nothing like that, Claude. . . . He was there because of me."

"You!" Van Hooten snapped wide awake, trying to make sense of what she meant.

"It was General Liu Wing. He went to Cheung Chau to have a meeting with me." Moia dabbed at her eyes again. "Claude, it was so stupid of me."

Van Hooten stared at the woman he loved. "Why, Moia? I think you had better tell me why."

"He has been a pest, such a pest! Once in a while I go to Tsuen Wan to the old villa, to pick up some clothing. He has been leaving notes at the gate. I think he is insanely jealous, Claude. It would not surprise me if he were the one that had Hargrave following me. Oh Claude, I was so stupid!" Moia dropped her eyes, staring into the teacup in front of her. "Years ago, Liu Wing and I were close. He was attending a military school near Shanghai. I was a student at a school nearby. Our relationship ended many years ago, as soon as I left Shanghai. But he has never given up. He has tried everything he can think of. He even made an effort to make a friend of my father."

"Why Cheung Chau?" Claude asked.

"I was to visit our bank in Shenzhen that day, so I knew you would not miss me. I suggested Cheung Chau once when Liu called. I wanted to have it out with him and get it over with once and for all. I thought no one would see us there. But someone did. I know from what Brandon Poole said today that somehow he knows."

"I see it all now," mused Claude, patting her hand. "It probably troubles him. He has no way of knowing what you just told me."

Claude Van Hooten stared grimly at the lights of Lantau in the distance. A chill ran though him as a cold sweat beaded on his brow. "Moia, you must remember then what Brandon Poole said on the elevator as we left the race track."

Moia's eyes met his own, tears now streaming from them. "Yes. He said that the same general was in Bangkok the night of the fire."

"I think we'd better have a serious conversation with Brandon Poole, in the morning, if possible." Van Hooten stroked his fingers through Moia's long hair. "Don't worry, it has to be a coincidence."

Moia shook her head. "No. Something is terribly wrong, Claude. I can feel it. I don't think Liu wants Phuket Color to be successful. He was angry with me in Beijing when we went to my father's conference. Oh Claude, what have I done?"

"Nothing, Moia. You have done nothing. If he had something to do with the fire, it is his twisted mind at work. I'll call Brandon Poole right now and leave a message that it is urgent that we talk again."

To his amazement, Brandon Poole picked up on his telephone as Van Hooten was leaving his message on an answering machine. The man was actually at work in his office before sunrise! "Brandon, now I know your secret to success. You stay up all night and make your plans while other people sleep."

"Hardly, Claude. Believe me, I could use a few hours' sleep. A friend of mine was picked up by the police last night on some trumped-up charge and I am trying to get the thing straightened out."

"Good luck! My opinion of the Royal Police runs very low these days," Van Hooten said, recalling Moia's recent to-do with Hargrave. "Brandon, something was said that went over my head yesterday afternoon at the races. Moia has just brought me up-to-date. General Liu Wing was an acquaintance of Moia's back in their school days in Shanghai. He's been making a perfect nuisance of himself, so Moia met with him the other day on Cheung Chau. She was bent on trying to talk some sense into him. I had no idea what you were driving at in the elevator until now."

"Aha, now I get the picture. I'm sorry to have caused either of you any distress." Poole was quiet for a moment, waiting to see if Van Hooten would volunteer any more information.

"Frankly, we are both worried about the general." Van Hooten winked comfortingly at Moia, listening wide-eyed on the receiver next to his. "Do you have any other information, Brandon?"

"As a matter of fact, I do. Pierre Boucher, a police captain in Bangkok, has told us that Liu was accompanied by Li Pao."

"Li Pao!" Van Hooten shrugged his shoulders toward Moia, who stared blankly at him. "That's news for concern. I can't imagine why he would meet the general there. Are you sure?"

"Absolutely, they stayed at the White Lotus, in separate quarters. Liu met Pao at Kai Tak and they flew to Bangkok together."

"That's crazy. However, Pao has a perfect right to be in Bangkok. He is our contact for Phuket construction in Beijing. But the general? It makes no sense." Van Hooten paused, glancing at Moia.

"I certainly agree with that," Brandon replied. "Pierre Boucher of the Bangkok police would like to question the general, but politics being what it is, he will not likely be permitted to. Claude, thanks for bringing me up to speed on this. Let's keep in touch. By the way, I meant it when I invited you to inspect the *Kowloon Eagle*. I have something of interest to show you. She is a very special vessel."

"Now you have me wondering. I'll check my schedule and get back to you today."

When Van Hooten hung up he felt relieved that Brandon Poole had accepted his explanation of Moia's meeting on Cheung Chau at face value. Poole obviously was using this information as a tool to probe his company's weaknesses. Van Hooten was concerned but he reasoned Poole was, at heart, just being a shrewd businessman. The information about Li Pao, however, was shattering. Now he was nervous. He lit a cigar and watched the smoke drift lazily in the still night air, then started to pace the veranda.

Moia looked as if she had been slapped. She had successfully explained the Cheung Chau meeting with Liu only to be shocked again with the news that her Beijing contact was in Bangkok on the night of the fire.

"Claude." She looked at him, wishing she could say something that would explain it all. "I remember the morning after the fire. I tried to reach Li Pao in Beijing several times. I became so desperate that I called his home and talked to his wife. She professed that she did not know where he was. That may have been the case. He is a secretive man. I think he was foisted on my father's committee by someone more important. You know how it is in Beijing."

Van Hooten nodded, then walked behind her chair and gently bent over her to kiss her forehead, then her lips. "Nothing changes . . . I love you, my dear. I think we had better get back to the business of running Phuket Color. But first, perhaps we ought to have a sunrise conference in the hammock over there."

Moia smiled for the first time that morning. "Claude, do you still think that is important now?"

"Very much so." He again bent over her and kissed her lips. "We've taken an emotional beating this morning. We've earned the right to feel good again."

Moia stood, letting her robe drop to the deck, sighing at the feel of the cool morning air on her skin, then walked toward the big hammock.

Chapter 36

BRANDON POOLE wondered if he had made a mistake. He had observed the affection Moia Hsu had shown Van Hooten in the box at Happy Valley. It had seemed genuine enough, but there was the matter of Li Pao. If he was a witness and party to the fire in Bangkok, was it possible that Moia had not known of it all along?

It raised the question of whether Moia's father had actually approved the disaster so as to weaken Van Hooten's hand and cause him to put Phuket Color on the market for a panic sale, perhaps to Moia's Chinese interests. Convoluted thinking? Perhaps not. Things like this were now going on in Hong Kong every day. He had heard of nothing quite so barbaric as his scenario, but nevertheless, the People's Republic was pushing its way in to every established level of business management here lately. Perhaps it was only a plot on the part of General Liu.

Brandon Poole pushed away from his desk and stretched. It was now six A.M. and he was tired. But sleep was a luxury he had not been able to afford for some time, relying on catnaps here and there between periods of intense work. He strolled to the window overlooking Victoria Harbor far below. The *Brandon Kowloon Eagle* was riding on a calm surface that mirrored the superstructure of the sophisticated vessel. He could see in duplicate the space-age navigation and communications systems that had been carefully fitted aboard the sleek freighter. It was the finest that money could buy, and that would include the systems aboard the most respected naval ships in the world.

He again glanced at the clock. Cecil Lo would be there in less than a half-hour. He stretched out on the long leather couch, hoping the punctual Lo would not be quite so punctual this morning.

After a fleeting nap, the buzzer sounded. Brandon flipped on the security monitor and the dapper Lo appeared on the screen. The slender investigator seldom looked ruffled, always as if he had stepped off some tailor's pedestal after donning a new suit. Brandon flipped another button and activated the door lock. "Come in, Cecil. You are right on the minute as usual."

Lo entered the office, looking questioningly at Brandon Poole. He stood before him, shirt from the day before hanging over rumpled trousers and a dark beard showing from a day's growth. "Oh my, Brandon. You haven't slept. You should have buzzed me. I could have delayed my visit for a few hours."

"Nonsense, Cecil. Time grows moss over everything. There is no news like fresh news. Now sit down and let me brew us a cup of tea while you talk."

Cecil Lo sat with a rare grin on his face, watching the billionaire deal with the task of bringing water to a boil in a tiny microwave oven located behind the wet bar in his office. "Our general has been distracted by the likes of Mary Lulu. They are to be off to Macau on the noon hydrofoil."

"Perhaps I do need sleep. I'd swear you said that General Liu was to be off to Macau with Mary Lulu."

"No question about it, sir. He sent her a rather lewd proposition written on one of his cards. A perky wait-

ress at the Typhoon Club delivered it to her backstage.
Mary Lulu invited the general into her dressing room,
looked him over and accepted his offer."

"I'll be damned!" Brandon turned from the microwave to face Lo. "That doesn't say much for his loyalty
to the affair of the heart with Moia Hsu, does it?"

"He didn't show much fidelity in Bangkok either. If
he slaps Mary Lulu around like he did that poor prostitute in Bangkok, he might get more than he bargained
for." Lo paused reflectively. "Strange man, General
Liu. His behavior is pretty outlandish for a man of his
standing. I wonder if Beijing knows of his peccadilloes.
Such officers in the People's Army regularly have better public ethics."

Poole nodded in agreement. "But I suppose the
nightlife of Hong Kong and the temptation of Macau
is so much different from the rigidity of life in Beijing
that he can't help himself. He can't be the cream of
the crop anyway. What kind of general would deserve
an assignment like his?"

"I've thought the very same thing, sir. In fact, I think
it would be wise to get to know him a little better. With
your approval, I want to ride that hydrofoil to Macau
with them." He sipped cautiously at the the hot brew
Poole handed him.

"You do exactly that, Cecil. Stick to them like glue.
I would like to get enough on the general to hang him
with the Chinese. If he is here to keep his eye on dissidents, he might well be responsible for Davy Wong's
troubles. Our Royal Hong Kong Police picked him up
last night. Lacy and I saw it ourselves in the night market. The commissioner is working on it. If they turn
him over to the Chinese, there will be hell to pay."

Cecil Lo looked stunned. "They wouldn't dare turn
him over. Half the population of Hong Kong would be
furious." Cecil stood, making ready to leave. "I have a
little packing to do and then I'm off for Bangkok. I'll

keep you posted as soon as they check in somewhere in Macau."

"Be careful, Cecil. If we believe our suspicions, our general could well be a killer."

"I know, sir. I'll be on proper guard." He smiled again as he opened the office door. "Perhaps I'll get a chance to try my luck at the tables. I haven't done that in years down in Macau. Let me know if I can help you with Davy in some way. I still know my way around the department."

As soon as Cecil closed the door, Brandon Poole turned on the world market monitors that covered a large section of the wall next to his desk. New York, Tokyo, London, Singapore, and Hong Kong monitors flashed up-to-date reviews of major stock market activity around the world. Money and commodity trading information was updated as quickly as transactions happened anywhere. He wrapped himself up in a morning routine that usually took him past ten o'clock. He stopped only on this morning to shower and prepare himself for the day, selecting quite casual clothes from the closet in the small suite connecting his office via a mobile panel.

By the time he returned to his office proper, the staff of Brandon Poole Ltd. had taken their places in the complex of offices that took up two floors of the massive bank building. The flashing light told him that a long list of calls to his personal number had accumulated.

There was a call from Davy Wong, obviously made while he was under close surveillance. "Hi Brandon. Sorry. . . . Hope to see you someday."

Brandon placed another call to the commissioner of police, who hadn't yet returned his call as he had promised.

Claude Van Hooten had called. "Brandon, thanks again for all those winners yesterday. I guess I should thank Cecil. Moia and I would like to take you up on the offer for a tour of your new freighter. At your convenience anytime."

We'll just see, thought Brandon, as he pressed Van Hooten's number. "Hello, Claude. I just got your message. Very opportune! I'm meeting a lighter at Fenwick Pier in Wan Chai in forty-five minutes. Can you make it?"

"Just a minute, Brandon." There was long pause at the other end. "You've got a deal. Moia wants to join me."

"Very good, you'll be back in your office shortly after noon. I'll warn the skipper that he'll have a boarding party soon." Brandon Poole hung up, then arose from his desk and stared at the *Kowloon Eagle* in the harbor. He debated with himself about the wisdom of showing Moia Hsu what he wanted Claude Van Hooten to see. Actually, he had no choice. If the woman shared a bedroom with Van Hooten, there would be no secrets anyway.

Poole arrived ten minutes early at the small pier facing north toward Kowloon. A small lighter identified as BRANDON POOLE LTD NO. 267, bumped against the dock, the result of a wake of a passing oiler bound for the outer islands. The harbor seemed especially busy that day. A steady procession of traffic flying the red flag of China made its way toward the mouth of the Pearl River to the north.

The skipper of the small lighter frowned as his vessel lurched against the dock again. "Our good friends up the river would do well to observe the rules of passage through the harbor. Too many of them leave an unpermitted wake."

"You are correct, Captain. Start writing their numbers down and give them to me. It is just a matter of time before some small sampan is swamped, or something worse."

"Yes sir!" the captain responded smartly. He lent a

hand to his legendary boss as he stepped aboard the lighter.

Brandon glanced down the pier and saw Moia Hsu and Claude Van Hooten walking briskly toward them. "Captain, have the aft bench cleared so that our passengers will have some protection from the spray."

While the captain was overseeing that task, Brandon Poole welcomed his guests, extending a hand to ease them aboard. "Welcome, on behalf of the captain. We are rewarded with a beautiful day for this." Brandon led them to the cleared aft bench, where the three of them sat as lines were withdrawn from the pier.

"Brandon, this is a fabulous treat. Our business days seldom include anything so diverting as this." Van Hooten grasped the hand of the smiling Moia as the engine rumbled and the lighter pulled away from the dock.

Within minutes they were approaching the fantail of the huge freighter. They swept close under the foot-high lettering, BRANDON KOWLOON EAGLE, almost directly above them. As they rounded to the port side they could see that a gangway had been lowered. Two uniformed mates stood at attention on the deck awaiting their arrival.

Moia talked excitedly to Van Hooten as they mounted the gangway. She looked over her shoulder to Poole, behind them. "It is so beautiful, just like the movies. I have never been on a big ship like this one."

Poole casually saluted her remark. "She is as swift and sturdy as any vessel afloat. The *Kowloon Eagle* would stand out in any harbor in the world." Brandon ran his eyes fondly along the superstructure and then onto the deck around them.

Moia nudged Claude Van Hooten and whispered in his ear. Van Hooten nodded in agreement to whatever she had said and then looked up to get caught in the steady gaze of his host. "Brandon, Moia just said that when you speak about the *Kowloon Eagle*, it is as if you were speaking of your own child."

"Young lady, you are very observant. I have always had a fondness for all the ships in our fleet. But this one is something special. Come, let me show you."

They followed Brandon Poole up a wide ladder leading from the main deck to a deck that started just beneath the bridge and ran aft almost two hundred feet. Poole entered the first of a long row of doors spaced along the companionway, Moia and Van Hooten following him. "We are on the passenger deck. The staterooms here will match those of the finest cruise ships. We have accommodations for a hundred people on this deck. It is not unusual for freighters to have facilities for a few paying passengers, but none I have ever seen have accommodations like these." Poole swept his arm around the stateroom. A massive king-size bed sat on a classically patterned Chinese silk carpet. There was a dressing table in polished teak and an entertainment center recessed in one bulkhead. A door led to a shower and sunken bath similar to what one might find in the best of hotels.

"On long hauls, the *Kowloon Eagle* will include some passengers willing to pay the price. But most of the facilities will be used by guests of Brandon Poole Ltd. wherever in the world we might be. There is a gym, a recreation room, and a captain's dining room to accommodate our passengers and guests. We have about four thousand employees worldwide, and I fully intend this vessel to be a source of restful relaxation for many of them over the coming years."

Poole led them quickly down another ladder penetrating several decks, and opened the door to one of several cargo holds. It was immaculately clean, about half the size of a football field in length, with massive doors in the overhead which slid open at the touch of a button on the control panel. "We will carry clean cargo, much of it highly specialized electronic equipment."

Thus far, for Van Hooten and Moia, it was an interesting show. The vessel was indeed spectacular and perhaps worth their trip as a curiosity. But up to now they had seen nothing that seemed to merit Brandon's insistence that they take time out to tour the *Kowloon Eagle*.

He took them down a passageway that ended at a closed door approximately amidships of the huge freighter. Inside was a large office that could accommodate perhaps twenty-five people. Scores of monitors along the wall were lit with the same information that filled those in Brandon Poole's office ashore.

"Look carefully at what you see, my friends. This is the beating heart of Brandon Poole Ltd. It is, in effect, our world headquarters. We may shift to the Andaman Islands, Grand Cayman, London, New York, or even to Shanghai to be near our new construction site. But this vessel is as much the headquarters of Brandon Poole Ltd. as is the office space in Hong Kong. I compare it to a cocoon, a life-support system for our worldwide enterprises."

"It's magnificent, Brandon." Van Hooten was taking in every nook and corner of the command center. "What flag will she sail under?"

"Right now she sails under British registry." Poole grinned at his guests.

"And in 1997?" pressured Van Hooten.

"Can you name a port in the world that would refuse entry to this vessel and all it stands for?"

"I distinctly feel that the *Kowloon Eagle* will still be gracing Victoria Harbor at the turn of the century," Van Hooten declared.

"Bravo, Claude. Well put. I think we ought to drink to that. Let's go up to the aft deck. I think they have prepared a bit of midday libation there. Moia, does

Claude always have such an uncanny knack of predicting the future?"

Moia smiled at their host. "Always. That is why he is so successful in the fashion and style business. He can predict what people will be wearing before they have an inkling of it themselves. There are many kinds of genius in our world, Mr. Poole."

Van Hooten began chuckling aloud as they approached the table set for them on the aft deck. "Brandon, what if someone decided to join your firm and turned out to be habitually seasick?"

Poole saw Moia narrow her eyes and look soberly at Van Hooten as he finished his question. "Not very likely, is it, Claude? Not aboard a ship that stays snug in some harbor as often as I intend this one to."

"Brandon, how about Bali, or Tahiti, or some such place? All those monitors below deck would bring the world to your door." Van Hooten smiled easily, sipping at a sherry at this idyllic moment in Victoria Harbor.

"It could be done, Claude! In this cyber age it could be done. Moia, can you see yourself administrating for Phuket Color in such surroundings?" Brandon asked, thinking how perfectly civil she was toward him today, after yesterday's to-do.

She shook her head, smiling at the two men. "Not really. I think that would be mixing too much pleasure with business. I am a big-city person at heart."

"Well, on that note I will let you people get back to work. I just wanted you to see some of the inner workings of Brandon Poole Ltd."

The three of them sipped at the tea and sherry, and nibbled at the cakes that the steward had provided. Several minutes passed before Brandon led them back to the lighter for transport to Central District.

"Thank you for coming. I'll be staying aboard for a while." Poole caught Moia's eyes before he spoke again. "By the way, I suppose you've heard that our Royal Police picked up Davy Wong last night in the night market. Davy is a dear friend. I'm hoping that our police don't do something silly, like turn him over to the mainlanders.''

Moia commented quickly. "I hope not! Davy Wong is a brave man. Everyone knows how he tried to save lives at Tiananmen Square. I had not heard of this until now. He has lots of friends in China as in Hong Kong."

"It is good to hear you say that, Moia. It gives me reason to hope. In fact, if you feel that way, there is hope. I won't worry about Davy so much." Brandon Poole watched them until they had boarded the lighter below, much impressed with Moia's straightforward reply. For an important Beijing woman, she was walking a narrow path. She was quite gutsy. No question about it, Van Hooten had himself a jewel in Moia Hsu.

Poole returned alone to the aft deck, pacing quietly as he savored the aura of his beloved Hong Kong which surrounded him as he stood alone on the freighter. His eyes now drifted from his villa on the Peak and focused on the Macau ferry terminal to the north. He looked at his watch. He smiled. That would be the noon hydrofoil to Macau, he thought, as he watched the sleek ferry pull away from the dock. Its untypical passengers included Cecil Lo, Mary Lulu, the racy blond rocker from New York, and her oddball companion, who purported to be a general of the People's Liberation Army.

Or *were* they untypical? He wondered about all the others on the hydrofoil, all so eager to dump their hard-earned money on the tables and hungry gaming machines of Macau. If only a few of the other passengers were anything like the three that he knew, Macau could be a very exciting place this evening.

Chapter 37

⊛

FROM HIS vantage point at a window seat on the Macau hydrofoil, Cecil Lo was perhaps a quarter of a mile from the *Kowloon Eagle*. He had watched the threesome sitting at the small table set on the elevated aft deck. He took the tiny roof prism binoculars from his pocket and smiled as he identified the faces of Brandon Poole, Moia, and Van Hooten.

The foxy Poole was no doubt working them over, making them feel at home with Brandon Poole Ltd. He was a master at such negotiations. Phuket Color would fall into his lap like a ripe plum one day soon. He would bet on it. Not that they would not be paid deservedly well for it. But it would no longer belong to Van Hooten. He had watched Poole gobble up company after company so adeptly that it would have put the taipans of old to shame.

He watched as Brandon escorted the couple back to the lighter. Even from his distance it had all seemed very chummy. The lighter now vanished from view behind the freighter, probably returning the couple to the pier at Fenwick Street. He tucked his binoculars away and cast a glance forward through his dark sunglasses into the passenger cabin of the hydrofoil.

Liu Wing had his arm loosely around the shoulders of Mary Lulu, pointing off into the distance toward Shenzhen in the People's Republic. Lo imagined that he was telling her that his homeland was only a few miles away, probably offering to take her there. But who would really want to go to Shenzhen? The tall buildings, from this distance, made it look deceptively like Hong Kong.

The hydrofoil now rose to full plane, skimming along the northern coast of Hong Kong Island. Even though Macau was perhaps forty miles away across this arm of the South China Sea, going there was much like being on a busy highway. The hydrofoil zipped easily past all the other ferries and boats that lined up to follow the well-marked course from buoy to buoy.

Mary Lulu, he observed, was almost as tall as the general. Their faces were on the same level when they talked to each other. Without theatrical makeup, she still turned heads among the other passengers. She wore form-fitting slacks and a dark, low-neck sweater that would have been more appropriate for evening wear. The general had a habit of touching her when he talked, even brushing her cheek with his fingertips now and then. She didn't seem to mind.

He glanced around at the other passengers. They were mostly Chinese. One large group, because of their austere dress, he guessed was from the People's Republic. A very few tourists, probably Americans or Australians, completed the passenger list for the noon run to Macau. Lo busied himself with a copy of the *Morning Post*. One short bulletin carried the story that a number of people were being routinely questioned by the Royal Hong Kong Police about a recent homicide near Tsuen Wan.

Included in the questioning was Davy Wong, noted political activist, who was purported to have information on the crime. Lo felt irate with disgust. Davy Wong had bigger fish to fry than the Sha Tin pickpocket. He suspected that Brandon Poole would take this atrocity all the way to the governor. He'd better hurry, thought Lo. Davy could be spirited away on the train to Lo Wu in a matter of hours.

Cecil Lo looked up from his newspaper. The general and Mary Lulu were now engaged in an intense conversation. Practically cheek to cheek, Liu was explaining something in great detail using his hands and fingers to emphasize some point. She was spellbound, and with no expression whatever on her face for the longest time, she burst into laughter, suppressed it with a hand in front of her mouth, then grasped the general's hand and kissed it.

Lo was amazed. Whatever else the evil general did, he seemed to have a way of captivating women. Quite a knack, he thought, to be able to do that. In comparison, his own life had been almost that of a monk. He could never quite discover why it was so many attractive women were driven to scoundrels.

The big hydrofoil skimmed the wavetops with scarcely a motion, moving at high speed between the ominous boulders that jutted from the water in that part of the South China Sea, which stretched from the western tip of Hong Kong Island to the shoreline of the People's Republic.

By the time Lo finished his tea and the paper, they were already slowing down. The hydrofoil dropped off its plane and rumbled slowly into the harbor of Macau. The pesky customs procedure in Macau would take perhaps a half-hour, so Lo prepared to exit the ferry long before Liu and Mary Lulu. He would secure a taxicab for the day and wait for the pair on the other side. Perhaps one virtue of Hong Kong becoming part of the People's Republic would be the elimination of all the red tape getting in and out of Macau. In these days the Portuguese really had little to do with Macau, so it should be possible.

Liu and his leggy companion piled into a cab and

became engulfed in each other's arms almost at once. His own driver was able to follow them easily in the light traffic. Quite predictably, they headed straight for the Villa Nova. The big hotel sat at the tip of Macau near the causeway to the island of Taipa, and housed one of the more elaborate gambling casinos in Macau.

Cecil Lo was getting excited. He was hoping that they would defer their bedroom activity until evening. He wanted to witness how they handled the casino. After all, he made his living by making a study of people. Bedroom doors were quite an obstacle.

No such luck. The pair retired to their suite and stayed there for hours. Lo decided it was time to do a little eavesdropping before calling Brandon in Hong Kong. The times in years past that he had squandered in Macau were about to pay off.

Felix Chen had worked with the security staff of the hotel for many years. The slender man grinned broadly when Lo asked him about the tall blonde and her escort. "Oh yes, she is quite something. Our staff has been fighting among themselves for the right to service their suite. Such a woman is like a small typhoon spinning her way through Macau."

Lo unsheathed the impressive wad of Brandon's money from his pocket just far enough so his old friend Chen could see it. "I would very much like to do a walk-by of their quarters. It is my job to see that she comes to no harm."

Chen nodded toward the entrance of the hotel and began walking. He didn't speak until they were outside in the blazing afternoon sun. "I am afraid that it is not possible to do that. Security monitors the halls with video cameras. It would be impossible to loiter there. Such a young lady and her friend deserve privacy."

Lo watched Chen's eyes drop to the pair of thousand-dollar Hong Kong notes he held in his hand. Working with the inexhaustible resources of Brandon Poole had always been a shortcut to inspire creativity in people. Macau was really not much different from Hong Kong these days. Selling information was a popular business that required no office expense or inventory maintenance.

"I have an idea," Chen offered brightly. "Perhaps you would like to stay in the hotel sometime. One of our finest suites is available. Come, let me show you should you be impelled to spend your holiday here."

Chen led Lo to the elevator and then into a corner suite on a high floor overlooking the causeway and Taipa in the distance. He put his finger to his lips and walked gingerly toward a closed door that led to an adjoining suite. Loud voices emerged from behind the door. An argument, a serious argument, was taking place, punctuated now and then by a slapping sound, almost assuredly that of leather on flesh.

Cecil Lo sank silently to the carpet and carefully placed his ear next to the seam of the closed door. Chen sat cross-legged next to him, head bent down. In the total silence, they were able to make out most of the spoken words that wafted from the adjoining room.

Another loud slapping noise came from the room. There was a short squeal of pain. "Okay, okay. That is enough. You win, my general. But how can I please you if you don't turn me loose?" There was another slapping sound. "You bastard! Look at what you've done. You've left a mark on my leg. Is that the chivalry you are taught? You've seen me perform. Would you like such a flaw in your performer?"

"Be silent! The walls may have ears here. Relax, I am in charge. I know what you capitalist bitches all want. I have read books about your decadence."

"Oh my God! I'll bet you have," came the muffled retort from Mary Lulu. And then there was silence, except for occasional sounds of movement, but no spoken words.

Lo thought back to the bruised Natasha in Bangkok. Impresario Sean Xiang had paid handsomely to bring

Mary Lulu to Hong Kong. Sean was, of course, an old friend of Brandon's. Lo made up his mind to call Brandon Poole immediately. His friend's valuable property could soon be damaged goods. "Felix, my friend," he whispered. "I have heard enough. I must call Hong Kong."

Felix Chen nodded. "Come, we'll go to my office."

Then, before they could stand up from their eavesdropping position, a loud masculine howl of pain came from the room, followed a couple of seconds later by footsteps and the slamming of a door.

When they peeked outside, Mary Lulu was walking swiftly down the hall toward the elevator, fussing with the belt of one of those terry cloth robes furnished by the hotel, trying to conceal her nudity. Apparently that was all she wore.

"Good!" mumbled Lo. "Funny thing, Chen. I knew that this one was a fighter."

Chen put his finger to his lips, urging silence. There was a gasp and then groan from the adjoining room and then heavy footsteps. "Well, at least she didn't kill him. Perhaps it was just a lovers' spat," he whispered.

Lo nodded, his thoughts returning to Mary Lulu marching toward the elevator in the hallway. "Where do you suppose she went?"

"Probably to the recreation area. She could relax there for a while dressed that way, or perhaps to one of the shops near the lobby to buy some clothing. Who knows what such a woman will do?"

"She is a woman of means," assured Lo, "an American entertainer. Please, let us go, I must use your telephone."

Brandon Poole answered his private line in Hong Kong on the first ring.

"I'm afraid our entertainer is getting herself in big trouble, Mr. Poole. She and the general had a big fight in their suite."

"Who won?"

"I think Miss Lulu did. She ran down the hall in a bathrobe. He is in pain. He is moaning in his room. I think she bit him or kicked him in the you-know-where."

There was a long pause in Hong Kong. "How do you know all this?"

"I found an old friend here. He helped me listen. I think Miss Lulu herself may be hurt."

"Thanks for the information, Lo. I will call Sean Xiang. He has a large investment in her. Keep me posted. Sean may want to intervene. I think he would not be intimidated by the general."

When Brandon Poole hung up the telephone, he debated with himself the wisdom of calling Sean Xiang. Sean was not a great favorite in Beijing. The nature of the entertainment Xiang imported to Hong Kong was held in low esteem. The stimulating and suggestive artists brought from the United States were considered irreverent to the point of moral contamination.

If Mary Lulu was so unstable as to become involved with Liu Wing, he wondered if Sean Xiang *would* intervene. Spending favors now due from Beijing shouldn't be used to achieve minor victories. He decided he would tell his friend what he knew and then wash his hands of the matter.

Brandon reached again for the phone and then hesitated. The thought had been recurring to him that his telephone line might somehow be tapped, despite all the assurances he had from his security experts. He decided to call anyway.

"Hello, you old dog, how've you been? Just wanted to remind you of our handball date."

"Handball? Oh yes! It's a good thing you called. I didn't write it on my schedule."

"You just know you're going to lose. See you in a few minutes."

"You betcha!" Sean replied with so much gusto that

anyone would have believed that they really had a handball date, when in fact they hadn't played in years.

Brandon arrived at the athletic club in a matter of minutes. Sean had a farther distance to come, so he picked up a copy of the *Morning Post* and sat in an alcove of the mossy old club to wait for him.

The paper was playing up a big story about the construction of the new twenty-billion-dollar airport for Hong Kong, now running behind schedule. Completion of Chek Lap Kok International Airport off Lantau would not happen until spring 1998, long after the lowering of the flag. Apparently the new flight path coincided with the Castle Peak Weapons Range, a military facility long used by the British in western New Territories. As a solution, the Chinese were asking that a new facility be built at British expense to accommodate the People's Liberation Army after the takeover in 1997.

Interesting, thought Poole. This was a matter that should have been taken care of years ago. It could be interpreted by the Chinese that the governor was dragging his feet toward the transition. It was another sign that the fateful year was approaching without many of the major problems being addressed. He pushed the newspaper aside as the energetic Sean Xiang approached.

"There you are, ready for battle." Sean slashed his palm through the air in mock handball play, grinning broadly at the stoic Brandon Poole.

Poole pointed toward a chair next to him. "Sorry, Sean, but I thought it best to talk in person. One of your investments is acting crazy. How much do you have committed to Mary Lulu?"

"Mary Lulu! Of all the things I expected you to talk about, it wouldn't be Mary Lulu." Then his jovial face grew dark. "Lots of dollars for me, Brandon. Up front. She pulls down big bucks, as they say in America."

"I think she has fallen into bad hands. An alleged

general of the People's Liberation Army has taken her on holiday, and is apparently treating her like a common whore down in Macau. Unless you can get her back into Hong Kong quickly, my informant says she may not be fit for star billing."

Sean, usually overflowing with high spirits, suddenly became morose. He listened intently as Brandon fed him the details given him by Lo. He looked at his watch. "Damn it, Brandon, I'll have to get the next hydrofoil. I'm afraid I have little good to say about the communists. But if this fellow is a general, his superiors would not approve such high-profile shenanigans. I have to get the facts quickly."

"How do you propose to find her?"

"One thing about Mary Lulu, Brandon. She is not hard to find. Perhaps your man can point the way for me."

"That much can be arranged." Brandon spoke slowly, not comfortable with Lo getting directly involved. "You must understand, Sean, that I am at present seeking important concessions from the communists. I cannot afford to go public on this matter and will deny knowledge of it if I am asked."

"Brandon, we understand each other. That is the way it has always been." The broad smile returned to Sean Xiang's face. "I must be on my way now. Thank you, Brandon. I hope our next visit is more pleasant."

Poole watched as Sean gave him an enthusiastic thumbs-up and watched him walk rapidly to the door of the athletic club.

When Brandon returned to his office, there was a message from the office of the police commissioner. It stated only that Davy Wong would be released within a matter of hours, and that he was no longer implicated in the slaying in Tsuen Wan. Poole felt a rush of relief, which was short lived and replaced by a vague uneasiness. The release had come too easily. It was not typical of the drawn-out, face-saving negotiations that were usually required.

Poole's private line winked its bright flashing light at him.

"Brandon, it's me!"

Poole recognized the exuberant voice of Davy Wong instantly and heaved a sigh of relief. "Davy, you are free. How wonderful! I want to see you."

"It will take some time, Brandon. They released me near Lo Wu."

"Lo Wu!" Poole exclaimed, picturing in his mind the bridge across the Sham Chun River at Lo Wu, which led to the People's Republic on the other side. "I was hoping to see you here in Central District by now."

"I have no idea why they released me here, Brandon. They know I live in Wan Chai. But let's face it. I'll take my freedom anywhere I can get it." Davy chuckled before speaking again. "I will see you in about an hour. We'll talk more then."

"Are you sure you are all right?" asked Poole after a pause.

"I am fine, Brandon. Perhaps they thought the sight of my homeland across the river would be tempting. It is funny, Brandon, isn't it?"

"Davy, put some distance between yourself and Lo Wu as quickly as you can. I won't budge until I see you here."

A feeling of helplessness swept Brandon Poole when he hung up the phone. He felt that Davy Wong would be released in the remote countryside for just one reason. That immediate area was beyond a boundary that was technically closed, though in recent times enforcement had been lax. He stared at the clock. The next hour would tell the story. Already the big second hand had swept around the dial, and Davy Wong was still near Lo Wu.

Chapter 38

Davy Wong decided to make his way through the remote New Territories countryside toward Sha Ling, where a much-traveled road would give him an opportunity to find transportation to Kowloon in the south. There was little doubt in his mind why he had been given his "freedom" so near his native land. The main road and the rail line southward would be heavily patrolled by communist observers. He was convinced that the expected route would end his freedom abruptly with his capture.

At the first opportunity he plunged into the dense underbrush of a ravine which led toward a stand of trees on a hillside a kilometer to the east. Now and then he stopped and listened to the silence around him. Satisfied that he had not been followed, he broke into a trot, crashing through the underbrush toward his selected haven on the hillside.

There was a narrow meadow now between him and the grove. He walked slowly through the tall grass, trying his best not to alert distant binoculars that might be searching. At last he reached the sheltering grove.

He heard the slam of a bolt inserting a bullet into the chamber of a rifle. He stood gasping as he felt the barrel of another prodding him in the back.

"Davy Wong, what are you doing way out here in the woods? Freeze! Do not move!"

He was grabbed roughly by several others, hand-cuffed, and led to a dusty old Mazda van hidden in the grove. From there, with five others packed into the small van with him, they roared full speed down the road to Man Kam To where they sped through a deserted checkpoint into the People's Republic of China. Davy Wong was home again.

Back in Hong Kong, Brandon Poole had watched the hands sweep around the dial, marking three hours since the call from Lo Wu. He leaned back in his chair and sighed heavily. It was growing dark outside. Davy should have been there long ago. Giving him his freedom in the loosely patrolled border area had to have been a planned event. Who in Hong Kong could have been bribed to do that? he wondered, and then answered his own question aloud. "Any of a thousand who might need a favor from Beijing."

Chapter 39

SEAN XIANG entered the hotel in Macau and was confronted by Cecil Lo almost immediately upon entering the casino. "Sean, you made it here quickly. I didn't expect you for another hour. Please sit down with me over here for a few moments." Lo motioned toward a couch in the vestibule of the casino.

Sean studied the aging detective. He had a good reputation around Hong Kong, not specifically for any of his personal accomplishments, but for the mere fact that he was known to be a long-time insider in Brandon Poole's complicated empire. "Cecil, Brandon sends his regards. I left him only a few hours ago. I was fortunate enough to catch the next hydrofoil just as it was leaving the dock. So what can you tell me about my fair lady?"

"Fair lady?" Cecil Lo grinned at the unlikely description of Mary Lulu. "She is in her quarters. About an hour ago a doctor left her. I am told she is in fine condition, except for a few bruises here and there. Of course in her act at the Typhoon Club the here and there is quite visible."

"Is this general with her?"

"Oh heavens, no. He left the hotel shortly after their to-do in her suite. He looked positively ashen. I believe

he walked with a slight limp that I did not notice before."

"Really! Bully for Mary Lulu! Sounds like she won
the fight. Do you suppose the general went back to
Hong Kong?"

"He took a cab to the ferry terminal. I think he was
quite anxious to leave Macau. Your star was making
noises about calling the police. By now I think perhaps
she has."

Sean smiled. "She's a tough cookie. She's a tall
woman, in fine athletic condition. I wouldn't want to
take her on ... in a fight," he quickly added. "Well,
let's see if she'll let me in to see her. Hang around,
Cecil, and I'll bring you up-to-date."

Lo nodded as Sean left to seek out a house phone.
He was a little puzzled by his lack of interest in pursuing the general. If local police would question him,
they might find out a little more about him. Like, for
instance, what he was really doing in Hong Kong and
Macau. Of course, Sean was a businessman who no
doubt wanted to assess the damage to his star entertainer first.

Mary Lulu opened the door to the length of the security chain. "Are you alone, Sean?"

"Yes, of course. Are you okay?"

She released the security chain and opened the door
wide. As Sean entered her suite, she threw her arms
around him and held him tightly. "Oh Sean, I was such
a fool. All along I knew he was a bastard. I guess I just
thought that a general in anyone's army would be more
of a gentleman. As soon as we were alone he became
an animal."

Sean kept his arms around her until she began to
relax. "Are you okay?"

"Look." She opened the short robe to permit his
inspection. There was a small bruise on her breast and

another larger one on her thigh. "That pig! The doctor said they will look worse tomorrow."

"You are very lucky. Some men feel that they are a gift for a beautiful woman, and will not be denied."

"Ah, but look." Mary Lulu walked over to the bed and threw back the covers. Smiling triumphantly, she pointed to the ample blots of blood on the sheets. "He won't be making love to anyone for a while."

"What have you done?" asked Sean as he stared at the sheet.

"I bit him! I had to, Sean. He was very strong. He would have beaten me to a pulp. It gave me time to jump up and leave the room."

"That was quick thinking." Sean looked at her beautiful blue eyes, trying to suppress a smile. "Did you report him to anyone?"

"Yes, to the hotel security. They will not let him enter the premises again."

"I think you had better return to Hong Kong with me. They will probably report it to the Macau police, who may take the matter up with the Chinese, since he is apparently a general."

"Oh Sean, I have been so bad. You are so understanding. At first he excited me. He was just so different."

Sean stepped back when she thought she was about to kiss him. "I'm a little surprised, Mary. You Americans confuse me sometimes. What would your friend Chad Grissom think of all this?" Then quickly he added, "I'm sorry, I guess that is none of my business."

Mary laughed aloud. "Chad Grissom! He does not like the ladies at all. He and I are just a publicity thing."

"Really? I had no idea. I would have kept a closer eye on you. I guess I just felt that he was sort of looking after you."

"Sean, will you wait until I get dressed? I would like to go back to Hong Kong with you. I don't want to explore Macau. Maybe some other time, but not to-day."

"That's very smart, Mary." He gaped at her flawless body as she dropped her robe, preparing to dress for the trip back to Hong Kong. "Before you return to America, I promise you I will show you the sights of Macau."

"And I will insist that you keep that promise."

Sean Xiang sat down in a chair to wait for her, won-dering about the powerful attraction the beautiful en-tertainer held for him. For a fleeting second he thought of spending the night with her in Macau. But the thought of the escapade she had had with the general was too much to push from his mind.

Chapter 40

LACY LOCKE pulled the drapes wide and stared at Kowloon across Victoria Harbor. The early morning sun cast long shadows, bathing Hong Kong in a light totally different than she had seen before. The sunlight dimmed in the far west where New Territories merged in an appropriate gray haze of the People's Republic. Brandon Poole had called the Mandarin, rousing her at the break of day.

He knew it was a terrible inconvenience, he had said, but something urgent had come up and he needed her input. Not fully awake, she had promised to meet him at his office within an hour.

Now she was having second thoughts. His car and driver would be here in forty minutes and she was moving about as if she had all day. Since the night when he had popped the incredible proposition that she have his son, she had busied herself with other business in Hong Kong, hoping that his unexpected ardor would cool. Despite all this, she was unable to muster the words to refuse his sunrise invitation. She wondered if anyone really got away with saying no to Brandon Poole.

His driver, not Cecil Lo to her surprise, was right on

the minute. The huge bank building was not yet open to the morning rush. Getting to Poole's office involved signing in and getting his approval before being escorted to an elevator.

Poole, coatless but in white shirt and tie, met her in the office anteroom. "Lacy, you look magnificent this morning, but then you always do."

He squeezed her hand firmly, but much to her pleasant surprise he did not give her the casual kiss that she had learned to expect. "Brandon, I must warn you that I am still half asleep, and if I truly look magnificent it is just dumb luck. Thanks anyway."

"Lacy, I have some tea and some coffee brewing in my office. We'll soon get you wide awake. I desperately need your brains this morning."

"I'll do my best, Brandon. I warn you, morning is not my best time." She sat in a leather chair next to a coffee table set with a tea service. Despite the fact that it was her brains that interested him this morning, she couldn't help notice his eyes sweep over her as he sat on another chair across the table. The rather severe black dress she had put on in haste was stylishly short as was the office mode in Hong Kong these days, but its brevity made it impossible to hide her legs with maximum modesty. She wondered if their business relationship would ever be quite normal after his startling proposition on their last meeting.

Poole sipped at his tea, put the cup down gently and wrung his hands together as he started to speak. As usual, his gray-blue eyes locked on her own when he spoke, with only a rare blink or side glance.

"Lacy, some people in this life mean a lot more to me than other people. Oh, perhaps there may be a dozen. They are people that have played the game squarely with me and over the years have formed a meaningful bond. There is an unspoken reciprocity of respect." Brandon Poole paused and broke his steady gaze for a moment to stare out the window.

Lacy decided not to speak, preferring to wait until he found his own words. She nodded slightly and sipped her tea. Certainly the man must be trying to say something important, having brought her to his office at this hour.

"Davy Wong is such a person." Brandon Poole spoke softly, his eyes again riveted on her own.

Lacy sighed. Actually it was a sigh of relief, but Brandon wouldn't know that. She was relieved to find that he hadn't brought her there at this hour to pursue his personal feeling for her. "Davy Wong?" she questioned and then remembered the phone call he had made on Nathan Road. "Oh yes! Davy Wong, the man we saw struggling in the night market."

"That's the man, Lacy, that's the man. The Royal Hong Kong Police jailed him that night on some trumped-up charges. I've done my damnedest to get him released ever since then, and yesterday afternoon they released him."

"That's wonderful, Brandon!"

"Wrong, Lacy. Something terrible has happened and maybe you can help." Poole rose from his chair, walked over to a computer printer and picked up several papers. "Here, Lacy, take a look."

One by one, Lacy read through the news bulletins datelined that very morning from Beijing. Davy Wong had been picked up, supposedly in Shenzhen, after entering the People's Republic illegally. Wong was identified as an enemy of the People's Republic, wanted for planning rebellion against the state, and for lying to the Western press about events during the Tiananmen Square incident in 1989. One of the reports stated that there were at least twelve charges pending against Wong that were punishable by death or lengthy prison terms, and that he would face trial for his crimes within a few days.

"Brandon, this is terrible. Your friend is in big trouble. Is any of this true?"

"Davy's only crime was telling the truth. He was one of the more vocal dissidents before the Tiananmen massacre. Since then he has been active getting a handful of his friends out of the People's Republic. Now he has got himself in a bind, trying to help others."

"You say I can help. How can I possibly help? First of all, why would he cross the border? I thought he was being held by the Hong Kong police."

"He was, but they released him. I, among others, went to bat for him. Davy is very popular in Hong Kong. He called me yesterday afternoon. The police freed him near Lo Wu, up near the border of Shenzhen. It is a dangerous area. No doubt he was abducted and taken across the border. It is rather easy to do these days. Davy is a brave man but he would never cross that border voluntarily."

Lacy shook her head. "Brandon, how in the world can I possibly help?"

"Your husband, Adam Locke, is a television news anchor in New York, right?"

"Of course. Adam . . . reads the news. Aha! I get the drift. You want Adam to tell the world about Davy Wong." Lacy paused. Her thoughts went back to her last phone conversation with Adam. She had reluctantly persuaded him to run a news story for her about the financial climate of Hong Kong in these days. He had agreed, but she hadn't sent him the story yet. "Brandon, all the wire services are here in Hong Kong. Why don't you just give the story to them?"

"I will. But if Adam Locke could pop the story as an exclusive in New York first, all the other news media would pound on their representatives out here to follow up. Sometimes Beijing will respond to excessive pressure, especially when they want something, like help in building their roads and dams."

Lacy turned her hands upward and shrugged. "I don't know, Brandon, I just don't know. I'm afraid Adam and I have not been very close lately. Our arrangement has always been that he does his work and I do mine. I spoke to Adam a few days ago about doing a story on the financial state of Hong Kong. He was so cool toward the idea that I have not yet followed it up."

"My dear, this is a story of heroic proportion. Davy Wong is a saint. His life the past few years has been selfless, totally wrapped up in securing freedom for those who deserve it. His seizure could be disastrous for him. Beijing will have to believe the world is watching or he will wind up in an obscure prison within days." Poole rose from his chair and started to pace slowly around the office as he talked. "This can be blown up as a news story of major international interest if it is handled quickly."

Lacy sat quietly, trying to figure out the best way to approach Adam. "Brandon, I will try. I know very little about the history of Davy Wong other than what you have told me. Can you have a release drawn up as you feel it should be presented?"

Poole walked quickly to his desk and picked up several typewritten pages. He turned to her, beaming with satisfaction. "I just happen to have it all prepared. It would be nice if it were to be used without substantial alteration." He handed the pages to Lacy and stood at her shoulder as she read them.

Finally she nodded her head enthusiastically. "Brandon, I think it is dynamite. Promise me that you will give Adam a few hours' exclusivity before you release it here in Hong Kong." She looked at the big clock on the wall. "Right now is the best time to call Adam. I should catch him in New York just before bedtime."

Poole pointed to a phone on his desk. "Be my guest. Line seven is a special rig to the United States. It should be as secure as any."

Lacy rose and walked over to the huge desk, much aware of Poole's scrutiny with every step. Here she was, getting involved in the politics of Hong Kong. She was sure that this would be a no-no when New World-wide Securities became aware of her active part in breaking the story. The mental picture of Davy Wong on the pavement, struggling with the police in the night market, was still vivid in her mind. Who better to vouch for him than Brandon Poole?

"Hello, Adam, were you asleep?" She could hear movement and mumbling at the other end.

"No, of course not. Just wanted to shut down the TV so I could hear better. How's Hong Kong?"

"Exciting, Adam. Lots of hard work. I still haven't had time to play tourist." There it was again, a voice in the background. "Who is there with you, Adam?"

"No one, honey, it must be a bad connection. When are you coming home?"

"When I'm finished. I can't tell yet." She noticed the connection was perfectly clear. "Adam, will you go to your den and activate the recorder. I want to read a news story. It must break in the morning. Remember, I told you I would have something. This is very big." There was a pause for several seconds.

"Hi, I just hit the switch, fire away." Lacy proceeded to read the press release that Brandon had prepared, word for word. "Okay, I got it. Hey, this is big. I'll get the staff to polish it up in the morning. Where'd you get this?"

"Beijing released a bare-bones report this morning. My story has all the background. Play it number one, Adam. You'll have a scoop. Don't let the staff fool with it. Read it as is, Adam."

"How do I verify?"

Lacy groaned. A break like this and Adam was trying to cover his wimpy tail. "Just tell them it is an un-impeachable source, Adam!" Lacy found herself shouting into the phone. "Adam, do you consider your wife an unimpeachable source?"

"Of course. Why do you sound so belligerent, Lacy?"

"Figure it out, Adam. A very brave person is in danger. You can help by making this number one in the morning. The other networks will jump right on it. So just read the news and don't worry so much about covering your ass. You'll be a hero." There the noise was again. There was someone humming in the background. "Who was that, Adam?"

A pause and then complete silence for a couple of seconds. "Who was what, Lacy? I can't hear it at this end. Hey, Lacy, it's a great story. I'll lead with it, for sure."

"Thanks, Adam. Call me tomorrow about this time, when you're alone." She hung up abruptly, stared at the phone and then looked across the room at Brandon Poole.

"So? Will he break the story in the morning in New York?"

"Yes."

"You don't sound very happy. Everything okay at home?"

Lacy smiled, then shrugged. "Everything is peachy. Adam has trouble getting his wits together after a hard day's work. I usually call him earlier in the morning from Hong Kong, because it is nighttime in New York and he is home from the station." She rose from the desk and walked over to the window overlooking the Peak. I wonder who was humming little ditties in the background, she thought. "I hope it helps Davy Wong, Brandon. It seems to mean a lot to you."

Brandon Poole got up from his chair and walked over to stand behind her at the window. "How do you like my Hong Kong in the morning? I like to stand here much earlier and watch it come alive. Look at the traffic. It's getting intolerable. We need more roads, tunnels, and bridges. So there is yet lots more money to be made for Brandon Poole Ltd. I suppose that is why I want to stay, Lacy. Hong Kong is really not totally constructed yet and I am just bull-headed enough to believe that the Chinese can't do it without me."

She felt his arms encircle her gently, as their eyes followed the wake of a junk in full sail, flying the red flag of China as it made its way north in the fresh morning breeze. "Brandon, it is beautiful. I understand why you want to stay a part of all this."

"Do you? Then perhaps you might even understand the little question I put to you the last time we were together." He paused and continued to hold her loosely.

"Yes, I understand, Brandon."

"Have you given it some thought?"

"Of course. You could hardly expect a woman not to give such a question some thought."

"And?"

"Your question is preposterous, but I still think about it." She felt warm and flushed and realized that Poole's casual embrace pleased her greatly. She moved quickly away from his loose grasp and turned to face a faint smile on his ruggedly handsome face. "But right now, I am thinking about breakfast. Will your busy schedule allow you to join me at the Mandarin?"

"Absolutely! The queen herself couldn't make me refuse such an invitation."

Chapter 41

GENERAL LIU winced with discomfort in his seat on a regularly scheduled Dragon Air flight from Hong Kong to Beijing. He had shunned all efforts of flight attendants to serve him anything during the entire flight. The two-and-a-half-hour flight seemed interminable to him. Finally they touched down at Beijing International Airport, made more somber than usual by a gray, drizzly day. The jet had parked some distance from the terminal, and passengers filed down an exit ramp to waiting buses on the tarmac. Unexpectedly, General Wing faced a quartet of military guards at the bottom of the ramp. One of them stepped forward.

"Please sir, you are to come with us."

Liu stood motionless in the rain for a moment and stared at the group, not expecting such a welcome. "That won't be necessary, I have my own plans, thank you." When he made a move to pass them, one stepped in front of him and handed him an envelope.

He quickly ripped it open and read the note inside, signed by General Chan, a judicial officer in the Liberation Army. "What's this all about?"

The young officer shook his head. "I don't know, sir. You are to come with us." Reluctantly, Liu piled into a limousine and was wedged in the middle of the rear seat between two of his escorts. Without further conversation he was driven to General Chan's office just west of Tiananmen Square.

Liu knew the name of the general well. He was noted for his unrelenting pursuit of officers of the People's Liberation Army who had abused or misused their command. His welcoming committee seated him in the anteroom to Chan's office and then left him alone. The door was left ajar so he could still see one of the group standing guard outside.

The small, austere anteroom did little to provide comfort to those who waited. Four straight-back wooden chairs and a small table with nothing on it made up the total furnishings. On the wall was a portrait of Deng Xiaoping and another featuring a group of officers, none of whom Liu could recognize.

Liu twisted uncomfortably on the hard wooden chair. The injury to his scrotum inflicted by the American entertainer made comfort impossible. It had been his intention to go immediately to a personal physician once he had landed.

The door to the general's office opened, and a short barrel-chested man wearing a fatigue uniform without insignia walked out. He scrutinized Liu from head to toe for a moment before speaking. "I am General Chan. You are to come in."

He closed the door behind them, pointed to a chair, then went behind his desk and sat down. Liu crossed his legs and tried to get comfortable.

"You are in pain, General Liu?"

"Yes sir, I injured my groin while rock climbing in the hills in New Territories."

"Not true!" Chan shook his finger at him. "You injured yourself while wrestling with a slut in Macau!"

All the color went from Liu's face. He shrugged and quickly realized that if Chan knew that, he must know a lot more. "Yes sir, I did. It is embarrassing, sir. I wanted to keep it to myself."

Chan waved his hand to quiet him. "I don't blame you, but it is of no importance. You'll go to a clinic from here." General Chan hesitated as he studied the papers in front of him. "Much more important is that you have made a shambles out of your assignment in Hong Kong. I'm curious. What do you think your assignment was?"

"My assignment is to observe the workings of the Royal Hong Kong Police, determine their techniques for law and order and make recommendations to guide our own security force in 1997."

Chan shook his head in agreement. "You are correct, General Liu. In fact you have it verbatim. I would have never guessed it. Before I tell you about your new assignment, it is pertinent to point out the failures of the last one. Let me see now." He stopped again, shook his head negatively and began to read from the papers in front of him.

"You bribed a policeman, Superintendent Hargrave, over a long period of time. That alone was perhaps a good idea. The problem is that half of Hong Kong must have known about it. Hargrave had a very big mouth. This folly led to the harassment of Moia Hsu, a daughter of a member of the staff of the trade minister of China. Hargrave himself was caught by Moia Hsu and arrested in Aberdeen on a direct assignment of yours. Idiotic!" Chan roared, and slapped his hand on his desk.

"I'm sorry, sir. Hargrave was a blundering fool."

"Yes, General Liu. But he was *your* blundering fool." Chan's whole face quivered when he spoke. "Then there was the matter of you having Moia Hsu followed for days, then arranging a meeting, well observed by others in Cheung Chau, like a lovesick puppy dog. Right?"

"Yes sir." Liu knew that another lie would not be tolerated.

"Then there was the matter of the prostitute in Bangkok. Not only did you beat her, but you did not pay her. That is of little importance. But because of the big splash you made there, authorities would like to ask you a few questions about the unusual fire at Phuket Color." Chan looked at him with a cold stare. "Luckily for you, we will not permit further inquiry concerning that incident. Now there is this mindless incident in Macau with a celebrity known to the whole decadent capitalist world. There is much more, General Liu. But you know it, so why should I read on. Agreed?"

"Yes sir."

"Now as to your promotion. As soon as you are ready to travel with comfort, you will be assigned to lead an important unit in Xinjiang, near the Russian boundary. The People's Army makes its headquarters near Kashgar."

General Wing shook his head in protest. The remote outpost was three thousand miles from Beijing. He had heard that if any place on earth most resembled hell, it would be Kashgar. "Sir, I know nothing about that area."

"In the next three years, you will learn and come back a much better leader of men. After all, the Russian border is much more important than the tiny outpost of Hong Kong."

Chapter 42

Are you absolutely sure?" Claude Van Hooten asked the question of Moia, who lay nestled next to him in the broad hammock. His arm circled her, his hand slowly stroking her shoulder.

"Yes, Claude. The doctor confirmed it. But I have known for a few days." She turned slightly and beamed a smile up at him. "Are you disappointed?"

"Of course not. Someday Phuket Color will need a new president. I knew it would happen. I wonder if it happened right here in this hammock?"

"Yes it did, Claude. I know. Is that strange?"

"I'll take your word for it. How big is our child now?

Moia squirmed her way to Van Hooten's lips and grinned at him with happiness. "About this big!" she left a gap of about an inch between her thumb and forefinger.

Van Hooten hugged her close. "Then it will be some time before we can start teaching it the wonders of Hong Kong."

Moia's face saddened. "Oh Claude, our child will never know the Hong Kong that we know. He will only know it as China."

"He?"

Moia smiled faintly. "I will hope, Claude. Sons have more opportunities in China."

"What about Moia Hsu? She found much opportunity."

"Perhaps Moia Hsu was an exceptional child." She laughed at her observation and then hugged him all the harder.

"Ah! Then we will not hope for a boy or a girl. We will hope only for an exceptional child."

"Listen, Claude. You can hear Hong Kong waking up. Do you ever listen in the morning? First there are a few planes in the pattern for Kai Tak. Then, if you listen closely you can hear the traffic start to build on Stanley Gap Road. There are horns and whistles from the harbor. And then there is you, grumbling that it would be nice to have your tea."

"I never grumble."

"Yes you do! Every morning." Moia kissed his lips and then sprang adeptly from the hammock. "Catch up on your morning news. I will prepare tea."

Van Hooten walked to a sheltered alcove on the veranda and turned on the television. He donned a robe and paced slowly, digesting yesterday's closing summary of the New York market. Then there was the usual series of brief news bulletins, one of which made him stop his pacing and listen intently.

Beijing authorities announced that Davy Wong, wanted for a long list of crimes against the state, had been arrested while pursuing illegal activity in Shenzhen. That was it, pure and simple. There were no further details.

Moia soon returned with their tea and found Van Hooten seated, looking glumly at the newscast. "The communists picked up Davy Wong in Shenzhen last evening."

"Really? That is strange. Whatever was he doing in Shenzhen? That would be a terrible risk for him to take."

Van Hooten shook his head. They had discussed Davy Wong several times in the past. They were in total agreement in their sympathy for the heroic dissident. "I find it hard to believe that he would be so foolish as to cross that border. I would bet that he was hijacked from Hong Kong." Van Hooten became silent for a while. "There will be much sadness in Hong Kong today. The sad truth is, Moia, that we will never know exactly what happened."

"Don't be so sure, Claude. Davy Wong is very much a high-profile dissident. There will be many questions, even from abroad." Moia became quiet, wondering if she could get further information from her father in Beijing.

"So, how does your day stack up? Where are you taking our child today?" Van Hooten rubbed at his unshaven chin and smiled at Moia.

"I have scheduled a meeting with Lacy Locke. We plan to go over the details of tomorrow's trip to Foshan. I still think it is important for her to see our workers in full production. Li Pao will be coming down from Beijing. I plan to bring up the subject of his trip to Bangkok. I want to know for sure that Brandon Poole is telling the truth." Moia was stern faced now.

"Moia, it would serve no purpose to pursue questioning of Pao beyond a casual mention. He had a perfect right to be in Bangkok at the time to review production of the factory." Moia was now in the process of dressing for her day as she conversed with Van Hooten. He became preoccupied with the procedure. "You certainly don't look at all pregnant. Could the doctor be wrong?"

"Claude! It will be months before you can notice."

"I want to be married by then."

Moia stopped fussing with her clothes and put her arms around Van Hooten. "I agree." They met in a lingering kiss. "In fact, I am going to tell my father very soon."

"Oh? I'm not sure he cares very much about the idea of you marrying a money-grabbing Dutchman." Van Hooten spoke only partially in jest.

"Remember, my handsome money-grabber, I am not asking my father's permission, or even his approval. I am merely going to tell him what we will do."

"Will he be happy about that?"

"Happy . . . ?" Moia's smile slowly turned into a sober face. "Happiness may come to my father in a long, long time. But then, he is the most patient man I know. I will remind him of that great virtue." Moia kissed him again and headed for the door.

Chapter 43

Hargrave sat on the edge of his bed in the dingy rented room on the Avenida de Almeida Ribeiro in Macau. He looked at his wristwatch. It was now almost two A.M. His fingers had trouble closing on the neck of a bottle of Mateus standing on a chair beside his bed. He swished his mouth with the last few swigs and swallowed, then stood the bottle at the side of the bed next to two others.

He figured he must have slept for about four hours. Reflexively he reached for his wallet and began to count the money, hoping his last night in the floating casino had been only a nightmare. There were ten thousand Hong Kong dollars left, about twelve hundred U.S. dollars. That was all. He groaned and tossed the money on the dresser. Three days ago he had left Hong Kong with over three hundred thousand Hong Kong or about thirty-eight thousand U.S. He cursed his decision to try to double his money in the Macau Palace before fleeing to San Francisco. His life savings had been scooped from the table in front of him by the stone-faced dealers.

He reached for the missing bottle, then remembered that he had just emptied it. He kicked at the bottles on the floor. Macau had been a bad idea. Once, the commissioner had told him that someday Macau would chew him up and spit him out. Not yet, he thought, looking through bleary eyes at the money on the dresser. He carefully stuffed his remaining ten thousand into his wallet. All was not lost, he reasoned. Many times he had come to Macau with a stake of just ten thousand and gone home a winner.

He walked over to the wash basin and rubbed cold water over his face. He combed his hair with the tips of his fingers, picked up the old poplin field jacket that now held all his worldly belongings and walked out the door.

The narrow street to the east was lit only by dim light coming from cracks in the shuttered retail stalls. Occasionally laughter came from behind closed doors, but more often cursing or yelling. He finally turned a corner and walked the remaining block to the waterfront. The sight of the garish red and gold Macau Palace gambling barge lit brilliantly in the dark night quickened his step. Luck ran in streaks. He had experienced it himself many times. Now was a time for a new beginning.

He inspected the row of blackjack tables on the second level of the floating casino, carefully avoiding the cadaver-faced dealer who had tapped him out the night before.

The ten thousand went in twenty minutes. Often it seemed as if the cards had barely touched the felt before the dealers scooped up his wager.

Hargrave rose from the table and walked down the stairway, out the door and down the cobblestone street. His hastily planned retirement from the Royal Police had lasted just four days. "It's those damn communists," he cursed. He toyed briefly with the idea of sneaking back into Hong Kong and into his office, as if nothing had happened. Of course that was impossible. He hadn't been a real policeman in years. He had lived on the bribery of politicians, felons, and now the Beijing general. He hadn't known of one instance of survival from a letter such as he had received from the Investigative Commission. His gambling debts were mountainous. Sha Tin had eaten him alive.

He groaned and jammed his hands into his pockets and felt the lump of change. There was probably enough there to buy another bottle of Mateus.

He came upon an old woman hosing down a three-foot pile of freshly cleaned shrimp on the sidewalk, a common sight along the waterfront in the wee hours. She cursed him when he got near the shrimp and threatened to squirt him with the hose.

He backed off and became aware of someone immediately behind him before being struck by a head-splitting blow. He fell clumsily on the water-slicked cobblestones. Blood ran from the wound.

The old woman stopped the peeling of the shrimp, rose from her squat and walked over to Hargrave. She looked furtively around her and then proceeded to go through his pockets. A few patacas jingled along the cobblestones. The Rolex disappeared into her bosom. Then a badge enclosed in a small leather folio fell from a pocket. She read the inscription: "Superintendent Terry Hargrave, Royal Hong Kong Police." She ran down the street and pounded on a door, shouting, "Quick! There was a fight!"

Two men emerged from the doorway and walked to the prone Hargrave. One bent down to look at him and noticed the badge folio lying on the stones. "He is a policeman!" He bent low, listening for breath. "I think it is too late."

Chapter 44

Brandon Poole took Claude Van Hooten's call in a matter of seconds. "Brandon, is it possible to see you this morning? Believe it or not, I want to talk about the Phuket Color proposition you offered."

"Why shouldn't I believe it? Of course I will see you. I'll send you transportation from the pier. I am aboard the *Kowloon Eagle* this morning. Set a time."

"Aboard the freighter? I called your office."

"The wonders of modern techology never cease, do they, Claude? I'd much prefer to talk to you out here if you can make it. The walls have no ears here."

"Mmm . . . How about in an hour?"

"Good! I look forward to it."

"Brandon, did you hear about Davy Wong on the morning news?"

"Nasty show. He should have been more careful. See you in an hour, Claude."

Poole hung up, leaving Van Hooten staring at the disconnected phone. That was a bit curt, he thought. Brandon Poole seemed more than a little paranoid about his privacy on the phone. Perhaps he'd been too trusting of the system in the past himself. Of course, he was but a tiny fish in this great pool.

An hour later the sleek runabout dispatched by Poole pulled alongside the *Kowloon Eagle*, gleaming in the morning sunshine. A steward led Van Hooten to Poole's private stateroom, positioned a few meters aft of the bridge.

Brandon Poole was seated behind a massive desk staring into a computer terminal when Van Hooten was shown in. "Welcome aboard once again, Claude!" Poole waved his hand at a chair across from him. "Give me just a moment. I'm getting a little more information on the Davy Wong thing. This time he apparently has dug a deep hole for himself."

Finally, Poole turned from the computer after activating a printer, which began spewing out pages into a basket behind him. "Claude, you have made a rather bleak day much brighter. I have been thinking a lot about Phuket Color here lately. I'm convinced that it can be one of the fastest growing partners in the family of Poole Ltd. But only if you run it yourself. Otherwise I am not interested."

"Whoa! I think we are getting a little ahead of ourselves here. I'm still in the thinking stage about this thing." Van Hooten shook his head in amazement at Poole's aggressive approach. "Who knows, Brandon, how motivated I would be working for someone else?"

"What motivates you?" Poole asked while leafing through a sheaf of papers on his desk.

"Money in the bank. Lots of money, preferably in a bank thousands of miles from Hong Kong." Van Hooten watched a flicker of a smile cross Poole's face.

"Claude, I am building factories, earthen dams, road cuts through mountains, and lots of other things for the Chinese in Beijing. If Poole Ltd. owned Phuket Color, I would have bargaining power for that company far beyond what you could ever dream of. In a nutshell, I could make more money and pay you more than you could ever take out of it as it stands. Your autonomy at the helm would never skip a beat."

Van Hooten opened a briefcase and pulled a folio from it. He flipped through it briefly and then slid it across the desk to Poole. "This is Phuket Color, all the stats as of this morning. Take a look and make an offer. We both have time not to do something hasty, I presume."

"By that, I assume you are thinking early 1997," probed Poole.

"Brandon, if we can strike a deal, I would like to have it buttoned up long before that. Frankly, there may be some static from the Chinese if we wait too long. Who knows?" Van Hooten shrugged. "Who can guess the political climate in the future with total accuracy?"

"I think you and I are in a position to prognosticate far better than most." Poole turned around and fished several pages from the basket in front of his printer. "You asked earlier about Davy Wong, and now about politics. Take a look at these."

Van Hooten read through the material, comprising mostly news bulletins from Beijing and New York. "This is fascinating. Who would have guessed that Davy Wong would attract so much attention so quickly?"

"A New York newsman picked it up and obviously saw the injustice. Now all the foreign press is digging for information all over Hong Kong. Beijing needs American investment, as well as a lot of others. I don't think that they will let the freedom of Davy Wong stand in the way. They have backed down before. After all, Davy is not a militant. He is guilty only of exercising free speech where it was unwanted. He wouldn't harm a fly. He has a lot of fans in Hong Kong, and now all over the world."

Van Hooten read through the rest of the dispatches carefully. "I hope you're right, Brandon. They did let Harry Wu go last year. I'll have to bounce this off Moia and see what she thinks. She is a far better judge of Beijing politics than I."

"Hey, that's a good idea. I'd be interested in what she thinks. I believe that she is visiting Foshan with Lacy Locke tomorrow, right?"

Van Hooten couldn't suppress a look of surprise. He didn't know that Poole knew the exact date of the visit to Foshan. "Yes, as a matter of fact they are. In fact, we are quite anxious for her to see Foshan. Production is far beyond our expectancy for this early in the game."

"Are all the arrangements complete for their one-day visit?"

"I left that to Moia. To do the trip in one day they'll have to fly to Guangzhou. It's a shame they don't have more time. Lacy would appreciate the trip up the river on the hydrofoil. A Phuket van will meet the plane and take them to the factory near Foshan. Sing Lee, our factory manager, will supervise their visit. Li Pao, Moia's contact in Beijing, will join them for the day, I understand. They will return from Guangzhou on a late afternoon flight to Hong Kong."

"Li Pao? His name keeps popping up. Say that we do come to an agreement to work together. I would prefer to use our own point man in Beijing. Is Moia really hung up on Li Pao?" Fresh in Brandon Poole's mind was Cecil Lo's expressed suspicion of Li Pao. The police in Bangkok also wanted to question him as well as the general.

"I think Moia would welcome the opportunity to use someone else. I suggest you ask her. Pao must be a busy man. Sometimes she has trouble locating him. I would much prefer we use the facilities of your company if we get together."

"Very good, Claude. We seem to come to agreements very quickly. I think we would work well together when it is necessary to do so." Poole looked up at a light blinking rapidly on a communications panel.

"Excuse me, this might be urgent." He listened for a moment and handed the phone to Van Hooten. "It's for you."

"Claude Van Hooten here. I'm very busy. . . . Oh." There was a long pause as Van Hooten listened intently. Finally, he spoke. "Well, I'll be damned. Keep me posted. I'll be back in the office within the hour."

Van Hooten shook his head in puzzlement before speaking. "I guess we'll never know why Moia was followed by the police. Superintendent Hargrave fell and cracked his skull in Macau last night. He's dead." Van Hooten then told Poole all he knew about the odd incident at the power plant in Aberdeen. "The police just called my office to tell them that the hearing on Moia's complaint was canceled."

"Strange," mused Poole. "Dead men can't talk, can they? Well, at least he won't be following your lovely Moia anymore. Maybe I can learn something from the commissioner. He's due to call me soon about another matter."

"It is upsetting, Brandon. You can't imagine how annoyed Moia has been. We saw the old car several times out on Stanley Gap Road. It is possible that Hargrave had been following her for some time. In fact, I am still irked that the police dragged their feet in this matter. I feel uneasy. General Liu must be out there somewhere. If you don't mind, I have made a decision to accompany the two women to Foshan tomorrow."

Poole nodded enthusiastically. "Good idea, Claude. I feel much better about the trip."

Chapter 45

THE CHINA Air flight leaped into a steep climb from Kai Tak, banked and headed west on a flight pattern that took them directly over the delta of the Pearl River. A light drizzle fell from the overcast that quickly wiped away the view beneath their plane. They sat three across in the jet, reminding Lacy of some of the crowded commuter flights back in the States. Because of the shortness of the flight, they never climbed above the clouds.

Moia Hsu was tireless. Sitting between Lacy and Van Hooten, she used almost all the forty minutes in the air to present Lacy with the miraculous construction details of the factory near Foshan. She assured her it was completed in record time despite the traditional rainy season. She even had a photographic story of the construction in her briefcase which ended with the presentation of the Phuket Color sport coat to Van Hooten.

"The Shanghai factory will also open months ahead of time, thanks to Mr. Brandon Poole, and a few favors from Beijing," she said proudly.

"Who is the Phuket representative working with the contractor in Shanghai?" Lacy asked the question remembering that the mysterious Li Pao was the key man in Foshan and Bangkok.

Moia's faced sobered perceptibly. "Li Pao . . . Right now it is Li Pao, but perhaps that will be changed." She didn't say why and went on to discuss the van trip that lay ahead of them. "Lacy, be prepared for a a slightly uncomfortable trip to the factory from Foshan. The road is not completely paved as yet, and this weather makes it terrible."

"I will survive. Rural roads in America are sometimes like that. Believe me, this trip is exciting. The business tempo of Hong Kong is exhausting, kind of like New York. I needed this change of pace. What is Foshan like?"

"It's been a trade center for centuries. Now Foshan will profit by the industrialization of China in the future. It is much more relaxed than Hong Kong. Too bad you can't spend more time there."

"Moia, I will be back someday and explore your country."

Moia suddenly became silent and pensive. Then, leaning forward to look at Van Hooten, she said, "Of course, my country is now Hong Kong . . . which will soon be China. But Hong Kong is so different. I will always live there."

"Oh look!" Lacy exclaimed. Their plane nosed below the cloud cover in their approach to Baiyun Airport near Guangzhou. A checkerboard of vivid shades of green interspersed with small lakes appeared as far as the eyes could see.

"Vegetables, fish, you name it. The produce of this land feeds a large part of southeast China including Guangzhou, which many of us still like to call Canton"—she paused, smiling at Van Hooten—"and even Hong Kong. You will see as we drive to Foshan." Lacy noticed there was always a hint of pride in Moia's voice when she described her native land.

The fully loaded plane thumped down heavily on the

runway at Baiyun Airport and taxied to a terminal apron where a portable deplaning ramp was pushed into place.

As soon as the three of them set foot on the apron, Moia spotted Sing Lee, the Phuket factory manager, walking toward them. "Sing, so good to see you again." Moia's greeting was returned by a nervous smile from Sing Lee, who immediately grasped her arm, turned her away from the others and whispered something to her in a low voice.

Van Hooten and Lacy watched as Moia looked quickly, almost angrily at the terminal ahead. Whatever Sing Lee had said to her seemed to be very upsetting. Then she motioned for them to join her, and the three of them followed Lee toward a different door to the terminal than the other passengers were led to.

Moia looked at Van Hooten, shrugged and said, "There has been a slight change in our plans, but I am asssured that it will not cost us much time."

"What's going on, Moia?"

Van Hooten's question was ignored as Moia picked up the pace and led them rapidly to the terminal. Just as they entered the terminal, she turned to Van Hooten. "I'm sorry, Claude. We'll get this over with in a hurry."

Sing Lee led the way to a small office and tapped gently on the door a couple of times. Sing Lee opened the door, and stepped to one side, allowing Moia, Lacy, and Van Hooten to enter.

The aging Dr. Ching Hsu, dressed in a dark business suit, stood in the center of the room. Li Pao stood at his side. Moia strode forward and briefly hugged her father, amost perfunctorily, without emotion. "Father, this is a surprise. What brings you to Foshan?"

"You do, daughter. Time and opportunity permitted it. When Li told me of his visit, I thought it would be a good time for me to come with him, and see for myself the fruit of my daughter's labor." So far the old man had not yet acknowledged the presence of Lacy and Van Hooten in the room.

Moia quickly turned toward the others. "Father, you have met Claude Van Hooten in Beijing, and this is Lacy Locke, a financial analyst from New York. Lacy, this is Dr. Hsu."

"Dr. Hsu, it is a pleasure meeting you. Moia has been so helpful. I have learned so much about China from her."

The trade minister touched her hand in more of a symbolic than real handshake. Dr. Hsu's eyes fixed on the blue eyes of the tall, dark-haired woman. "Financial analyst . . . New York . . . Wall Street," he mused, nodding his head. "Welcome to the People's Republic of China. Have you visited our Hang Seng market in Hong Kong?"

Van Hooten, still ignored, winced. The old man was already calling it "our Hang Seng." The traders on that Hong Kong market would be amused at that.

"Not yet, Dr. Hsu, but I plan to," replied Lacy.

There were several seconds of awkward silence before the old man nodded at Lacy. "Forgive me, but I must have a few minutes with my daughter. We have some business to talk about, and then I will turn her over to you. Li Pao will stay here and make you comfortable until we return."

As he and Moia left the room, he walked past Claude Van Hooten and almost imperceptibly touched the lapel of his jacket. "Very nice coat." He spoke almost in a whisper, never meeting Van Hooten's eyes.

"Thank you, Dr. Hsu." Van Hooten spoke to the back of his head as they left the room. He shrugged at Lacy, wondering if the old man knew that the jacket he wore was not a Phuket Color product. Van Hooten considered the cold reception by Moia's father a virtual snub. If the others hadn't been there, he probably wouldn't have said anything.

Sing Lee, who had disappeared for a moment, returned with several bottles of chilled Coca-Cola.

"Ah, there is a man who can read minds." Lacy took one of the soft drinks and sipped. "It's warm and humid here. I can see why the crops grow so well."

"Did you have a nice flight?" The question came from the stone-faced, scrawny Li Pao.

"Yes," Lacy replied. "It was cloudy, so we couldn't see very much. But we landed safely. Landing safely always makes it a nice flight." If Li Pao saw any humor in her remark, he gave not a flicker of evidence.

"Li," Van Hooten began, "Perhaps you can tell Lacy and me how the construction is coming up in Shanghai."

"Very good." He replied quickly and did not elaborate.

Van Hooten wondered if the strange introvert was any more loquacious with Moia. He wondered how she ever did business with him. "Well, we might as well make ourselves comfortable." Van Hooten proceeded to open some folding chairs leaning against the wall and once again addressed Li Pao, determined to pry a few words out of him. "How are things coming along in Bangkok? Will they ever get back into production there?"

"No, it was a big fire." Pao shook his head in emphasis.

"Claude, let's take a little walk. It is stifling in here." Lacy nodded toward the door, and the two of them went outside and stood under the narrow eave. "Mr. Pao may be very good at something but it is not communication."

Van Hooten smiled weakly, obviously concerned about the conversation between Moia and her father. "I wonder what is going on in there, Lacy."

"I can't imagine. Perhaps I shouldn't have come. Maybe it's upsetting to Dr. Hsu."

"Nonsense, Lacy! We'll learn from Moia, sooner or later."

* * *

Inside the Baiyun terminal, Moia and her father sat at right angles to each other at a table in a small customs office. They were alone in the room.

"It is time for you to return to Beijing. The Trade Ministry needs you." Dr. Hsu spoke slowly and firmly. It sounded very much like an order.

"To be another bureaucrat, like Li Pao." She shook her head resolutely.

"That is another reason you must return to Beijing. My daughter is beginning to talk like a capitalist." Hsu stared at his daughter sullenly.

"Perhaps it is a good thing. It was you who sent me to Hong Kong to learn their ways. China must rise from its poverty, father. To do that, the people must have hope and incentive. You told me once that a thousand Phuket Colors would make China strong. You are wrong. It will take many more. All kinds of business, all over China. It can be done! But not by party members in Beijing."

"Now you are wiser than your father? I need you for sure in Beijing." The old man's patience was being pushed to the limit. "I expect you to conclude your visit here and return to Beijing." Both of his fists were clenched in front of him on the table.

"I could never do that to Claude." Moia waited for the chastisement from her father.

"Ah. Now I see. So life is cozy there on Stanley Gap Road." He spat the sentence at her in disgust. "Capitalists! You now have their good ways, and their bad ways."

"I am sorry, father, that you see things this way. I am in love with Claude Van Hooten. In fact, I am going to have his child! I did not plan to tell you that yet, but you must know."

"Return to Beijing. We can take care of your problem there."

Hsu reached forward as if to pat her hand. She

jerked it away. "I have no problem, father. A child is not a problem. It is you that has a problem. Father, tell me, was it you who had Liu Wing following me all over Hong Kong? Did you have him bribe the police to follow me?"

"Are you not my daughter?" Dr. Hsu looked at her, eyes pleading. "Liu Wing was a fool. He made many mistakes because he was in love with you. In Beijing you will not be bothered with him. He has been sent to a new command in Kashgar."

Moia looked at him in amazement. "The answer is no! Hong Kong is my home now." Moia rose from the table. "There are people waiting in that room who want to help me help China. We need their help, and all the other people like them who have resources. Please try to understand."

The old man looked at her bitterly. "You have become like Davy Wong."

"Davy Wong? I will tell you something. He would help China also if they would just let him. All of Hong Kong is shocked that he was taken. The rest of the world is angry, father. The people we need desperately are angry. If you can figure out a way to influence Beijing, you will try to get him set free."

"You seem to be very concerned with Davy Wong."

"That is true, father. Right after Tiananmen Square, you yourself said that the army acted too quickly and with unnecessary force. Remember?"

The old man was silent. He knew she remembered correctly. "Moia, come close, come close to your father." She walked back to the table and sat down, weary with the argument.

"What if I . . ." He paused, faltering for a moment. "What if I could get Davy Wong released through my own influence and the influence of others. Would you then return to Beijing? Perhaps for a year or so, just to give it a try."

"Father, the freedom of people like Davy Wong is

more important to China than anything. It has nothing to do with me returning to Beijing. It is not fair of you to ask such a question. I can best serve China in Hong Kong. Now, father, I am going to leave. We have a factory to inspect."

The old man clasped his daughter's hands in his own, squeezed them firmly, then rose from the table and walked to the door. He opened it and left without looking back.

Chapter 46

THE TRIP to the factory at Foshan on the dark, rainy day had an additional pall descend on the visitors when Moia emerged from the meeting with her father. Her attitude became less personal and her enthusiasm waned visibly on the drive to Phuket Color.

"I thought Dr. Hsu was coming with us," Van Hooten said as they got underway without him. He felt that it was no small breach of courtesy for him not to say good-bye to Lacy in particular, who had come many thousands of miles to assess the wisdom of a stock issue for Phuket Color. Perhaps the old man didn't understand.

Moia stared through the van window into the gray bleakness of the day. "Dr. Hsu has urgent business in Beijing. I am sorry he could not spend more time with us, but it was not to be."

Van Hooten, who sat in the front of the van next to Sing Lee, twisted in his seat trying to catch Moia's attention, but she continued to stare out the window. Li Pao had unexpectedly joined Dr. Hsu on the trip back to Beijing. No doubt this irked Moia, who had a few questions for him. Perhaps that was why she was so depressed, Van Hooten thought.

"Oh look!" exclaimed Lacy. Across a water-filled ditch beside the rutted road, water buffalo were yoked to a plow, driven by a field worker wading through the mire. "I've seen that on postcards."

"You still see it all over South China," said Van Hooten. "Farm machinery is still one of the big necessities in short supply. Perhaps we should be making tractors instead of clothing." His quip brought no comment from Moia, who still appeared to be lost in deep thought.

Sing Lee wheeled the van into the driveway of the factory a few minutes before noon. Van Hooten noticed that the access road had been completely paved since his last visit, and also, that all of Brandon Poole Ltd.'s construction equipment had been moved from the grove of trees at the perimeter of the property.

Moia's spirits picked up considerably as Sing Lee led them through a whirlwind tour of Phuket Color. There must of been a couple of hundred people hard at work. Finished racks of clothing and huge crates were ready for shipment on the broad loading dock. Moia and Sing Lee asked many questions of workers on production lines and translated their answers for the benefit of Lacy and Van Hooten.

Once inside the building, Lacy realized that she could be in any modern similar factory in the United States. This spot of ground had been transformed into a modern miracle, still surrounded by an ancient China.

"Lacy, look at this!" Excitement returned to Moia's voice as they stood at a workstation in the computer room. "Here are production figures for the month. We are up fifty-one percent over our projection!" Then she turned to Van Hooten. "Oh Claude, isn't it wonderful!" She beamed a genuine smile toward him, the first since the abrupt departure of her father from Guangzhou.

Van Hooten looked at Moia intently, then winked at Lacy. "Well, now we know what makes Moia happy, don't we. Success is an exhilarating experience when you start with a muddy field and get this in five months."

Sing Lee was beaming at the threesome. After all, it was he who had done the heavy lifting to bring the unit into full production.

Van Hooten spoke an aside to Moia. "Maybe we should get a manager here and ship Sing Lee up to Shanghai to get them started."

"I will discuss it with Li Pao." Her mood reverted to her previous soberness. "Oh, the hell with it, Claude, we'll just do it. I'm sure Brandon Poole would welcome him there."

Van Hooten grinned. Now she was sounding like the real Moia who got things done.

The tour ended with everyone in high spirits over what they had seen. But the bleak day still surrounded them on the drive back to Baiyun Airport. "Now the plane will be late," Moia advised the group with a smile. "The plane is always late."

The flight back to Hong Kong turned out to be a white-knuckle trip in the foul weather. "Landing at Kai Tak when the weather is fine is bad enough. But believe me, Lacy, this flight always makes it," Van Hooten assured her.

After clearing customs in Hong Kong, Lacy found a smiling Cecil Lo awaiting her in the arrival area. Poole had insisted on the accommodation. "Can I drop you somewhere?" Lo asked Van Hooten and Moia.

"That's nice of you but we have made arrangements to get to Stanley. Thanks anyway." Van Hooten seemed anxious to be on his way with Moia.

"Lacy, I just remembered something," Moia said. "Tomorrow afternoon we will run the promo tapes that Chad Grissom did at Sai Kung. Please drop by the office. I would like to look at them with you."

"Oh, that would be interesting! I'll try to make it. I'll call in the morning."

The two disappeared to meet their limo, and Cecil Lo led Lacy to the area reserved for VIPs. He opened the door to the big silver Rolls-Royce, and there sat Brandon Poole, beaming a broad smile of welcome.

"Brandon, what a surprise!" She brushed his cheek with a kiss as she settled in the seat next to him. It was a spontaneous gesture of thanks and relief after a tedious day. "I'm afraid I'll be poor company. It was an exhausting day. There is so much to tell you."

"You look magnificent. If you had an exhausting day, you hide it very well." His eyes fixed on her with the half smile that she now accepted as his natural visage. Nevertheless, it sometimes served to mask his true feelings. She had watched others try to puzzle it out. "I want to hear all about your trip. I've arranged to have dinner at the Mandarin, so you will be close to home."

"That's so nice, Brandon. I love all your little adventures, but I'm happy we're not dashing off into the night this time."

"There's always tomorrow. Were you impressed with the factory?"

"What I know about factories you could put in your pocket, but I was very impressed. Moia said that production was fifty-one percent over expectation for the first month."

"Hmmm . . . Sounds like someone is doing their job."

"I think it's Sing Lee. Van Hooten talked about moving him to Shanghai. Oh, Brandon, I haven't told you the most important thing. Moia's father, Dr. Hsu, met us at the airport with Li Pao."

"Really!" Poole's half smile faded. "What did he think of the factory?"

"Brandon, it was so mysterious. He didn't go to Foshan. I don't think he said more than a dozen words to us. I thought it was rude. When we first arrived, they were waiting. He and Moia met alone in a closed room while the rest of us sat. Van Hooten was visibly shaken." Lacy went on to give Poole all the details of their visit.

"Strange . . . It's hard to know what to make of it. The old man is hard to read. Actually, he has very limited real power. It sounds like somebody must have jumped on his case up in Beijing." Poole grasped her hand in both of his, apparently in deep thought. "What did Moia say about the meeting?"

"Nothing. She was sullen for hours after it. She perked up at the factory, but never really seemed herself for the rest of the trip. It's not like her. I could tell that Van Hooten was concerned."

"I'd like to be a little bird on the veranda at Stanley Gap Road tonight. I would guess there is trouble in Van Hooten's little paradise."

"Does that mean trouble for Phuket Color?"

"I doubt it, Lacy. It's just another of those things that make Hong Kong so interesting these days. If you can figure out what all the coming and going of bureaucrats from Beijing really means, you'd have to be a clairvoyant. What did you think of Li Pao?"

"He's a cold fish. He didn't utter ten words. He sat like a dummy with us while Moia had her private meeting. Then he left with Dr. Hsu." By now they were out of the harbor tunnel and approaching the Mandarin. "Oh, by the way, Moia asked me to drop by tomorrow and look at some promotional stuff they filmed near Sai Kung. I can't wait to go. Maybe I can learn more."

"They've got their problems with Pretty Boy—what's his name?"

"Chad Grissom."

"I guess he's in love. He ran off to Bangkok with a male Thai dancer."

"Brandon, you're joking!. How do you know that?"

"My dear, I received word through my carefully fertilized and watered grapevine." He returned to his half smile as Cecil pulled the Rolls in front of the Mandarin.

Inside, they were seated immediately in a cozy corner of the grill, where Lacy continued to fill Brandon in on the whirlwind visit to Foshan. "I had a very good feeling about the factory. In fact I feel strongly that Phuket Color is in good hands. Their stock issue should be a wise investment for risk capital. Given the political situation, it should be sold as high risk. Don't you agree?"

"I'm afraid I may turn your high risk into a low risk very soon, Lacy. I plan to make an offer for Phuket within a few days. Keep that under your beautiful hair, my dear." Poole was back to his enigmatic smile again. He looked at his wristwatch. "We had some very big news about an hour before you arrived. Did you hear about Davy Wong?"

"No! What happened?"

"It seems the bastards had tried him in absentia along with others. He's already been sent to prison for four years, for telling lies about the state and spreading propaganda to the foreign media."

Lacy again pictured Davy Wong on the pavement, as he was apprehended in the night market. "Four years? Oh Brandon, that is so cruel. Is there any recourse?"

"Actually, the sentence is not unexpected. Sometimes they sentence people and then find a way to deport them if pressure builds and, at the same time, if they can get something in return. You might recall the case of Harry Wu a year or so ago. So there is a miracle now and then. I believe that it was your Adam that got the ball rolling for Davy. I have a tape of his news story. It is almost verbatim. Now we expect demonstrations in Hong Kong. You'll see them in a couple of days." Poole sipped at a snifter of brandy. "Enough of this business talk and speculation over politics. That will be best done with a fresh mind tomorrow."

Then came his biggest smile and a toast. "To us! . . . Have you done any more thinking about our son?"

Lacy looked at him in disbelief, smiled, then started laughing. The laugh grew into a low, almost hysterical giggle, which she tried to squelch but could not. Finally she regained her composure.

"Brandon, let me tell you about my day. I got up at five o'clock, packed, then flew to China for the first time in my life. Despite the rain and a bumpy flight, it was quite a kick. Met the sour-faced trade minister and then drove an hour and a half through the rain and mud. Saw farmers in sun hats plowing fields with water buffalo. Amazing! I toured the factory, listened to Moia's sales pitch for at least two hours, then it was back through the mud to Canton. We finally got on a two-hours-late flight for a roller coaster ride to Hong Kong. Met you at Kai Tak, a sight for weary eyes. Now, while having a very nice dinner, Brandon Poole, local billionaire and a perfectly nice man, inquires about my having his son." Her wide-open eyes gazed on Poole's now serious face. "Brandon, it's been a busy, busy day."

Poole looked at her for a few moments, then asked, "Are you poking fun at my perfectly serious little idea?"

"Of course not, Brandon. But I am closing my mind at the end of this very long day to any perfectly serious thoughts of any kind."

"Thank you, Lacy, I can live with that." Poole glanced around to make sure they had no audience, then kissed her gently on the lips. He moved away from her and took a sip of his brandy. "By the way, Lacy, if I were to purchase Phuket, would you hire Moia Hsu along with Van Hooten?"

She stared at Poole. To her surprise the kiss did not upset her. In fact, it seemed a natural thing. "Okay, you win. I will answer one more serious question. As far as those two lovebirds are concerned, you don't get one without the other."

"Lacy, you are the most exciting woman in Hong Kong."

"Hey, Brandon, watch it. That's serious. Besides, there is Moia Hsu and Mary Lulu. Take a good look. I'll bet they would both make fine mothers."

"You have a sense of humor, even after a long day."

Chapter 47

CLAUDE VAN HOOTEN rolled and tossed. Try as he did, sleep was impossible. Ultimately, he gave up and tiptoed from their bedroom out to the veranda. It was two A.M. He had watched the digits on the clock spin laboriously though the hours from the moment he went to bed. Moia's account of the conversation with her father, and his plea for her to return to Beijing for "a year or so" in return for his effort to release Davy Wong, was totally unexpected.

To put their love and their life, and now their child on the back burner for the freedom of dissident Davy Wong, no matter how courageous he was, was unthinkable for Van Hooten, and thankfully for Moia. This explained Dr. Hsu's coldness toward him at Baiyun Airport. The old man had tried and failed to get Moia to leave Hong Kong. It must have been a major disappointment for him. Of course, it was a trauma for Moia too, to take such a stand against the wishes of her father.

He lit a cigar and watched the smoke waft slowly through the still night air. As angry as he was with Dr. Hsu, he had to be proud of Moia. The consistency of her love for him made his spirits soar.

He wondered now if the old man would go to bat for Wong anyway. Dr. Hsu was certainly midlevel or lower among the thousands of bureaucrats in Beijing. Yet, if he made such a proposition to Moia, the old man must at least think that he could do it. If he was instrumental in getting General Liu assigned to Kashgar, perhaps he had more pull than Van Hooten thought.

"Claude." Her voice came softly from the doorway behind him. "I cannot sleep either. I feel terrible. Something is wrong about what I have done, but I don't know what it is. What can it be?"

Van Hooten turned, put his arms around her and pressed her to his chest. "It is not wrong to have compassion for your father. But it was wrong for your father to confront you with such a proposition."

"I know it was. But I got the distinct feeling that my father was not himself, that he was under some pressure, or he would not have asked me such a thing."

"I love you, Moia. Perhaps I don't deserve the love of such a noble person. Everything will be fine for us. Someday your father will understand."

The two of them walked to the broad hammock nearby and lay motionlessly entwined together for a long time, still wide awake.

"Moia, are you awake?" Claude whispered.

"Of course I am."

"I have something very important to say. I want you to marry me. I mean now, before you might have to go to Beijing again on business."

"Of course I will." Moia looked up and smiled at him.

"I'll get right on the details in the morning," Claude promised. "We'll feel much better afterward. And someday your father will be proud and pleased."

"Yes, perhaps. But it will take a long time." Moia spoke softly into his ear. "I love you." Within minutes they were both sound asleep.

Chapter 48

THE NEXT morning Lacy Locke arrived at the Phuket Color office in Central at ten o'clock pursuant to the invitation to look over promotion material for their new line. Moia Hsu met her in the outer office, brimming with energy and warmth. Whatever had caused her moodiness of yesterday had completely disappeared.

"Lacy, you're right on time. I wish I could say the same for Chad Grissom. He is not here, so we will go ahead without him." Moia led her to a small conference room where an attendant was setting up projection equipment for the showing.

Lacy almost blurted out that Grissom was in Bangkok with his Thai lover, then bit her tongue. Brandon hadn't told her his source, or whether or not it was confidential information. Perhaps Moia knew and thought it unimportant.

"Lacy, before we get started, I have some wonderful news I want to share with you. But first how long are you going to be in Hong Kong?" Moia was absolutely radiant.

"It's funny you ask. I was trying to figure it out this morning. I've already stayed longer than I had planned.

I'll probably be here for another week at the most."

"Very good! Claude and I are going to be married in two days. I want you to come to our wedding."

Lacy was startled by the unexpected announcement from the effervescent Moia. "That's wonderful news! I am so happy for you." She embraced Moia. "You kept that secret all day yesterday. How could you?"

"We made the decision early this morning," she said, blushing. "Claude has already made arrangements today. It will be at St. John's Cathedral on Thursday. Just a few people, in the chapel. Please say you'll be there."

"I wouldn't miss it for anything. What a way to cap off my trip to Hong Kong!"

Claude Van Hooten entered the room, obviously in a spirited mood. The tall, rugged Dutchman was usually quite sober faced. He looked at the two women and grinned boyishly. "Well, I can see that Moia has brought you up-to-date on our plans. Lacy, I'm a lucky man." He put his arm around Moia and squeezed her affectionately. "To celebrate this day, I have made Moia president of Phuket Color. Hell, she does most of the work anyway."

"Congratulations to both of you. If the world knew what I know, Phuket's stock would jump off the charts."

Van Hooten stayed until the first of the Chad Grissom shots were flashed on the screen. "I'm going to leave you two together. Moia's judgment is much better than mine about these things. All I know is that it's about time to put the catalog together, so I hope most of the shots are as good as that one." He nodded at the jaunty pose of Chad Grissom waving from the aft deck of a schooner, then left them alone.

The two examined the photographs one by one as they flashed on the screen. Whatever problems Chad Grissom had with his sexual identity didn't affect his work. His modeling of the Phuket men's line was masculine and appealing. Moia was ecstatic. "We can use almost all of these. You like, Lacy?"

"Grissom is very photogenic. It's strange. He has a boyish quality in person that vanishes in most of the shots. I think they're terrific."

Van Hooten returned to the conference room just as the two were wrapping up their meeting. Lacy was preparing to leave. "Ladies, I have some news. In my haste to get plans made for Thursday, I neglected to monitor the morning news reports. Beijing has just announced that Davy Wong was sentenced some time ago, in absentia, and now has been sent to prison for four years."

"Oh Claude!" Moia gasped. "I feel so terrible." She shook her head in disappointment.

Van Hooten spoke softly. "Sometimes, they send people to prison in Beijing before deporting them. Who knows?"

Lacy watched the exchange between the two. "I'm sorry. Brandon saw the news report last night and told me about it at dinner. I just assumed you knew. Brandon said the same thing that Claude just did, that sometimes they deport them after they are sentenced, like Harry Wu."

"There is a difference," Moia said quietly. "Wu was an American citizen. Davy Wong is originally from Hong Kong. We can hope, but it is not the same." She shook her head pensively. "Claude, I am going to call my father right now. He must know something of this."

Van Hooten shrugged. "Give it a try, Moia. In view of the news, he must expect your call."

Moia left to place her call to Beijing. Van Hooten walked with Lacy into his office. "How about cup of coffee, Lacy? You might as well stay and see how Moia makes out with her call. As you must gather, Dr. Hsu told her only yesterday morning that he would push for the release of Wong. What did you think of Dr. Hsu?"

"He was so aloof that I really didn't have time to form an opinion. Moia seemed upset after he left."

"Oh, you noticed that. Moia was very upset. Usually she has been able to communicate with her father." Van Hooten crossed his fingers. "We will hope for the best. Do all of our problems, so unique with Hong Kong, confuse you, Lacy?"

"It's different but it is exciting. Now that I have been here, I'll be on pins and needles until 1997."

"As we all will." Van Hooten picked up a copy of a news item clipped from a local journal. He handed it to Lacy. "Things like this make us a little nervous."

Lacy scanned the brief article. There was a rumor afoot that the Chinese planned to march ten to fifteen thousand troops of the People's Liberation Army through the streets of Hong Kong on July 1, 1997. "For what purpose?" asked Lacy.

"A celebration, a show of power, I suppose. For whatever reason, I don't know. It's totally unnecessary."

Moia entered the office again to join them. She was upset, her eyes wet with tears. Van Hooten leapt to his feet to hold her in his arms. "What is it, Moia? What is it?"

"I could not reach my father. I finally talked to one of the members of the Trade Ministry I know. He read me an announcement that was circulated a few hours ago. It said that Dr. Hsu had been dismissed from the Trade Ministry for reassignment to work with an agricultural committee." She shook her head in disbelief. "Oh Claude, something is wrong. Something is terribly wrong."

"Did you try Li Pao?"

"Yes, he was also dismissed."

Lacy couldn't think of anything comforting to say about the news. She had no way of assessing it. Moia's sober face of yesterday had returned.

Van Hooten picked up a phone in response to a blinking signal. "Bring it right in, please." His secretary entered the office with a single sheet of paper.

Van Hooten read it in silence as Lacy and Moia watched, and then summarized the contents. "Well, it seems that the officials of the People's Republic are demanding to examine the travel documents of one of my employees. They point out that it is illegal for a pregnant citizen of China to cross into Hong Kong. Indeed, it is even illegal for them to visit relatives and friends in Hong Kong."

"What a strange law," Lacy murmured.

"Not from their point of view," explained Van Hooten. "There are thousands of pregnant women in China who would like to cross that border to get citizenship in the free world for their unborn child. Many are turned back each day. Some manage to slip through."

Moia, eyes still teary, faced Van Hooten. "There is only one person in all of China who knows of my condition. That is my father. He had to have been the one to tell the authorities."

Chapter 49

BRANDON POOLE worked feverishly at his desk in the command room aboard the *Kowloon Eagle*. Captain Guy Bridges, skipper of the vessel, sat across from him totally absorbed in the instructions that lay before him.

"From Friday, thereafter, I want you to be able to leave Hong Kong on twenty-four hours' notice. I believe that all cargo will be stowed at the end of this day, right?"

"Yes sir. The electronics installation for the Cayman Islands is now all aboard. The major tonnage for Baltimore and New York will be in place by tomorrow. The passenger list is incomplete, I believe. I am showing twenty names, four of them bound for the Caymans and the others for New York. Here is your copy of the list, sir."

Captain Bridges watched as Poole studied the list. He had served in Poole's fleet for ten years after retirement from the Royal Navy. His last command had been as skipper of a missile frigate very similar to the *Kowloon Eagle*, especially its complex electronics. His weathered face and steel gray hair attested to many years at sea. Intent gray eyes under a heavy brow now fixed on Brandon Poole's.

"Guy, I think perhaps we'll hold the passenger list at that level. A lot of others are anxious to go, but I'd rather keep this first voyage easily manageable." Poole paused in thought for a moment. "Keep the four staterooms immediately behind my own quarters empty for the time being. Put Cecil Lo in the nearest occupied stateroom to my own. If other space is to be assigned later, I will do it myself."

"Consider it done, sir." Bridges clasped his hands behind his head and stretched away from the table. "I don't mind telling you that this trip is a beauty, sir. It is the longest single run from home base that I have ever made. It's a very satisfying voyage for an old war horse like me."

Poole smiled and looked up at the world chart on the bulkhead. "It is exciting, isn't it. Well, Captain, with the future of Hong Kong being the riddle that it is, I would guess that we will see a lot of water in the next few months."

"I'm curious, sir. Do you expect to headquarter Brandon Poole Ltd. in the Cayman Islands?"

"Absolutely not. We are a Hong Kong company. The titular home office will be here long after I'm gone, I hope. However, Captain, the wonders of modern technology make it possible to have multiple functional headquarters. For instance, there is one aboard this vessel, and one to be in the Caymans, all connected by electronic banking, computers, and cutting-edge communications." Poole rose and walked over to the world chart. He pointed to the big circle around Hong Kong. "Of course, Hong Kong is my home. My heart will always be here in this harbor, and in my house on the Peak, as will, hopefully, my person and my heirs."

Captain Bridges gathered his papers and left the command room, leaving Poole studying the world chart. Brandon checked the time. Van Hooten would be here in a matter of minutes. He properly stowed the papers he had studied with the captain, with the exception of the passenger list.

The only other thing left on his desk was the bound proposal for the acquisition of Phuket Color. He flipped the pages without really looking at them. All the work had been done. It had been checked and rechecked by his financial people. Phuket would be only a very minor holding in the vast worldwide network of Brandon Poole Ltd.

He picked up the passenger list and ran down the list of names, chuckling aloud when he read the names of Sean Xiang and Mary Lulu. They were taking a little vacation, to try things out as Sean had put it, and would leave the *Kowloon Eagle* in Hawaii for a flight back.

There was a rap on the door, and the first mate led Van Hooten into the command room.

"Congratulations, Claude! I can't say I'm surprised after watching the way you two look at each other. Moia is one of a kind. I will certainly be at the chapel on Thursday."

"I really never thought I would do it, Brandon, but then I never thought they made women like Moia. Incidentally, Moia and I have gone through a bit of hell over the last few hours. I think you ought to be brought up-to-date."

"Fire away. I want you to get that worried look off your face. I want you in a good mood when you look at my proposal."

Van Hooten told him of the discussion Moia had with her father concerning Davy Wong, and of their subsequent amazement that he had been sent to prison so promptly. "When Moia called to question her father, she was given information that Dr. Hsu had been dismissed, along with Li Pao. Brandon, I have no idea what to make of all this."

"Simple. The old man exceeded his authority. He is a relatively minor expeditor up there in Beijing. They will just throw him another desk job, probably even less important. It does amaze me, but it really doesn't concern me at all. I have my own tangled web to deal with in Beijing. Moia should not worry about it."

"Well, there is a little bit more to the story, Brandon. Moia made the mistake of telling her father she was pregnant. Now the People's Republic wants to examine her travel papers. You know, they forbid pregnant single women to cross that border."

Poole tried to force a comforting smile. "Well, in a couple of days, that matter will be taken care of, won't it? After all, the old man has been dismissed. It could be called sour grapes on his part. Believe me, the matter will never be brought up again with Mrs. Moia Van Hooten, and an appropriate new visa."

"Think so?"

"Certainly. China has too much on its plate." Brandon paused and then slid the acquisition proposal across the desk. "I'd like to make this a reality as quickly as possible."

Van Hooten fanned through the pages. "Hmm . . . twenty-six pages. They can never nail this stuff down in about six paragraphs, can they?"

Poole shook his head. "Lawyers plus accountants equals monotony and procrastination. How about I send out for lunch and we'll roll up our sleeves and get it done. At least we'll know if we're close."

"Sounds good to me." Van Hooten randomly flipped the pages before settling down to read the proposition. He stopped at one page listing executive salaries which Van Hooten had given him. "Oh, by the way, I made Moia president of Phuket just this morning—and I gave her a fifty percent salary increase."

"Sounds logical to me, old man. If that is the only stumbling block, we've got a deal. Read on!"

Chapter 50

LACY LET the phone ring endlessly, it seemed. Finally Adam answered. "Adam, I can never catch you when you are supposed to be at home. I guess it's one in the morning there."

"Yeah. Jesus, Lacy give me a minute. I was sound asleep. You still in Hong Kong?"

"Yes, Adam, I'm thinking about living here."

"What! I'd swear you said you were thinking about living in Hong Kong."

"That's right, Adam. In fact, I won't be home for several weeks. I don't want to spoil your fun. I want you and Babs Billings to have a ball. But I want you out of our apartment by the time I do get back. It was mine in the first place, remember?"

"Lacy, have you been drinking?"

"As a matter of fact, I have had a couple. And in perfectly delightful company. Where's the music coming from?"

"Guess I left the TV on."

"It wasn't on a few seconds ago. You see, Adam, you live from one lie to another. It's been that way for years."

"Lacy, are you serious?"

"Yes I am, Adam. Remember, you once told me that if I ever wanted to leave to make sure you were the first to know. Well now you know, Adam."

There was a long period of silence before Adam spoke in a whisper. "Lacy, you better see a psychiatrist. You've turned into a real bitch lately. We'll talk when you get home."

"I want you out of there, Adam. My name is on the lease, remember?"

"Who in the hell do you think you are to talk to me like that?" Music now swelled in the background.

"Good-bye, Adam." Lacy hung up the phone. I might as well face it, she told herself. Things started going downhill with Adam before our honeymoon was over. She felt relaxed. Her eyes were dry. She couldn't believe she had done it—and having done it, she was amazed it had taken this long.

Lacy sat at the desk in her suite at the Mandarin looking at her appointment calendar. She reviewed the list of her contacts in Hong Kong and then studied the file kept on each. Her work was very nearly completed. She was prepared to make carefully considered recommendations to New Worldwide Securities that she felt would enhance the success of their Pacific Rim holdings.

She pictured her office on Wall Street. Eric, her assistant, had done a whale of a job keeping things going. His daily communications were up-to-date. Some of her clients probably were not even aware of her travel.

Brandon Poole was probably right. Cutting-edge electronics had made the entire world capable of minute scrutiny from a single computer workstation anywhere. She thought about her office, the commuting, the people, the lunches, the dinners, the tightly woven routine. She pictured Adam, reading the morning news. Then a single dominating thought burst free from her subconscious. Now that her mission was nearly completed, she really wanted to stay in Hong Kong.

She checked the time. It was now one-thirty in the morning in New York. She certainly couldn't pester Whitney Gordon like she had Adam. Whit was a prince of a CEO, but calling him now would be pushing a good working relationship to the limit. But she had vacation days piled up. She would even offer to continue her daily communication with Eric. She wanted more of Hong Kong. She turned to the mirror and smiled. Of course, what she now knew was that it was really Brandon Poole she wanted, with that damned enigmatic grin of his.

What the hell, she thought, she'd call Whit right now. If he was a bit grumpy about being awakened, it would be a kick of a story to tell someday.

Still anchored in Victoria Harbor, bustling activity filled the decks of the *Kowloon Eagle*. Lighters ringed the vessel, waiting their turn to lade cargo. Brandon Poole was handling the business of Brandon Poole Ltd. from the command room aboard. A steady stream of water taxis brought appointments as the schedule demanded. It was evident to veteran harbor watchers that the sleek freighter was preparing to sail.

At desks within the business quarters below deck, a staff numbering more than fifty routinely carried on the worldwide business of the company.

Poole was all over the ship, greeting everyone and personally checking the viability of each workstation. Two deck officers followed him, taking notes pertaining to last-minute problems. When he finally completed his inspection, he returned to his command room aft of the bridge where he could see the preparations on the deck. In a few moments he would be joined by Captain Bridges.

At five in the afternoon, Lacy Locke arrived by water taxi. Met by a steward, she was shown the way to Poole's command room. A double-faced, black silk sheath dress moved just enough with each step of her svelte figure to catch a quick appreciative glance from the men working the lighters. Glistening jet hair tossed lazily in the light breeze.

"Lacy, welcome aboard! You're becoming an expert at getting around our harbor. Captain Bridges, this is my special friend, Lacy Locke. Lacy is visiting from New York."

Captain Bridges smiled affably, touching his brow in salute. "I'll add my welcome to that of Mr. Poole. New York! My, my, it's been many years since I've taken a vessel to your great city. Doing it again would be a fine adventure."

"Victoria Harbor is beautiful, Captain, so busy!"

"Ah yes, I'm afraid it's much too busy. Very crowded out there." He waved his hand toward the scores of ships moored between the *Kowloon Eagle* and New Territories. "Also, we have some very special problems once in a while."

Poole interrupted. "Captain, tell Lacy about the little problem with the Chinese and their missiles. It's a fascinating little game we play at times."

"Surely. Ms. Locke, allow me to show you the chart." He motioned to a chart projected on the bulkhead. It showed Southeast Asia with shipping lanes to Hong Kong.

"Because of weather conditions down here"—he pointed to an area of the South China Sea near the Philippines—"we considered a passage north, moving west of Taiwan and into the East China Sea. However, our dear friends in the People's Republic of China are testing their missiles again. They are firing from inside China to a target landing area about eighty miles north of Taiwan, in the East China Sea. So we would rather deal with the weather than the missiles."

"It's frightening! When did this start?" Lacy could not remember reading anything about it.

"Oh, it has been going on periodically for years. I suppose they have to test them someplace." The captain winked at Lacy. "Of course, by landing them in this target area, it shows clearly that all of Taiwan is within range of their missiles.''

"It's just a bit of sword-rattling, Lacy," interjected Poole. "The People's Republic regards Taiwan as one would consider an errant child. They firmly believe that the child will assuredly come home someday."

"Interesting. I have read a little about that," Lacy said. "But, Captain, you will find no such excitement around New York harbor."

"Oh, it's nothing to worry about. The Chinese keep everyone well posted as to when they are going to practice," assured the captain. He excused himself, leaving Lacy and Brandon alone in the command room.

"Lacy, I've used the word *magnificent* before. I will have to consult with the poets. But for now I will just say again that you look magnificent!"

"It's a perfectly good word, Brandon. Thank you."

"Lacy, tonight I want you to experience a bit of Poole tradition. Whenever Brandon Poole Ltd. acquires a new company we welcome the new member of our family by having dinner at the Peak. There will be about a dozen people including you and me to toast the success of our new colleagues. Chelsea is roughing up a caterer to make sure he serves the best of Hong Kong food."

"And who are the guests of honor?" Lacy asked, intrigued by Brandon's confident, enigmatic smile.

"Guess!"

"Claude Van Hooten and Moia Hsu." Brandon nodded emphatically as she spoke. "Already, Brandon? That's impossible!"

"The deal is done, my dear. Even now as we speak, the Phuket computers are being linked to our own right here aboard the *Kowloon Eagle*."

"Brandon, it is so exciting. Thanks for including me tonight. This tops everything." Lacy hugged him and kissed his cheek with excitement. Outside, the lights of

Hong Kong circling the *Kowloon Eagle* began to twinkle around them.

Brandon Poole pulled her firmly into his arms. The half smile was gone. He gently kissed her lips, then spoke. "I knew your trip to Hong Kong would end. I suppose you think you have to leave. I just want you to know one thing . . . I love you, Lacy." Poole dropped his arms and walked to the window. "Well there, I've said it. I can only tell you that I would feel dishonest if I hadn't, and also very guilty."

Lacy stood rooted to the spot, looking at Brandon silhouetted against the lights. She was struggling to find words. "Brandon . . . I love what you said . . . I'm flattered, and speechless. Oh damn it! Brandon . . . come over here and hold me, please!" Brandon joined Lacy, wrapped his arms around her snugly and kissed her again.

Finally Brandon turned them to face the panorama of Hong Kong all around them. "I'll behave now, Lacy. Just think, we've got all the way until the end of our lives to finish this adventure."

Poole walked over to the desk and picked up the intercom. "This is Brandon Poole. Prepare the launch. Ms. Locke and I will be leaving for Central immediately." He opened the door for Lacy. "We can't keep our guests waiting. Chelsea might get violent."

The small parking area near the private tramway on the Peak filled quickly with an assortment of Rolls-Royces and Mercedeses. At the top of the tram, guests were shown to the main terrace for cocktails. The stone terrace wrapped around two-thirds of the villa, offering an unparalleled view of the city below.

Brandon Poole's guests were an elite group of businessmen, all very prominent leaders in Hong Kong's capitalist aristocracy. The celebration of Phuket Color's acquisition was turned into an even more festive event because of the next day's marriage of Moia Hsu and Claude Van Hooten. Despite the comparative secrecy of their quick union, news of it had swept through Hong Kong society virtually overnight. The affair of the hard-driving Dutchman and the attractive woman from Beijing had been watched by many for a long time, and Brandon's guests felt it a distinct privilege to socialize with the couple on this night. Broad smiles and good fellowship dominated the evening.

The dazzling Lacy Locke, constantly at the elbow of Brandon Poole, did not go unnoticed. One of Brandon's fiercest competitors, a shipping magnate, edged close to him and nodded approvingly at Lacy. "Eh Brandon, you scoundrel, I'll bet you'll be next."

"There could be a worse fate," retorted Brandon with his lazy smile.

"What about young Davy Wong?" the magnate asked.

The smile vanished. "The man will be set free, my friend. Sometimes miracles take a little time, even in Hong Kong."

The guests were on their way promptly after a relaxing dinner, but not before a traditional round of toasts. Poole raised his glass three times, toasting to the good health and long life of Moia and Claude Van Hooten; to God giving strength to Davy Wong; and to the future well-being of the people of the Crown Colony of Hong Kong.

After the guests had left, Brandon and Lacy sat next to each other on deck chairs, sipping at brandy.

"Brandon, your dinner party was a highlight of my visit. It seems that every day brings another one. Those men have so much respect for you. They hang on your every word."

"Nonsense! They'd have a rowdy toast if I were to go belly up." He chuckled easily at his remark, meant only partly in jest. "They listen because they are all in this same odd boat. They make a game of reassuring each other. But in fact, they are all deathly fearful of the future—and the Chinese. It's coming swiftly now, like a runaway freight train. There is no stopping it."

"My money is on men like you working things out. I just know it!"

"Lacy, I am a little different from the others. I have a lifeboat. I have the *Kowloon Eagle*. I can be here in name, but stay away as long as I like." Brandon paused. "All this brings me to a serious proposal, Lacy. When do you plan to return to New York?"

"I've really just begun to seriously consider it. All of a sudden, I am in no hurry to leave."

"My dear, I have a perfect solution. Hear me out before you say a word." Brandon sipped at his brandy and then began. "In thirty-two hours from now, the *Kowloon Eagle* will slip out of Victoria Harbor with the rising sun. We'll move swiftly into the South China Sea, skirt north of the Philippines, and go full speed to Hawaii. We'll drop several passengers there, including Sean Xiang and Mary Lulu." He stopped and smiled broadly at the thought of the unlikely couple.

"From there we will continue eastward, dropping down to about eight degrees north of the equator. We'll go through the Panama Canal. Less than a day later, we'll anchor at Grand Cayman. We are dropping cargo there and leaving a nucleus of staff to man an auxiliary headquarters for Brandon Poole Ltd. But the first thing we do when we get to the Caymans will be to take Lacy Locke to the airport so that she can catch her plane to New York, less than four hours away."

"Brandon! What makes you think that I want to go to New York?"

"Now hear me out, Lacy. You promised you would. You will have your own private stateroom, even your own computer if you want one, and lots of very special people aboard who are making this trip as passengers. Consider the whole thing a twelve-day learning seminar. I can't imagine a company with the status of New

Worldwide Securities looking unfavorably on such an experience.''

Lacy sat for perhaps a full thirty seconds, staring out into the glitter of Hong Kong below the Peak. She then met his eyes, determined to say what was on her mind. "What about your other proposition, Brandon? The little thing about your future son. Do we get five thousand miles from nowhere, and then talk about it?''

"I promise never to talk about it unless you bring it up. My dear, you can't stop me from thinking about it, but I won't bring it up.''

She found it impossible to meet his intense gaze. She had to look away. "I like your proposition, Brandon. Both of them. Thirty-two hours?'' She looked at her wristwatch. "I'll be ready to go.''

"Very good!'' Poole leaned toward her, framed her face gently with his hands and kissed her, intensely and unrushed.

Later, Cecil Lo drove them back to the Mandarin. For most of the trip they were silent, until Lacy spoke. "Brandon, I'm very curious. If I were to give you a daughter instead of a son, what would you name her?''

"There has been only one name in our family for as long as I can remember. I suppose I'd have to call her Brandon.''

Chapter 51

THE NEXT morning, the wedding of Moia Hsu and Claude Van Hooten in the old Gothic Cathedral of St. John was brief and simple. There were about twenty guests in the small chapel, most of them associates of Van Hooten at Phuket Color. Van Hooten was evidently well liked in his capacity. The atmosphere was one of lighthearted gaiety all through the brief service. At its conclusion the men were quite vocal with their congratulations and the women dabbed at their eyes.

A spate of tears burst forth down Lacy Locke's cheeks. In a short time she had come to feel much empathy for Moia Hsu. Somehow Moia symbolized the yet obscure future of Hong Kong. Here was a brilliant, highly educated Chinese woman, intensely loyal to Van Hooten and Hong Kong. Yet she was consumed with the necessity of doing all she could to help pull her homeland into the next century.

Lacy scanned the small group as they left the chapel. Aside from Cecil Lo, there were only two other Chinese there. "Does her father know about the wedding, Brandon?"

"I don't see how he could. If he did know, I'm sure he wouldn't do anything about it. It will take lots of time for the old man to get over this. But I think he will."

They watched as the newlyweds hustled to their waiting limo. Amidst much waving and cheering, the limo eased onto Garden Road and sped away.

"Where do you think they are going, Brandon?"

"I don't think Van Hooten would share that knowledge with anyone. I did ask him if he wanted to leave with us and spend a few days in Hawaii. He wouldn't hear of it. Said they couldn't spare the time. He said they've planned a delayed honeymoon in Bali, but for the next couple of days, they'd just string up a hammock somewhere."

"Don't you think Van Hooten is sort of an odd duck, Brandon?"

"Absolutely not. He's decisive and he's honest. He tends to speak his mind. That can get him in a lot of trouble. But he'll make a fine executive for us." He walked Lacy back to his Rolls, where Cecil Lo stood waiting. "How about you, Cecil, are you all packed and ready to come aboard tonight? We leave at daybreak, you know."

"Sir, I am already stowed away on board. Marvelous stateroom, sir, you'll have me spoiled for sure."

Listening to their conversation, Lacy suddenly turned slightly queasy, overcome by a nervous excitement. She, too, would be moving aboard the *Kowloon Eagle* this very evening, leaving the staid, comfortable security of the Mandarin Hotel. She was still amazed at her quick assent to make the voyage to the Caymans. She glanced at the man next to her. What did she really know about Brandon Poole? What on earth made her agree to sail halfway around the world with this virtual stranger? "Brandon . . . I, I'm wondering . . ."

"Yes, what are you wondering about?"

"I'm wondering if Moia will be happy," she lied. "Oh no! Brandon, it isn't that. I'm so damn nervous about the trip. I wish I could be unflappable, like you."

"Really! I must confess I'm quite flappable, actually very nervous about the whole thing. Remember, here I am leaving Hong Kong to set up in the Cayman Islands, all just in case. In case of what? I don't really know, nor will anyone until 1997. I daresay I am more nervous than you." He put his arm around her and pulled her closer. "So let's call our nervousness a draw. You and I can steady each other through the few days to the Caymans. Agreed?"

Lacy nodded and stared out the window.

As they approached the Mandarin, Brandon instructed Lo to wait for him, then entered the hotel with Lacy. "Lacy, in all the excitement of the wedding, I almost forgot something." He led her to a darkened corner of the cocktail lounge just off the lobby.

When they were seated he pulled an envelope from his pocket and opened it. "Now cup your hands, please." He shook the envelope and a ring fell into her open hands. It was a simple gold ring, set with a ruby the size of an almond. "Just a little going-away present. Chelsea found it in the back of a drawer that hadn't been opened for fifty years. It belonged to Sir Brandon."

"Oh Brandon, no, no. I can't possibly accept this."

"Nonsense! It is customary to leave Hong Kong with a little gift. Chelsea's find was opportune. With everything happening, I haven't had a speck of time for shopping. Now take it. It would be insane to pop it back in the drawer and let it lie for another fifty years." He grasped her hand and closed her fingers around the ruby. "Behave now. You're making me nervous. Wear it to the captain's dinner tonight, or toss it into the sea. It's yours."

Lacy opened her palm and looked at the huge ruby, shaking her head. "It's truly beautiful, Brandon. We'll talk about it later. I'll borrow it for the captain's dinner. Would that make you happy?"

He didn't answer her directly. "I suspect Sir Brandon

picked it up in Burma. He spent a lot of time there."
Poole stood up and prepared to leave. "I must get back
to the ship. There's lots of last-minute things to attend
to. Cheer up, Lacy. Everything will be just fine."

Poole left quickly, leaving her with her hand tightly
closed around the ruby ring. How, she asked herself,
how does one say no to Brandon Poole? And more
importantly, did she want to?

Chapter 52

LACY SAT bolt upright in her bed and looked around her in the dim light. She was alone. She was perfectly safe and had slept soundly for several hours. It was four in the morning. She remembered clearly that Brandon had asked her to join him for breakfast in his command room at five o'clock. She could already hear sounds of activity around the giant freighter. Bells, whistles, and occasional shouted commands that were unintelligible to her seemed to come from every direction.

In another half-hour, she was dressed in slacks and a sweater and ready to explore the deck. She opened her door and was engulfed by the sounds of the vessel coming to life. Outside on the passenger deck, other passengers had gathered here and there along the rail. The lights of Hong Kong still glimmered all around them in the faint morning light. A few feet away she recognized Mary Lulu in a long robe, looking very tall but perfectly normal, as compared with her outlandish appearance on stage. Sean, standing next to her, caught Lacy's eye and waved. She returned his greeting, then made her way forward to the command room. Brandon and several others were standing around sipping at coffee and nibbling from a buffet of fruits and pastries.

"Lacy!" When Brandon shouted, the others looked her way. "You're just in time. Guy Bridges has invited several of us to the bridge." The engines of the big freighter were rumbling to life, and now they were moving slowly from the mooring. All the lighters and attending vessels had disappeared.

Captain Guy's selected route would take them along the north end of Hong Kong Island, then south through the West Lamma channel into the South China Sea. In the distance was a small island on the port side. Everyone now gathered along the rail as the light grew vivid orange in the eastern sky. Appropriate oohs and ahs came from the spectators as a thin sliver of sun popped out of the sea just beyond the small island.

"Magnificent, Brandon!" Lacy exclaimed. "Such a sunrise I've never seen. What is that little island?"

"That's Lamma Island, a fisherman's island. A charming little temple to Tin Hau is there. Tin Hau is the patron saint of fishermen. I'll have to take you there some day." He beamed down at her, as if he knew he would do it.

"I'd like that, Brandon."

Poole continued to talk softly, only to her. "Look behind you, Lacy. See that small group looking back at Hong Kong? They have good reason to wonder if they will ever see it again. Three of them are dissidents, unwelcome in China. The stocky one in the middle is Davy Wong. That's a secret you and I must keep for a while."

"How! How did it ever happen! Only yesterday I heard he was in prison."

"It's an axiom in Hong Kong that occasionally an awful lot of money, along with good luck, can produce your choice of miracles."

Hong Kong was now fading from sight, fusing with the mist of the Pearl River delta as the daylight grew stronger. Around them, passengers were returning to their quarters.

Lacy continued to stand on the bridge with Brandon for a long time until the last trace of land fell beneath the horizon. "Oh, Brandon, it's so sad. What will really happen in 1997?"

Brandon shook his head and shrugged. "We will hope and work for the best. But for now the only certainty I know of is that on July 1, 1997, the sun will rise again out of the South China Sea beyond Lamma Island and shine on the temple to Tin Hau, just as it did a hundred and fifty years ago."